The Flight of Torque

Blood of the Nagaran

Book One

Rebecca Laffar-Smith

The Flight of Torque

First published in Australia in 2014 by Rebecca Laffar-Smith
Third edition Copyright © 2018 by Rebecca Laffar-Smith

National Library of Australia Cataloguing-in-Publication entry:
Author: Laffar-Smith, Rebecca, author.
Title: The Flight of Torque / Rebecca Laffar-Smith
ISBN: 978-0-6482286-1-5 (Paperback)
        978-0-9925395-1-1 (eBook)
Dewey Number: A823.4

Cover design by CirceCorp Design (Carolina Fiandri)

For Forge, the ideas man,
and Matt, who always believed.

Thank you both
for inspiring me,
believing in me,
and following me
through to the end.

Contents

Prologue

The riot of his golden curls captured her attention. Despite the tension in his shoulders and his unusual haste to settle her to sleep, the familiar wave comforted her. Tori reached for the fuzzy mop, so different from her own dark crop. Her father tucked the sheets around her and leaned forward to kiss her forehead. "Just one more story, Daddy, please?" she pleaded, moving to sit up again. He shook his head and she watched his hair swirl as he settled her back down into her bed.

"Not tonight, Sweetheart. I have to work." He tucked the sheets around her again and then stood. "You get some sleep and I'll see you in the morning."

Tori nodded as he stepped away, drawing the bedroom door almost closed behind him. She watched his shadow flit across the sliver of light that remained and smiled, burying herself deeper into her blankets. Drifting on the edges of sleep she listened to him moving around the house. A gentle knock on a distant door, muffled voices; memories fluttered behind her eyelids as she slipped into sleep.

The room was darker when, startled, she blinked her eyes open. The light through the doorway was gone and Tori quivered under her blankets as she listened to the unusual night sounds around her. She could hear raised voices from across the hall, but she did not understand her father's angry words. "Daddy?" Tori whispered. She slid her feet to the ground and crept out of bed to peek out of her room. The hall was dim. Light escaped from beneath her father's bedroom door, but directly across from her, his office stood open. The lamp on his desk glowed.

A woman's voice bit out a response, "You know nothing, Rick. She betrayed you. Even now she shrouds you in lies and you do everything she asks. Why do you trust her?"

Tori tiptoed across the hall. When she saw there was no one in her father's office she slipped inside. The adjoining door to her father's bedroom was open and light filtered across the coffee table and touched the edges of his desk. She snuck behind the desk and gazed at the leather-clad back of a tall, young woman with thick red waves of hair.

"She's my wife. She wouldn't betray me," her father responded. Tori could see him standing across from the woman. His hands waved in front of him, "Em, please, you can't be here." He touched her shoulder, urging her out of the room. Tori ducked under the desk and peered through a gap in the wooden backing as the two adults came into the room.

"Join us, Rick, please. I don't want you on the wrong side of this."

"I can't. You know I can't," he replied.

The woman turned away from him. She closed her eyes as she clutched something tight to her chest under her jacket. Tori leaned forward trying to see. Her father stepped up behind the woman and pulled the door closed behind him.

As the woman drew her hand from beneath her jacket, Tori saw the black and red inked tattoo of a snake coiled around the woman's wrist. A flash of light glittered from the slender object in the woman's hand. Tori froze as the woman whispered, "Then I'm sorry, Rick. I have my orders. They won't let you protect her lies, or her blood." The woman moved so quickly that Tori could only see her father and the woman struggle against each other as they fought. He shoved her backwards and her hip slammed against the desk. She gasped in pain and then hissed in anger before lunging at him.

A quiet gasp escaped Tori's lips. Her father glanced down at her and their eyes met between the slats of the table. His eyes widened. "Don't," he grunted then gasped, his hands dropping away from the woman's shoulders.

The woman stepped backward. She gazed at the blossoming stain of red that spread across Rick's belly. Her hands were smudged with darkness. Blood trickled down the length of the blade still clutched in her hands. It stained her fingers. "I'm sorry," she whispered again.

Rick stepped toward her. One hand clutched his stomach. "Em, why?" he asked, then gasped. His eyes closed against the pain and he fell forward to his knees. His body shuddered and his head struck the coffee table as he sprawled, twitching, on the rich cream carpet. Breath dragged through his lungs in shallow gasps and his arms twitched. The woman stood over him as his convulsions slowed and then ceased.

"Why couldn't it have been me, not her? *She* did this," the woman said. Her voice was full with bitter anger. Tori watched the woman stroke a tear from her cheek with her sleeve as she whispered, "I'm sorry." Her voice quivered and another tear fell as she turned away. She shook her head, lifted her chin, then strode from the room, and disappeared down the hall.

Tori quivered when the front door slammed. Her eyes were fixed on her father. He lay face down with his head tilted. Glassy, unseeing eyes gazed at her as blood pooled onto the carpet around him. Tori whispered, "Daddy?" Frozen in place she willed him to move.

Time seemed to stand still, but in the distance, Tori heard a flutter, like doves landing on the windowsill, then a young man knelt beside her father. Tori's eyes widened as the man's shoulders flexed and two giant white wings tucked themselves behind his back. His bare chest held a soft golden glow in the warm light of the lamp. His hands, strong and gentle, turned her father onto his back. The man leaned close over her father's chest, putting his ear near Rick's lips. The gentle waves of his flaxen hair fell across his face. Tori could see the crease of concern in his brow and the flash of pain in his steel blue eyes. "Dammit, Michael, why today? If I hadn't had to go looking for you I would have been here. I should have been here." The man sat back, his head bowed, wings trailing on the ground behind him. He looked down at his blood-soaked hands. "Too late," he whispered.

The piercing wail of emergency sirens approached; red and blue light flashed through the office window. The man raised his eyes and stepped toward the glass. He shook his head and frowned as he looked down to the road below. "What purpose does getting the authorities involved serve them?" After an incisive glance around the room, his eyes briefly settled on the body one last time.

He sighed, then stepped through the open window, spread his wings, and launched himself into the dark night sky.

Tori shivered, rocking back and forth with her arms wrapped around her legs, as chaos in blue uniforms burst into the room.

Chapter One
A Shadow In Black

20 years later

"I can't do this anymore, Tempany. Give me something else. Send me to a desk somewhere or put me back on messenger duty." Lucas's voice echoed with anger. Even he could hear the edge of grief that scuffed his throat as he forced back unshed tears. He grimaced and tossed aside the heavy book he had pulled from the vast bookshelf. As he spun away from the cabinet his pale wings lifted to prevent his feathers from trailing on the carpet.

Tempany gazed across at him. He could feel the compassion in her sapphire eyes. She stood still, her presence calm and her voice tender, "Lucas, I understand how this most recent loss affects you, but we need you. Michael is still missing. There is no one else who can take this case."

"You don't understand, Tempany." He threw up his hands in frustration and turned to face her. "I've lost people before; it comes with the job. We can't save them all; I accept that. But I'm not just losing one from time to time. Fourteen people; everyone I've tried to protect for the past twenty years has been killed. These people, they've not reached the end of their time. They didn't pass peacefully in their sleep. They've been murdered." He turned, pushed a hand through his hair, and then paced across the office floor. "I'm supposed to stop that from happening. What's the point if I can't save them?"

She remained calm, standing beside her desk in a beam of sunlight from the window. Her straight, blonde hair was a golden cast so pale it seemed almost completely devoid of colour. She looked regal, like an ice queen. Lucas tried to tamp down the bitterness he felt over her innate calm. *Didn't she ever get pissed off?* Her quiet voice and steady gaze irked him all the more. "You are not infallible, Lucas. We all have limitations here. We can't know what will happen and when. We can't always be there to protect them. You aren't expected to be super human."

"But I am, aren't I? That's why we're here."

She shook her head, "There is only so much we can do. Fate plays its own cards and people write their own histories. But this girl, she needs you, Lucas. Her life is turning upside down and she has no one else to keep her from straying into the darkness."

"I can't protect her, Tempany. That's just it. Don't you see?" Lucas turned and stood his ground before her.

Chapter 1. A Shadow In Black

The muscles in his shoulders flexed causing the white curve of his wings to flutter slightly behind him. "Fourteen innocents, fourteen people who needed me. I couldn't protect any of them."

"So you won't even try?" Tempany's voice pitched slightly and Lucas felt a smug satisfaction that she was not as unruffled as she appeared. She took a deep breath before continuing in a steady tone, "She's not involved in any of this, Lucas. All I'm asking is that you keep her from getting involved. She doesn't need a guardian, she needs a friend. Just look at the case. Go see her. I need more time to find Michael, but I can't do that unless I know I can depend on you for this. It's not even really an assignment; it's just until I can get Michael back here, and convince him to finish what he started."

Tempany's soft pleading disconcerted Lucas. He was not used to her begging him to take a job. He could see the concern in her eyes and, as he finally faced her directly, he noticed the lines of fatigue and worry that marred her normally flawless features. He sighed, frowning. "He'd better get back here and clean up this mess. Look, give me the file. I'll do what I can, but I don't want this case, Tempany. You need to line up someone else to take over."

She nodded handing him a manila folder. "I promise, Lucas. Thank you. I'll see what I can arrange to get you off the protection detail if that is really what you want, but I don't want to lose you. You've had a bad run, but you've always been one of my best."

"Just focus on finding Michael," Lucas replied. "Things've been falling apart since he left. We need him back here." He flipped through the pages, frowning, and then nodded. "All right, I'll check in again shortly."

The grass looked exceedingly chipper, Tori decided, a rich, freshly groomed green that was vibrant in the sunlight. Even the day seemed unnaturally cheerful as Tori's gaze wandered, absorbing details in the landscape. People were stark blobs of dark black, red, and grey against the bright yellow and green of the sun and grass. A disturbing blob of darkness hovered over a deep hole in the rich earth. The wooden casket's walnut finish gleamed.

Tori swiped at another drop trickling down her cheek. The cool breeze chilled the smear against her skin. She could feel the looks of pity prickle around her as the minister's voice droned on and on in a solemn but artificial manner. A soft hymn filled the air and Tori glanced up as people began to chatter in low voices. As the song came to an end, they shifted on their feet as if eager to move on.

Tori felt the lump grow in the back of her throat and bit back another sob. She wanted to yell at the people milling around her, "Stop it! Don't you have any respect? My grandmother is dead!" Instead, she clutched her gloved hands together and let another tear fall as she watched the coffin descend into the ground.

An elderly woman, with hair a shock of tight, white spirals, approached Tori. Tori felt her skin crawl as the woman patted her arm. She shifted uncomfortably, turning to face the woman, but at the same time stepping out of reach. "Oh, you poor dear," the woman said, her voice a scratch of nosey interest rather than concern. "Your grandmother was a wonderful woman."

Tori forced a smile to her lips. "Thank you for your kindness," she muttered in return. She buried the snide retort regarding the woman's vindictive gossip and ignored her horrendously smug air. "I loved her very much," she added instead.

"I'm sure you did, dear. We all did." The comment was offhand and the old woman was already moving away. A stream of others just like her moved past Tori in a procession. They bestowed their condolences, and now the service was over, retreated to their parked cars.

The Flight Of Torque

As the cemetery emptied, Tori was left alone with her thoughts and the cool afternoon breeze. She startled as a soft Irish voice spoke in gentle, comforting tones from beside her, "Oh Tori, that darling woman, how she'd be hurtin' to see you cry so many tears. Anna loved you, oh how she loved you."

Tori lifted her dark eyes to meet the calm ocean spray in the gaze of her Grandmother's friend, Jess. She attempted a watery smile. "I don't know what I'll do without her. She was my rock, Jess; all I really had left in the world to hold on to."

Jess nodded, her skin crinkled around her tender eyes. "You'll do a'right I think," she said, her voice holding more certainty than her words. "She thought the world of you. I don't think even this ghastly illness could've forced Anna to leave it if she thought you might still need her." Jess gestured at the casket, then bent to pick up a handful of rich dark earth. She trickled it across the wood finish with a gentle wave of her hand. With a satisfied nod, she dusted her hands together before turning back to Tori. "You're grown now. I expect she thought it was well time to let the old sleep. Besides, it's past time you brought your own young'uns into the world."

Jess's eyes sparkled and Tori felt the day's first real smile tilt her lips. "I certainly have no plans of it, Jess.

Chapter 1. A Shadow In Black

Much to Gran's disappointment, I'm sure. But Gran knew I liked to walk the path less travelled." Tori's cheeks ached with the effort to smile. The smile faded quickly, but knowing she still knew how to smile was reassuring. Surely she would not be sad forever.

"She did at that. She admired your independence, your spirit. So don't you go letting her passing get you down too long. She lived a grand ol' life and, much as her getting sick stole the last of it from her, I think she'd have been satisfied with the legacy she left behind."

Tori nodded, "Thank you, Jess. And thank you for coming today."

"I wouldn't have been anywhere else, Love. But I best be getting on now before it gets much later in the day. These old eyes o' mine don't like to be out on the streets after dark."

"Of course, thank you for staying so late. Would you like me to see you home safely?"

"Nonsense, nonsense," Jess said, touching Tori on the shoulder, "Lovely of you to offer, dear, but I can manage. You stay. I expect you want a few more moments alone to say goodbye."

Tori nodded and touched the older woman's fingers with her own. "Thank you," she whispered as Jess tottered away.

The Flight Of Torque

Tori turned back to the grave. The men who had lowered the casket had moved away. She stood alone, as the late afternoon crept toward evening and even the birds began to settle down for the night.

Long minutes passed until Tori shivered. The setting sun brought a cool breeze that lifted goose bumps on her bare shoulders. She rubbed her hands against her upper arms, blinking as she glanced around. The graveyard was empty except for a man that stood under the shadows cast by a tree in the distance. The cool grey of his long jacket fitted his broad shoulders. In one hand he held what looked like a folder.

Tori shivered again as she watched him. He gazed down at a grave marker near his feet, but Tori could not help feeling as if he had been watching her. She watched him crouch and touch the stone at his feet with his free hand and then stand again. The movement was somehow familiar. She wondered if it was the way his pale blonde hair fell across his face, hiding his features, or maybe the gentle strength in his hands or the tightness in his jaw. Transfixed, Tori could not draw her gaze away.

He lifted his chin and met her eyes across the distance between them. She felt a tickle of awareness ripple through her. A flush warmed her cheeks. She saw his lips tilt in a smile and he tipped is head in acknowledgement. Tori glanced away, feeling conspicuous, then looked back. He was gone.

The darkness of descending night cast a gloom over the graveyard. Tori shook her head and then carefully picked her way through the grass toward the gate.

"Damn it!" Tori swore softly and winced. A thick river of blood welled along the gash in her palm. Shards of glass littered the bedroom floor and blood splattered onto an old sepia photograph that had fallen out of a broken picture frame. She gasped as she pulled a blood-smeared sliver of glass from her hand. The shard slipped from her fingers and it clinked against the other fractured pieces on the floor. Then, staunching the bright red flow with a tight grip, Tori lifted both hands to her chest. Drops of crimson splashed on her pale shirt. She swore again as she moved to the en suite bathroom. The cool water from the basin soothed the jagged pain that lanced across her hand and the water ran clear before she turned off the tap. She wrapped a hand towel around the wound and reprimanded herself in the vanity mirror, "Stupid, clumsy." Tears welled in her still burning eyes. She took a deep breath, gave herself a last look, then shook her head and turned away, returning to the bedroom.

The Flight Of Torque

This time, taking more care as she nursed her wounded hand, she gathered the broken shards of glass and piled them in the small wastebasket near the door. The wooden frame was intact, but the picture it had held of a much younger Anna, face radiant with delight and cradling a newborn baby in her arms, was already stained. Tori used a clean corner of the hand towel to wipe away the worst of the smears. She carefully lifted the edges of the picture to wipe the back and frame. A slip of paper slid out from behind the photograph and fluttered to the floor.

Tori finished wiping the frame then replaced it gently on the bedside table. She bent to pick up the fallen paper. It was creased in several places and aged to a soft, honey yellow. The blue scrawl of handwriting on the paper was unfamiliar, reading simply, "Me and M. 1987". Tori turned the page over to reveal a set of photobooth-style photographs. The woman in the pictures shared Tori's dark eyes and the same raven-hued river of hair. A thick gold chain hung around her neck. Its intricate pendent, a serpent coiled around a silver vial, disappeared into the curve of her cleavage. Tori's breath caught as she looked down at the woman in the photograph. She was clearly blooming with health and youth. She leaned into the strong arms of the man behind her and gazed up at him, eyes filled with love-rich awe. Tori swallowed as a lump gathered in her throat. The final picture in the set of four showed the woman, head tilted back and the man's head leaning over her shoulder as they shared an intimate kiss. The woman's rounded belly was a swell that stretched her top and the man's arms cupped her gently, as if cradling the child within.

Tori let the pictures flutter to the floor again as she sat down on the edge of the bed. Confused, she glared down at the photographs. Somehow they taunted her as light reflected on the glossy paper. Although Tori had never known her mother, Anna had shared a few captured memories of her with Tori when she was a child.

Tori had grown more and more like the woman in the old photographs. Seeing them always brought an ache of longing to Tori's heart. Anna had kept fewer and fewer pictures of her daughter on the walls. Perhaps she had sensed the pain Tori still felt over losing the mother she had never known.

But the man in the photograph was not Tori's father. Although the two shared loosely curled locks that wove around their ears, their hairstyle was where similarity ended. Where her father's face gentled into soft curves and his eyes into pale pools of azure sky, the man in the photograph had sharp cheekbones and a firm jaw.

His hair was washed with shades of ash. His eyes, shades darker, were like raging seas. They held a piercing alertness that gentled only in the photograph where he gazed down at the woman beside him. Tori sensed an aloofness about him that contrasted with her father's welcoming warmth. His muscular body stood rigid, as if ready to react to any provocation. He cupped Tori's mother in a protective, almost warding, embrace, as if she was somehow precious and breakable.

"M. Who are you?" Tori said. She reached down, snatched the photograph from the floor and shoved it into the pocket of her jeans.

Chapter Two
Bound By Blood And Duty

Through the upstairs bedroom window, he could see the silhouette of Tori, as she moved around her grandmother's bedroom. The lamp cast a golden glow through the room. The light entwined with the moonlight streaming in from outside. He perched on the balcony railing of the house across the street and dangled his feet as he rocked on the metal bars. From time to time he fluttered, almost having to flail his wings, as he corrected his precarious balance on the rail. He was restless. Waiting was never his strong suit and watching her made him itch to knock on the door and introduce himself. He wanted to be closer.

He forced himself to keep still. His role was to keep her safe. He should have maintained the guise of humanity, but the hidden hours of darkness were the only time he could truly feel the wind. It was tempting to move; free of the restraints and bindings he wore throughout the day.

"Just look at the case. Go see her," he mimicked Tempany's words. "As if she didn't know this whole thing was likely to explode into this mess." He thumped a hand against the railing. Again, in higher pitch, he echoed

Tempany's prim and proper tone, "She's not involved in any of this, Lucas." He paused, changing register, "Involved up to her pretty little neck is what she is. Not involved. Huh, if anything it all started with her. If she really is as clueless as she seems, then Anna did a thorough job keeping it all from her." His brow furrowed and he traced the iron rail with his fingers. "Though I can't begin to guess why the old woman didn't simply brainwash her into believing like the rest of them. She was right there with her coven of Nagaran witches when her daughter gave birth to the girl. Anna swaddled the young thing before passing her into Rick's arms. She sent them away as Charlene bled out all over the cold stone altar." He sighed then said, "I bet their scaly queen smiled on."

He grimaced and his lips tightened as he forced them closed. He returned his focus to the woman beyond the soft lace drapes. Tori picked up the photo-frame she had placed on the bedside table. She added it to the box where several others had already been packed between pages of old newsprint. She moved quickly now, perhaps sensing the darkening night. She gathered her grandmother's belongings, packing away precious mementos. As the evening wore on, he could see her exhaustion in the droop of her shoulders and the shuffle of her feet. She had gathered several boxes; some to take back to her own apartment and others she would deliver to charity in the morning.

As the old grandfather clock in the hall rang out twelve resounding chimes, Tori flicked off the lamp on her grandmother's bedside table, plunging the room almost into full darkness. Moonlight still shone through the curtains. For a moment, Tori stood, fully illuminated by the moonlight, as she reached either side of her to draw the curtains closed. He thought she was lost to his sight, but moments later he saw her shadow move through other rooms. Darkness shrouded the windows of the old house as she drew more curtains, turned out other lights, and closed doors.

Lucas huffed a breath from his lungs and pushed himself off the railing, flapping his wings to land gently in the crisp, dew-damp grass. He walked silently across the empty street. He could not see her now, but as he got closer to the house he heard the hiss of hot water in the upstairs bathroom. When the water ceased, he listened to her soft feet pad across the hall. They dragged, with the ache of tired muscles and her sorrow.

He settled against a wall near her bedroom window and tipped his head back. Moments later he heard her pull back her crisp, clean sheets and sigh. As she settled into her bed, he could sense the heaviness that weighted down her heart. He sat in the darkness, listening to the soft rhythm of her breathing, until her breath slowed in the rest of dreamless sleep. Then he rose from the damp grass. Broad, white-feathered wings arched out from behind him as he launched himself into the night sky, finally free to soar.

The old grandfather clock rang with the discordant clang of splintered wood and shattered glass. Tori startled awake and threw back the covers of the bed. She sat on the edge of her bed, listening to the muted noises that broke her sleep, and realised there was a struggle downstairs. Hesitantly, she touched the floor with her toes and inched across the room. Her bare feet padded on the wooden floorboards as she crept out the door and down the hall. She stumbled to a standstill at the top of the stairs. She could see the fractured wreck of antique cherry wood; the clock's gears still spun but the hands clanked against the decorative plate, unable to turn.

Beside the clock, she could see a trail of books and papers strewn through the entryway. The door of the library stood open. Tori watched as dark shadows danced in the beam of light cast by the moon through the library window.

Chapter 2. Bound By Blood And Duty

Two beasts battled in the darkness. Their lithe movements swirled in rhythmic steps as if the two were somehow in sync with each other. The silent grace of the dancing shadows contrasted with the clomp of booted feet, the grunt of muttered oaths, and the clatter of furniture. A large picture frame fell from the wall and crashed to the floor. It startled Tori out of her frozen state. She darted down the carpeted stairs and stood in the doorway of the library.

Inside, two people, a male and female, struggled against each other. Tori's mind flashed backwards, remembering a similar struggle through the eyes of a frightened little girl. Her breath caught in her throat; a quiet gasp that she attempted to silence by cupping a hand over her mouth.

The woman had the same waves of red hair, lithe figure, and black leather jacket as the woman in Tori's memory, but the man was vastly different from the father she remembered. His hair, a glistening midnight black, gleamed in a moonlight. Black swirls on his muscular chest arrowed down to the corded black pants that hung from his waist. His large, bare feet stepped between the woman's smaller boots as he shoved her back against the wall. She hissed with pain, and then, with an angry scream, she clawed sharp nails down his back. He grunted, leapt to one side and flexed his shoulders. Behind him, rich crimson feathers rippled, fluttered, and then tucked tightly against his skin.

The woman took the opportunity to dart out from beneath his strong hands. She drew a blade from the belt at her waist and gripped it between her fingers. She snarled at him, her back arching, cat-like, as she faced him across the room. They circled each other, around and around the room, while their equally dark eyes glared as they sized up one another.

"There is nothing here, witch. They left nothing for you to find." The man spoke with a defiance.

She snarled back, "You know nothing of what Anna and Char hid here, Uriel. Nor the secret they shared that they kept from the Nagaran."

He shook his head. "I know Anna's death came slowly. She had time to fold, rather than play an unwinnable hand."

The woman hissed. "Anna was out of her mind with the pain her illness brought her final days. She didn't even tell the girl. You think she had the sense to hide the record?"

"I think she knew better than to have ever kept it," he bit back.

"Then why are you here?"

Chapter 2. Bound By Blood And Duty

"My business is none of yours."

She lunged at him with the blade but he thrust her hand away. The blade snagged on the edge of the desk, running a dark grove through the wood as it glanced off the edge. It spun out of the woman's fingers and tumbled to the floor. She growled, then raised her hands and shoved against the man's chest. He stumbled backwards and winced as the fragile bones in his wings crunched against the bookshelf.

"Witch!" he muttered. He gripped her arm between the thick fingers of one hand and dragged her toward him. She flailed against him, her own hands landing ineffective blows on his chest and shoulders. He shook her and she uttered a violent expletive as she launched herself at him. Blood welled in streaks across his skin where her sharp nails tore through the flesh of his chest and arms. He tossed her backward in an almost effortless fling. Her body flew across the room and landed in a crumpled heap on top of the glass coffee table. It shattered beneath her. Her breath huffed out of her lungs as she panted. His dark eyes followed her as she dragged herself upright and pulled herself out of the shards.

"The Seraphim use brute force to still the wicked now, do they?" Her words taunted as she straightened.

She lifted her eyes to glance at him from beneath shuttered eyelids.

"When needs must," he muttered, glaring back. "Enough of this! Neither of us will leave here with what we seek. Much as destroying you would elicit some small measure of satisfaction; I am not willing to pay the price for your life. And though you might think your toxins could overpower me, they will not."

Her chin rose and she hissed, "You think yourself so superior, Uriel. But your arrogance will sever your wings if you do not watch your pride."

He chuckled. "You think you know me? I am the shadow that stands behind your closed eyes when you scream in terror at the darkness."

"I know you would withstand even the deadliest of my toxins, but do not delude yourself into thinking me defanged."

The long black cord of a slick whip snaked out from behind her as she flicked her wrist toward him. He swept his head backwards to avoid the blow, but the tip glanced a sharp crack that oozed a trickle of blood from the cheek beneath his left eye. When the cord whipped out again he lifted his wrist and caught the coil in his fist. It snaked around him. The snared thorns lining one edge, shredded his skin, and he gritted his teeth against the pain as he yanked on the cord.

The woman stumbled forward a few feet before she was able to pull back. She released the whip's handle. Hissing in fury, her whole body vibrated with her anger as she glared. The silence between them grew until, suddenly, she spun on the toe of one boot. She lunged down to snatch up the dagger from the floor where it had settled and then strode from the room. She shoved Tori aside as she sped through the door and sprinted from the house.

Tori winced as her arm was crushed against the doorframe. She rubbed the tender muscle as she righted herself. The man stood, a silent statue, in the corner of the room. His dark gaze followed her movements. Then, with quick, sure fingers he unwound the whip from his wrist and coiled it. He threw Tori an icy glare. She froze, her breath catching in her throat. Seconds later, with the whip still gripped in his hand, he turned his back on her, sprung out of the window, and soared into the air.

The young, uniformed police office raised an eyebrow. "Wings?" he sneered. "You're telling me the intruder had wings? Like a bird?"

Tori sighed, growing increasingly frustrated as the same questions were asked again and again with varying shades of disbelief. *They think I'm crazy,* Tori thought with a grimace. *I bet they think I'm making this stuff up, but who could make this stuff up?*

"Okay," the constable drawled. "And what did the second intruder look like? I suppose she had wings too?"

Tori stood, flexing her tired limbs. "Look," she said, gesturing to the young constable. "I've answered your questions. There is nothing more I can tell you. If you've finished can we please end this? I'd like to get some sleep before sunrise?"

He glanced out the window as if expecting the early morning light to shine, but grey pre-dawn darkness filled the panes. Tori felt reassured by the solid glass between her and the outside world. The frown on the policeman's face, however, was not reassuring. He glanced around the library at the disarray of shelves, the broken coffee table, and the clutter of books and papers strewn across the floor. Tori's gaze lingered on the black smudges of fingerprint dust marring the polished wood surfaces and the heavy, mud-caked boots of the men tramping filth into the rug.

"I think we still need to dust a few places for prints and take some more photographs," the constable said.

He received an affirmative nod from one of the overall-clad, booted men. "Yeah, another," he paused, glancing at the men working around him, then added "ten minutes?" His voice was tinged with uncertainty. The furrow across his brow matched the frown on his lips.

The police officer turned back to Tori and smiled. The curve of his lips did not crinkle the young man's eyes. "We shouldn't be much longer. We'll get out of your hair shortly, but the detective might want you to come in and answer some questions at the precinct." Tori sighed and nodded. She crossed her arms across her chest and turned away to gaze, again, out of the library window.

A sharp knock rattled the wood frame of the door. Tori tensed, her breath catching in her throat. She lifted a hand to her mouth as she spun around.

"Sorry. Didn't mean to startle you." The man's reassuring tone held a ring of sincerity. Tori absorbed the broad lean of the man's shoulders under the fine wool of his grey coat as he pushed himself up from the doorframe. As if in defiance of the fastidious and professional cut of his clothing, the man's hair hung a little too long, brushing his shoulders. The pale wash of blue in his eyes glittered with suppressed mirth. "Detective Lucas Caelum," the man added. He moved across the room and reached a hand out to her. "Tori, isn't it? I understand you've had an incident here tonight?"

Tori's gaze lingered on the honey-tan of his strong and gentle fingers and she heard him clear his throat. She blushed and reached out to return the handshake as she finally replied, "I'm sorry. Yes, that's right."

His smile was warm and Tori could see the light of compassion in his eyes. "It's fine. Please. I know it has been a late night and I appreciate your cooperation in this matter. I hope we can find the intruders and secure your safety."

"Thank you," Tori replied. His soothing tone was the first that rang with any sort of respect for the difficult position she was in and she was truly grateful for his concern. "I can't begin to describe," she said, her voice dropping low before falling away leaving the sentence unfinished.

Lucas reached a hand to touch her shoulder. "Please," he said again, "I hope you'll try. Anything you can tell us can help in our investigation. But, of course, you must be exhausted. We should save this until tomorrow." When he took away his hand Tori felt the chill of the night air replace the warmth that had seemed to radiate from his touch. He reached into his jacket and drew out a card. "If you need anything, please call me."

"Thank you," Tori said again.

"I'd like to go over your case," he continued. "Make sure we haven't missed any details. Would you come into the office tomorrow? How does eleven o'clock sound?"

Tori's brow furrowed. Somehow, the brisk tone of business did not sit well in his voice. It was like the soft compassion he expressed a few moments ago was in sharp contrast with the stiff formality of his professional manner.

"Detective," Tori began.

"Lucas, please call me Lucas," the detective interrupted.

"Lucas, then. I really do think I've told your officers everything," she began.

He interrupted again, "Oh, don't think of our meeting as an interrogation, Tori. What I'd really like to do is share with you what we learn tonight. We'll match your case against others in our database and find out what we can. Perhaps something we find will help you make connections about who the intruders were and what they might want with you or your home."

Tori lifted an eyebrow. "Is that something you normally do with victims of a home invasion?"

He shifted on his feet and glanced away for a second before looking her directly in the eye. "I think yours is a special case," he admitted. "Certainly, some of the particulars make your case unique. I think we could help each other."

She nodded, "I see."

"Yes. So, eleven o'clock?"

Tori glanced at the card. The address was across the city. "I suppose I can be there then."

"Perfect," Lucas said with a smile. "You should get some rest, is there anyone you can call? Family you can stay with?"

Tori shook her head. "My grandmother recently passed away. She was the only family I had left. Really, I do think I will be fine here. It's almost morning."

Lucas's brow crinkled in concern. "You really should," he trailed off as Tori shook her head, then sighed, running a hand through his hair. "Fine. Please, leave this room alone for the time being. Avoid touching anything; we'll put some tape across the doorway and may need to come back in the next day or so. I will let you know when things can be cleaned up without endangering the evidence."

Tori nodded and walked with him across the room. It felt strange being shepherded out of the library but she let him lead her away. At the door he stood, as if barring her from returning to the room. "Get some sleep. We'll lock the front door when we're finished."

"I really should stay," Tori began, her voice full of uncertainty.

"There's nothing to worry about," Lucas interrupted again. "We'll be a few more minutes yet. You might as well go up and get some rest." He put a hand on her shoulder again; the warm tingle where his fingers touched her soothed the bruised muscles in her arm.

Tori blinked, feeling the exhaustion of the late night sweeping over her. She rubbed her brow with two fingers and sighed. "I suppose," she mumbled, yawned, and then nodded. "Yes, okay. Please make sure you do lock up when you leave." She turned away and, with one hand on the wooden railing, headed up the stairs.

Chapter Three
Honour If Not Faith

Lucas watched Tori stumble, half asleep, up the stairs to her room. She trailed a hand along the wall as if guiding herself through the darkness. *Maybe her eyes are closed*, he thought with a smile. As she disappeared down the hall he lingered a moment, listening to her bare feet pad along the thick carpet to her bedroom. The cool sheets whispered as she climbed into bed. Almost instantly her breath slowed to a soft, rhythmic hum.

He straightened from where he had been leaning on the doorframe and turned to face the men in the library. "Wrap up, guys," he ordered. "This is taking too long." He kept his voice low but firm. The officers looked up and then shuffled as they rushed to pack away their equipment.

Lucas ran a hand through his hair and crossed the room to gaze out of the large casement windows. He wondered who had closed the windows after one of the intruders had left through them and if protocol had been followed to dust the glass and frame for prints. He glanced down at the dark earth of the garden bed below. It was flawless, untouched. Obviously, neither intruder had stood there when coming inside.

Chapter 3. Honour If Not Faith

Lucas ran an expert eye over the sill. No dust, but… His eyes narrowed at the dark shade caught in the stay that held the window in position. He brushed his fingers against it and tugged it free; a black contour feather. The warm glow in the shaft was unmistakably Seraphim; the lightless blood red swirl of the fine vanes, unmistakably Uriel. Lucas frowned and tucked the feather into the pocket of his pants. He drew the curtains closed against the early light of the rising sun and turned to see the mess strewn across the room.

The evidence of a skirmish was everywhere. No surface had remained untouched by the two intruders in their struggle. There were trails of dark powder across most of the flat surfaces with swirls of it coating the desk and bookshelf. Lucas frowned and muttered beneath his breath, "Lot of good that'll do. Neither intruder will come up in any database." His constable crossed the room toward him and Lucas closed his lips firmly.

"Sir, I don't know how much of her story we can credit," the constable said. "Woman alone in a big house, it's no wonder she's let her imagination get away from her." The constable ran his fingers over the notepad in his hand. "Although, maybe we ought to take her to the station right now, get her tested. Did you hear? She claimed one of the intruders had wings. Maybe she's on something."

Lucas shook his head, "Like you said, her imagination probably. She seemed reasonably rattled but exhausted. Didn't really seem the type for drugs."

"Yeah, well, who the hell knows these days," the constable replied.

Lucas's chin dropped. "Good cops know," he said. His voice held a sharp note of censure.

The constable straitened. "Right. Well, beyond the wings she claimed to have recognised the other intruder, a woman. Like a woman could have held off some massive hulk in a scuffle to make this kind of mess."

Lucas swung his head back up and raised sharp eyes, skewering the constable. "She said she recognised the woman?"

The constable nodded, "Right. From before. Something about the woman who killed her father?"

With a frown, Lucas replied, "That case is twenty years old. Unsolved." His voice trailed off as his thoughts, turned inward, and darkened.

"Twenty years? She'd have been a kid," the constable scoffed.

"She was six. Saw the whole thing from under his desk." Lucas's tone was flat.

Chapter 3. Honour If Not Faith

"You know someone who worked that beat?" the constable asked.

"Something like that," Lucas replied. He scowled and turned away. Raising his voice, he called to the other men, "Come on, wrap up. I want to get all this back to the office before the traffic gets bad." They scuttled for the door.

With a final frown at the disarray, Lucas shepherded the men out of the room. Then he strapped thick black and yellow tape in a large X across the library door. As the men clattered into trucks parked on the verge, Lucas locked the front door, tugged it closed, then walked across the drive to his car.

"You're sure she said it was the same woman? She was certain?" Lucas asked the constable, his voice tight. He gazed down at the report the man had given him. The folder was little more than the few pages of her statement. The photographs and fingerprint analyses had not come back from the labs yet.

"Exactly the same. She said the woman looked exactly the same. Even down to the black jacket, boots, and ornate dagger. She's an unreliable witness. You said before, that case was twenty years ago, she was a child."

"Possibly," Lucas muttered, his attention on the report more than the constable's words.

The constable raised an eyebrow. "Possibly? A good attorney would discredit her in a second. She's an unreliable witness."

"Yeah," Lucas replied, although he still looked as if he had not been listening to a word the constable had said. He snatched the folder from the desk. "Look," he said, finally lifting his gaze to meet the constable's, "leave this with me."

The constable nodded.

Lucas turned and strode toward the door leading out of the offices. As he reached it he turned back and called, "And send me the lab results as soon as they come in."

"Can I ask, sir, where are you going?"

"I want to check out something," Lucas said before he strode out of the building. He sensed the confused and frustrated huff of the constable but ignored the wave of angry energy that surged toward him. As he stepped out into the early morning sunlight, his thoughts were already turned back twenty years, and as he drove across town he thought about the pictures a little girl had drawn; a flame-haired witch dressed in black and wielding a wicked-edged blade; snakes curled up the woman's arm, their tongues flickering as if they leapt from her skin.

A loud, percussive knocking woke Tori from a dream. She ignored it, still held by dreams She lay in bed a moment trying to capture remnants before they disappeared, but all that remained were the clouds and dancing pairs of wings trailing a rainbow of feathers. She blinked as the knocking began again and a muffled call rose up the stairs. The words were indistinct and Tori frowned, glancing at the clock; a little after nine. She could not remember the last time she had slept so late.

With a sigh Tori pushed back the blankets and pulled herself up out of bed. She slipped her feet into her slippers and pulled her robe over her shoulders. As she padded down the stairs she tightened the belt of the robe, then crossed the hall to the front door.

"Tori, you there? You must be home," a soft Irish brogue swept through the glass panes in the door.

Tori smiled as she pulled it open. "Jess," she said, her face warm with welcome as she continued with a grin, "you're pounding on my door first thing in the morning?"

"Right as, I surely am," Jess replied. "Sarah heard from Ruth that the cops had been here in the middle of the night, 'cause someone broke in to Anna's house. Oh, my heart's been jumping about, imagining you upstairs, asleep in your bed all the while." Jess shuddered and pulled Tori close in a tight hug. "Oh, I don't want to imagine what they might have done to you." She stepped backward and ran her gaze from Tori's head to her feet and back again. "Please, tell me you're all right."

Tori lifted a weak smile and stepped back to invite Jess into the house. "Oh, Jess. I'm fine. Really. It was, I don't know, surreal, I suppose, but after the police came," she paused, considering, "I don't know," she said again, then continued, "somehow, it seemed easy to feel safe. I slept," she added as they moved across the entryway to the kitchen. "I don't remember the last time I slept so well. Maybe not since Gran got sick."

"For the life of me, I was right worried. And to think you were snug in your bed, sleeping like a babe." Jess fussed and busied herself filling the kettle with water from the tap as Tori stood in the kitchen doorway.

"Oh please," Tori pleaded, stepping forward. "Let me do that, you're the guest, I should be waiting on you," she said.

"Nonsense. Sit down. Let me fix you something to eat. Regain your strength."

"Really, it wasn't all that bad. I'm fine. It..." Tori bit her lip then ran a hand through her hair before continuing,

"I guess it's just that it brought up memories." She pictured the woman she had seen last night and shuddered as she drew out a chair and sat down at the breakfast counter. "You know, about my father, that night," Tori drew a ragged breath trailing off as she sat down at the breakfast counter.

Jess turned to face her, gaze full of concerned warmth. "Oh darling, you poor dear. Here's your tea. You can talk with me, if you want to."

Tori smiled. Jess seemed to have the same warmth and kindness Tori missed most about her Grandmother. "Thank you, Jess. You're a treasure."

As Jess moved around the kitchen preparing some toast and marmalade, Tori let her mind wander. In her dreams, a strange, harmonious discord had somehow woven last night with the night her father was killed. "Angels," she muttered, shaking her head as she trailed her fingers over the cold countertop.

Jess lifted her head from a low cabinet. "Pardon dear? I didn't hear you."

"Oh, it's silly, really. It must have been my imagination. Like when I was a child. It's just, last night, I thought one of the intruders had, you know, wings." Tori replied.

"You saw them! I thought you said you were asleep!"

"I didn't say that, you did. When the grandfather clock was broken the noise woke me and I came downstairs. I saw them, two people, a woman, that woman, and an a..." she paused considering her words, "and, a man. They were fighting about something. I don't really remember what they were saying. I don't know what they were talking about," Tori explained.

"What do you remember? What did they say?" Jess asked. She gazed at Tori intently, the marmalade-smeared knife forgotten in her fingers.

Tori drew her hands back and cradled them in front of her, as she let her mind wander, trying to recall the words. "They," she began, then changed track, "it was something about cards. And they said Grandma's name. The woman, she said that gran kept a secret. A secret about the Naga," she drew out the name as she tried to remember it, "Naga, well, Naga-something. Oh! And something about Seraphim. She called him Uriel." Tori looked up at Jess, her brow creased. "What does it all mean?"

A strange glint of light passed through the older woman's eyes and she turned away, suddenly, before replying, "It all sounds mad to me. Maybe you really did imagine it, muddled it all in with your dreams. You really do have that creative way about you." Her voice dropped trailing away as she turned spread the marmalade on the toast.

Tori shook her head. "None of it made any sense. But it was strange. The woman, she looked like the woman who killed my Dad. I mean, really looked like her. Like she was her. And the man, I," Tori swiped a tear away and sniffed, "I thought he had wings. Like the Angel that came after, when my Dad," she took another shaky breath, "you know, when he died. They were darker, the wings, red not white, but they were like before."

"Really, dear," Jess said with a sigh. She placed a plate in front of Tori then picked up a cloth. Wiping it vigorously across the counter, she continued, "It must have been your imagination. It's no wonder, really. You'd been woken suddenly, and it is such a shocking thing to find strangers in your house in the middle of the night. You must have been terrified."

"That's just it, Jess, I wasn't afraid. I was surprised, yes, but not really afraid," Tori replied. "They didn't even seem to care that I was there. The woman just shoved me out of the way; she didn't even really look at me. She didn't say anything to me, neither of them did."

"Maybe it really was a dream. The police will figure it all out, dear. You just let them do their jobs. Now, eat your toast. It'll put some zest back into you and you'll be right as rain."

Tori smiled. "Thank you, Jess. You're right. I'm fine, and I'm starving. This smells delicious. I hope you won't mind if I eat this then pop upstairs for a shower?"

"Not at all, dear. You go. The hot water will do you wonders." She smiled and waved Tori off with the damp cloth. She was already returning her attention to the sink as Tori left the room.

After breakfast, Jess left in a tizzy of farewells and coiffed hugs of frothy lace and wool. Tori finally felt warm. The tea, the shower, and the sizzling plate heaped with a dripping breakfast had taken the chill from her bones and she felt like herself again. As she stood in the doorway and waved to Jess who pulled out of the driveway in her compact little blue Kia she let her mind wander over the normal course of her day.

By now I should be at the office, Darcy would rip me over the coals if I were this late getting in, Tori thought with a grin. She pulled the door closed and crossed the hall to the phone.

Chapter 3. Honour If Not Faith

After several long rings she heard the other end get picked up and her editor's voice cut crisply in her ear, "Jordan Darcy, here. Speak fast, you're holding up the news."

"Darcy, it's Tori," Tori began.

His voice clipped her off before she could say anything more. "Tori! When are you getting your butt back in here, woman? I need you. A rocking story just came across my desk about some underground network of smugglers. It could be the city's first crime syndicate, Lightening. Big news."

Tori smiled at the use of the nickname she had earned in her junior year. "That's what I was calling about, Darcy. I have to go into the police station later this morning but..."

Darcy interrupted her. "Police? Why aren't we going to print with that right now?" he demanded.

"It's filler. Just a run of your mill home invasion, nothing to make headline. They didn't even take anything," Tori replied. *Least that's the only story the world at large is getting about it.*

"Huh, right." Darcy replied. The clatter of printers in the background and raised voices made Tori wonder if her editor could even hear her. She could tell his attention was already wandering. "Well, get the police over with. I'll have Sue email you what we got so far on the smugglers and you can jump on it. I want it asap, you hear? Don't let those bastards at ICP steal this story, Lightening. I want the scoop on this Nagaran thing."

Tori gasped, remembering the word from the conversation between the intruders last night, but before she could reply the buzz of the signal disconnecting rang in her ear. She grimaced, glancing at the phone in her hands. She was tempted to call him back but shook her head as she put the phone back in its cradle. She bit her lip between her teeth and, as she went to walk away, she glanced at the mirror above the phone. She ran a hand through the curling chaos of her hair. It hung past her shoulders, down her back, and was impossible to tame. Giving up, she sighed and snatched up her keys and purse.

Chapter Four

Blood Ties

"You said she wasn't in any of this, Tempany," Lucas shouted as he stormed into the penthouse office. The morning sunlight streamed in from the window. It gave the room an aura of warmth and peace. The thick cream carpet sprung under his feet as he strode across the room and slammed three folders on her desk.

Tempany turned her strong sapphire eyes on him, her brow creased. "Lucas," she said.

"Why didn't you tell me the truth?" Lucas demanded.

"I didn't think it applied to her," Tempany replied as she brushed a hand over the top folder. "She was just a child then. I didn't think the trouble had anything to do with her."

"Well she's in it up to her neck now," Lucas snapped in reply. He flicked open the folder and drew two pictures from deep among the papers. They were a child's drawings; the one of the woman he had remembered as he drove, and another, of a white winged angel bent over a body.

"She had remarkable artistic talent, so young," Tempany whispered, tracing a finger over the carefully detailed wings.

Lucas jabbed a finger at the other picture. "The woman, Tempany. Who is she? Who is she really?"

Tempany looked down at the woman in the drawing as she replied, "We don't know, Lucas. Honestly. She's one of them, I would suppose. But we've never had the opportunity to make an I.D. with any degree of certainty."

"You've had twenty years! Surely something has come up about this. I thought they were looking into her. You mean to tell me the conclave have left Rick's murderer free to roam around, killing people, whenever and however she pleases?" Lucas shoved the papers back into the folder. Tempany remained silent and Lucas glared down at her as he continued. "She was in her house, Tempany. Right there, inches from her. Hell, she brushed right past and my charge has a bruise or two to prove it."

Tempany pushed her chair back and stood, gaining the several inches needed to meet Lucas's eye. "Watch your tone, Lucas. I can appreciate your anger but there is no call to be disrespectful, especially a man of your standing," Tempany reprimanded him.

He snarled, his voice low, "I'm not a man."

She ignored him and continued, "We did not know Tori was in such imminent danger."

"I don't believe you. It's the whole reason I was put on this case, isn't it? You knew this might happen. Uriel was there! Did you send him?"

Tempany blinked in surprise and then gave a heavy sigh before answering, "Uriel no longer answers to me." She drew herself upright and lifted her shoulders in a graceful shrug and then settled herself down in her chair again. "Since Michael," she began.

Lucas snapped, interrupting her, "Michael! It always comes back to Michael. Is that who Uriel takes his orders from now? Michael vies for a right to lead the Heavens?"

"I don't know. But we'll find him, Lucas," Tempany replied, finding the quiet calm that was so characteristic of her interactions with others. Lucas threw up his hands and hissed an exasperated sigh as he spun away from her. He stalked across the room, pacing the length of it with heavy steps. Despite his obvious disapproval, her tone softened, and with greater conviction she said again, "we'll find him."

"You haven't found him yet. He's been gone too long already."

Tempany's reply was a soft croon that was barely audible, "Time moves slowly here, but it's nothing more than the pause between two breaths. A moment is a lifetime; a decade, a millennia."

Lucas turned, spinning back to face her. "Two decades, and far too many deaths. We should have put a stop to the Nagaran centuries ago, before they ever became more than a rabble of sheep herders splitting the guts of newborn lambs to read their fortunes and drink their blood. Before they were influential enough to cause dissent within the conclave."

Tempany's head tipped forward and her eyes closed. Lucas could feel the wash of pain that flooded over her. "None of us could have seen what they would become."

"Michael saw it, even then."

"Lucas," Tempany kept her voice gentle but persuasive.

"Look, forget it, Tempany. You said I could get off this case. I want off it, now!"

Tempany bit her lip. Lucas, distracted from his anger and frustration for a moment, thought the movement seemed almost endearingly youthful. Then he snapped the stray fancy away with an angry huff and straightening to glare across the room at her.

Chapter 4. Blood Ties

"Lucas," Tempany began more carefully. She felt around the words, "I've tried. I really have tried to find someone else, but there *is* no one else."

"You promised!" Lucas stroked a hand through is hair, rumpling the golden curls. His eyes closed a moment before they opened, slightly moistened with the glisten of unshed tears. "I can't do this Tempany. I can't do it again."

"There is no one else who can, Lucas. You have to do this. You can't just abandon her."

Lucas drew his hand down his face and then choked a strange, empty laugh. He strode across the room and glared down at her. "What makes you think I can protect her? I didn't protect any of the others." He shook his head. "This one is on you, Tempany," he said. He snatched the folders from her desk then turned his back on her and strode from the room.

The front desk at the police station reminded Tori of the newspaper offices; a mass of papers, strewn in some strange, organised chaos. She joined the queue at reception and sighed as she looked down the long line in front of her.

Men in blue strode around the room. Somehow, they all moved with the same air of confidence, as if they were going somewhere of vital importance. *Probably even swagger like that when they head for the men's room*, Tori thought with a smile.

Finally, she reached the front of the queue and was able to speak to the clerk. "I'm supposed to meet with Detective, ah," Tori paused, realising she had forgotten the detective's last name. She drew the card from her pocket and glanced down at the sharp-edged print. "Detective Caelum."

The woman behind the desk nodded and tapped her pen on the page in front of her. "Name?" she snapped, her tone brisk.

"Tori, I'm Tori Sapera. He asked me to come in this morning. It's about the people who broke into my home last night."

The woman sniffed and lifted her head, pushing her spectacles back up her nose. "He's not in yet," she drawled. "You'll have to come back later."

Tori glanced down at her watch, "But he asked me to meet him at eleven."

The woman shrugged. "Don't know what to tell you, honey. He's not here. You can sit and wait if you want. No idea how long he'll be."

A cool breeze drifted through the front door of the office as another pair of finely polished black leather shoes sauntered across the threshold. He clutched a selection of folders in his hand. His dark scowl seemed unnatural on his face. His eyes sparkled as they caught sight of Tori standing at the desk. He spoke crisply, "Miss Sapera, good. Come with me."

Tori turned a quick smile on the woman at the desk before turning away. The woman at the desk shrugged one shoulder, sighed, and called out sharply, "Next!" She waved the next person forward before Tori had even stepped away from the desk.

Tori turned rushing to catch up with Lucas who was striding away down a brightly lit hallway. They entered another shared office space. He led her across the room to another door, which he opened. He gestured for her to enter before stepping in behind her and closing the door.

Although the room had no window, it was bright and airy with a sense of spaciousness that defied its size. The walls, painted a soft yellow, complemented the pale blue carpet. A broad oak desk seemed to fill the room, its surface scattered with haphazard piles of paper. A large, clean whiteboard was tucked behind the door.

"Right," Lucas said, placing the folders onto the desk. "Thank you for coming in."

He trailed off, distracted by a post-it on a folder. Tori read the upside-down words in black marker, "Photos and Labs."

"Oh, perfect. Just a moment. Bear with me, please." Lucas's tone had the detached air of professionalism that Tori remember from their earlier meeting. He was already flipping through pages and scanning information, but he lifted a hand to gesture at the empty seat opposite his desk.

Tori sat and lifted her chin to peer at the photographs that had scattered out of the file when he had flicked it open and pulled out the printed pages. They were of the mess her house had been left in. Tori frowned, feeling the sting of tears in her eyes. She bit her bottom lip as she blinked them away and turned her gaze to Lucas's face. His eyes, the same pale blue as the carpet, were sharp and alert as he studied the pages before him.

Moments later he looked up at her from the pages. "Unfortunately we have very little to go on, but the fingerprint analyses does confirm that at least two sets of fresh prints from your home invasion last night match prints found at a crime scene twenty years ago. Relative size would indicate one set belongs to you, and the other seems to be those of the woman you described," Lucas explained.

"So you can trace her, can't you? You can finally catch my father's killer?" Tori weaved her hands in her lap, clutching her fingers as she leaned forward.

Lucas swallowed and Tori saw the flex of his Adam's apple before he replied, "Unfortunately, those prints have no identification in our database although they are linked to another unsolved crime. I'm not at liberty to discuss that case with you. I can tell you, however, that we are doing everything we can to positively identify the woman and bring her to justice."

Tori quivered, drawing in a shaky breath. She felt a well of anger building in her chest and grasped at the fire it gave her to push away the tears dampening her lashes. "You didn't catch her twenty years ago, what makes you think now will be any different?" she asked, her tone lashed with bitterness.

"Our technology has improved over the years and we have more to go on. We had fingerprints on file from your father's case and possibly a sample of hair from the other. This time we recovered two samples of fresh blood from the scene. We are coming closer all the time to discovering her identity and we have an idea of who she works for."

Tori shook her head. "Who she works for? What do you mean?"

"In your transcripts, from your father's case, you said the woman had demanded your father join them." Lucas shuffled through the file searching for a page. "Here it is. "Join us", you said the woman had said that to your father."

"I was a child," Tori cried. "I was terrified, and traumatised. You take the word of children who draw pictures of snakes and angels and scream in their dreams?"

Lucas stabled his hands on the edges of his desk and looked across at her. His gaze had gentled. It soothed the anger she was trying to hold on to. "I trust a witness to a crime," he said. "I admit, it's not evidence that would hold up in court, but I trust it."

Tori shivered, "You trust it? The snakes, and the wings, do you trust that too?"

"You're not crazy, Tori. You weren't then, and you're not now. I can't explain it to you, but I trust that what you described, what you drew as a child, I trust that is what you saw."

Tori gazed up at him. His eyes burned with sincerity and she felt the smouldering flames of her anger dissolve in a flood of tears. Her breath hitched and she caught her face in her hands, feeling moisture gather on her fingers as her shoulders shuddered with noisy sobs.

Chapter 4. Blood Ties

Seconds later his hand was on her arm, a quiet strength that burned warmly through the sleeve of her shirt. She felt enveloped by him, as if he had pulled her into a hug, but only his hand touched her, cupping her arm and rubbing a single thumb up and down so softly she barely felt the movement. If not for the burning flame of his fingers she might not even notice the motion. Her tears dried and the sobs slowed until she no longer shook with them. She lifted her head from her hands and wiped the pad of her thumb across one check, stroking away the dampness.

"I'm sorry," she said. "I don't normally fall apart like this."

Lucas gave her a compassionate smile and reached behind him to snatch a tissue from the box on his desk. "Here," he said, handing her the tissue. "You've been through a great deal."

Tori sniffed as she wiped the tears from her eyes and cheek, then brushed the tissue against her nose. "It's just, I never had anyone believe me, well, except my Gran," Tori said. Her lips quivered and she drew a shuddered breath as she blinked back more tears. "I'll be okay now, thank you."

She noticed for the first time how close he was. He had crouched in front her, barely an inch from her knees, and his arm reached across her to touch her shoulder. His thumb still stroked her arm. His soothing warmth tingled along her skin.

Lucas blinked, seeming to gather himself, then snatched his hand away. "Right," he said gruffly, then cleared his throat. "Well, is there anything else you remember of last night that you didn't tell the constable?" Lucas asked as he stood. He stepped backwards and leaned his hips against his desk. His hands gripped the edges either side of him.

Tori swiped away a final tear and crumpled the tissue between her fingers in her lap. "I don't think so," she began, her voice tentative as she let her mind wander backward playing the scene through her memory for missing fragments of detail. She shook her head and added, "I don't remember any more. Is it enough, you know, to catch these," she paused, "uh, people?"

"I'm piecing together the information and will do what I can. In the meantime, I recommend you keep your home secure. Perhaps there is someone you could stay with? At least until we determine what the intruders may have been searching for and if there is a possibility they might return."

Chapter 4. Blood Ties

Tori nodded. Lucas pushed himself off the desk and held his hand out to her. She stood taking it and felt his warmth tingle through her fingers.

"Thank you for coming in. I will contact you when I have more information," he said. His tone had turned sharply professional again but his warm hand and gentle eyes were soft.

"Thank you, detective. I appreciate all you are doing," Tori replied. His hand lingered in hers before breaking apart. Tori blinked, then smiled at him as he stepped past her to open the door.

Chapter Five
Behind Crumbling Walls

Tori shivered in the chilled air, her dark-eyed gaze intent on the aged stone and moulding timbers before her. She pulled her thick, woven coat tighter against her shoulders. The length of her well-worn blue jeans, ragged and mud-splattered, clung to her legs. Tori looked ahead of her. She moved with cautious, but steady steps.

The gate hung on dilapidated hinges and squealed in protest as Tori leaned against it. It gave, grudgingly. Tori brushed a strand of raven hair out of her face then stood on the threshold as she spoke into a small voice recorder. "This church is, perhaps, the oldest in the city. It appears to have been out of service for many years. There's no sign of recent activity, but according to my sources it's a frequent location for the exchange of illegally smuggled exotic animals." She flicked the device off and slipped it into her pocket before trudging through the damp grass.

The doors of the church loomed, gaping like an open maw, with nothing but darkness within. Tori let a sliver of fear chill her as she glanced around. She could not shake the sense of being watched that hung over her. Since the break in last night her uneasy tension seemed almost constant. An impending sense of doom lingered in the air. She tossed her shoulders in an attempt to throw it off and glanced around the deserted churchyard again.

As she leaned on the rotten timbers of the old door, she gasped, snatching back her hand. "Oh, don't be ridiculous," she muttered under her breath. She shook her head, pushing away the sense of unease and discomfort that had pulsed though her. "It's just cold."

She rubbed her arms to ward off the late autumn chill that lingered in the shadow of the old church. Then she pulled the sleeve of her coat down over her hand and shoved again with her covered fist. She forced the door wider and pushed her way inside. The door swung behind her as she stepped past. It clanged shut, closing her into the darkness within.

Tori stood, waiting for her eyes to adjust to the gloom. Slowly two rows of pews came into focus. They stood, facing the far end of the church, like two-dozen devotees listening intently to a long silent sermon.

A shaft of light bloomed through the round window that spread the greater length across the farthest wall. Crossings of colour cast shadows on the ground. Through fragments of broken glass Tori could see the sky. Even damaged, she could see the magnificent stained-glass apparition of a handsome angel; its face full of tenderness. In its glorious, winged embrace lay an infant. The child's smile lit with serenity, peace, and contentment; radiant with the knowledge that he was safe and loved.

The church appeared to have been cared for in its time. Even in the faded years it had retained a charm and life all its own. The building appeared to have fallen into disuse. The outside world had started to reclaim the stone. Vines crept through crevices in a fallen segment of wall. A steady drip of damp echoed from an unseen corner.

Tori drew the voice recorder from her pocket again. Her voice a soft, reverent, whisper, barely stirred the eddy of dust in the air. The husky tone echoed from the stone around her. "This beautiful old church is deserted. Nothing seems out of order. There's no sign of disturbance or recent use. Nothing that would indicate illicit activity." She clicked the recorder off again and sighed.

She walked further into the long room. Half way down the aisle she gazed up, surrounded by the light of the stained glass. "It's a shame no one comes here anymore," she said into the stillness.

Chapter 5. Behind Crumbling Walls

"Why would she come here of all places?" Lucas muttered. He glared at the two old doors that had swung closed. They blocked his view of Tori. He tapped his fingers against the steering wheel of his sedan as it idled on the curb outside the church. A long minute passed.

Lucas huffed an impatient sigh and twisted the keys in the ignition. He opened the door and drew himself out of the car, then tossed his coat across the seat before slamming the door shut. He leaned back against the warm metal. The afternoon sunlight warmed his skin, but the dark coldness of the church seemed to taunt him. Something about the place left an uneasy rock in the pit of his stomach.

A flicker of movement caught his eye. The shadow of motion danced so quickly he wondered if it were just a play of sunlight through the trees. The hair on the back of his neck prickled. Lucas pushed himself up from the car. He scanned the contours of the church, frowning at the darkness in the windows.

There it was again, a dark flicker in the shadows. It slunk along a far wall then disappeared behind the church. Lucas's gaze narrowed. He caught a glimpse of a black booted heel as it stepped around the distant corner.

Lucas strode across the yard and slammed his hands against the twin doors, shoving them wide. As he strode into the building he fixed his eyes on his charge. She stood in the centre of the room, unaware and unprotected.

The squealing protest of the outer door lifted gooseflesh on Tori's skin. The hinges of the old wood splintered and the doors crashed with a resounding shudder against the inner walls. Tori spun, her hair fluttered against her shoulders and her breath froze in her lungs. The voice recorder tumbled from her fingers and clattered against the stone floor. Her eyes widened as she gazed down the length of the church.

The detective strode toward her with his hand lifted. Tori blinked in surprise. He emitted a rippling aura of confidence and strength from his broad shoulders. Honeyed strands of hair framed a softened face.

"Tori," Lucas called out. Spears of blue cut across the room and held Tori's darker gaze. His eyes seemed to glow with the reflected sparkle of sunlight and then darkened as they drifted away from her. She could see his throat convulse, a sharp swallow, an indrawn breath, before strangling out a cry, "Tori!"

Thick hands grabbed her shoulders and Tori tensed. A shudder of revulsion coursed through her.

Instinctively, she jerked away from the black-gloved fingers but could not free herself from their steel grip.

Her eyes caught on Lucas in the distance. He looked like he had been coming toward her, but his step faltered. She could see his hesitation as his gaze swept the room before coming back to her face.

She caught and held the darkening azure depths. He was closer now, but still several feet from reach. Tori registered the emotions flickering across his features; helplessness and failure disappeared as swiftly as they had shown themselves. Her own gaze pleaded with his. An instant later self-preservation rippled through the churning fear in her belly. She clawed at the gloved fist that had threaded across her shoulders and bit the thick, course fibre covering her assailant's arm. His yelp of pain encouraged her, but his grip tightened.

Tori lifted her foot, kicking her insole backwards and connecting with the solid leg of the man behind her. He grunted, accepting the pain, and then yanked her backwards off her feet. Off balance, Tori felt herself falling and flailed to catch herself. The arm around her pulled her against a thick body.

Tori's gaze whipped around to see dark eyes, and the shaved head above them. "Let me go!" she demanded finding her voice. She strained her neck, ignoring the ache in her muscles, as she fixed a glare on the stranger who held her.

His voice was a course rumble, hissed between callused lips, "No can do, Missy. You're intended for the Sacred Mother." He did not meet her gaze. His focus across the room drew Tori's attention to another presence: the woman.

Tori glared at her. She was clad in dark leather again; this time a skirt slit up both sides flowed around her long legs. The flickering tongue of a small black-, red-, and gold-banded snake touched her cheek. The woman watched it a moment with a smile through lips painted crimson. The snake curled around her wrist. As one, they turned to gaze across the room.

The woman was not watching her, Tori realised. She was watching the detective. Lucas seemed frozen just within the doors of the church. His gaze remained transfixed on Tori. "Look out!" he cried. She winced as a sharp blade nicked the skin at her neck. An arm wrapped around her waist. She turned her head to lighten the pressure and felt the man behind her tighten his grip again.

"Silence!" he hissed, but the warning had been enough to spur the detective to action. Lucas turned, backing away. Tori held her breath, watching him. Her mind raced. *He can't leave me here.*

Instead of backing toward the door, Lucas turned. He circled around the room slightly to bring all three people into view. Tori gasped as his new position revealed a pair of magnificent feathered wings. Tori's mind conjured the soft white contours of the wings she had seen in the stained glass window behind her. Her gaze wandered over Lucas, seeing him again as if for the first time.

Somehow, she recognised him. Beyond the features of the detective she had met earlier in the day, there was a sense of knowing him. "I've known him my whole life," she whispered, suddenly realising why she recognised the curve of his chin and the strong caress of his hands.

The knife dug against her chin again and the man behind her grunted, shifting his grip into a painful crush against her ribs. A drawl of laughter from the woman drew Tori's attention. She bit her lip against the pain, and pushed her head back against her captor as she gazed up at the redhead.

"You're timing is immaculate, Seraph. What a pleasure to see you with your lovely Charmer." She drew a long, coiled whip from her leather belt with her free hand. She caressed it in agile fingers. "You couldn't save your precious charge before, and now you will fail again. So unlike Uriel," she said with a wicked smile. "Have *you* tasted my venom, boy? Let's dance with the pipes."

With a sharp crack, black wiry tendrils whipped out several feet. Tori flinched. Her breath grew ragged as she watched in growing horror. The detective's eyes narrowed. He lifted an arm to swipe away the uncoiled whip. Sharp spines cut his forearm as he swatted the cord away. Tori could see his lips harden as his eyes darkened.

The woman moved several feet closer with a hiss. Her fingers flexed on the whip's handle. Her brows drew together as his voice called in soft menace, "I do not fear you, woman."

Her lips curved in a smile and her wrist dropped the length of whip allowing several feet of slack. "You will, pretty boy," she spat, eyes darkening.

He gasped and staggered backwards. Tori's breath caught in her chest as she watched rich red blood course from his shoulder. A hard bolt splintered a chip of wood from the pew behind him and sunk deep into the stone floor. Tori searched the rafters. A third darkness-clad figure steadied the spent crossbow, a smug grin on his face. His eyebrow lifted as he looked down on them, waiting.

With a shuddering breath and flutter of wings, Lucas fell to one knee. Air hissed between his teeth and he glanced at his shoulder before returning angry eyes to the woman. Dark black swirled in the red rivulets of blood that coursed from his shoulder. "Poison," he winced, a single word on exhaled breath. His eyelashes fluttered on his cheeks as he tried to fend off the swift spreading toxin.

From the rafters above them the man with the crossbow leapt, landing with lithe grace as he brought the full weight of the heavy crossbow with crushing accuracy against the shoulder it had already wounded. With a groan, Lucas sought Tori's gaze again. She saw pain blurring his vision and felt her stomach flutter at the deeper pain she saw within the depths of his eyes. There was an anxious helplessness within this giant soul that spoke through the cold autumn air of heart-breaking failure. The crossbowman dealt him a kick to the ribs and he doubled over.

A melodious chuckle echoed off the walls and the woman swayed toward them. "Oh my, this prize is barely worth the blood we've spilled to be so easily taken." She spread her feet as she reached him and gripped his chin between the fingers of one hand, forcing him to see her.

"Does your charge mean so little to you, Seraph, that you won't fight to protect her from our kind?"

Tori could see the anger that flared within him in the hardening of his jaw. He tore himself out of her grasp and struggled against the numbing poison that ran through his system. "You will not harm her!"

"She is already ours, boy, and we will do with her as we please. Who could stop us? You? Weak as a lamb and even now inching closer and closer toward slumber?" She nodded to the crossbowman. Course fingers gripped Lucas's shoulder.

Lucas gritted his teeth. "Enough! I won't play your games."

Her laugh tinkled again but her eyes remained cold. As the bells of laughter faded her lips curved in a dark scowl. She nodded at the crossbowman who clipped the crossbow to his belt and unclipped a rough set of manacles. They jangled in his hands as his quick fingers rattled the length of chain. "Come, little boy. The High Priestess has a use for you, too," he taunted.

A swift glare from the leather-clad woman silenced him and, with brow furrowed he jammed a knee between Lucas's drooping wings and dragged the angel's arms beneath them. Lucas groaned again as his shoulder pulled tight. Another flurry of blood coursed down his shirt.

His pale feathers fluttered until the crossbowman slapped them aside with a roughened mutter and clicked the manacles into place. The detective's body crumpled, he drooped forward and slumped to the ground, unconscious.

"Ah, your protector has succumb, Charmer," the woman whispered, leaning close to Tori. Her ruby lips brushed against Tori's cheek. Tori drew back from the intimacy then winced as the sharp steel blade nicked her throat again.

"Who are you?" Tori demanded through gritted teeth. "What do you want with me?"

The woman stepped backward. She looked Tori up and down as she slapped the coil of her whip against her gloved fingers. A cruel smile curved her lips, but her dark eyes remained impassive. "I? Why I am Marlena and I have no desire for you at all, Charmer. But for your family connection I would care nothing for you at all."

Tori's eyes narrowed, "You killed my father."

Marlena chuckled darkly, "So I did, and you saw the whole thing, didn't you. A little mouse hiding under your daddy's desk."

"I saw you. I saw you stab him," Tori said, her voice laced with a pain.

"Yes, but you know nothing of that. You were a child. I asked him to join us, to be with me. He should have been with me, but your wretched mother," Marlena trailed off. Her chin had dropped as she remembered. Now it snapped back up. "You look like her you know. She and I were friends once, before she mated with filth and had delusions of grandeur. Rick was blind, even then. He thought the world spun from the core at her heart. He wouldn't believe me when I told him the truth. No one ever believed me."

Tori glared at her. "You expect my pity?" The crack of the woman's hand against her cheek stung. Tori turned back, her gaze full of hatred.

"I expect respect. I deserve it. I demand it," Marlena snarled. "You know nothing of the trials I've been through, child. Nothing. Your mother had it all, the wealth, the status. She hoarded it all. Even your father. Once something was hers she never gave it up. Not until you." Marlena's lips curved in a smile and she tilted her head. "She gave you up, even as you came into the world, a mewling brat. She gave you up and never saw you again."

Gritting her teeth, her eyes narrowed, Tori bit back, "My mother died."

Chapter 5. Behind Crumbling Walls

"Did she? I suppose she did. At least that is how Anna would have described it. She was gone, and you were here, and she was never my best friend again."

"My mother's alive?" she asked in a tentative whisper full of a child's senseless hope.

Marlena blinked at her as if seeing her again for the first time, "What?"

"My mother, she's alive?"

The woman grunted. "I've no idea," she muttered. "What you should be asking about is what secret Anna kept from you all these years. Did you know your grandmother had a secret?"

Tori swallowed and blinked back the tears forming in her eyes. "Don't speak of my grandmother as if you knew her better than I did," Tori spat.

"Ah, but I did, for a time. Enough to know she didn't tell you everything. Enough to know you've not learned the truth," Marlena said, her lips curved in a taunting smile.

"I learned she loved me. They all loved me. I was precious to them," Tori snapped back. She drew the warmth of those three truths around her like a blanket to fend off the coldness of Marlena's words. She wriggled against her captor's arms and shouted, "Let me go!"

"But you've come so far, Charmer. You've learned so much already. Surely such a talented journalist would not abandon the truth so close to uncovering its secrets. So close to knowing about you mother's connection to the Nagaran." The woman paused as if gauging Tori's reaction.

Tori felt baited but could not stem her curiosity. "The Nagaran?" she asked. "What does my mother have to do with the Nagaran? What is it?"

Marlena chuckled again, "Ah, so you are interested. Come, Charmer, it's time you learned the truth." She turned away from Tori and moved into the darkness of a distant wall. Tori heard stone grinding on stone but could not see through the shadows until an eerie red glow seeped outward. "Bring them," Marlena demanded, her sharp command startling the two men into action.

Tori stumbled as she felt the man behind her push forward. He grunted, relaxing his wrist and the dagger to create more space. He leaned close before taking the next step and whispered, "Wouldn't wanna slit your throat 'fore Mistress Marlena has the pleasure of running ya through."

With a gasp Tori thrust her elbow backward and attempted to spin herself out of his grip. Her eyes widened in renewed fear as his arms clamped back around her.

"Be still, woman," he grunted. His guttural tone and the swaying glow of red light heightened Tori's fear. She kicked and scratched, careless of the damage she was inflicting on her captor. He grunted again as blow after blow landed against shin or stomach. Tori struck out with her fist and scored a glancing blow against the side of his face. "You..." he bellowed before raising his own fist.

Tori's teeth rattled with the blow and her head whipped backwards. Her vision spun and her body slumped. She felt herself falling, unable to stop the dizziness spreading over her. Her eyelids shuttered and she disappeared into darkness.

Chapter Six
Torque Rises

The air hummed and resonated in warm steady beats. A rich, heady heartbeat thrummed within Lucas; building, rising, and echoing until it throbbed like a dull roar inside his skull. Heat scorched his throat and his nose tingled with the acrid scent of thick smog and burning embers. A strange perfume spiced the humid air. It hung over him, sticking to his skin.

Groggy, he pulled at the edges of his mind. His thoughts were scattered, but as he came out of a deep lethargy he started to hear low chants in the throbbing around him. Blasphemous words uttered with deep conviction formed from the fragments of meaningless hum.

Lucas stirred. His muscles bunched, tight and slow. He registered pain, in his shoulder, his back and legs. Hard iron chaffed against his thighs and wrists. He attempted to pull himself upright. Chains jangled, hanging heavy across him. His shoulders cramped, slamming against hard metal on all sides.

His eyelids fluttered open. They too were heavy and uncooperative. The muted red light sent another wave of pain through his skull and Lucas grunted, blinking with slow and deliberate flickers as his vision began to adjust.

A cage. He could see the iron bars now. They surrounded him on all sides and dug into his legs and wings. Manacles held his wrists on a short chain that looped around the edges of the cage, binding him to the box. His hair brushed the bars above him.

As he shifted his weight the chains jangled again. The sharp edges dragged against his skin. Blood oozed around torn flesh and Lucas gasped short sharp breaths as he tried to still his shoulders. One shoulder ached more than the other. The dark spread of his blood against the soft white cotton of his shirt brought memories rushing back to him.

Tori! The thought flickered through his mind amongst the dozen others that reminded him of the confrontation in the church. *How long ago?* He could not be sure. It might have been hours, days, or weeks.

His gaze scanned the room around him, hunting, seeking. An eddying throng of red hoods swayed to the pulsing beat of the chant. A hundred voices joined in varied pitch. The red glow flickered and smothered them in shifting shapes. Shadows darkened the rough-hewn, earthen walls every few feet where the light between each brazier faded.

Lucas surveyed the room; the robed heads were turned toward the front of the chamber where a woman stood, raised on a semi-circle dais, before a blackened altar. Beneath her, a ragged pile of soft cloth writhed and quivered.

"Tori!" The word ripped from his raw, dry throat. A handful of the nearest faces turned toward him. They skittered away from him, their eyes wide, before one by one they returned their gazes to the front of the room.

Lucas could not take his eyes from the altar. Draped in folds of white silk, Tori struggled against the bindings that held her down. He could see her lips moving, begging and pleading. Stains of blood blackened her wrists, ankles, and face. A dark bruise pooled against her jaw.

Lucas tugged again at the manacles holding him in place and ignored the pain as they cut into his skin. Baring all his weakened strength he could not get them to give him even another inch, let alone his freedom. He slammed his hip against the cage then grimaced as the iron bars cut across his skin, adding new bruises to his already beaten body.

The chanting faded and Lucas found his gaze returning to the raised dais. The woman who stood behind Tori was covered head to toe in flowing red robes. Her face was concealed in the shroud of the crimson hood. In one hand she held a sharp curved athamé. The blade glistened with flecks of red in the strange flickering light. She held it in a gentle caress, poised inches above Tori's throat. "NO!" Lucas's voice rose and echoed off the walls.

The woman's hand froze and her head rose. Her pale blue gaze stabbed out at the crowd gathered before her. As her eyes fell on Lucas they paused. Her lips curved in a smile, baring her teeth. Her voice dripped with cruel malice, "Seraph, you awaken."

With a sensuous twist she turned and leaned down to whisper in the ear of the brutish, bald and heavily muscled man at the foot of the dais. She ran a finger along his jaw as she turned his face toward her own. The man leaned into her, breathing deeply, then snapped alert. He turned abruptly and wove through the crowd toward the cage.

Lucas's lips drew tight as he watched the man approach. His strength was returning, but he still struggled to hold himself upright. He could not imagine a confrontation with anyone while his muscles burned with lethargy-inducing toxins. He pressed himself backwards in the cage as the man clattered the hinges open. The metal bars cut across his back, crushing his wings and grinding hard into the tender bones.

He could not push himself any further into the cage, and even pressing backwards, as hard as his worn muscles and aching bones would let him, Lucas was still within arm's reach of the cage door. Thick fingers gripped the heavy chain. Lucas toppled sideways as his hands were yanked to the edge of the cage. He winced as the manacles bit into his wrists. A heavy set of keys jangled against the chains before they fell away and Lucas grasped first one wrist and then the other, rubbing the broken skin. Before the sensation had returned to the tips of his fingers, a large hand gripped the sleeve of his shirt and tugged. Lucas stumbled out of the cage and steadied himself on his feet.

"Bring him forward, Orton," the lady called. Her voice rang out through the room and echoed down the corridors. The earthen cavern amplified the sound like an amphitheatre.

The muscled brute, Orton, half dragged, half shoved Lucas back toward the dais. Robe-swathed worshipers scrambled out of his way as the Seraph stumbled forward.

As they approached the raised platform the woman reached down, gripping Lucas's elbow. Her fingers pinched his skin leaving a claim on him that reminded him, more than words might, that he was still a prisoner.

"You will bear witness to her suffering, Seraph," she crooned, "and then you will serve the whim of the Nagaran or we will condemn your soul to walk the blackened earth for all eternity." Her lips curled at the threat.

Lucas glared at her. He stood an easy head over her, but she held his gaze. Her hazy blue eyes burned with fervour and, as Lucas held her stare, she stood straighter, hands on hips, her stature a dominant aura in the room. Lucas broke the standoff first. His gaze flicked to the stone altar where Tori whimpered but no longer struggled against her bonds. "Let her go," he muttered in a low-pitched voice.

The woman's laugh grated against his nerves. She turned her back on him, raising her arms to the cultists before her. They took up their earlier chant with greater reverence than before. Anger fired within him and Lucas reached for the ropes binding Tori's ankles. He had tugged one foot free of the bonds before three strong-armed men could tackle him to his knees.

"Now, now, precious, your Charmer is far too important to us for you to be desecrating her awakening ceremony," she soothed. She ran a hand down Lucas's chest. A false smile graced her lips and gave her an almost manic appearance.

The Flight Of Torque

"Don't touch me!" Lucas thrust her away from him and struck out at the nearest man as he rose to his feet. The men holding him stumbled, knocked off balance, and Lucas used the advantage to fight his way free of them. His fist landed a solid blow in the gut of one man and his foot took the legs out from another before he had reached Tori's side again.

He grabbed at a dagger laid above her head and cut ragged tears through the bindings at her wrists. She sobbed and struggled against the cords that held her down. Lucas could feel her shivering body press against him as he leaned close to cut at the ropes. One hand came free and she reached out, clinging to him with a desperation that made his movements more agitated and frenzied.

The room had grown quiet as worshippers watched the struggle for power before them. Lucas could not tell when the din of their chanting had ceased but the sudden quiet, broken only by Tori's whimpering, sent a quiver of unease through his skin.

"Take him in hand, now." A sharp voice rose from the back of the room. Marlena strode through the parting wave of crowding cultists. They bowed their heads, some bending in half as she glided past them. Her golden robes seemed to flow and float as she swayed across the room.

Chapter 6: Torque Rises

Lucas was torn out of Tori's grasp by several strong hands and shoved again to his knees. He winced as his hip banged against the sharp corner of the altar. The stone ground against skin.

One particular hand added pressure against Lucas's shoulder sending sparks of pain through the unbound injury. Fresh blood coursed down his chest from the wound. Lucas's angry glare caught the malicious grin of the crossbowman who had dealt the injury in the church.

With swift steps Marlena rose to stand beside them. She ripped the dagger from Lucas's hands and turned to red-robed woman. "Explain this," she demanded.

The cultist dropped to one knee and bowed her head. "I'm sorry, High Priestess. He came to bear greater strength than I expected after so recent an exposure to Veliserum."

"You're a fool, girl, to think so watered a toxin would temper a Seraph for long." The High Priestess turned her gaze back on Lucas, "And you, still attempting to save your charge? Have you even begun to wonder why she is here with us? The Charmer is a Child of the Nagaran. You should feel honoured." Marlena's fingers caressed the double-edged blade as she fondled the hilt in one hand and ran her thumb across its piercing tip with the other. "I have fond memories of this blade." She turned and let the blade catch the red-orange light of the flickering braziers as she lifted it over Tori. "Do you recognise it, Charmer?"

Lucas thrust his chest outward. "Let her go!" he demanded again.

Her hand struck a stunning blow against his cheek. The smile on her lips faded, replaced by an angry scowl. "You really do not know your place, Seraph," she spat. "I shall teach you to respect the gift I give in allowing you to live." Her eyes darkened with malice and her hips swayed as she walked around him in a slow circle.

Lucas watched her movements. He felt her step behind him and the men holding him down shuffled their feet. She stepped closer, running a hand through the soft feathers of first one wing and then the other before rounding on him again. The smile was back on her lips.

"Yes, I think we need to teach you a lesson." Her eyes gave a cursory glance at each of the men holding him then settled on the hulking brute who had unlocked his cage. "Orton, you've strength enough. Take this dagger," she said, passing the blade to Orton who took it in one calloused hand while never taking the other from Lucas's arm.

"Yes, Mistress. I am your servant." His deep rusted voice held a rich ring of worship. Lucas felt sickened by the affection in Orton's tone.

"Hold him down, boys," Marlena crooned. She ran a hand in gentle caress over each of the men in turn. "Now Orton, thrust that steel between the blades of our dear Seraph's shoulders," she said, each word dripping with a saccharine sweetness, before her voice lowered to a cruel sneer, "and sever those pretty wings from his body."

Lucas flinched, then thrashed against the hands holding him down. Feeling pain lance through his shoulder, he gritted his teeth as he yanked himself forward out of the crossbowman's grasp. He turned, swinging a fist into the man's gut and stumbling as he tried to draw himself up onto his feet. Orton slashed at him with the dagger and Lucas felt the blade cut across his ribs as he tried to step backward out of their reach. He slammed against the altar. The hard stone crushed fragile bones in his wings and he cried out. Pulling away he fell into the arms of the men. They caught his heavy weight and threw him backward again. The crossbowman lifted his foot and kicked Lucas in the stomach then spun, his foot cracking against Lucas's jaw.

The Flight Of Torque

Lucas fell to the floor and the third man yanked him up. He felt the hard grip of the two men claw his shoulders as they lifted him and turned his back to Orton. Their grip tightened and they shoved his hips hard against the stone altar. He bowed under their weight feeling the rock cutting into his flesh. His chin brushed the soft folds of white cloth that covered Tori's ankles and his hazy gaze sought hers. He felt the strain in his muscles as he struggled to free himself, and felt himself grow weaker and weaker as blood coursed from his wounds.

Orton gripped a wing in one hand. It flexed beneath his fingers and he tightened his grasp, crushing the fragile bones. Lucas clenched his teeth with the pain. He felt the dagger thrust into the soft flesh of his back and he howled with agony as Orton severed the sinewed muscle, tendon, and bone of first one wing and then the other. Fresh blood coursed down his shoulders and back. It splattered the ground before soaking into the ochre rock and turned pink the white silk robes that covered Tori.

"Are you learning, boy?" The High Priestess asked.

Smothered in pain, Lucas could not find the words to answer. He struggled to hold onto the threads of consciousness that were trying to steal away from him again. He saw her grimace and nod to an unseen hand behind him. Searing heat cut into his throbbing flesh and the smell of putrid flames hit his nostrils. Waves of dizziness blurred his vision and he struggled to fend off the darkness descending over him.

Tori's eyes glistened. Tears coursed down her cheeks. Her heart ached as she glimpsed the piercing pain in the features of the angelic creature at her feet. She tilted her head at an awkward angle, afraid to take her gaze from him, and struggled against the ropes still binding her to the cold, dark stone. When he crumpled to the floor she moaned and willed him to remain strong; to fight; to live.

The shirt on his back hung in tattered threads from swollen flesh. Blood pooled in dark wells where half-submerged bone logs bobbed with each ragged breath. Skin puckered around the gaping wounds, the edges black where the flesh had been seared by flame.

The High Priestess sneered and the crack of her hand on Lucas's cheek silenced the restless muttering in the crowd of worshippers. "You are weak, Seraph," she said between gritted teeth when his eyelids quivered, and flickered open. "Without your wings you are still very beautiful, but just a man. You will watch as all you care for is taken from you. Your insolence will be rewarded, with pain."

Her fingers flickered in command to the men holding him. Orton passed the bloodstained dagger to the young cultist and then gripped Lucas's arm. Lucas groaned as another man pulled his shoulders back and together they lifted his crumpled body onto his feet. The crossbowman gripped his hair, forcing his head up until he was certain the Seraph could see the altar.

Marlena crossed the dais and settled herself into an ornate throne at its centre. She scrutinised Tori, a look laced in a cutting hatred that Tori did not understand. With a careless wave of her hand she motioned for the ceremony to continue.

Tori gazed at the angel; his corded muscles and hot skin brushed against her legs. She could feel his heat through the soft folds of silk and sensed the dejection in his spirit. She let her eyes wander over him. She was beginning to remember his face as the one that had grown familiar in her dreams. She remembered it from the night her father had been killed.

She gasped as cold metal was placed against her throat. The sharp blade forced back her chin. Warm blood trickled down her neck and into her hair. She turned her face up to the woman looming above her. Malicious eyes sparkled with pleasure and a soft, pink tongue darted between the young woman's painted lips. "Now you are mine, pretty Charmer."

"Why are you doing this?" Tori asked with short, sharp breaths. The rapture in pain apparent on the woman's face sent chills across Tori's skin.

A sigh of impatience from the throne caused Tori to look again at the regal woman sitting there. "Corelle! Continue, now!" Marlena demanded.

The young cultist's brow creased with anger, but she moved with careful grace. The dagger lifted away from Tori's neck and the cool blade brushed her breast before Tori heard her silken robe ripping, torn down the middle. The edges of the robe fell aside, baring her flesh from neck to navel. Her pale skin flushed in the flickering light from the braziers. Tori thrashed against the ropes binding her arms. Her pert breasts swayed with each movement and her breathing quickened as she felt the caress of Corelle's breath across her nipples. She clenched her thighs, feeling the tug of rope binding her ankle, and glared up at Corelle whose dark red lips moved in chant.

"Sacred mother, grant us beauty. Sacred mother, grant us wealth. Sacred mother, this we offer; blood for blood and health for health." Her warm breath brushed

Tori's face and hair. Her hands moved over Tori's soft, pale flesh.

Corelle stroked her fingers through the blood pooling in the hollow between Tori's collarbones and then painted Tori's wrists with the dark stain of crimson. She traced up the length of Tori's arms, following the curve of muscle. Her agile hands moved in sure motions drawing an arching line either side of Tori's eyes, along her collarbone, across her midriff, over her ribs.

With each stroke the woman's chant grew stronger. It wove with the voices of the cultists around her, rising to crescendo.

Tori's breath came in quick bursts, her chest heaving. She had given up the struggle against the rope and instead worked with one hand in an attempt to loosen the knots that held her down. She watched with wide eyes as Corelle's bloodied fingers gripped the curved dagger.

One hand held the blade. Its hilt almost touched Tori's chin as she looked down her body. Corelle's free hand disappeared beneath the folds of her dark robe. She withdrew a vial and flipped the cap with her thumb. A bitter smell filled Tori's nostrils and she whimpered growing more frantic.

Corelle's lips moved to the same rhythm but the words of the chant altered as she poured the thick green liquid with careful precision along the length of the blade. "Sacred mother, grant us courage. Sacred mother, grant us guile. Sacred mother, so anointed; tooth for tooth and bile for bile."

The toxin, like a viscous honey, sizzled as it burned along the blade of the dagger and blackened the blood that pooled along its edges. Tori's eyes widened. "No, don't do this," she pleaded. Tori could see the light change in the woman's eyes, but she did not falter in her meticulous enactment of the ritual. Tori cast a desperate look across the dais to the woman who watched with an impassive and unmoved expression from her throne. "Why are you doing this?"

Tori's breath caught as she felt the air move above her. Corelle dropped the glass vial and it splintered on the hard stone floor. She gripped the hilt of the dagger with both hands and poised the pointed blade above Tori's heart. Her voice rang out at fevered pitch. "Sacred mother, grant us glory. Sacred mother, grant us might. Sacred mother, take our daughter; life for life and blight for blight."

The blade cut deep into Tori's flesh and Tori sank into the pain. "No," she moaned, her breath stolen by the agony of the twin-edged dagger thrusting toward her heart. She felt a rib give under the pressure and her tear-filled focus blurred.

Forcing herself to concentrate, she turned her gaze on the beautiful Seraph and used the gentle features of his face to fight the waves of nausea and dizziness that threatened to drown her. The sky in his eyes calmed her mind as her body quivered and shook. Her chest reared up from the altar and her lungs burned as she gasped for air. Her shoulders arched; her arms, dragged down by the ropes binding her wrists, wrenched at a painful angle, tugging at the tendons holding the joints to her torso. Every muscle wracked with spasms, tingling through her skin like thousands of needle pinpricks torturing the molecules across every inch of her body. Convulsions shook through every limb.

Tori's teeth chattered and she bit her tongue to hold back tortured cries. The taste of blood in her mouth sent a wave of hunger through her whole body. Her ragged breath quivered between her lips, hissing between her teeth, as she tried to quell the violent reaction. Her body defied her. She could see the horror and defeat in the eyes of her would-be saviour and ached for him. Despite the pain in his own body he still struggled against the men holding him back. Every time a cry betrayed the agony coursing through her he quivered as if his own skin were being flogged from his body.

Her stomach turned as she watched her angel struggling against the hands that held him back. *He wants to save me.* The thought caressed her mind with wonder and confusion, drawing her away from the pain.

As her body began to still, Tori shivered against an icy chill that crept through her from the surface of her skin, sinking deeper and deeper into her core. The fuzzy darkness that had lingered behind her eyes brightened. She felt aware of everything at once. Her mind crystallised in the moment. Her body tensed and gave a final shudder. Her eyes widened in fear and her voice keened from her, a cry with no words. Her fingers fumbled on the hard rope before falling away. A flurry of searing pain rippled over her tingling skin and she screamed as it lanced through every nerve ending.

Every inch of Tori's flesh felt like it was peeling away from her body. The chill grew and a raw hunger confused her senses. She felt as if she had come away from herself. Somehow she was removed from herself, detached from her body, looking down at the blood soaked dais, the flickering red pulse of light, the swaying mass of worshippers. As she rose above them, she recognised the startled and horrified vibrations radiating from the men and woman around her.

Something was happening that was not right for them and Tori knew something terribly wrong was happening within her. A consuming anger drove out her sanity. She felt swallowed by the cold that weighed down her limbs and could not contain the hunger rising within.

Time seemed to still, waiting, then twirled to catch up to the stolen moment. Tori sucked air into her lungs and shuddered. Every nerve returned to life with agonising intensity. She reared up, free of the bonds that had restrained her.

Surprise, followed by swift fury, turned on Corelle. Tori reached for the dagger then realised that her arms would not co-operate. As rage overwhelmed her, Tori felt a sense of falling, fading. Her body reacted to commands she could not remember giving. Her head and chest swayed like the flickering light and then snapped forward. Sharp teeth sunk into soft muscle at the curve of Corelle's neck and shoulder.

Tori tasted blood on her tongue and swayed into the rich warmth before she could drag her thoughts away from the strange ecstasy that filled her. She hissed a snarl, her tongue flicking between her lips. Her body quivered.

Chapter 6: Torque Rises

Horrified, the young cultist dropped the dagger. It clattered to the floor. Her hands came up against Tori's chest. The limp pressure felt more a caress than the brutal shove the weakening woman intended. Her warmth was already ebbing. Tori could smell the trickle of death that stole across the woman's skin. It grew stronger with the fading beats of her heart.

Drawing back, she tilted her head to look down on the woman. Her tongue flickered between her lips. Confused thoughts brushed through her mind too swift to grasp. Corelle's body crumpled to the floor, blood still oozing from the twin punctures at her throat.

Tori slithered forward pulling her tail from beneath the torn and bloodied silk. She landed with graceful poise on the ground. Twin eyes with slitted irises gazed down on the young priestess as Tori's scattered thoughts came together one by one. Her memories of the last few moments lanced through her. Horrified, she gasped. Another hiss flickered from her mouth. She turned to see members of the cult dropping to their knees. The cacophony of their voices roared in reverent pleas. They begged for mercy, weeping and prostrating themselves on the floor.

Tori hunted for the sight of the Seraph and found him. His mouth hung open on a frozen breath and his pain-filled gaze washed over her. The men holding him dropped to their knees, their eyes wide with shocked disbelief. Their hands fell away and without their support Lucas fell on one knee. Tori watched him struggle to rise. Her lips moved in supplication. She tried to call out to him but her voice was frozen, she could not speak. She felt trapped, unable to move, her scream silenced by a hiss that snarled from the back of her throat.

Then, as she and Lucas gazed at each other through the incense-thickened air, a cold darkness fell over her and consciousness faded. With it, Tori's naked human limbs fell in a scarred and battered heap against the hard stone floor of the dais.

Chapter Seven
Cold Dreams And Darkness

Lucas thrust himself forward but was too late to catch Tori. He knelt beside her, brushing his fingers against her cheek. He could not quite understand what he had seen. Strange images flickered through his mind's eye; mottled scale, blended with Tori's dark flowing hair and sad eyes. Then she was gone and a giant serpent had swayed before him.

Quivers shuddered through his body. His limbs burned with exhaustion. Pain spiked through him as he rotated his shoulders. He felt his freedom of movement with surprise. His body ached but was no longer held down by callused hands.

At snail's pace, awareness gathered around him. The worshippers were frenzied, their voices raised in anger, horror, and awe. The High Priestess had risen from her throne, but stood motionless at its foot. Her lips were parted on a silent gasp and her wide-eyed gaze was rooted to Tori's unconscious body.

The men who had bowed and scraped to the hissing serpent gathered their wits faster than their mistress. Orton rose at their centre and ambled, brow furrowed, toward Lucas and Tori. His lips were tight and his eyes glistened with malice. The men around him mirrored his movements. They wove forward with careful, stalking steps. Lucas felt caught between the urge to flee and a will to fight.

As Orton's thick fingers grabbed Lucas's shoulder Lucas yanked backward. Orton stumbled forward and Lucas spun cracking his elbow across the brute's back. The man tumbled forward, catching himself on his hands in a crouch before whipping a leg around and taking Lucas's feet out from under him. Lucas rolled, wincing at the tug in his shoulder as he pushed himself up from the floor. Orton stood, his chest heaving as he glared at Lucas.

"You ain't getting another lick in, bird boy."

Lucas smiled. "You do know what I am, don't you?"

"Pathetic. Yep, I know that. Should have seen how you crumpled when Jackson got you good. Almost laughed myself wet at the look on yer face. O'course I couldn't, not with the mistress watching, but I wanted to mind." Orton's lips curled up. He paced a careful circle around Lucas.

"What are you waiting for then? An invitation?"

Orton's eyes narrowed. He huffed a breath. "I ain't afraid of you, no matter what you is."

Chapter 7. Cold Dreams And Darkness

Lucas lifted his chin in challenge and the other man ground his teeth together then lunged forward. Lucas's agile step took him out of the bull's path. His foot snaked out catching Orton's ankle. The man sprawled to the ground. He spluttered as he pushed himself upward.

"Fight like a man, ya pansy," he bellowed.

"But I'm not a man."

"You ain't no angel either. Can't be 'n angel without wings." Orton sneered, inching closer.

Lucas winced, swivelling his shoulders and feeling the lightness, free of the heavy weight of his wings. Taking advantage of the his distraction Orton thrust a fist forward. Lucas snapped his head back, but the blow caught a glancing cut across his chin. He shook his head, bringing his hands up to shield his face from the barrage of blows that followed the first strike.

Each punch snapped against his wrists as Lucas thrust Orton's arms away. The brute seemed to have endless energy, but his precision was miniscule. Lucas waited, fending off the blows. Orton pushed forward, crowding his space. Lucas pushed back, but inch by inch Orton gained ground against him, until Lucas felt the cold, hard thrust of the altar behind him.

Caged, Lucas grimaced as he fended off another iron fist. An opening showed itself and Lucas took it, striking a hard blow into Orton's chin. The man's face felt like rock, but the blow snapped back the brute's head and he grunted, stumbling backward. A glowing brazier toppled in his wake sending a rain of hissing embers across the floor.

Lucas watched the haze in the man's eyes. A low rumble roared from the back of Orton's throat as he pushed forward again. Lucas thrust his shoulder into the man's chest and struck a hard punch into his ribs. Orton doubled over and Lucas's knee crushed into his face. A rush of blood spurted through Orton's fingers as he grabbed his nose.

Lucas smiled. "Are you learning anything?"

Orton's mumbled reply was lost behind the bloody nose and cracked lip. He glared up at Lucas. Lucas moved to strike down but the other man moved surprisingly fast, thrusting his head upward. The thick skull cut Lucas's jaw and his teeth clashed together, barely missing his tongue.

Lucas's breath hissed from his lips and he reeled backward but stopped short as the altar butted against his hips. Orton burst forward with an angry scowl. He thrust a shoulder forward. Lucas twirled sideways out of the brute's path and lifted his hands to shield his face as Orton turned on him again. The man's fist punched forward and Lucas stepped aside, flicking a fist under the man's arm and into his ribs.

Orton grunted but parried back catching his other fist against Lucas's cheekbone. Lucas could feel the sting of the bruise blooming under his skin. He thrust out again then gasped as a blow came from behind, cracking between his shoulder-blades. The skin tore and a gush of blood seeped down his back. He spun toward his new attacker.

"Right on, Carny. Give him hell." Orton chuckled, rubbing his ribs as he stepped back.

Carny was a wiry fellow. Dark haired with a grin on his thin lips and a wicked sparkle in his eyes. He shifted the weight between his feet, dancing back and forth. Lucas watched him, wary.

"Carny, is it?" he asked.

"My friends call me that. You're not no friend of mine."

"What do I call you then?"

Carny smiled. "You call me death."

Lucas shook his head. "I don't know. Carny just seems so much more fitting. You look like a side show from a carnival I once saw. The gypsies knew how to throw a party in those days. Likely as not you would have been the sort to finagle his way out of a mess of knots, or, I don't know, locked chains maybe."

"I'm not no carnival freak." Carny glared, his narrow eyes sharp above his hawk-like nose.

Lucas shrugged. "Well, if you're ever considering a new line of work." With an angry hiss Carny leapt forward. He kicked a high side kick and Lucas blinked as he snapped his head backwards to avoid the blow. He raised an eyebrow. "Well, you've got some moves. Maybe you'd make a good lion tamer. I imagine those guys have got to be quick on their feet."

Carny spun low on the ground and brought his foot behind Lucas's leg. Lucas stumbled but caught himself before falling.

"You gonna be the lion then?" Carny grinned. "I could probably find a chair some place. Get you a hoop of fire to jump through."

Lucas chuckled. "Quick and witty. You must be a smooth one with the ladies."

"Never had no complaints." Carny shifted from foot to foot.

They stepped around each other in a careful dance. Carny surged forward with a flurry of open-handed blows and powerful kicks. Lucas fended him off, blocking the man's quick moves. He grunted as a kick to his ribs got past his guard. As he spun out of Carny's reach a hard fist crushed against his skull, just missing his eye.

Lucas stumbled and Orton gripped his shoulder as he jumped up carrying his fist down with the weight of his body. Lucas shifted, catching the blow on his shoulder instead of his face. He gasped as pain rocked through his body. Carny took the advantage, kicking against Lucas's shoulder again and again. Blood coursed from the crossbow wound and Lucas crumpled to his knees.

Orton gripped his shoulders with one arm, arching Lucas's spine backward so that Carny could strike out at Lucas's bared ribs and stomach. Lucas heaved ragged breaths, his muscles grew weaker but he tugged against the iron grasp that held him still as Carny continued to pummel into him. His fist was arcing forward and Lucas flinched away then blinked as another man caught Carny's wrist and shoved him out of the way.

"Enough, Carny. He's about done. For now at least. I'll give you another go at him later." The newcomer lowered a loaded crossbow in front of Lucas's face. Lucas looked up into the arrogant gaze of the crossbowman. His jaw squared and he ground his teeth. "Happy to see me again I see."

"Jackson," Carny whined. "I was just getting into it."

"Back off, Carny. Jackson's gotta get this under hand."

"That's right. You two were too busy beating the hell out of him to hear but The High Priestess said to be done with him. Get him down to the cells she said."

Carny and Orton both glanced at the dais where Marlena was shouting orders. The worshippers were already scattering. Some of the cultists gave wide eyed looks at the still unconscious Tori sprawled on the cold stone.

Lucas jerked forward but Orton's crushing fingers bit into his arms.

"You ain't not going no where, pretty boy."

Jackson tightened his grip on the trigger, "Don't try anything, Seraph. The High Priestess wants to keep you alive but I'm not so attached to you. You give me any trouble and the next bolt from this crossbow will blow your brains across the altar. I figure The Sacred Mother will find it a fitting sacrifice. You might even get a place in the hallowed halls of the Nagaran."

Lucas glared up at him. "Maybe she might. You can ask her when I send you to see her."

The crossbowman laughed. "You're spirited, Seraph. I'll give you that." He stepped back, keeping the crossbow trained on Lucas. "Orton, get him to his feet. We're going."

Carny moved to one side of Lucas, and Orton, still gripping Lucas's shoulders, pulled him to his feet. Lucas grunted as another gush of blood trickled down his chest.

Despite the scurry of worshippers there were still a few stunned faces gawking up at the raised platform. Their jaws were slack, still shocked. As the four men advanced down the stairs and into the crowd, the onlookers parted, scattering to either side of the cavern. They blinked, some brushing a hand over their faces before turning away and scuttling down the halls. Their whispers echoed muted hisses off the walls.

"Slow, Seraph. I'll be watching, and just remember this is a hair trigger. It won't take much, just a squeeze. Oh, and I never miss."

Carny chuckled. "That's right, he ain't not never missed nothing." His fingers cut into Lucas's arm as he dragged the limp limbs forward. "Come on then, don't be 'specting me to carry you."

Lucas's legs were barely beneath him when Orton shoved him forward. Lucas stumbled but the grip on his arms held him upright. "Walk, pretty boy."

They wove through the dark, dank corridors. The halls criss-crossed through a dozen caverns. Most were empty but here and there small groups of cultists whispered, heads together. As the four men clambered into through rooms the worshippers wide eyes would turn to watch them. As the men passed the worshippers' whispers became more frantic and hushed.

The gap between braziers of burning coals and reeking incense increased the further into the bowels of the underground temple the men walked. The darknesses between red glows were heavy with the fog of acrid smoke and haze of sickly scent. Lucas grimaced as they passed another shadowed hall.

As they reached a narrow staircase the braziers ended. Carny snatched a torch from the wall and lead the way down the tiny carved stairs.

"Watch your step, little lion. Wouldn't not want you to break your neck in a fall. This stairway ain't not nothing but a long, long way down."

Orton's sinewed arm cut across Lucas's shoulders and pressed against his throat. "Don't mind, Carny. I got him good. He's going no place."

"Come on you two, I haven't got all day."

"Aww, Jackson, you used to be more fun than this."

"He's sweet on a girl, Carny. Gotta never leave the ladies waiting for long."

"I'm not. I've got things to do, that's all. Come on."

Chapter 7. Cold Dreams And Darkness

The stairs opened out on a dark row of cells. The iron bars were cut into the hard rock of the cavern roof and floor. A large gate clanged open and Carny thrust the torch into the cell, waving the flickering flame side to side above the ground. The light bounced back and fourth in the few feet from one side of the cell to the other.

"Look, see, ain't not no rats to make a meal of you. Least not yet. O'course if one comes along there ain't no one to hear you call for help neither." Carny laughed and drew the torch back. He stepped out of the way as Orton threw Lucas into the cell. Lucas stumbled, catching himself against the back wall. Pain shot up his arms and through his shoulders, coursing down his back.

"One of you should stay here. Keep an eye on him."

Orton grunted. "Why? It's not like he's going someplace. These cells are locked tight."

"Yeah, Jackson. There's not no angel voodoo gonna get 'em open. 'Sides, he's weak as a kitten, little lion cub. See, he can't not barely stand."

"The High Priestess will be pissed if anything happens to him."

"So, we'll take turns checkin' on him. Com'on, the boys've got a match going upstairs. I got good coin on the outcome. Ain't not no way I'm giving it up for babysittin'."

"Eh? What's odds?" Orton asked.

"Seven to one, Hissyfit verse Clawless Tooth. Man, Hissy can be a right nipper but I reckon it's 'bout time Clawless took down. He's not no pitbull but he's got fire in his beady eyes."

"Jackson, we gotta go. You got yeh thing to do an' we got ours. Carny and I'll check on him after the fight. Swear."

His crossbow lowered, Jackson gripped the bars and shook them. They jangled, but held fast. He sighed. "Yeah, I guess he's not going anywhere. You check back on him, mind. And not just after the fights, every hour."

The three turned away and began walking up the stairs. Carny's whine echoed back as the torchlight disappeared and darkness smothered Lucas.

The dank cold chilled his aching muscles and Lucas lay on the floor a long moment, breathing slow breaths into his bruised ribs. His back roared with a burning fire against the rocky earthen floor of the cell. He rolled to his belly. Every inch of his body stung. He huffed, dust clinging to his face and scattering across the floor. His ribs complained at the weight of his body but the pain of the bruises was dulled by the flames licking across his back and shoulders.

Chapter 7. Cold Dreams And Darkness

Lucas took a few short gasps and then, with the last of his strength, he pulled himself over to the bars of the cell. They shuddered, jangling in the iron lock as he shook the cell door. He shouted, over and over, knowing no one would hear him. As his horse voice gave out Lucas sunk against the bars, his head leaning on the cool rods.

"Tori, I'm so sorry," he whispered into the darkness. "I failed, again."

The strange murmur of voices, staged in hushed whispers, threaded over Tori's skin and she squirmed against the hard cold floor. A dark weight of exhaustion gripped her limbs and lethargy dragged down her eyelids but her ears heard the movement throbbing around her. Her breath heaved through her lungs and her dry, cracked lips tasted of dust and blood.

"Bring her!" Marlena's sharp voice bit through the muttering voices. Soft, warm arms lifted her from the floor and she snuggled into the warmth. Tori heard a soft unfamiliar chuckle. She wanted to pull herself awake, urged herself to wake up, to fight back, but the ache in her belly rumbled with hungry desire and her arms crept around a warm, muscled neck. Her hair tumbled backwards over the curve of his arm. Her conscious thoughts drifted away again as the pain in her chest stabbed and the arms holding her shifted her weight, pulling her closer against the hard muscles of his chest. She felt a ripple of pleasure blossom through her, pooling between her thighs as her breasts brushed against soft wool.

In the darkness of her mind she felt a slithering caress. It hissed curling around her. Then her body arched as it snapped against her mind. It sifted through her thoughts, twisting them, turning them against her memories as if it were threading itself through every moment of her life. Fragments chased across her, drawing into the most painful thoughts and lingering over them as if enjoying the pain she had suffered and relishing the anguish. Tori whimpered and the arms around her tightened. She fought against the nightmares filling her mind, tortured flashes of her most broken moments played over and over in her mind.

The grip around her tightened and she sucked a ragged breath into her lungs. Pain stabbed across her chest, and lanced through her entire body. She welcomed the sweep of agony because it blanked her mind. The curl of darkness snarled against her thoughts one last time, sending a wave of nausea roiling in her gut as it faded. She felt her stomach retch, felt the sticky splatter of vomit against her lips and chin, smelled the acrid scent of bile and bit back the second wave of sickness that raced through her.

Before the fog stole her away again she heard the snarling voice of The High Priestess. "Get her cleaned up and see to that wound. Put a guard on her. She's not to leave the room." A swirl of robes brushed Tori's skin as the woman passed. Footsteps faded as they crossed the room and paced down the hall.

A gentle hand brushed strands of her fringe from her sweat-soaked forehead. "All will be well, dolce uno. I have you." The lilting accent in his voice soaked a honeyed warmth through her skin. Her eyelids fluttered open and she saw the dark curl of his hair before they fluttered closed again.

Tori felt pain stab through her ribs with every step he took, it seemed to grow fainter and fainter as her body, nerve endings overwhelmed with sensation, began to shut down. Her head lolled against the crook of his arm. Her whole body went slack as her muscles refused to support her. Darkness pulled her down again, slithering over her as if coiling around her legs, her chest, her throat, she felt the cool embrace of stiff sheets. As her mind gave itself over to nothingness, shielding itself from the torment of tortured terrors that were beginning to play through her thoughts again, she heard a soft feminine voice and felt a warm damp cloth brushing against her tingling skin.

The room throbbed with echoes of running water and Tori swirled in the depths of a strange dream. She felt a wash of security she had not felt since she had been a very small child. The memories that tingled through her were unfamiliar, as if they belonged to someone else, but somehow she knew they were her own. The forgotten tendrils of her life that were lost in the shrouded places in her mind. Shadows, late whispers she heard while she was sleeping, secrets hidden in her childhood memories.

She felt moist tears on her eye lashes but, entranced by the wonder of seeing parts of her life she never realised still existed within her she let them trickle across her cheek and splatter against the pillow beneath her head. Her child-mind wove backward through time. Snippets of fragile moments passed in seconds then flittered further backward, backward, backward. She felt the soft caress of a blanket around her tiny limbs. Her whole body ached. Her head throbbed. As she opened her eyes the light stabbed through her. She saw only the fuzzy edges of the world. Voices chattered around her. The memory held the words crisply although Tori realised that she could not possibly have understood them. Her newborn self was placed in the arms of a woman whose face was white. Her hair a rag of sodden waves sheeting past her shoulders. Her smile was the only radiant feature, it brightened her face but could not brighten the sparkle of tears and the shadow of sorrow in her eyes.

Tori cried out; an unfamiliar mewling burst from her lips. The woman thrust her away, sobbing. The man who took her had tight blond ringlets of hair. He leaned over her, crooning.

"She will be cared for." Tori recognised the voice of her grandmother.

"But not by me." The young woman's voice broke on a sob. Her arms reached out as if she wished to pull the infant Tori back and cradle her against her chest. The man stepped away and her arms fell beside her, laying limp against the bed. She whispered, "I've already given so much."

The wisps of memory faded as Tori's mind woke. Grogginess dulled her movements. Her limbs, muscles weighted down by lingering lethargy, were stiff and sore. She tried to capture the memory of her mother, to hold it so that it would never be lost again but it faded with her returning senses. She felt the tug of warm sheets against her skin. The pungent scent of smothering incense and haze of smoke clung to her skin. Her mouth felt dry, the taste of blood and salt lingered on her tongue. As she stirred, she heard a faint murmur of voices in the hall outside her room. They wove through her with a strange sense of displacement.

"How much time?" Tori whispered against the soft creases of the thick white pillow.

Her eyes fluttered open. She gazed at the blank whitewashed walls as the blur of her tears faded. The sharp edges of the walls, and the dark wood of the bed-frame appeared out of the haze. The stiff sheets felt rough against her bare skin and as she shifted to sit up the folds fell to her hips. A stab of pain ricocheted across Tori's ribs and she sucked in a breath, her chest rising and falling. She touched a hand to her breast where a patch of bandages strapped across her shoulder. They clung tight around her ribs and back, holding a wad of gauze against the throbbing wound.

A low whistle blew across the room followed by a throaty chuckle. Tori's head whipped upward and she pulled the sheet up to her chin. Two men stood by the door across the room. Their eyes glittered as they watched her, admiration clear in their faces.

Tori glared back at them. Inside her head she heard a snarling hiss and felt a wave of nausea crash over her again. Her eyes sparkled and the hiss slipped through her lips followed by a throaty growl. "What do you look at?"

The two men paled. The youngest's back hit the wall and his hands flattened against it.

"Perverted thugs," the voice whipped through her lips and then Tori felt the heavy weight constricting around her thoughts lift. She blinked, taking a shuddering breath into her lungs. Then fumbled, tugging the sheet as she twisted, placing her bare feet on the floor. The cool tiles sent a chill through her body. Her breath caught in her throat and she bit her lip, raising one hand to her brow. Her head tipped forward and she slid to the floor, dragging the sheet with her.

Leaning her back against the bed frame, Tori wrapped her arms around her legs. The pain in her chest and ribs pushed back her racing thoughts. Her body shuddered and her breath gasped through her lungs. Flashes of memory surfaced as she forced back a violent stirring in her stomach that made her feel as if she were going to be sick. "No," she groaned, doubling over. Tears dripped from her eyes onto the sheet. Her body shook and her breath came in short, sharp gusts. Memories flashed through her mind and she gripped the sides of her head, shaking it from side to side as if she could banish the images from behind her eyes. "No, no, no." Her breath hiccupped from her lungs.

Tori ran a hand through the thick folds of her hair and searched through the confusing scraps of memory for something solid to grasp and hold on to. She tried to banish the dark anger and the strange compulsions that rose within her. A deep hunger called her from the pit of her stomach. It roiled and churned within her. The young cultist, Corelle, flashed through her thoughts. The woman's horrified, life-ebbed eyes burned in Tori's mind.

Lucas swirled to the surface. His face swam in the fragmented vision. She felt the wave of horror that had raced through him, the crushing defeat that had chased it from his face. Her heart ached, feeling the distance between them. Her eyes flickered open as the darkness within her wove through her thoughts. Somehow, the coil reached out, weaving its way through the temple on a thread of her senses and clung to a warm cord of golden light. Tori felt Lucas's warmth wash over her as if he had wrapped his arms around her. She let herself sink into that feeling, embracing it in her mind. Her heart ached for him, seeing again the agony that lanced across his face as first one, then the other of his wings were cut from his body. She could feel the pain lingering like a thousand whips lashing through his whole body.

Chapter 7. Cold Dreams And Darkness

"I'm sorry," she whispered, "I'm so, so sorry." She thrust the sheet against her lips as another shudder of tears wracked her body. The compassion in his eyes warmed her skin, but slowly the chill that had swept over her returned. She grew still, tears drying on her cheeks.

She tipped her forehead against her arms crossed over her knees and sat there, clinging to the memory of Lucas's beautiful face as if he could hold back the darkness and fear that threatened to drown her.

Chapter Eight
Tool Of The High Priestess

Lucas tossed in the darkness. His body sprawled in a heap across the earthen floor. The cold of the ground beneath him seeped through his sweat-soaked skin as he slept. "No!" he shouted, jolted out of sleep by the nightmares that raged through his dreams. His body jerked upright and he slammed against the bars. The hard iron jarred his hip and shoulder. His muscles ached.

The darkness shrouded him and the air smothered him. His chest heaved as he dragged rank, humid breaths into his lungs. Lucas listened to the silence, his thoughts wandered through dark, haunting memories. A crumble of stone shifted across the room and the darkness wavered into flickering shadows. Quiet footsteps followed, each placed carefully, almost soundlessly on the fragile steps. Torchlight flickered around the corner. Lucas shut his eyes against the sudden stabbing light. A man crossed to the cell but stood several feet from the bars.

"Seraph?" The meticulous and accented voice was a throaty murmur in the room.

Lucas's eyes fluttered open and he glanced at the pale faced, dark haired man who stood across from him. The man's dark eyes shadowed a mask of firm resolve.

"Here to deliver a fresh beating?" Lucas asked. "I suppose I could go another round but I'd rather not waste my time with you."

The man shook his head. "I am Crey de Luca Vento, leader of the Uprising. You are no friend to the Nagaran, and so you are friend to me."

Lucas chuckled. "Uprising, huh? So the Nagaran have themselves a one man resistance?"

"Hardly." Crey's smile mocked Lucas. "We are several hundred strong, spread through many sects of the Nagaran. The Uprising intends to bring the Nagaran to their knees. We will end their dark arrogance and shameful selfishness by undermining their sinister machinations. We must restore the integrity of our people.

"And you propose doing that how?"

"Piece by piece. Small, carefully calculated victories win a war more quickly and with fewer casualties than a beleaguered battle. You are one piece, the Charmer another. This sect of the Nagaran is due a downfall."

"Where are you from, Crey?" Lucas asked. He used the bars of his cell to help pull himself onto his feet. He grimaced as a sharp lance of pain ran the length of his ribs. His breath caught in his throat as he waited for the pain to subside.

Crey reached forward to assist, but stopped inches from the bars. "I apologise, there is nothing I can do for your pain."

Lucas shook his head. "It's nothing. Broken rib probably, but not much you could do about it. It'll heal."

"Of course," Crey replied with a nod. "To answer your question, I am from Luca Vento. My father is Conte Vincento Marque Sonto."

"You're a Count's son, and he abides you running a rebellion?"

Crey grinned. "He was my father, not my master. He probably would not have encouraged my endeavour, but the Uprising calls to the cause those it must. I was called, and so are you."

Lucas smiled. "I think you've got the wrong guy. I've already got a calling and I don't think it's the sort to take a back seat to a petty power war."

"I know what you are, Seraph, but your calling is in line with the Charmer's and so it is in line with mine."

"I don't understand."

"She is the Charmer. It is her destiny to bring an end to the Nagaran. I did not expect her to arrive in my lifetime, but perhaps she is the reason I was called."

"Tori?"

"Yes, so you call her."

"But she died. I saw her body in a crumpled heap turning cold on the stone of the dais."

Crey shook his head. "I felt her chill too, but she is not dead. The serpent sleeps through the winter."

"What does that mean?"

"It does not matter. Just know that she lives. Her situation is, perhaps, better than your own. As the Charmer she is given a place of honour here. Although, the High Priestess is most displeased. I've not seen her this angry." He chuckled. "It is quite pleasant to see her so put out. Not so kindly to those who happen across her path as she rages, but her discontent has the Uprising here in great spirits."

"I can imagine."

"Yes." Crey glanced to the stairs and rose to his feet. A rowdy laugh echoed down the walls from the hall above.

"Ah, my next barrage of bruises," Lucas said. He grimaced and shuffled back to brace himself against the rock wall.

"I must go, Seraph, but I will work to arrange your freedom. You are no good for the Uprising, or for the Charmer, if you are stuck behind bars." Crey touched two fingers to his forehead in a respectful salute before turning. The stiff formality straightened his spine as his silent footsteps started up the stairs. The flickering torchlight faded and the room was plunged back into blackness for long minutes.

The laughter above broke into a rambunctious riot of verse sung in drunken stupor. The noise ricocheted off the walls and rang in Lucas's ears. His head throbbed and he tilted it back against the wall. The noise grew louder and the torchlight flicked a glowing corridor of light up the stairs. The tromp of feet were heavy and each verse of the song grew more and more ridiculous.

"Ha, ha! Right on!" Orton's voice bounced off the walls.

"Heh! Woah!" A tumble of stones scattered down the stairs followed by a heavy grunt. Carny slumped in a heap at the foot of the stairs. He lay there, his face a blank slate of surprise before breaking into a hyena-like laugh. "I ain't not hurt. Get me up ya big lump."

Orton stepped the last few steps almost doubled over with laughter. The torch wavered in his hand, scattering the shadows across the walls. Lucas grimaced. Even against drunken idiots he suspected he would wear more blows than he could deliver in his current state. He closed his eyes, and waited for it to begin.

Chapter 8. Tool Of The High Priestess

Tori pulled herself up from the floor. She dragged the sheet around her stiff shoulders. Holding her back straight she ignored the calculating look in the men's eyes and demanded, "What are you doing in my room?"

The young man winced, lifting a hand to swipe across his brow as he looked away. The other cleared his throat before speaking, his voice a shudder of nervous tension. "Sorry miss, it's orders, we have to keep an eye on you."

Tori raised an eyebrow. "Then I suppose you are doing a good job, but surely I am entitled to some privacy."

He shrugged. Then, glancing away, he muttered, "Orders."

The door crashed against the wall. The men jumped, stepping aside. A flush of guilt crept across their faces as Marlena strode into the room. Tori watched her hawk-like movements and recognised anger in each jerk of the woman's head. Her chin lifted in defiance.

"You!" The woman spat.

"What is the meaning of this?" Tori demanded, her haughty tone was tainted with an uneasy quiver.

"Meaning? I go where I please Charmer. You hold no command here."

The Flight Of Torque

The High Priestess's gaze dug against her bare skin and Tori cinched the sheet tighter around herself. She opened her mouth, trying to scrape the memories of the creature within her together in her mind. She wanted the dark power to refute the other woman's claim. Surely what had happened changed her status. The elegance of the room she had been given betrayed some significance in her captivity. The beast would not rise to the bait. Tori berated her weakness, searching for words.

Her jaw froze as the lancing pitch of the Marlena's voice cut her off before she could protest. "Silence! You will listen to me. *I*, am Marlena, High Priestess of the Nagaran. These are my people and I will have no blood-traitor usurper claiming an unsanctioned place amongst their loyalties."

"Unsanctioned? This would never have happened if you had left me alone. You did this to me. These people, the Nagaran, are nothing to me."

"Nothing? How dare you lie to me, you little bitch. Do you think I am ignorant of what the Nagaran is to you, to your family?"

Tori's breath caught and her gaze searched the other woman's face for the traces of truth that lingered in her eyes. "What are you talking about?" she whispered.

Chapter 8. Tool Of The High Priestess

The High Priestess's sharp laughter rang against the marble walls. "You really don't know, do you?"

"Tell me! Damn the Nagaran. What is this all about?"

Marlena crossed the room in a two swift steps and Tori's head jerked back at the sharp blow against her cheek. She felt the flames of the slap burning a handprint in her skin. A shudder of violent rage stirred through her body. "Watch your tongue, filthy blood-traitor. The Nagaran are your life, the blood of your blood. I will not stand to hear you defile them with your ignorance and blasphemy. You do not deserve your heritage. Your blood is all that preserves you from the wrath of the Sacred Mother."

"What do you mean?" Tori held a hand against her stinging cheek.

"The Naragran is an ancient people, descended of the Four Fathers, whose powers conquer the world. We are the serpents of the earth. Born to the land and blessed by its riches. Years before you or I the Nagaran ruled these people. The Sacred Mother gave her worshippers the wealth of the earth and from its soils mankind has blossomed." She paced back and fourth across the length of the room.

Tori stood, her stance filled with impatient confusion. "What has this got to do with me?"

With an irritated sigh Marlena turned to face Tori. "You, are the daughter of our people's blood; a direct descendant of our people. You, are a Charmer, perhaps the only one who still lives. Don't interrupt!" Marlena snapped as Tori opened her mouth. Tori recoiled, rocked by flashes of violent compulsions which flittered through her mind. The High Priestess nodded, as though satisfied with what she perceived to be Tori's show of deference and respect. "Were you any other I would snuff the irritation of you from my sect, but instead I am forced to make use of you as I can. You will stay here until commanded and speak to no one. Do you understand?"

Tori glanced up, trying to push the horrifying thoughts from her mind. The High Priestess, glared down and Tori gave her a timid nod. She watched as the High Priestess crossed to the door, then whispered, just loud enough to be heard across the room, "What are you going to do with me?"

Marlena chuckled as she turned the door handle. "You will serve a purpose, and you will live, if you control yourself and do exactly as I tell you." She stalked out of the room and slammed the door closed behind her.

Chapter 8. Tool Of The High Priestess

Tori lowered herself to the edge of the bed, the sheet still wrapped around her. She tried to control the dragging breath that shuddered through her and forced back the menacing rage that tried to pull her into the blackness of her thoughts. She shuddered as the violent fury hissed back at her, then sobbed as she felt her own anger and frustration, at herself, at her helplessness. From time to time she glanced at the door. The two men standing either side of it watched every movement she made. Occasionally they shifted on their feet, but it was clear they were resolute to follow their orders.

Hours seemed to pass. Tori grew more and more restless. She stood. She tugged the sheet tighter around her body as she turned to face the two men. "Don't I at least get food? Water? What about clothes?" she said. Her voice whipped across the room as a snarl and Tori bit her teeth together.

The men flushed. "I'm sorry miss," said the eldest. "I'm sure they'll send someone."

Tori sank back to the bed and scuttled across it to lean her back against the headrest. She stretched her back, wincing as the tightness in her chest and ribs tugged against the bandages. She watched the two men just as they watched her. From time to time they glanced away. Their increasing discomfort was apparent and Tori smiled.

"I suppose, you're tainted in the presence of the blood-traitor? You must have done something heinous to be forced to be babysitters to a helpless woman."

The two remained silent, but their wary gazes flinched away.

"Of course, perhaps Marlena is hoping I'll lose control and deal with you both for her."

The youngest shifted his feet and Tori saw the bob of his Adam's apple as he swallowed. The other man shook his head, keeping his eyes on the floor. "We've our orders, Miss. Nothing more than that," he said.

"It's actually an honour to be trusted to protect the Charmer," the young man said, his voice cracking with tension.

Tori's eyebrow rose. "Protect? Is that what you think you are doing? You're my captors, nothing more. Your kind has kidnapped me, assaulted me, and now you hold me captive." The pitch of her voice increased as anger washed over her again. Stabbing pain rippled across her skin, and then flushed away. Her breath hitched in her throat as it faded and she blinked away the flood of tears that had filled her eyes.

Chapter 8. Tool Of The High Priestess

The men were not looking at her, their eyes cast to the ground as if afraid to meet her gaze. The young man's cheeks flushed. "There was no other way. I'm sure the High Priestess..."

A soft knock on the door interrupted his reply. It opened slowly. One of the guards glanced at the newcomer then reached out to pull the door wide so she could pass them. She moved carefully into the room, balancing a tray between her hands and stepping around the door before they closed it behind her. She glanced up at Tori, her gaze wary, but a smile lifting her lips.

"You must be hungry," she said as she approached.

"I am," Tori replied. "And I'd appreciate some clothes." She lifted her chin at the men. They had closed the door and again stood either side of it, watching her.

"Of course. I'll see to it. I'm Zara, by the way. I've been asked to see to your needs."

"Asked? I got the impression Marlena doesn't *ask* anything of anyone."

"Why do you stand it?"

Zara smiled. "I admit, it was not a request I could refuse."

She sat on the edge of the bed and lay the tray before Tori then shrugged her shoulders. The movement was graceful, her lithe, pale-skinned body looked like that of a dancer. Her long-lashed eyelids dipped over the calm sky of her eyes. "I've a purpose," she said. The words were laced with a deep conviction at odds with her delicate features and hesitant movements. She tilted her head, her chin lifting in a gesture that indicated the two men beside the door were privy to their conversation.

Tori nodded. She did not understand, but she suspected there was more to the situation than Zara could say.

"You'll come to know," Zara whispered, leaning forward. She hid her voice beneath her breath so she would not be overheard by the men across the room. "For the moment trust that I'm on your side. I will do what I can to protect your welfare, and to ensure you are safe and comfortable here. I can do no more, for the moment."

"Is," Tori stopped, clearing her throat. Swallowing, she forced the tears back. Her chest ached with the effort and she felt a quiver of tension shudder through her muscles. She took a deep breath, wincing as it burned through her ribs, then began again in a whisper, "Is he?" Her voice hitched. She swallowed again but could not continue.

Zara leaned forward, touching Tori's hand with her cool fingers. "He lives, they have him in the cells below."

Chapter 8. Tool Of The High Priestess

"His wings, I didn't think he'd survive it. What will they do to him down there?"

"I'll go down to him, see to his wounds as I did yours."

Tori's lips twisted up in a grimace of a smile. "I appreciate that," she said. A growl rippled through her stomach. It felt like a mixture of desire and hunger. She glanced down at the tray Zara had placed in front of her and raised her voice above their shared whisper, "So what have you brought me?"

"Breakfast," Zara said, arranging the cutlery on the tray. "I'm sorry it's not much. We're accustomed to living simply here."

"At this point I could eat anything. I'm starving."

As Tori reached forward the sheet slipped around her shoulders and she grimaced as she tugged it back into place.

Zara smiled, a gentle bow of lips that creased her compassion-filled eyes. "When you've finished eating I'll see to getting you something to wear."

Tori glanced at the two men.

Zara turned to look at them over her shoulder. They were grinning. Their smiles knowing.

"And ensure your privacy while you change," Zara added. The men cast their eyes down at her glare.

Tori touched her wrist. "I'm grateful, more than I can say."

Zara nodded. "Eat."

The cold soothed his skin. Lucas's shoulder, back, and ribs ached. He was sure new bruises where blooming across his chest. The cold darkness felt like a shroud, soothing his burning skin. He gazed up at the ceiling but could not see it.

"Tori," he whispered. He could feel her. He felt the radiation of her agitation through the layers of rock between them. "At least she's safe," he muttered.

Light flickered off the walls. A soft gasp followed the muted glow into the room. "And in better shape then you."

Orton grunted, "Get him done and get out, Zara."

"You sick bastards," she spat. "What did you do to him?"

"He don't not deserve your pity. He's a filthy freak. 'Sides, he got his own licks in. Right on broke Orton's nose, he did. Right, Orton?"

"Shut up, Carny. He ain't got the better o' me."

"Let me in there and then get out," Zara said, glaring at the two men. "I swear, if you give me any grief I'll break more than your fat, ugly nose."

Orton chuckled. "Like to see you try. Nothing but a feather. Bet you couldn't hurt a fly."

"You're right. I wouldn't want to break my wrist messing up your face. But Jackson would have your hide if I told him you'd been messing with me."

She glared at them and Lucas smiled at her feisty defiance. "You should be a redhead," he said. "Temper like that."

She smiled at him and her tone gentled, "My father thought so too. He figured I got it from my mother. Apparently she could be hot-tempered."

"Apparently?"

"I never knew her." She turned on the men again. "Come on you slow oxen, I haven't got all day."

Orton clambered over to the cell door. "Don't move or I'll help Carny give you another broken rib."

Lucas watched him but remained laying on the floor. He raised his arms and tucked his hands behind his head. "Actually, I'm quite comfortable. Besides, I'm about to have the company of a beautiful woman. I doubt you've had the same without having to pay for it."

Orton stepped past the cell door and gave Lucas a hard kick.

"Get out!" Zara shouted at him. "I swear, Orton. If you touch him again I'll have you both seen into the torture room."

Carny snorted. "We ain't not go no torture room. That's just a rumour."

"Is it? Would you like to know for sure?"

He stepped back from her, holding his hands up. Orton stepped past her and she slipped into the cell.

"Thank you," she said, kneeling down beside Lucas. "You can leave now."

Orton frowned, "You sure? He might hurt ya."

"After what you two did to him? I think I'd be lucky to save him from infection. I doubt he could move if he wanted to. Besides, he's a Seraph, sworn to protect the innocent. He's not a stupid brute like you two lumps."

The two men glared at her. "I hope he slits your throat, bitch," Orton muttered, then turned and stomped up the stairs.

Carny glanced at her, at Lucas, and at her again. "You don't not know nothing of nothing. Cornered snake'll bite anything. Serve you right if he does."

"Out!"

He shrugged, then turned out of the room and followed Orton up the stairs. The soft hue of the lantern light flickered across his disappearing back.

"Thanks," Lucas said. She returned his smile, her face a pretty pale ghost in the muted light.

"Don't thank me yet. These wounds aren't going to be fun to tend to."

"Tell me about it. I suspect at least two of my ribs are broken and I don't even want to imagine the mess of my back."

Zara bit her lip. "I should probably start there. Do you think you can sit up?"

"Probably, but I'm not sure I want to."

"Come on, is the big, brave Seraph a baby when it comes to a bit of pain."

He chuckled. "I'd say a little more than a bit." He grunted as he pushed himself upright. The muscles in his arms bunched and he felt bruises he did not know he had.

Zara gasped as she saw the full extent of the injuries to his back. "I can't believe you're alive. How can you even bare to move?"

Lucas shrugged and then winced. "Gingerly, and as little as possible. I usually heal pretty fast, but even I'm not sure how long it'll take this time. Without my wings-" He took a pained breath. "They said I'm not an angel, not without my wings. What if they're right?"

"Angel blood," Zara said. "Despite how much of it you've lost it still runs in your veins. Besides, you can't take it out of your soul. That part of you can't be cut away."

He closed his eyes. "Hearts can be broken, maybe souls can be too."

"Ribs can be broken, and then they heal. Hearts can be broken, but they heal too. Souls, always survive." She smiled, seeing the sapphire flecks in his eyes glisten in the muted light of the lantern.

His half smile barely hid his doubt.

She placed a box on the floor beside her and opened it. Inside was an array of gauze, bandages, and ointments. She poured a dark amber liquid on a square of gauze and leaned toward him. "Let's see to these wounds. I'm sorry, this will sting, but it's the only way to stave off infection."

"It's ok. It can't hurt more than the rest of me already does."

He sucked in his breath as her soft touch burned on his skin. Even behind him, where he could not see her face, he knew she was crying.

Chapter Nine
Secrets And Lies

Zara had left hours ago having brought Tori's washed and pressed clothes. Tori had been glad at the time to be in her own things, but now as she tossed and turned, trying to sleep, her denim of her jeans were heavy and tight around her hips. She pulled her knees up to her chest and then gasped as the pain in her ribs stabbed through her. She gripped the pillow, smothering her scream in the thick crush of soft lumps. Between trying to sleep and pacing the room she felt her agitation growing. At some stage the guards at her door had been replaced by two others. She tried to sit on the bed, staring down the two men, but she could not sit for more than a few minutes at a time before getting up and pacing back and forth across the room. The soles of her bare feet padded across the floor. The sound of each footfall echoed through the silence that hung over the room.

Tori sat again and the bed shifted beneath her. She raised a hand to her throbbing head. With her eyes closed, she felt the chaos of her thoughts burn behind her eyelids. Dark memories curled around her, wrapping tendrils through every inch of her body. She shuddered, against the fire of them over her skin. She pushed back at the hissing fury building in her mind. She fought against the drowning darkness that crept up in her. Her skin crawled with frustration and she pushed herself to her feet again. Her chest tugged. Under her shirt, the bandages pulled tight and she winced. Her breath hissed out of her and she sucked air into her lungs in the following breath. The clinging musk of the crimson braziers washed through her.

She paced across the room then leaned her head against the wall. The cool stone soothed the fire across her brow, but it flared the anger within her. She hit the wall with both fists and shoved herself backward. Turning, she strode across the room and stood in front of the two men, glaring at them.

"I have something to say to Marlena," she said. The older guard's eyes widened and he shuddered. The other cocked his head, running his eyes up and down her body. He lifted an eyebrow and whistled low. This was the first time Tori had spoken to them since they had taken their shift. *How long ago?* Tori wondered. She had lost track of the hours. Day or night? She could not remember. *Was the funeral only a day ago?* Maybe several days had past. She could not be sure.

"Boy, ain't you not no stunnin' looker. They said ya was a hotty. That snake thing ain't not nothing to look at, but, damn, when ya fell down all naked. God, breasts like sweet, ripe grapefruits. I ain't not never been so hard. Wanna give me a piece of that, babe?" He rubbed his hand over his crotch, rocking his hips forward.

Tori shuddered, then drew herself up to loom over him. She looked down, hands on her hips. Her eyes narrowed and her voice hissed from her in a furious snarl. "I demand you take me to the High Priestess at once."

He glared back at her. "Ain't not no way, missy. We can't not be doing that. We got orders. Gotta keep ya here. So we ain't not going no place."

"What is your name?" she said, her voice a sharp bite that lanced through her lips.

The man swallowed, licking his tongue across his lips as he ran his gaze over her body again. He put his hands on his hips, and thrust the swell that strained against his pants forward, then lifted his chin, "Carny, that's me. The old fogey there, he's Renold. Say hi, Renold." The other man shifted his feet and looked away.

"Well, Carny. I'm certain that should the Charmer wish to speak to the High Priestess, it would be loath to deny the request." The haughty tone of her voice was unfamiliar, the words delivered before she had a chance to gather her thoughts. "Given the situation, I suspect there are unpleasant consequences for anyone who displeases the High Priestess."

Renold swallowed and glanced at Carny. "Maybe," he began.

Carny shook his head. "Ain't not going no place, Renold. We gots our orders."

"But what if she's right. She's the Charmer. You know what that means."

Carny pressed his lips together. "I know it don't not mean we not got no orders. That sure ain't not what it means."

"We'll take her right there and bring her right back."

The edge of darkness licked at the pungent taste of their hesitation. She felt it play on their uncertainty as her lips hissed out the words, "I'm certain the High Priestess would want to know what I have to say."

The men glanced at her, then Renold turned his gaze on Carny. Carny snapped, "Damn it, Ren. We got orders. There ain't not no way. The High Priestess'd skin our hides for even considering it. I ain't not doing it. No way, not never."

The snarl that pressed through her tingled over her skin and shuddered across her shoulders. She felt herself quiver as tension build within her. Her forehead smashed into Carny's face. He flew backward and crashed against the wall. Renold stepped in front of her and she snarled, lashing out at him. Tori felt a wave of horror as her body snapped forward, teeth sinking deep into his throat. Tori felt trapped inside her own head, watching her actions with terror, but helpless to control herself.

Carny's shocked face, watched with horror as Renold's heavy body crumbled to the floor. He turned, mouth hanging open and leaned back against the wall. Tori could see the daze of concussion in his eyes. His breathing shuddered in heavy gasping breaths. Fear wove thick in the air, Tori's tongue darted across her lips as if she could taste it. "Now, Carny, I will not be denied. You will take me to the High Priestess."

He nodded, then turned. His eyes snapped to Renold as he fumbled over the door handle. Once he got the door open he hurried through the corridor. Tori's body slinked close behind him. She felt the tingle of hairs that stood on the back of his neck as her warm breath whispered down his spine.

The corridor was dank and hazy. Tori shivered, feeling her own thoughts crowd back into her mind. She took a shallow breath and squared her shoulders.

Carny's step faltered on the uneven ground and he grunted, stumbling. He shivered as Tori brushed up against his back. He winced as he recovered, then grimaced with each slow step he took down the hall in front of her. They turned through several corridors before entering a large, cavernous room. Red robes shifted like a churning sea of reverent frenzy. Carny lead Tori through the crowd, he glanced wide eyes either side of him, searching the impassive faces of the swaying crowd. Moving with careful steps between the hands, heads, and legs of the cultists, Tori stayed close behind him. The devout voices around her rose and fell in practiced cadence. The sounds wove together in a pulsing heartbeat that filled the room and echoed off the cavern walls.

Tori scanned the room, seeing it clearly for the first time. The careful detail of the chamber had been blurred by the sheen of tears and mask of terror that had filled her as she had been tied to the altar. The memory of it lanced through her with crystal-edged sharpness. Smooth rock walls were carved from the rich earth. Flickering torchlight cast muted shadows of orange and red on the ochre clay. Thick stone pillars were spaced at regular intervals along the walls. In each, marble serpents were raised in hissing fury above nests of splintered eggs. Braziers burned beneath them, the light flickering from marble flecks.

As her gaze wandered, Tori began to take in the details of those prostrating toward the dais and the raised throne where the High Priestess lorded over the proceedings. There were men and women, even children, consumed by their piety and given completely to their prayers. Each was dressed in dark robes ranging from crimson to ebony. Their eyes gazed forward and gleamed with the reflected flames or perhaps with manic devotion to their faith.

Zara caught her gaze as Tori passed. She reached a hand to grasp Tori's wrist, but her fingers fell away as Tori shook her head. Zara's eyes pleaded, and her breathing quickened. Her lips moved in a pleading whisper, "Tori."

On the dais ahead of them a man, dressed in flowing black robes, looked out at the throbbing crowd. His voice, raised above the hum of worshippers, rang out crisp devotions that he read from a scale-covered tome. He caressed the book with his fingers and cradled it in his hands like one might a newborn baby. As Tori came nearer the dais, he placed the book, with reverent care, onto a stand beside him and picked up the ornate staff that rested against it. The man thrust the staff into the ground. The ring of metal clanking against stone ricocheted outward. The sound washed over the cultists who dropped to their knees, dipping their heads to the ground.

Carny veered his path between the prostrate cultists and approached the throne positioned to the right of the raised platform. The High Priestess watched them, her eyes dark with fury. Tori stumbled up the step then lifted her chin and focused on the woman ahead of them.

As they reached her, Marlena's whispered voice whipped out at them. "What is the meaning of this?"

Carny glanced at Tori, whose lips were pressed together. Her tongue slid across her dry lips as she felt a shudder of unease lace through her. The man shivered and then stuttered, "I'm sorry, High Priestess. The Charmer's gotta speak to ya. She weren't not gonna let me live if I didn't never bring her to ya."

"Your orders were clear, Brother. You were to ensure she did not leave her room."

"Yep, that be right. I gotta be knowing that, but she, Renold, there weren't not nothing I could do," he stuttered into silence. Marlena's eyes narrowed and she stood, her lips twitching.

She turned her sharp gaze on Tori. Her dark eyes studied Tori as if she could peal back Tori's skin and crawl into her soul, pulling the thoughts from her mind. Tori cringed, feeling as if all her weaknesses were exposed. With a shudder, her spine stiffened and she felt the shutter between her own thoughts and the slithering darkness within fall into place inside her mind. Her thoughts sharpened and she returned Marlena's look with a glare. Her chin tilted and her lips curved in a smile.

Marlena swallowed, glancing away, then cleared her throat. The priest faltered and glanced uncertainly at her. The crowd of worshippers stilled, the hum muted, and an uncomfortable silence descended upon the room.

"Thank you, Brother Josiah," the High Priestess said. The priest bowed low to her and then stepped back, offering her centre place on the dais. Marlena stepped into it and turned to face the crowd. "Nagaran, join me in giving thanks to our Sacred Mother." Her voice bounced back from the walls of the room. Her words rose and fell with tempered piety and the cultists joined their own soft chant with hers. "We thank you, Sacred Mother, for your life sustaining milk and for the safety of your people. We thank you for giving us the strength and commitment to overcome our enemies. We thank you, Sacred Mother, for all you have given us. We thank you."

As her dulcet tones of her reverence faded, the room fell silent. As one, the cultists rose to stand, their rigid lines facing the throne. "We thank you, High Priestess, for giving voice to our Sacred Mother," they said as one. "We thank you for your guidance, understanding, and knowledge. We thank you, High

Priestess, for all you have given us. We thank you." Marlena smiled and smoothed her robes, gently preening herself as the Nagaran finished their prayer.

The cultists waited and Tori sensed their communal breath held until the High Priestess tilted her head. "My brothers and sisters," she said, addressing the crowd with a wave of her hand. "Standing before me is the Charmer. Shall we hear what she has to say?"

An uproar rose from the audience. Tori could not be sure if the majority was for or against her being given the opportunity to speak. Some more eager cultists had leapt to their feet and were shouting angry suggestions that it would be better to bring about her very painful death. Others seemed keen to hear her. For a moment, Tori stood uncertain, her breath shallow as she looked out at the churning wave of red and black below. A coursing ripple of decisive resolve wove around her. Bravado lifted her chin and Tori felt a reptilian smile curve her lips as she nodded her head to the gathered crowd.

She turned, acknowledging the High Priestess who took her seat on the throne. "I thank you for hearing me, High Priestess." Tori's voice rose, echoing back to her from the cavern walls.

Her limbs tugged her downward and she dropped with a hiss to her knees before the throne. Her body doubled over and a stab of pain radiating across her ribs as her forehead touched the ground. The dramatic gasp that swept through the room washed over her and her eyes sparkled. Her smile disappeared before she lifted her head and looked into Marlena's shocked gaze. Her features hardened into a glassy facade of respect and gratitude. A tingle of power shuddered through her belly and she closed her eyes, feeling the slithering crawl of the darkness within.

"What is the matter, my dear Charmer? Are you feeling like you do not belong here?"

Tori felt the serpent pull from within. Her body quivered with a foreboding fear and the urge to run was overwhelming, but she could not force her limbs to cooperate. Her breath shuddered through her and her shoulders pulled back. Her spine straightened as her lips curved in a mocking smile. "Not at all, High Priestess," she said. Her tongue flickered, hissing the final syllable of Marlena's title. "I feel I am exactly where I am meant to be, in the service of the Sacred Mother."

"Really," Marlena said, her eyebrow raised and she ran her gaze down Tori with a look of distain. "And how do you feel you could serve the Nagaran, Charmer?" Her eyes narrowed, their glare felt like razors cutting across

Tori's skin. Tori's muscled clenched and she clung to her thoughts as they slithered in and out of her mind.

A short hiss escaped her lips before she could bite her tongue and Tori battled with the raging instincts within her. Her voice hissed out of her soft lips. It sounded strange in her ears. "I am Torque," she said. Tori's brow furrowed, wondering where the name had come from. She felt the darkness well up within her and realised it was the name of the serpent. Tori pushed back the traces of anger that threaded through her mind, but the determination of the beast within forced her to act the part it had come to play. "I give my allegiance to you, High Priestess, and to the Nagaran. I am the Serpent. I am the Charmer. I am yours to command under the guidance of the Sacred Mother."

Silence tingled across her skin. Tori felt the shudder that pressed against her head and pushed back against the turmoil tugging her insides. She could feel roaring hunger within. It bubbled in snarling fury near the surface of her skin. She pushed back the malevolent darkness, afraid of its power to control her actions, her words. She quailed at the strength of its compulsion to bring harm upon the cultists.

As she fought back the serpent within her, Tori became oblivious to the continued silence behind her.

Chapter 9. Secrets And Lies

When the High Priestess rose to her feet Tori blinked in surprise, but her limbs would not move as she tried to stand. Marlena took a step toward Tori. She bent and gripped Tori's chin with her fingers. Sharp, painted nails dug into Tori's soft skin. "You pledge allegiance?" Marlena asked. Her eyes were dark with suspicion.

Tori's breath dragged through her lungs before answering, "I do, High Priestess." Torque pushed hard and Tori felt the swift hiss that slithered through her lips before the weight of her limbs seeped into her mind and she realised she again had control of her own body. Terror flooded through her and she quivered under Marlena's glaring fury.

"You have a sharp tongue, Charmer. I sensed this even before I heard you speak. Your anger vibrates in the air. You should be careful to quell your instinct to strike. You must learn to subjugate yourself before the might of the Sacred Mother. Your allegiance, after all, is to her."

Anger boiled through her and Tori felt the wisps of her control flee. Her eyes closed and a split tongue darted between her lips. The High Priestess gasped, her hand falling away as she stepped backward. Tori felt the transformation of her body, the warmth of her flesh turned to a chill of scales and she rose, her height towering over the woman before her as her muscles flexed through her entire body.

Her head tilted and she glared at Marlena through slitted eyes. Her tongue darted between her lips with a soft hiss. "You should be careful, High Priestess, that *you* do not displease the Sacred Mother by underestimating my loyalty. Be certain that should she call to question your self-serving piety she would find fault. My reverence, however, she would favour. My worship would be her greatest boon. After all, I have given myself to her completely, mind and body." She rose to her full height and stared down at the High Priestess.

The woman blinked, understanding her meaning. Torque licked her lips, feeling the quiver in the air and smelling the scent of the High Priestess's fear. Her fangs gleamed through a serpentine smile and she tilted her head in an acknowledging nod as warmth returned to the softening flesh of her human skin. Tori felt the anger within fade as a whispered sigh passed through her. She felt her limbs returning, the warm breeze of muggy air caressed her skin. Her mind raced. She flushed as she realised she stood naked before them, her clothes lay in tattered threads at her feet, but she could not move to cover her modesty. Instead, her mouth twisted with a husky murmur, "How may I serve the Sacred Mother?"

The cultists watched with awe, their gazes fixed to the curve of her spine, their mouths gaping. The High Priestess shuddered, her breath ragged, as she quailed. Tori could see the way the silk folds of Marlena's robes shivered as she shook. She sensed the turmoil that ran its course through Marlena's body before the woman's features smoothed back into proud arrogance and her gaze cut down at Tori. Tori watched her with lidded eyes as the woman raked her gaze down Tori's naked body, the pulse of jealousy that flooded from her washed over Tori's skin and her spine straightened. Tori saw the transformation as the woman pulled herself together. The High Priestess shook off her shock and recovered her poise. "You will stay out of our way, out of our sight, and we will call for you when we can make use of you." Marlena looked out at the crowd, her eyes stilling on Zara. She waved the young woman forward. "You will go with Zara," Marlena said, directing the command at Tori. "She will show you where you can be fitted with robes and teach you where you are expected to be and when. I will send notice when I have more specific commands for you. Meanwhile, I expect you to remain within the temple at all times."

Tori felt the strength and power that had raged through her body fade away. Her muscles stiffened as she urged herself to stand. She gave a slow nod as she rose to her feet, then bent, low enough to acknowledge the command, but not so low that the bow would be mistaken for submission. The High Priestess turned on her heel and strode from the room. Wisps of her gown streamed behind her. Tori's lips curved in a satisfied smile. As Zara wove through the crowd of departing devout and stepped up onto the platform, Torque's voice whispered from between her lips, "A freedom of sorts perhaps?"

Tori tugged the silk cloth from the altar and wrapped it around herself before she turned to the crowd. Cultists, huddled in groups, seemed to watch every move she made. She grimaced, pulling the sheet tight around herself as she turned to Zara. Tori caught the dark anger burning in Zara's eyes. She bit her lip, forcing back her tears, and stepped forward to meet her.

Tori winced as Zara's fingers bit into her wrist. The grip was firm and she kept a swift pace as she crossed the room. Zara glanced back once as her new 'Sister' trailed behind her. She strode down the long, flame-lit corridor. A large black door swung open as they neared it. The room beyond was blindingly bright. The stark contrast between the pulsing red against the walls of the corridor and the pale off-white walls and fluorescent lighting stung Tori's sensitive eyes. A young woman came to a standstill in front of them. She flushed, glancing at Tori and, cowering, stammered an apology as she stepped around them and hurried down the hall.

Zara spun Tori into the room. Tori stumbled as the floor fell away at her feet a little. She regained her balance and turned to face the woman behind her. Zara's eyes sparked with blue fire. Her voice, a bare whisper, spat in muted anger, "What are you doing?"

Tori blinked. "What are you talking about?"

"You, I know what you are, Tori. There is no way you would swear allegiance to this cult. You could unravel all we have done here. Have you any idea what you have gotten yourself into?" She moved across the room and pulled open the double doors of a large mirrored closet. Dark robes hung inside and she gathered one after another, tossing them onto the pale cloth covering a large table.

Tori shook her head. "I don't understand," she said on a whispered breath. She tried to mimic the resonating power that had hissed from her lips in the chamber, but it quivered in her throat as she said, "I am Torque, the Charmer. I swear allegiance to the Nagaran and to the Sacred Mother." Tori stood in the centre of the room. The cool air chilled her skin and she could feel her pulse throb through her ears. She felt Torque hum inside her with curiosity and insatiable desire. Tori clenched her fingers, her nails cutting into the soft flesh of her palm. Closing her eyes, she fought down the hunger that tore through her.

When she opened her eyes, Zara had turned her steel eyes to her. "You really don't, do you?" She ran her gaze up and down Tori's agitated and restless body. She gestured to the table. "Come here and put one of these on. You'll be required to wear robes at all times in the temple. These are sacred garments and as such should be worn with regard to what these symbols mean to the cult. The serpent is their power. The temple is like a nest. The Nagaran live a communal life here, dependant on one another while remaining true to their own inner power."

The robes were a thick wool and Tori was drawn to their warmth. She pulled the soft material over her head and adjusted the folds feeling as if she had crawled into a second skin. The robe cocooned her and she felt enlivened by the warmth. Torque reared within her and Tori shuddered as a throb of desire pulsed through her. She sucked a sharp breath into her lungs. Then closed her eyes as pain lanced through her. The raging blaze of the serpent's fire faded as she let the breath whisper out between her lips.

Tori took another breath, shallow and careful, then opening her eyes, she said, "You talk as if you're not one of them." She glanced at Zara.

Zara bit her lip then sighed before continuing. "You will be expected to attend dawn and dusk services in the chamber. If you do not attend, you will not eat. I suggest you never negotiate on that account, it will call instant suspicion on you and I'm certain you will be watched closely as it is."

Tori nodded. "Why are you helping me?"

Zara paused and looked at Tori, her expression compassionate. There was a hint of desperation in her eyes, and something else, a secret. Their was more that she was not saying. "Please, Tori. Be very careful here. You don't understand the mess you've stepped into. I want to help, if I can. I'm not sure how much I can tell you. It's all," she stopped as a gong rang out through the walls. As the sound faded, she shook her head. "I'm sorry," she said. "We've no more time. That calls us to dinner. We must not be late."

Chapter Ten
Uprising

Zara had been gone what must have been several hours. The darkness after her lantern-light had left him seemed more oppressive than before. His skin crawled despite the fresh bandages. She had bound his ribs but every breath still burned through his chest. Each movement tugged at the wounds across his back and his shoulder ached. He had finally pulled himself upright and stood beside the bars.

"Hey!" Lucas shouted. He shook the cell door, then shouted again. "Hey! I need food if you don't want me to die down here."

Upstairs, a door creaked. Light flickered down the stairs. Orton's rough voice echoed down, "Shut up! Else I come down an' give ya another beatin'. Zara'd be pissed if she hadda come patch you up again."

"I need to eat, and drink. That is so long as your High Priestess intends to keep me alive."

Orton grunted and slammed the door. Lucas grimaced then paced the length of the cell. It was not a big room. Perhaps two metres from length to length and half that from the rough stone wall at the back to the bars at the front. With careful steps, Lucas paced up and down the cell. He shuffled his feet but there did not seem to be anything inside the cell. No bed, no amenities of any kind. The room was empty, except for him. Other than the bars that stretched across the front of the cell the walls were solid rock.

"Likelihood of escape? Next to nil," Lucas muttered.

"Oh, I don't know. The odds could improve if you had friends in the right places."

Lucas smiled, the darkness had only faded a little and he had been so preoccupied with exploring the cell that he had not heard Crey descend the stairs. He glanced behind the man but the stairs behind him were empty and dark.

"Do not worry, we are alone."

"Well, I do hope the odds are in my favour."

"Certainly, although perhaps not today. Today, you get fed. It is not much. They will not permit me to bring you better and will not allow the use of cutlery. Still, the food will curb your appetite for the time being."

"I appreciate that, Crey," Lucas said. He reached down as Crey slipped the tray through the small gap beneath the cell door. "Have you seen her?" he asked before dipping a piece of bread into the bowl of soup. He began eating as Crey replied.

Crey frowned. "She is a strange creature. I am not sure her loyalties are in line with our own."

"What do you mean?" Lucas said between mouthfuls.

"She swore allegiance to the Sacred Mother. She has joined the Nagaran."

Lucas's brow furrowed. "She," he paused. "I don't understand."

"The Charmer came to the great hall. The devotions were interrupted so that she could speak. Then, she pledged allegiance to the High Priestess. She transformed, in part at least, into the great Serpenthrope. Even the High Priestess could see the power radiating from her. She is truly the chosen, but I do not understand why she would choose to ally herself with the Nagaran."

"She is smart. I am sure she has a play here. She can't mean to become one of them."

"They have changed her. Perhaps they have convinced her that she is one of them."

Lucas shook his head. "I won't believe that. I can't."

Crey shrugged. "It is no matter, at least at this time. The Uprising can still act in defiance in this sect. The Charmer is not essential to our plans, for the moment."

"I thought you said she and I were pieces in your chess game against the Nagaran."

"Her destiny will unfold. Nothing can prevent her fate coming to pass."

"What do you mean?"

"I have no time to explain. I must return or the men guarding the door will cause trouble for me. I must be very careful to avoid suspicion."

Lucas laughed. "You play your part with subterfuge but you don't believe Tori could play her own?"

Crey frowned. "Perhaps, but while I am not certain I cannot assume. She does not know what we fight for, or why." The door above them jangled and Crey glanced back to the stairs. "I must go. My loyalty to the Nagaran must appear resolute, if it is called to question I will be unable to help you."

Lucas guzzled the cup of water that had come with his meal as Crey rose to his feet. "Thank you," Lucas said. He passed the tray to Crey, who nodded, then turned and disappeared up the steps. Lucas sighed as the light disappeared with him and he was again plunged into darkness.

Tori felt like she was under constant guard. She was never alone. Zara had been replaced by another devout when they had joined the worshippers for evening meal. The meal was limp and bland. Most of the vegetables had lost their colour. The only part of the meal that was actually palatable was the rich mushroom soup. The woman who had stayed with her through dinner had, for the most part, ignored her presence. The other worshippers in the room had been less apathetic. Tori felt their eyes on her as they watched every move she made. Their whispers tingled down her spine.

After the meal she had been escorted back to her room by a third female devotee. They had crossed through the confusing weave of rooms and corridors at a crawling pace. The girl was a bubble of energy. She reminded Tori of the cheerleaders she had hated in high school. The girl had actually bounced and tossed her pony tail when she had introduced herself. *Tiffany*, a bubbly, cheerleader type name. Tori wondered how someone like her could be drawn to the Nagaran.

As they had walked Tori glanced through the arched doorways they passed. Most rooms were interconnected with others. Tori felt as if they were walking in circles. After turning another unfamiliar corner she realised they were back at the room she had been kept in.

At the door Tiffany turned to Tori. "You'll want to sleep, now."

"What time is it?" Tori asked.

The girl shrugged. "Well," she drawled, "dinner is at five. So I suppose it would be closer to seven by now. We don't exactly keep watches. They clash with the robes." She swirled around, tossing her hair again. It swung behind her as she pranced away.

"Seven? My bedtime was later than that when I was a child."

A soft chuckle behind her reminded Tori that she was not alone.

"So, you're my new babysitter?" She eyed the man. His soft brown eyes sparkled with humour and his skin held a dark olive colouring. He was the first of the Nagaran that was not the pallor of having spent too much time out of the sunlight.

"I am Crey," he said. "You do not remember, but we met earlier."

"We did?"

"Indeed. In fact, we were quite intimate. You clung to me. It was very gratifying." His dimpled smile lit up his face.

Tori flushed. Dark hunger bloomed low in her belly. She felt Torque stir within her and swallowed. "I remember," she said and then paused. The heat of his skin was like a lode stone, calling to the cool blood that pulsed through her veins. Tori swayed forward and a smile curved her lips. "I," she stuttered, her voice stolen from her as her breath caught on another wave of desire that pooled between her thighs. She clenched them together, stepping backward with a gasp.

He chuckled again, but deep in his eyes she could see a flash of curiosity. He watched her face as if he was deciphering every expression that chased across her features. His voice low, he replied, "I am certain you had no intention of giving me the wrong idea."

His eyes lingered on her and she sensed the lie hidden in his words. *He's not certain at all.* The slither of the serpent hissed through her thoughts. "Yes," she said instead.

"Now we are alone."

A purr of desire swirled through her and her voice hitched in concern, "What do you mean?"

He smiled. "Only that we may talk freely. It can be," he paused, considering his words, "difficult to do that. However, the Nagaran sleep early and rise late. I am fortunate to have this opportunity."

"What would we have to talk about?" Tori asked.

"Much it would seem. Your friend is certain your loyalty to the Nagaran is a ruse. I am tempted to believe him."

Chapter 10. Uprising

She gasped, then stammered, "No. I am devoted to the Sacred Mother."

He tilted his head, tracing his gaze over her face. A moment passed before he answered, "Perhaps. We will see."

Tori stepped backward, moving away from him. She crossed the room to the bed. It had been remade in her absence. The sheets were crisp as though freshly laundered, but the clinging odour of the musky incense that threaded through every inch of the temple was woven through them. Tori wrinkled her nose as she pulled the sheets back. She turned back to him, standing beside the bed. "I think I would like to sleep now. As you said, the Nagaran sleep early and rise late."

"Tori, I really had hoped to talk with you."

"I don't know you," she said. She felt the burn of curiosity that washed over her skin. She glared up at Crey, giving a furious shake of her head. "I don't know what you could possibly want to say to me."

"Perhaps that is why you should allow me. Your Seraph asked me to look in on you. He is concerned for your safety."

"You've seen him?" Tori stepped forward, then stopped. She dropped her hand to the sheet.

"You should sit. There is much to explain." She sank to the sheets of the bed, but sat stiffly on the edge. He crossed the room, lowering himself to the floor opposite and leaned back against the wall. "I am Crey de Luca Vento. I am keeper of accounts among the Nagaran."

Tori settled further back on the bed and crossed her legs. "What does that mean, keeper of accounts?"

Crey smiled. "It means I am in charge of keeping account of the Nagaran histories. I suppose you might think me some what a librarian."

"The Nagaran have a library?"

"Of sorts."

"You said you'd seen Lucas?"

"Your Seraph, yes. I took his meal to him earlier."

"Is he?" Tori stopped, afraid to ask if he was hurt. The memory of the cruel severing of his wings flashed through her mind. A hissing fury flurried with it and coiled around her chest. She sucked a breath into her lungs as it slithered away.

"His wounds have been attended to and he will live. He is concerned for your well being also. I assured him that you were safe."

"I am not sure that I am."

She felt Crey's eyes on her. His head tilted and his smile faded. "Why would you doubt it? You have sworn allegiance to the Nagaran. You are their Sister now."

Tori shook her head. "I don't know that is what I am. You are here, sent to watch me. Tiffany, Sarah, Zara. I am never left alone. The High Priestess does not trust me."

"I suspect she is most put out by your arrival." His smile returned.

"Why?"

"You are the Charmer."

"But was does that mean? I don't understand. They did this to me." Tori could hear the frustration in her own voice and grimaced. A lick of the serpent's anger flickered through her mind. Tori took a breath, feeling the swirl of the serpent stirring in her mind before it faded again. She glanced at Crey. "I mean no disrespect, of course, but you must understand my confusion."

"Indeed. Given the Nagaran's treatment of you, I thought your resentment would linger. Yet, not even a day later you swear allegiance."

Tori pressed her lips together. Torque stirred within her, again. It clawed from within, vying for supremacy. Its dark, reptilian suspicion crawled through her mind and she felt the shutter falling across her control. Before it had snapped shut there was a soft knock on the door and her mind cleared. She drew a shaky breath, glancing at the door. Crey stood and crossed the room to open it. The soft voice from the doorway was familiar. Tori watched Crey lean past Zara out the door and glance up and down the corridor before shepherding her inside.

As Zara stepped into the room, she glanced at Tori, her gaze full of angry rebuke. "Well, has she told you yet?"

Crey touched her arm. "We have barely begun to speak together."

"Why are you stepping around this, Crey. Either she's with us, or against us."

"It is a delicate issue, and perhaps not black and white. Her angel believes she is acting a part."

"Well? Is she?"

"I have not ascertained. I cannot be sure where her loyalties lie."

"Crey," Zara began, but Crey interrupted her.

"Zara, give me this opportunity to speak with her."

She looked at him a long moment before shaking her head. She turned on Tori. "Surely you have no intension of serving the Nagaran?"

Chapter 10. Uprising

Crey reached to grip Zara's arm. "Zara!" He said in an angry whisper. She glared at him and yanked her arm away.

"I'm sorry, Crey. I have to know," Zara said. She did look sorry, Tori decided. The angry crease in her brow had smoothed and she turned back to Tori, crossing the room to stand beside the bed. Her mouth tilted in a hesitant smile and Tori felt the caress of the serpent's curiosity in her mind again. "I'm sorry, Tori," Zara began, "I feel as if I know you and I can't understand why you did this. We are taking a very big risk, coming to you like this, but we have to know. Do you mean to serve the Nagaran as you say you do?"

With a sigh, Crey crossed the room and slid down the wall again. "Forgive us. Zara should know better then to speak about these matters so openly."

Confusion washed over Tori and overwhelmed by the emotion she felt Torque rise up within her. The serpent reared, anger bubbling through her. Fury rippled on the surface, a dark anger that throbbed through her whole body. Curiosity gave way to a penetrating hunger, and with it disturbing thoughts turned her body. She felt the slither of the serpent mind caressing her own. The scent of blood tingled through her nostrils and she licked her lips at the phantom taste on her tongue. Her whole body rocked forward, and she rose to her knees.

Crey and Zara gasped and stepped back as a keening cry came from between Tori's lips. She felt as if her skin were splitting, shedding her body as the serpent tore through her. Impassive eyes gazed down at the two. A forked tongue flicked between her lips as she swayed on the bed. The heavy robes still fell around her, torn at the throat it shivered around the scales of a serpent and down the tail which twitched among the sheets. The serpent loomed up over Crey. Its head swung downward, nostrils flaring as it drew the warm scent of the man into its throat, the smell was tainted with the cold chill of fear. The creature snarled, its teeth wicked points that hovered near Crey's throat. Crey swallowed, quivering beneath it.

Tori screamed behind the shield in her mind. The powerlessness that throbbed through her pounded against her as if she were pummelling herself as she bashed her fists against the barrier that kept her from her control. In her thoughts the serpent's hunger licked against her mind. Flashes of a nightmare flogged her, pools of blood, Crey and Zara laying white across the stained floor, their throats torn open by sharp fangs. She shuddered, feeling the images crushing her and her heart raced. The furious lash of thoughts whipped through her and piece by piece began to soften. A calculating shimmer of the serpent's rational thought glimmered through as it considered the choices laid before it.

Almost as quickly as the serpent had slipped over her she felt the shedding of its scales and the cool brush of the sheets across her legs. The robes clung in loose shreds and tangled around her legs, pooling at her knees. Her breath slipped through her lips. She sobbed, rocked back and pulled her knees to her chin. The pain in her chest nagged at her, but the ache within her soul drowned out the agony.

"I'm a monster," she whispered, her voice breaking. Her tears ran down her cheeks and dripped a damp stain across the white sheets.

A look passed between Crey and Zara that seemed to communicate a hesitant understanding. It washed across their faces as their terror began to subside. Their shared look lingered on each other and Tori sensed between them a fear for each other that spoke of deep caring, of love. The flashes of insight flittered past in an instant. Words slipped with a gentle hiss from between her lips, "Why do you ask these questions?"

Zara and Crey flinched at the whip of the serpent's voice from Tori's mouth. Crey's gaze snapped back to

Tori, his body stiffening. Crey composed himself quicker than Zara. "So," he said, his voice a low croon, "it is true."

"Oh Tori, what have they done to you?" Zara whispered. Here own eyes were filled with tears. She swiped them from her cheeks and reached out. She tugged the folds of white sheet and pulled them around Tori, her fingers brushing over Tori's hand.

Tori looked down at her fingers, feeling the warmth of Zara's skin on hers. She heard the deep compassion in Zara's voice and a ripple of wonder fluttered in her mind. Her breath shuddered from her chest and she blinked the tears from her eyes. "I don't understand." Her voice broke as another sob wrenched through her. She pulled the sheets, holding them with her arms resting on her legs. Her head fell forward and she lay her forehead across her folded arms.

"It is the gift of the Charmer." Crey's soft voice carried an edge of quiet awe.

She looked up at him. "Gift? It doesn't feel like a gift to me."

He smiled, but a trace of sadness lingered in his eyes. "Perhaps not, but in the prophecies of the Nagaran, it is considered a great honour to have the gift of Serpenthropy bestowed upon one. The Nagaran have performed the ritual for decades, but there has not been a true Charmer in all that time. The Sacred Mother was the first, and last, until you."

"Why me?"

Crey shrugged. "I do not know."

Zara said, "Your parents, or perhaps your grandparents, must have been descendants of the Nagaran at some point, Tori."

"No," Tori said. She shook her head. "That's not possible."

"How can you be sure?" Zara asked.

"My mother died in childbirth and my father," Tori paused, gasping. "Marlena murdered him."

Crey glanced at Zara. They shared a knowing look.

"The Nagaran killed my father," Tori whispered.

Crey leaned forward. "My parents were also killed, four years ago. I was twenty-two and away at university. When the news of their murders reached me, I came home. The authorities had few leads. The case remains unsolved, but I have traced their deaths to the Nagaran."

"Esmerelda and Vincento were the kindest people," Zara whispered, her voice wavered and she wiped a tear from her cheek. "They had a remarkable library. I was just the daughter of their friend, but they allowed me to spend long hours there, reading. Vincento loved the books." She reached out and gripped Crey's hand in her own.

"I have come to learn a great deal about what lead to my parents' deaths. My father had purchased an old tome from a traveller who was passing though Luca Vento. According to my father's journals, the book was truly remarkable."

Tori shook her head. "I don't understand. What has this got to do with why you are here, with what I've become?"

Crey looked up at her. She felt as if his eyes were peering into her soul, weighing her loyalty. Finally, he answered, "The Nagaran. Tori, the book was a true history of the battle between the Four Fathers and the birth of the Sacred Mother."

Chapter Eleven
A Story Of Four Fathers

"Do you think they're asleep now?" Zara whispered. She glanced at the closed door.

Crey looked down at the watch hidden beneath the long sleeves of his robe. "It is likely," he said. Lifting his gaze to Tori he smiled. "Time to go, I think."

"You're leaving? But I thought," Tori trailed off as Crey shook his head and chuckled.

"No, I am to watch you always. I do not defy the High Priestess." He winked at her. "*We* are leaving. There is someone who needs to be part of our conversation. As he cannot come here, we must go to him."

"Who?"

"He means your Seraph," Zara said.

"Lucas?" Tori's breath caught and she felt her pulse quicken. "You're taking me to see him?"

Crey nodded. Zara handed Tori a robe from the small collection sent to the room while they were at evening meal. Crey crossed the room to the door, keeping his eyes averted as Zara helped Tori pull the folds of the robe over her head. When Zara crossed the room to him, Crey turned a smile on Tori and whispered, "We must be silent. No one must know you left your room this night."

Tori nodded, following him as he turned and stepped into the hall. Zara drew up behind them, closing the door. The snick of the door catching seemed to echo down the hallway. They moved through the dark weave of halls. Occasionally Crey would pause at an intersection and hold up his hand. They stilled as he glanced around the corner before waving them forward again.

Some minutes later the light in the hall grew brighter. Rowdy laughter ahead of them drowned out the soft pad of their feet on the earthen floors.

"An' she was not nothin' but a right looker, breasts the size of melons."

A rough voice spluttered. Tori heard the splash of liquid on wood. "Ain't no woman like that take a second look at your ugly mug."

"She right did, I swear."

"Oh boys, I'm sure you've both had a harem of beautiful girls take you to bed." Tori blinked, glancing behind her as Zara stepped past her into the light around the corner of the hall. Tori went to step forward but Crey held her back, shaking his head.

"Zara, ya beautiful wench. Why ain't you getting the zees like everyone else?"

"I came to see if you and Carny had eaten something," Zara said.

Chapter 11. A Story Of Four Fathers

"We don't got not nothing to eat. Not never had no break either. Shift change didn't never turn up."

"You two must be exhausted, and even hungrier I bet. Look, the guy down there's not going anywhere. He could barely move when I was patching him back together. Everyone else has gone to bed. Why don't we sneak down to the kitchen and grab something to eat real quick."

"I don't know, Zara. We ain't s'posed to leave our post."

"You're not supposed to be left to starve either, Orton. Come on. I'm sure they've got something still hot in the kitchen. It won't take long to snatch some soup and bread to bring back with you."

"Come on, Orton. I'm starved. Zara'll cover for us if anyone asks, right Zara?"

"Sure. I'll swear black and blue that I saw you at your post when I came by at all hours of the night."

The scratch of wood on rock grated on Tori's eardrums. Crey winked at her and motioned to a nearby corridor. They ducked into the darkness. Moments later Orton and Carny passed them with Zara a step behind. She flicked her hand beside her hip in a wave then lifted three fingers, closed them to her fist, then blew Crey a kiss with a cheeky grin.

Crey chuckled quietly as the three disappeared down the hall. "Come," he said. "We have thirty minutes only." He moved back down the hall and fumbled with the door, jangling a set of heavy keys. "This door can be difficult."

"You have the key?"

He glanced up, a grin across his face. "Of course, I am an adept spy. Ensuring I had free access to every room of this temple was the first thing I did when I arrived. It is difficult to pursue information through locked doors."

The click of the lock turning over drew the breath Tori did not realise she had been holding. "It works," she whispered.

"Certamente."

She looked down the dark stairs into the pitch blackness below. "He's in here?"

"Yes, take this, it will light the way." He handed her a lantern and, as she took the first few steps, he pulled the door closed behind them. Tori felt like each step she took echoed through the whole temple. Behind her, Crey's footsteps made no sound.

As they reached the bottom of the stairs Tori peered around the corner. The lantern barely lit the darkness and looking into the cell Tori searched for Lucas. "Lucas?" Her voice quivered as she drew the lantern higher, turning the beam of light across the iron bars.

Her name on a heavy exhale of breath startled her. "Tori." She bit her lip as she saw him, leaning against the wall in the farthest corner of the cell. He grunted, swallowing as he pulled himself upright. He stumbled forward and leaned on the bars. Dropping to his knees in front of her, he reached his fingers through the cell door. "Tori," he gasped again. She thrust the lantern behind her, Crey almost could not take it as she stepping forward to catch Lucas's hand with her own.

"Are you okay? What did they do to you?"

Lucas's grim smile looked like a grimace through his bruised and split lips. "Nothing more than I deserve." He closed his eyes, letting his hand fall away. "I'm so sorry, Tori."

Tori shook her head, reaching through the bars to touch his face. "Don't," she whispered. "Please don't. There is nothing for you to feel sorry about." His breath on her fingers sent a flurry of tingling warmth down her spine, pooling in her belly. Within her, Torque stirred. A growling hiss rumbled through her thoughts and Tori flinched.

Lucas's eyes, cast to the floor, flickered with pain. "I failed, Tori. I was supposed to protect you and I failed."

His voice was laden with a deep grief Tori could not understand.

"I don't understand."

"No, I suppose you don't. It doesn't matter. I *will* get you out of here. I can't undo what has happened, but I can make sure they never touch you again. You don't deserve the pain you've had in your life."

Tori tilted his chin up and looked deep into his eyes, then ran her fingers through his hair. "I remember you."

Lucas blinked. He lifted his chin to look at her through the bars. "What?"

"I remember. You didn't see me because I was hiding under my father's desk, but I saw you."

He shook his head and Tori's fingers fell away. "It seems like I've stood behind every sadness in your life. I was too late then, too. I can't begin to earn your forgiveness. I told them I shouldn't be a part of this. Too much has already happened."

Behind her, Crey cleared his throat. "You two have much to talk about, certamente, but we have not enough time."

"Is my friend in the right place to help me?" Lucas asked.

Tori furrowed her brow. "What?"

Chapter 11. A Story Of Four Fathers

Crey chuckled. "Unfortunately not. I can do nothing tonight. We have only one half hour to speak. You both need to know."

"About the war you mean, and your father's journal?" Tori asked.

He nodded. "Yes, about that, and about you, Charmer."

"Me?"

"About Tori? What does that mean?"

"Let us sit and I will tell you," Crey said as he settled with grace on the floor facing the cell bars. Lucas winced as he rotated his shoulder and then sat across from him. He leaned forward near the bars and watched Tori, his eyes intent as if he could not stand to lose sight of her.

As Tori settled herself on the floor she felt the warmth radiating from his body. Torque tugged within her, urging her to move closer. Tori had scooted closer to him before she realised she had not intended to move. Her breath escaped in a hiss as she felt Lucas's soft exhale against the back of her neck. He reached his arm through the bars and threaded his fingers through hers.

"It's okay," she whispered. "I'm not going anywhere."

"I," he began, then shook his head and turned guilt-filled eyes to Crey who had begun to speak.

But she is, thought Lucas. He could not get out of this cell and she could not stay. Even with her fingers curled in his he knew he was powerless to protect her. The little food he had been able to swallow churned in his stomach. He forced down the urge to be sick, then realised he was thankful for the sickness, for the guilt, for the helplessness, because the pain of those things, of his failure, made the ache of his body seem inconsequential. He had meant what he said before, the wounds were nothing more than he deserved.

"…they forged an alliance that united their lands. It ended the conflicts between their peoples. Theirs was a treaty that lead each land into prosperity and created a decade of plenty." Crey's voice finally penetrated the cloud of dark thoughts that crowded Lucas's mind.

"Who?" he asked.

Tori glanced at him over her shoulder. "The Four Fathers," she said, then turned to face Crey again, "but I don't understand, who were they? I thought you said there was a battle between them. Was that before the treaty?"

"That came after. About a century ago, the Four disputed. They dissolved the alliance and, between them, waged a war.

"Why would they do that?" Tori asked.

"Why are all wars started?" Crey said with an effacing smile. "Because of a woman." Lucas coughed hiding a smile behind the hand he raised to his mouth. Crey nodded at him. "The histories tell of an exotic beauty with olive skin and long dark hair. She was lithe and lovely, and moved with grace and poise. The Four men became entranced with her and fought over who would be the one to make her give away her innocence."

"They caused a war between their people because of a woman?" Tori's shocked voice reminded Lucas how innocent she really was. She knew about the world of course, as a journalist she had to have faced some of the darkest elements within it, but she did not really understand the way people, the way men, moved through the world.

"It happens more often than you might think," Lucas said. He grimaced. "Many of the wars through history began for one reason; a dispute for status. Often that status symbol is land or wealth or power, but the most powerful symbol of a man's prowess is the woman who loves him. Wars were won and lost by men who were in the thrall of an entrancing woman."

"And so it was with the Four Fathers. They had become like brothers. Their falling out over this young woman destroyed all their holdings. Their lands fell to ruin. The people who had made their homes there abandoned them. The swift decimation of the peace and prosperity they had taken years to forge is not, however, the highlight of their histories."

"The significance of that would mean little to the Nagaran," Lucas said.

"That is right. The Nagaran do not revere the Four Fathers for their standing. They are esteemed for what came after."

"You mean with the woman?" Tori asked.

Crey nodded. "Indeed. She was the Sacred Mother."

"Four Fathers and a Mother?" Tori whispered.

"She was not a mother before all this of course. The Nagaran refer to the time as the birth of the Sacred Mother. The story is not pleasant. As I said, the men vied for her affections. Her heart, however, was already taken and could not be stolen from her beau."

Lucas felt Tori lean forward, captivated by the story. Her profile in the flickering lantern light was entrancing. Her dark beauty, rich black hair, soft pink lips, all called to the core of a man. He imagined what it must have been like for the Four Fathers, each obsessed with a woman they could not have.

"As you can imagine, the men grew more and more furious to be denied. Indeed, their mutual dejection lead them to unite, one last time. They plotted together to steal the woman away. Together they would hold her captive until she chose from among them the one who would be her husband."

"They kidnapped her?" Tori gasped. "How could they do that? She couldn't choose who she fell in love with."

Crey smiled and Lucas squeezed her fingers. He told himself he meant to comfort her, to calm her agitation but a betraying thread wove through his heart.

"You are a romantic, little Charmer. These men were not so inclined to think a woman's emotions should be so steadfast."

"I suspect they believed that, denied the man she loved, she would take another."

Crey nodded at Lucas. "Perhaps," he said.

"So did they? Did they kidnap her?" Tori asked.

Crey nodded. "Yes. In the night the four took her and for many weeks they held her captive in a dark cell."

He glanced around them. "Much like this one, I suspect, only, hers was home to creatures less friendly than the rats who occasionally sneak into these depths."

Tori shuddered. "Rats?" She asked, glancing around into the corners of the room.

"Yes. Her cell had few rats for they were the feast of her other companions."

"Something worse than rats?"

Crey smiled. "Snakes, of course. The Nagaran are the people of snakes. They must be in this story somewhere."

"I don't understand."

"One night, after the Four had spent long hours," Crey paused, swallowing, "*convincing* her to submit, she lay battered and worn, near death, on the floor of her cell. The serpents came to her. To them, I suppose, she seemed a helpless feast, but the legend says the Sacred Mother charmed the snakes and that her blood ran with the venom of a thousand serpents."

"What does that mean?"

"I do not know. Whatever it means, it says she survived when she should not have. That she took on the form of the serpent, broke from her restraints, and escaped."

"So she was the first Serpenthrope?" Lucas asked.

Chapter 11. A Story Of Four Fathers

"Yes, and the Mother of all Serpenthrope."

Tori frowned. "How does that make her a mother?"

Crey sighed. "Because when she escaped, she was *gravidus*, pregnant."

"You mean," Tori sucked in a breath biting on her lower lip.

Crey lowered his eyes. "The histories called it the gift of progeny. Remember, the Nagaran worship the Four Fathers. They are considered the givers of life."

"But they worship the Sacred Mother. Surely her situation is the one they are more compassionate toward."

"I have not had an opportunity to learn how the Mother influences her people. The records indicate, however, that she abides this belief of the Nagaran."

Lucas leaned forward, grasping a bar with his free hand. "Perhaps she came to sympathise with her tormentors. She carried a child for them. That can change the heart of a woman. Not to mention that the ordeal may have hardened her."

Crey shook his head. "Not a child, children. Four of them. Each as distinctly akin to their individual fathers as they were unlike each other."

"She got impregnated by all four of the men?" Tori's voice rose with indignant anger. Lucas felt a shiver quiver through her fingers. He brushed his hand up her arm, running his fingers across her shoulder. They brushed against her neck and she turned her chin toward them. He felt the wave of desire that rushed through her like an echo within his core. His breath snagged in his lungs as the curve of her lips parted and her tongue darted across them. His hand fell away and he clutched at the bar, closing his eyes as he rested his head against it. He exhaled, feeling the burning air leave his lungs.

"The histories portray it as a nestling. As snakes give birth to a clutch of young, so did their Sacred Mother." Crey's words sounded as if they had been memorised from a book. He seemed oblivious to the tension that thrummed through Lucas.

Lucas blinked his eyes open. "What happened to the children?" he asked.

"They became the Nagaran royalty. They were ruthless, although the accounts praise their calculating and violent nature. It tells that they propagated the world with the children of the Nagaran. I take it to mean that they spread their seed in similar vein as their father's but that is not clearly defined as you can imagine. The children of the Nagaran are uncountable as records were not kept, but as there is only a single generation, or perhaps two by this year. One might imagine their numbers limited."

Chapter 11. A Story Of Four Fathers

Tori's mouth quivered. "But they call me a Charmer? Does that mean I'm one of them?"

Crey looked at her, meeting her eye as he answered. "It is unclear exactly what you are, Tori. The High Priestess, indeed the priestesses of many sects, have taken the children of the Nagaran for the ritual. You are the only one to have survived."

"What makes me different?"

His dark eyes looked deep into her own before he shook his head. His throaty voice, rich with sorrow, answered, "I do not know."

Silence fell between them. Lucas watched the emotions chasing across Tori's face in the flickering light from the lantern. He felt the anguish turning in her stomach. Somehow, being this close to her heightened his ability to sense her emotions. They tangled with his own, an urge to flee, fear mingled with a hint of dark fury. A chill passed through him, a cold slither of shadow that disappeared as if hidden by the wave of her other emotions.

Her breathing was rapid, her heart racing. "What-"

The question was interrupted by a loud clatter from above them. Feminine laughter followed by a heavy grunt echoed down the stairs. Crey pushed himself up from the floor in a fluid movement and reached down for Tori's hand. Lucas passed it to him as Crey blew out the lantern, plunging the room into darkness. "We must go."

He tugged Tori's hand and pulled her up, dragging her across the room. He dropped his arm across her, holding her pressed up against the rock as he leaned back. The clang of the heavy door rang down to them and Tori held her breath, pressing herself back against the wall. Torchlight flickered from the stairway and heavy feet tromped down the stairs.

"I just gotta check him's still breathing," drawled Orton's voice, thick with intoxicated slurs.

"You can barely stand up." Zara's voice echoed down to them.

Orton stumbled down the last of the stairs. The torch dropped from his hand, scattering ashes on the ground. The light wavered, sending a scatter of shadows around the room. Zara stepped down behind him, she glanced sideways at them, waving them behind her as she faked a laugh. "It's a good thing Carny couldn't hold his liquor or he'd give you grief for that tumble."

Orton grunted, climbing to his feet. He swayed as he stood. "I got it, I got it. Where's the damn torch?"

As Crey and Tori disappeared up the stairs, Zara reached down and picked up the torch. She glanced at Lucas and winked before turning back to Orton. "See, the

Seraph is safe and sound. You've done your duty. You really should be in bed."

"Right, gotta go wake those lazy you know, things, gotta get a'sleep."

Orton wavered then fell forward, hitting the ground hard. He snorted, eyes closed, his breathing heavy but regular.

Lucas raised an eyebrow. "What did you do to him?"

Zara gave him an impish grin. "Oh, he's just a little worse for triple shots of tequila. Hope you don't mind the company for a few hours. Someone will come across him eventually and drag him off to bed."

"Great," Lucas drawled. "I bet he snores."

"Probably," she said, giving him a wave before disappearing up the stairs with the torchlight.

Chapter Twelve
Searching For Unity

In the very early hours of the morning two young men came to take Crey's place as Tori's guard. Crey glanced at Tori. He could see the exhaustion in her weary limbs, and the waned pallor of her skin. He said in hushed tones, "She has not slept this night. She will not sleep while watched. Guard her, but from outside the door. Leave her to rest. I will have the morning meal sent." The two men hesitated, glancing at the ground. The white floor-tiles still held a faint stain where Renold's blood had pooled beneath his body. Their eyes drifted upward, watching her with wary gazes. Crey cleared his throat. "Do you understand?" Their attention snapped back to him and his steady gaze lingered on them, stern and demanding.

Their eager nods sent a stab of hurt through Tori's heart. *They're afraid of me.* She bit her lip, feeling tears well up in her eyes. Crey glanced across at her. An encouraging smile curved his lips and he nodded to her as he drew the door closed between them. Tori stared down at the dull stain near the door. The image of Renold's body, sprawled and bleeding, burned in her mind. She shuddered, closing her eyes. "What have they made me?" she whispered, her voice catching as tears streaked down her face. Sobbing, she turned away and buried her face in the thick pillows.

Hours passed. Tori still lay awake, tangled in the sheets where she had turned, over and over. She thumped her fist down on the tear-damp pillow again and kicked the sheet to the end of the bed. Her mind raced with all she had learned, all she had seen, all she had done since she had been taken. Nothing made sense. The images from her memories flickered through her mind like blazing bushfire. She wondered if they were shaped by her naivety. *Was anything she remembered true?*

"What have I become?" she whispered, feeling her breath bounce back across her lips as she buried her head, and a fresh wave of sobs, in the pillow. The slither of the serpent coiled around her thoughts, tormenting her with the ease with which it could alter the course of them within her mind. "Get out of my head." She sobbed, grasping her head, her nails digging into her scalp as her fingers laced through her hair. The hiss flickered through her, licking a dark trail across her skin. She shivered and her body recoiled from the sensation. "Leave me alone," she cried, wiping the tears from her cheek as she pushed herself upright on the bed.

Pain rippled through her chest and ribs at the violent movement. She welcomed it, embracing the sudden silence that rippled through her mind. Her thoughts were her own again and she sighed. She closed her eyes, tracing the memories of her family in her mind and trying to piece together the fragile fragments with the new information. She remembered the glimpse of her mother, of her infant self passed into her father's arms. "But not by me." The heart-broken words whispered through her mind again. *Were all the children of the Nagaran stolen from their mothers? What happened to the women who gave them life? Is my mother really dead?* The chase of unanswerable questions raced in circles around her mind. "Did my father lie to me?" she whispered.

The hiss in her mind felt like a concerned croon attempting to comfort her, but Tori's whole body tensed in violent rejection. Her breath shuddered out of her and she wrapped her arms around her body, crushing her chest to her knees, thrusting her ribs hard against her thighs. Searing agony swept through her, stilling her thoughts. Waves of pain drowned out the dark whispers in her mind, washing through her ears in a frenzied roar. As it ebbed away other memories surfaced. Late night whispers between her father and unseen faces while she slept. She could not hear their words, only the muted mutter of their voices.

Then, light wavered over her eyelids and she heard her father whisper, "She's only a child." Tori clung to the words and the sound of his voice in the shadows of her memory.

"She's the Charmer, Rick. She does not have the luxury of childhood." Tori winced at the harsh whisper of her grandmother. *Was this the secret Marlena had said my grandmother had kept from me?* In her memory a heavy door closed and the voices faded. She whimpered, biting her lip as a horrifying possibility occurred to her. *Was her father one of the Nagaran royals?*

Crey's soft voice echoed through her thoughts as she remembered their conversation. The memory, like all her others now, was crystal clear and exact. "It is unclear exactly what you are, Tori. The High Priestess, indeed the priestesses of many sects, have taken the children of the Nagaran for the ritual. You are the only one to have survived."

"What am I?" Tori whispered. She rocked back and forth on the bed, her head resting on her knees and her arms wrapped tightly around her legs. "What am I?" Her breath shuddered through her with raking sobs and tears coursed down her face.

"Charmer." The word hissed insider her mind. Tori shuddered. Whimpering, she buried her face in her hands. Her breath shuddered from her aching lungs. The curl of the serpent within her pressed upon her thoughts and wove a slithering sickness deep through her body. She felt constricted, as if her soul were suffocating beneath the crushing scales of the darkness within. Her breath hissed out of her lungs and the creeping tug of her skin sent a shudder of awareness through her tingling nerve endings. The pain in her chest faded as her whole body shivered. Her lips quivered and she felt her thoughts disappearing into the shadows of her mind.

"No," she groaned. Her skin felt like it was tearing away from her body. She tried to scream but her mouth would not open, her throat gripped tight in the grasp of the serpent. Tears streamed down her face as her arms fell away from the scaled coil that had been her legs. She gasped, the exhale shuddering through her body but not escaping her lips.

"We are the Charmer," hissed that serpentine voice from her lips. Tori's thoughts recoiled and she felt as if she shrank inside herself, hiding in the darkest recesses of her mind. The smothering tightness that throbbed through her head faded and her teary eyes flickered open. "We are the Charmer," the voice said again.

Chapter 12. Searching For Unity

Tori could hear the echo of her screams within her head. *No!*

"We are the Charmer," the serpent hissed through her lips.

I never wanted this. They made me this. Tori's own voice ripped through her mind. The ripple of the serpent's thoughts caressed her and she quivered. Her body shuddered in response.

"They," she heard the voice from her lips and felt her head tilt, "did not make us. They, awoke us."

"I don't understand." Exhaustion wove over her and the darkness within began to fade.

Hold on, Tori, just a little longer. The heat of Lucas's gentle voice tingled through her thoughts and her wracking sobs faded into soft whimpers. Her breath gasped from her lungs, her chest heaving. Her arms fell heavy beside her and her legs collapsed beneath her. She fell against the sheets of the bed and the tangled, torn rags of her robe. She wrapped her arms tight around herself and felt her mind seeking Lucas's warmth. She ached to feel his comforting arms around her. The caress of his masculine energy, reaching out to her, flickered across her thoughts, calm, strong, safe.

With a sharp inhale, she grasped the touch, feeling Lucas in the faint traces that grew stronger as she pulled the sensation about her. She rocked, like a child in the arms of her mother, as her tears dried on her cheeks. Tori let her mind wander, reaching out with her thoughts. She felt the traces of emotion in the air. A fog trailed through her; the wave of it swept across her. A flush of fatigue weighed her down and she curled into a ball. Her head sunk into the soft folds of her pillow.

"Lucas," she whispered, letting her eyes drift closed.

As she balanced on the edges of sleep the serpent's voice caressed though her thoughts, "Sleep."

Lucas had slept in fits and spurts. The pitch blackness had swept over him like a soothing blanket and the hard floor ached through his tired muscles. Orton's gentle snore had broken the still silence for a while, but what must have been hours had passed since someone had come down and roused him. He had grunted away, shaking off the young guard's hand and grumbling as he clambered to his feet. "Ge' off me," he slurred, pulling his arm away when the man had reached to help him. They had stumbled up the steps and the blackness had swept down the stairs as they disappeared above.

As Lucas lay in the still air, staring into the ink around him, he let himself search out the soft wave of energy that thrummed from Tori's soul. The caress of her through his mind touched the pit of his stomach and he swallowed. He felt the wretched torment of her nightmares churning through her and pushed himself to his feet. Pacing across the length of his cell he focused in on the feelings that channelled through him from the frightened woman above.

"What are they doing to her?" His voice husked out of his dry throat and his tongue darted out to moisten his cracked lips. The roiling fits of emotion jerked through him. Dark throbs of heart-aching tears burned deep inside him. Her tears, her sorrow, her tormented fear of herself. "Tori," he groaned.

He stopped pacing and felt his way around the cage to the cell door. With angry jerks he shuddered the gate as if he could pull it from its hinges. The door groaned, iron grinding on iron, but even as Lucas rocked it with the greatest strength his aching muscles could bare, the joints held. He dropped his head, resting it against the bars. His thoughts raked over him. Failure, helplessness, crushing responsibility.

"I should have kept her safe," he whispered, "Why can't I keep any of them safe?"

The door at the top of the stairs clanged and light flickered off the walls. Footsteps padded down the steps and whispered voices echoed through the room. "Could you have done that any more loudly?" Zara snapped.

"I apologise. The lock was stubborn. It needed cajoling," Crey responded.

"Cajoling? You think shoving it until the lock gave is cajoling? Now we've no way to hide the fact that someone has been down here."

As they crossed the last step, Lucas saw Crey's careless shrug. "They will discover he is gone. They will think he forced the door himself."

"Only if this cell door is worse for wear," Lucas said, shaking the iron bars.

Crey smiled at him. "I am prepared."

Lucas raised an eyebrow. "Then lets get this cage open. I need to get Tori out of here."

Zara stepped forward, shining the flickering torch across the bars as Crey bent down. He dripped an acrid liquid across the lower hinge. It sizzled and hissed, leaving a stain of rust down the bolts.

"What is that?" Lucas asked.

Crey shrugged. "It is why I could not help you sooner. The labs that cultivate the serpent toxins and other chemical compounds, they are complicated to infiltrate. There is always a person within. I had to wait until that person was of the Uprising rather than the Nagaran."

"You have someone in the lab?"

"Yes. There is little she can do without raising suspicion, but she makes copies of all the notes that pass through the lab. Her intelligence is invaluable. I hope my requisitioning of these chemicals will not inhibit her position there."

"Kayleigh is smart. She'll find a way to cover it up."

"Indeed. That is why she is so valuable to us." He stood again and lifted the glass vial to the upper hinge. The liquid dripped down the metal, burning a singe of rust through the rods. "Do you have strength enough? Pushing from your side would be simpler than pulling from ours."

Lucas nodded. "Step back."

Crey stepped away from the bars, crossing his arm in front of Zara. Lucas shoved at the bar, wincing at the tug of his shoulders and the twinge of his bruised muscles. He grunted, leaning his weight into the bars. They groaned, the iron twisting until the metal splintered, cracking the hinges. The cell door clattered, crashing to the ground. Lucas, tumbled forward. Crey reached out and gripped his arm before he could fall. Lucas groaned as the wrench on his arm sent a wave of pain through his shoulder.

"Sorry," Crey muttered, stepping back again.

Lucas shook his head. "It's nothing. Thank you."

Zara bit her lip, gazing at the bandage that crisscrossed over his chest and shoulder. Lucas glanced down and grimaced. A bloom of blood spread across the white stretch of cloth. "I didn't bring anything," she said. "I didn't think," her voice fell away.

"It's nothing," Lucas said again. "Come on, we have to get Tori."

Tori ran, faster and faster, down a tunnel of darkness that never seemed to diminish. A corridor glistened in the shadows. She wondered how she could see the line of doors disappearing into the blackness ahead of her, then realised that each door stood open, the darkness a shade lighter from within. She raced toward the nearest glimmer of light and felt herself slam into the door that was suddenly closed. Door by door she turned and every time the door slammed in her face. The darkness grew darker. The pinpricks of light that had traced lines up the hall disappeared as if winking out of existence. Instead, Tori stood, rooted to the void. Suddenly, a serpent reared up in front of her, lancing forward at her she raised her arms to protect herself. As the serpent curled around her, she thrashed and screamed.

Thick hands gripped her shoulders, forcing her down. A frantic scream cut through her ears and as her eyes blinked open Tori realised it was her own. Above her, two men struggled to hold her down. "Get her," one said to the other.

"I'm trying. She ain't exactly a feather."

Tori struggled, clawing at the man closest to her. He jerked his head back, his fingers digging into her skin. "No! No!" she shouted, shoving at him and kicking her feet. Her skin crawled under their fingers and pain shot through her, rippling over her like a cold shroud. Anger filled her, a flaming rage of hissing fury. It burst through her and Tori felt iron doors crash down around her thoughts. She gazed out from her own eyes, helpless to do anything as the serpent rose, rearing back on its thrashing tail.

She felt her body flick forward, striking out at the man. His keening cry froze and he crumpled beneath her. His blood cascaded through the raw flesh that hung from his throat. Like a torrent, it gushed through the fingers of the hand he had clapped to the wound. His wide eyes gazed up at her in horror. Tori quivered, feeling her own horror bouncing back at her from the wall around her thoughts. The taste of blood in her mouth tingled through her skin. Tori shuddered at the pleasure that rippled through her body.

The serpent turned as the other man, cowering, tried to crawl away from them. Torque hissed, snarling fangs dripping between scaled lips. Tori felt herself lurching forward again. The serpent's tail flicked across the floor and Torque soared forward with graceful poise. She slunk between the man and his escape. "Help!" he shouted. The cry echoed through the room and bounced off the walls down the hall. "Please, don't hurt me."

In her mind, Tori felt as if Torque was considering the plea. Her own thoughts begged the serpent to leave him alone. Her tongue flickered between her teeth. "You wish to live?" hissed the serpent's voice from her mouth.

"Please, I don't want to die," the man pleaded. The serpent tilted its head with curious interest. Tori could feel the pulse of the man's heart in the air. It raced, thrumming, in a frenzy of fear.

"You are afraid," Torque said. "Fear is weakness."

The man shuddered, flinching away as Torque curled forward, wrapping in tight coils around him. He screamed as the serpent's scaled body twisted around him, constricting him, crushing him. His heartbeat slowed and his thrashing stopped. His body hung limp, cooling against the chill scales. Torque slinked away, swaying across the floor. The serpent wove its way out of the door and swished back and forth down the hall. Already, the vibration of footsteps charging down the corridor pulsed up through the floor. Tori's tongue whipped out across her lips and a hiss slipped between her fangs.

A door swung open and a young blonde girl peered out. She looked down the hall toward the approaching guards. Her pony tail bobbed as she bounced on her feet. "What's going on?" she called, her voice a trill of excitement. The two men in front stopped several feet from her. The men behind them crashed up against their backs and they tumbled forward. They both scrambled backwards, their gazes fixed behind the blonde girl's head. Tori felt them staring at her and cowered. Her body remained a tight spring of agitated swaying. "What is it?" the girl asked. She turned, and screamed as the serpent snapped forward at her. Tiffany's body crumpled to the ground. Tori screamed within the walls of her mind.

The men attempted to scramble backwards down the hall. Their feet stumbled and their fingers flexed around the handles of their weapons. A whip cracked out. Tori felt it crack against her cheek. Torque snarled, swaying back and forth as she slithered forward. She moved faster than the men as they tried to weave their way backwards down the hall. A young guard waved a dagger in front of himself. His hands trembled and the blade almost slipped from his grip. Tori could smell the fear rippling off him like streams of icy sweat. *No,* she begged as she felt her muscles tensing. Torque rose to strike, the dagger clattered to the floor, blood splattering against the wall.

The remaining men froze. Tori's head tilted as her gaze wandered over them. Her tongue flickered back and forth, tasting the ripple of emotions thrumming through the air. Her tail swished and she wove between the men, slithering down the corridor. They cowered against the edges of the hall, whimpering. The serpent glided away but they remained there, frozen in place by their terror.

Tori's breath shuddered and she thrashed from inside her mind. "No," she cried out. The word burst from her lips and she felt her legs under her again. She stumbled, then pushed herself upright. Shouts rose up around her and she quivered, riveted to the spot.

The serpent hissed within her mind. *Run!*

She had control of her body. She could have ignored the urge from within, but her own racing heart, her own churning gut, was urging her to escape. She gasped air into her lungs and raced through the shadowy halls, searching for a way through the maze of empty rooms and corridors.

Chapter Thirteen
An Emotion-Charged Bond

The dark corridors, lit by flickering braziers, were barren. The walls were stained dark red by the glowing embers of fire. Tori ran, her chest heaving as she wove through a maze of chambers. The halls were empty, but from time to time she would stumble into a startled crowd of robed worshippers. They stared at her. A women flushed as Tori ran past her. A gasp spluttering through her lips. Tori glanced back at her, but her feet carried her forward across the room and she darted through the doorway on the far wall. A scandalised whisper behind her danced off the walls, "Not a stitch of clothing."

Tori cringed, wrapping her arms across her body. The muggy warmth of the incense thick air clung to her skin like a blanket, but her bare limbs shivered. Tears streaked down her face. She sprinted on, her chest heaving as she sucked the reek of smoke into her lungs. The temple wound and wound, corridor after corridor, room after room. Her legs burning, Tori wove through the maze. *I'm running in circles.* Her frustration grew as she chased though another corridor. It looked just like the others, a weave of rooms, blazing braziers, rock hewn walls. "Let me out!" Tori shouted.

Chapter 13. An Emotion-Charged Bond

Over time, the floor seemed to slant upward. Tori pushed herself harder, faster, higher and higher. She twisted and turned through the halls, following the rising rock beneath her feet. Darting around another corridor, Tori tripped over a step and fell. The cluster of stone stairs bruised her hip and thigh. She winced and gritted her teeth as she got back to her feet.

She looked up the dark well of stairs. A heavy door stood at the top. Tori glanced behind her, then scrambled up the stairs. She shoved on the door at the top. It opened and Tori felt the chill of frosted night wrap itself around her as she stumbled forward. She glanced around the vaulted room. The shadows of pews, stood like eerie black ghosts in the gloom of the old church. Moonlight glittered through the fragmented shards of stained glass. They cast a faint silhouette across the ground, the wings of an angel, the frosted blue eyes, the infant child. "Lucas," Tori whispered. She hesitated. Swallowing, she swiped away the tears that were drying on her cheek and glanced at the door. The cold iron was swinging closed behind her. It crashed shut. The heavy clang bounced off the crumbling stone walls.

Torque threaded through her mind, drawing her away, drowning Tori's thoughts of the gentle hands, the wave of hair, the sad eyes. Tori struggled to remember. "I have to go back," she said through gritted teeth. Torque dragged her into the blackness of her mind. Tori felt the grip of the serpent crawling across her skin and screamed, slamming herself against the walls in her mind. They crumbled and she fell, shocked, back into her own body, back into the burning fire of her aching limbs. "No!" she shouted, her lips moving. The sound echoed around her. She gasped as the cold air tore through her.

Tori raced across the room, slamming into the cold iron double doors, the way out. They clanged, shuddering, but would not open. Tori shoved against the doors. "No," she whispered, her eyes flooding with frustrated tears. "Open!" The doors held, the hard chilled metal burned Tori's skin and she bit down on the scream of pain that was bubbling up inside her.

Frantic, she shoved again, but the doors would not move. She turned, rubbing her hands over her arms as she looked around the room. A spiral of stairs at the back of the chamber drew her forward. She crossed the room, fighting inside herself against the clawing sensation of Torque in her mind as she raced up the spiral of stairs. They wound in a tight corkscrew, step after step. Tori's thighs burned and her calves quivered. Her whole body ached with the torment of her frantic attempt to flee. She gripped the carved wood rail and dragged herself forward.

Chapter 13. An Emotion-Charged Bond

The stairs spiralled through the wood rafters to the landing above.

The platform wrapped around the ceiling of the church. Tori ran their length, her hands tracing the wood wall. Her pace slowed as her fingers brushed the nooks in the wood. She circled the square of rafters and then huffed. "Nothing." She glanced up at the spiral staircase, it continued high into the roof disappearing into another platform several metres above.

Tori gritted her teeth. She ignored the weight of her aching muscles. She ignored the huff of the chilled night air burning through her heaving lungs. She pushed herself to carry on upward through the church. The thread of the serpent in her mind drove her onwards and she shook off the lingering doubt that she was in control. She wanted to run, she wanted to escape. Their desires were mutual, nothing more.

As she reached the second landing the space narrowed. The slant of the roof forced her to stoop. Against one wall, a beam of moonlight trickled under a small wooden door. Tori burst through it, splintering the aged wood, and stumbled into the bitter wind. The door opened out on a small balcony, carved into the recess of the roof. Battered shingles clung to the church, rising to a magnificent apex.

The Flight Of Torque

The frost of late night air crept through her. She felt the serpent within recoiling from the chill and her heart roared a triumph. Tori gripped the stone railing, leaning into the wind that wove through her hair. Her breath caught and she felt a tingle of fear trace down her spine. Torque reared up at it and Tori felt the hiss of fury sweep through her mind. She fought against the shutter that hovered over her thoughts. She thrust back against it. "No!" she shouted, her voice whipped away in the wind.

She stared down at the ground, stories below her, and searched for a way down. Jasmine bloomed their pale white starlight flowers. The vine crept up the wall in a tangle of weaving threads. Tori reached for it over the railing, her fingers traced along the rough stone walls, but she could not reach. She pulled herself up onto the smooth stone railing, creeping along it with slow, jerking movements. She clung to the rail, reaching one hand to touch an intricate carved stone gargoyle. Its toothy grin and obsidian eyes glared out at the dark night. She leaned her weight against the icy wings and sharp horns, reaching down to the vine-traced trellis. It taunted her, just out of reach.

Lucas trailed behind Crey. The other man's steps fell in silent footfalls on the rough rock. He moved down the corridor, creeping to each door and glancing within. Each time he stopped he held up a hand. Lucas and Zara stopped, waiting. When Crey waved them forward Lucas sighed in relief. *This is too cautious. Too slow.* Grimacing as they crept past another empty hallway, another barren chamber, Lucas gritted his teeth. Inside him, Tori's emotions churned in a quiver of terror, horror, torment. "Hold on, Tori. Just a little longer," he whispered.

Zara touched his uninjured shoulder as she pressed close behind him. "She'll be okay," she whispered against his back. Crey glanced back at them, raising a finger to his lips. They crept forward another few feet before stopping again.

Lucas felt a slick of cold quiver through him. A shudder ran down his spine and his breath hissed out through his teeth. Tori's racing heartbeat thundered through him. He could feel the waves of pain that throbbed through her muscles. "Tori!"

He heard Crey shout out to him as he tore past, chasing the tingle of Tori that wove through his senses. He ignored the pounding feet that raced after him and wove through the criss-crossing chaos of weaving corridors.

She drew him onward. Her heartbeat pulsing through him, her breath chasing his own in his lungs. He felt the frost of wind against his skin and in the same moment the muggy smoke burning through him. Her emotions rumbled through him and he felt like she lingered on the precipice between herself and the darkness. He raced forward, his pounding footsteps moved with certainty as he turned each of the corners through the maze of hallways and rooms. As he climbed higher through the temple, more and more Nagaran worshippers flashed by him. Their startled white faces blinked through his mind.

"Hey! It's him!" A man shouted as Lucas darted past. Thick fingers jerked on his arm but Lucas shoved back and the cultist tumbled into the people gathered behind him. Lucas did not pause. He swerved through the crowd and disappeared down another corridor. He slammed through a doorway and ran past a row of darkened rooms, turning up a small flight of stairs until he slammed open the hard door at the top.

Cold shivered across his skin. Lucas glanced around him, surprised at the faint glow of moonlight and the clean, fresh night air that filled his lungs. He hesitated. "Tori?" he called. His voice echoed back at him from the walls of the church. He closed his eyes, focusing on the wave of emotions that flushed through him. His lungs heaved and his chest thudded, but from above him, high above, her quaking tremor threaded through him.

The door behind him crashed and his eyes flashed open as he spun around. Crey almost collided with him as he strode through the doorway. Lucas raised a hand to steady him. Crey's breathing was heavy. He doubled over, catching his breath. His chest heaved with effort and his voice trembled. "Where are you going?"

"I have to get to Tori."

"You do not know the way."

"She's here," Lucas said, glancing around the room. The spiral staircase loomed in the darkness. "She's here," he said again, his voice firm with conviction.

"She cannot be. She could not leave her room."

Zara stumbled through the door and Crey caught her as she almost fell. Her eyes wide, her voice trembling, she said, "Crey?" He gripped her tight. Lucas swallowed, watching them. He closed his eyes and felt the thread of Tori tugging him forward.

"I have to find her," he said, crossing the room to the stairs. "She's up here." Pulling himself up the rail, he thundered up the steps two at a time. Circling higher and higher, he did not pause at the first landing, but pushed onward, upward. At the top he looked around disoriented before seeing the scatter of moonlight that shone through the fragmented door. He shoved shards of wood aside and stepped through, straightening as the night sky rose above him. His eyes searched the balcony. Tori stood on the railing, the fingers of one hand threaded around the wings of a gargoyle. She dangled over the edge. Lucas's breath caught in his throat and then shuddered out of him as he shouted, "Tori!"

Her bare feet on the railing felt frosted as they clung to the ice-cold stone. As Lucas's voice cried out her name from behind her Tori wobbled. Her hand slipped and she wavered in the air trying to regain her balance. Her breath hissed out of her lungs in a snarl as the serpent twisted around in her thoughts. The weave of it through her mind was graceful and she felt her muscles move in unfamiliar ways. She felt herself spin, her feet turning an elegant pirouette. Her legs trembled beneath her as she swayed between the safety of the roof and the plunging fall behind her. The serpent reared up within her, flickering a flare of angry hissing out at Lucas.

"No!" Tori shouted. She was not sure if she had meant the cry for the serpent or for Lucas. She held up a hand. "Don't come near me, Lucas."

He stepped closer, reaching a hand toward her. Torque rioted inside her and Tori shuddered against the burning chill of the serpent coiling around her mind. *I want him. We are the Charmer.*

"I won't be this thing," Tori cried. Her breath shuddered through her chest. The serpent hissed and her tongue flickered between her lips. Tori sobbed, biting her lip. The wind pressed against her skin and she shivered. A shudder of darkness washed through her thoughts and Tori closed her eyes, trying to fight against the shutter in her mind. "I won't let you take me," she whispered, her heart aching inside her chest. "I can't let you. I can't let you hurt anyone else."

Torque snarled, tingling across her skin. *Mine*, it whispered inside Tori's head.

Tori cried out, agony ripping through her body, as she felt the ripple of the serpent crawling through her. Her legs weakened and she clenched her thighs together, stiffening her knees. "No!" she cried, her voice quivered and a trail of salty tears washed down her cheeks and over her lips. Flashes of Torque's thoughts flickered through Tori's mind. Desire, hunger, violent yearning for a burning fire of throbbing sensation. Longing pooled through her, deep in her core she felt the pulse of it. Tori gritted her teeth, shoving at the thoughts within her. "You can't have him," she shouted.

Her eyelids fluttered open and her lips curved in a smile. The serpent's voice slipped between her lips. "He is ours. We are the Charmer."

Lucas's hand reached out to her, his eyes riveted to hers. A hoarse groan wrenched her name through his lips, "Tori!"

She gazed down at him, teardrops glistening on her eye lashes. The wind gusted across her skin. She whispered, "I'm sorry. I can't be a monster." Lucas's hand touched her wrist as she let herself go. The serpent reared up within, rippling over her skin. It thrashed, chasing through her as she threw herself into the gust of wind and off the edge of the balcony railing.

Chapter Fourteen
The Power To Choose

Her breath rushed out of her lungs as the crisp air whipped across her skin. Her hair blew across her face and fear drummed through her body. She twisted, turning through the air. Her body sprawled, leaden legs heavy. Her arms and head dropped back. She screamed, her terror building, as she watched the railing, and Lucas's beautiful face, drift further and further away above her. Her voice ripped out of her lungs, but the only sound she could hear was the rush of blood pulsing through her ears. The stars faded, as if every second she fell further and further out of their reach. The darkness swarming around her grew, blacking out the moonlit trees, the wisps of cloud, the scatter of night sky.

Torque reared up within her. Tori felt the rip of scales shiver over her skin. The serpent's tail whipped through the air, flailing. Its head swayed, swimming through the air, but unable to change the course of her fall, unable to return to the balcony above them, unable to climb through the sky or slow their descent. The serpent's tongue flickered a hiss through her lips. The darkness closed around her mind and Tori clawed at it. *No!*

The tail disappeared and her quivering legs trembled. Her arms stretched either side of her. Her soft flesh felt the brush of ice in the wind that swept through her as she tumbled, closer and closer to the ground. Her breath caught.

Inside her, Torque screamed. Tori could feel the serpent reeling and thrashing. Its teeth bit through her mind and Tori felt as if her head would tear apart. She remembered the sprawled bodies the creature within had left in its wake. Like a carpet of death, their faces frozen in terror, their cheeks streaked with tears, their throats stained with blood, they blanketed her thoughts. Guilt crushed through her and the darkness rose on it. Swirling through the flicker of each victim's last moment. The serpent rejoiced at the thrill of hunger and desire that pulsed through her. Tori shuddered, horrified at the wave of pleasure.

The serpent thrashed, splitting her skin again as scales burst to the surface. Tori's keening cry split through the darkness, through the throbbing pulse of blood pounding her ears, through the whipping wind. The crack of her voice, like a banshee's wail, cut through her. *No, no, no,* she cried. Her voice echoing off the walls in her mind. Anger flared within her and the serpent snarled back. Tori thrashed against the walls in her mind. With each lash she felt Torque quiver in her thoughts. *Let me go!*

Spitting fury lanced over her then faded. The shudder of the serpent's retreat rippled through her. Her breath shivered out of her with a sigh and the tightness in her chest eased. The ache of her heavy limbs returned. She closed her eyes. "I did that," she whispered. *I have the power to choose.* The thought whispered through her mind and the serpent within quivered, lingering in the back of her thoughts.

Doubt, fear, and anger flickered through her. Torque beat against the barrier between its thoughts and Tori's. Thrashing, it challenged her. She shook her head. "No! You cannot take me." The serpent's anger flickered through her again, and then faded as Torque retreated to the dark recesses of Tori's mind. The thought trickled through her mind again, *I have the power to choose.* As the inches closed between her and the ground, another realisation wove its way through her. *I don't want to die.*

Lucas hung over the railing. "Tori!" His eyes searched for her. *No! I can't fail again!* The shout passed through his mind as he reached for her, his hands catching the air as she tumbled away from him. She was falling, faster and faster, toward the hard cobblestones below. Her skin, painted silver by the moonlight, seemed to shimmer. The weave of the serpent rippled through her and then shimmered away again. He saw a wave of shock cross her face, and felt fear welling within her. Inside him, a wave of terror, shrouded with anger, washed over him. Triumph rippled through him, the thread of Tori strengthened and then he heard her scream, felt the terror grip her as the wind whipped over her face.

"NO!" Lucas shouted. He launched himself over the railing, throwing himself at her. The air caught over him, and pain shot through him as his limbs thrust against the wind. He twisted, turning in a spiral, and dove through the sky. Plummeting, he rushed toward her, dropping through the air like an anvil. The heavy weight of his body rippled past the whip of wind. His eyes watered but he refused to blink. He refused to let Tori's face disappear behind his eyelids.

Inch by inch the distance between them closed. Lucas's thoughts wavered. *I'm not going to reach her.* The flicker of doubt felt heavy in his heart and he drew the weight into himself, accepting the burden of it, half hoping it would rocket him closer and closer to her. He clenched his muscles, flexing the tendons in his arms and legs. They screamed in protest, the agony of his bruised joints burning through him. He gritted his teeth against the pain and kept his gaze locked on Tori's face.

Fear, a gut-deep wrench of fear gripped him. He shuddered, feeling the waves of it wash over him and wrenched against the thread in his heart that reached out for Tori. The taste of it filled his mouth. The terror of it drowned out the sound of the wind in his ears. The smell of it, rank and icy, penetrated his nostrils. It tingled over his skin and sunk deep into his bones. He could see that terror on Tori's face. He could feel it ripping through her, drowning her.

He swallowed the dry husk in this throat. His lungs burned with every breath and pain shot through every part of his body. He pushed it all to the back of his mind. "Tori." Tears blurred his vision, but through them he could see the rock hard ground rushing toward them. The distance seemed to close every second. *I can't save her.* The betraying thought wove through him.

Even certain that she would die, he could not bring himself to stop gazing at her face. Her eyes were closed and the moon glistened on her cheeks. Her hair whipped around her like a billowing trail of black silk ribbons. As he drew closer, Lucas reached out. His fingers closed around her ankle and he tugged her toward him. She flailed, fighting back against his grip. He pulled her against his chest and wrapped his arms around her. Tears streamed down her face and she pummelled her fists against his chest. "Tori," he whispered in her ear and her body shuddered. Heavy sobs ripped from her throat and she relaxed against him. Wrapping her arms hard around him, she clung, whimpering against his shoulder. He held her close, closing his eyes as he felt the wind sweep over them. They fell through the air. It thrust between them as if it were trying to rip them apart. Lucas dropped his chin, resting his cheek against hers. "I can't let you go," he whispered.

The ground drew closer and closer. Lucas turned Tori's face away from the dark rock beneath them, tucking her close against his shoulder. He saw the distance closing. Felt her fear tremble through her. Felt the echoing wave of it deep inside him. He ached for his wings. The burn across his back tormented him. His shoulders felt tight, missing the heavy weight of the ripple of feathers. "I'm so sorry." Tori's whisper tore through him. A rush of defeat washed over him and he closed his eyes, holding her close against him.

He held her tight in his arms and gave himself over to fate. *I have no power.* The thought lashed against him and he felt his helplessness tear through him. Anger bit back. *No! I'm meant for more than this!* He shouted within his mind.

A wave of energy pulsed through him. He felt it ripple through his muscles. A lick of fire ran down his back and his shoulders wrenched, catching on the wind. The breath he had been holding burst from his lungs. He felt a jolt of power kick through his stomach and he clenched his arms around Tori as their bodies thrashed against the wind. Scant feet from the ground a rocket of triumph shouted through him and he twisted in the air. He dragged her body against his as they skimmed the green stalks of grass and then climbed back into the air.

Pulsing golden waves of energy cascaded from the tangle of raw skin between his shoulder blades. Shimmering wings of power rippled in the air. Flexing, he spread them wide and felt his joy spreading out from within. He dipped and twirled through the sky, holding Tori in his arms. She shivered against him as his wings beat the air and they climbed higher and higher into the sky.

Tori's eyes flashed open as the wind shifted around her. Lucas's arms held her tight against him as they neared the ground and then the ground flashed past them. They wove through the tall grass that grew over the graves in the graveyard, twirled through the trees, and then soared upward, upward into the night sky. The crystal stars flickered above them. She gazed up, her chin tilted to the sky.

Lucas's hand cupped her face. The pad of his thumb traced over her cheek warming the cool stain where her tears had washed down her face. He seemed to glow, a vibrant golden light in the darkness. His face was radiant. Joy quivered through him and she felt the waves of it against her skin. She leaned closer, embraced in his warmth. Torque stirred within her and she pushed the dark taint of thoughts away. *This moment is mine,* she said. Her voice rang with commanding presence inside her mind. The serpent drew back and a wave of joy flushed through her body. Tori was not sure if the wash of joy was her own, or Lucas's, perhaps it was a weave of both.

Against her fingers, the ripple of his wings caressed her. The warm flush of energy tingled through her skin and wrapped around her wrist. She lifted her hand, feeling Lucas's grip around her tighten as she leaned closer toward him to gaze over his shoulder. She ran her fingers through the sparkling glow of feathers. "Your wings," she whispered, her lips against Lucas's ear. She felt the lift of his cheek and tilted her head back to see his face again.

"Wings," he said, his lips bowed by a radiant grin. His eyes sparkled.

"You don't even know do you?"

He glanced into her eyes. "Know what?"

"They're nothing like your old wings. These are," she paused, searching for a word. She shook her head. "They're incredible. I can't even begin to tell you how glorious they are."

Lucas shrugged. "They work. Does anything else matter?"

Tori blinked, she felt the shudder of fear tremble through her as she remembered plummeting toward the ground. "You saved me," she said, reverence threaded through her throaty murmur.

He shook his head, his eyes closed and he pulled her face against him, whispering into her hair, "You saved me." Tori shivered, feeling the treacle of his voice and breath tingle through her hair and over her scalp. The sensation rippled down her back, pooling in her belly. She inhaled his musky scent, tainted by the still lingering reek of incense, but wafting from his bare chest. She closed her eyes, tipping her head to rest her cheek against his shoulder. He tucked her head close under his chin, and his voice washed over her, "Let me show you how to fly." She trembled in his arms, closing her eyes. He chuckled, the rumble of his laughter tingled across her cheek. "Open your eyes, Tori."

"I don't want to fall, Lucas. No matter what happened back there, I don't want to die."

He swallowed. "I won't let you fall. I'll never let you fall again." He held her tight in his arms and she flickered her eyes open as they swirled through the sky.

They dipped and twirled under the stars. Lucas wove through the rise of buildings as they soared over the city. City lights flickered beneath them. Trails of red and white wove across dark rivers that wound through the rows of skyscrapers below. Tori gazed down at them. A shudder ran through her and Lucas's grip tightened around her. He rose higher, his thumping wings beating the air.

They swirled through a slick of moisture. It clung to Tori's skin, sending a chill deep into her bones. She shivered. "Cold?" Lucas asked, his voice a ripple through the air. Tori nodded.

A wave of heat flooded over her. "What?"

Lucas smiled. "I don't feel the cold. I'm cloaked by my aura. Now you are too."

"You can cloak me in your aura?"

"If I choose to." They fell silent as he wove between pockets of dampness. He twirled, rolling like a barrel through the air. Tori felt her breath shorten as they crept closer and closer toward the looming stars. Lucas brushed his hand down her hair, tilting her head back. He looked into her eyes and smiled. "High enough?" Tori nodded. "Then hold on."

Tori bit her lip. "Why?" He did not answer. Instead, he tucked her head close again, tightened his arms around her. She felt the flutter of his wings as they closed over her hands, wrapping snug against his back. The air rocketed past them and they plummeted through the air. Her scream pierced the silence and Lucas laughed. They tumbled, faster and faster. Tori closed her eyes, trembling in his arms.

He tilted his head down, whispering into her ear, "Open your eyes, Tori. I promise I won't let go. Soar with me."

She opened her eyes and looked down at the snow crusted mountains in the distance. They grew larger and larger. Tori's breath caught and she felt a shudder of fear quiver through her. Torque snapped on it, snarling. Tori bit it back, clinging to Lucas's joy and using it as a shroud against the darkness within. The sensation rippled over her. As the wind whipped past and the ground grew closer his wings tugged open catching the blast of air. They soared, gliding high above the rolling hills. He wove through the trees. The twirl of wind through his wings and the ripple of air over his body quivered through Tori's skin. His rejoicing was infectious. His radiance bubbled through her and she gave herself up to it, leaning into the wind.

She let her fingers fall away from Lucas's back, spreading her arms to catch the waves of air that rolled over them. She laughed, leaning back into the wind. Her hair whipped over her shoulders and across her face. She watched the trees swirl past them in a flicker of colour. An owl hooted and fluttered up from the branches, flapping away.

Lucas looped upward, turning through the tips of the great pines. They soared over the top of the forest and wove through the froth of mist that sizzled around them. Tori gave herself up to the thrill. She felt the wind streaming over her. She felt the warmth radiating from Lucas's skin. She felt the strength of his arms gripped tightly around her. She trusted him, she realised, letting him support her weight as she gave herself over to flight.

Grey predawn lit the sky. Tori blinked as the sun glistened over the horizon. Lucas sighed. "Time to land," he said against her ear as he pulled her close again.

Tears sparkled in her eyes. Her breath chased out of her lungs in a whisper, "Thank you for this. Thank you for," she bit her lip, burying her face into his neck. His hand ran through her hair, his thumb curved around the shell of her ear as he cupped her head against him. His wings beat strong, hard strokes as he wove his way around the buildings that rose up as they grew closer to the city. The streets below were grey. The streak of car lights flickered from the lower levels of stone, steel, and glass skyscrapers.

Lucas and Tori rose higher, gliding up the side of a building that loomed above those around it. A large helipad and an array of antennas sat on the rooftop. Lucas drifted toward the large H. His wings tucked close to his body as he landed and then sizzled away. Tori gasped. "What?" Lucas asked. The sky reflected in his eyes and Tori looked up at his face. His features shimmered through her tear-filled eyes.

"Your wings," she whispered.

He stroked the tears from her cheek, smiling down at her. "Hey, they're still there."

"But," Tori blinked, shaking her head. "But they're gone." She ran her fingers over his back, tracing the lines of his spine, the curve of his shoulder blades, and the honey-toned satin skin that spread across his muscles where torn flesh had once been. Warmth burst across her hands and a flutter of flame-licked feathers erupted through her fingers. She gasped. The golden shimmer tingled against her skin before she withdrew her hand.

"See, still there." His fingers stroked her cheek.

His breath caressed her face. She felt a rush of warmth pool through her. Her lips quivered and her breath rushed out of her. She lifted her face to gaze into the blue sky of his eyes. Tilting her chin up her lips touched his. A rumbled groan rippled around them. Tori was not sure if it was his or hers, but she felt him sigh against her mouth. His lips hardened as he sunk into the kiss. His fingers wove through her hair, gripping the strands as he tugged her head closer, deepening the kiss. His other hand ran over her belly, brushing a warm stroke of heat across her hips as it curved around her back and cupped her rear. Holding her body pressed hard against him his tongue tipped deep into her mouth. Their tongues chased each other, tasting each other. Passion rippled through her as his tongue traced the curve of her lips and delved deeper into her mouth. Her own danced across his tongue. Desire sunk deep into her skin, sinking through her body and pooling between her thighs. Her breasts, tingled, her hard nipples throbbed brushing over the soft curl of hair on his chest. Her hips pressed against the hard heat of him.

Chapter 14. The Power To Choose

Hunger burst through her and she gasped, her breath cutting through her lips as she felt the serpent rear up inside of her.

Chapter Fifteen
Darkness Rising

Lucas felt as if his whole body was burning, lit on fire by the caress of her soft lips on his. The nubs of her nipples pressed against his chest. Ripples of desire shot down through his belly. The lick of it trailed over his skin, sinking deep into his core and torturing his heart. His heartbeat raced, throbbing in a chaos of uneven thunder. Heat rose within him and he felt himself harden against the moist heat between her thighs. He groaned at the sweet torture of her in his arms. The soft flush of her skin against his fingers tingled up his arm and shivered down his back.

"No!" she said, her voice a hissed whisper as she pulled away from him.

His breath heaved through his lungs. His chest rose and fell in a flurry of gasps sucked deep into his lungs. Her lips quivered, the soft curve of pink glistened. Her tongue darted across them and he felt his groan through his whole body. His mind refused to work. Refused to make sense of what he was feeling. Her emotions tangled through him, weaves of passion, longing. He gazed into her glassy eyes. They seemed to see into his soul. She held a hand against his chest and her hard breathing washed over his skin. Inside him, a dark desire rose up and he felt it shudder between them as she stepped away. It was not his, he realised. It had reared up from deep within her and a wave of panic chased it.

Her tortured rejection stung. He felt the chill of it whip over him and tingle down his spine. Humiliation, and then sharp trail of guilt washed through him. "I'm sorry," he said, "that should not have happened." He dropped his hand away from her hair. The other brushed her bare hip as it fell to his side. The flicker of his wings fluttered across his back and then tugged tight as they sank beneath his skin. The tearing ache of the wounds in his back and shoulder were gone but the torment within his heart and the hard pulse of his manhood throbbed through him.

Tori shook her head. Her hair wove around her face. She bit her lower lip, her own chest heaving as she gasped for breath. She ran her hands up and down her arms and Lucas could feel the sliver of fear slipping through her. "No," she said again, her breath catching in her throat. "I can't do this."

"It won't happen again, Tori. I shouldn't have let the moment take me."

"It's not your fault. I," she trailed off.

"It *is* my fault. It is my duty is to protect you. I failed once, but I refuse to fail again."

"You didn't fail. You saved me."

"This should never have happened."

"I'm sorry," she whispered. He felt a shiver of cold trickle down his spine as the tug of his guilt tore through him again. The wave of it slithered through him, rippling over his skin. Tori gasped and the slick sheen of sweat on his skin chilled as he felt a bitter darkness coil around his heart. An intense fear threaded through him that he could not understand.

Torque sizzled on the surface of her emotions. Tori struggled against the shutter pressing in on her thoughts. Flashes of erotic images rushed through her and desire pooled between her thighs. The shiver of cool on her skin soothed the burning thrash of passion that licked over her whole body. The serpent within rose, pushing up through the churning ocean of her emotions. It wrapped itself in her mind. The hissing voice of the serpent soaked into her thoughts, *Mine.*

No! Tori shouted as she felt her mind drop behind the trap. She struggled, throwing her thoughts against the shield that stood between her mind and her ability to maintain control of the darkness within. *No!* Her frustrated cry broke across the barrier and her thoughts thrashed within her. The hiss of the serpent flickered through her. Tori felt it quiver along her nerve endings. Her whole body washed with the chill of Torque's darkness as it rose up within her. She sobbed, her tears crashing against the wall in her mind.

Tori's head tilted and her lips parted. Her breath shuddered from her lungs. Her skin drew tight against her ribcage. The pain in her ribs shot through her and the serpent growled. Shock flitted over Lucas's face and her lips curved in a smile. His wary eyes watched her. His confusion caressed her, tingling down her spine. Torque licked her lips, relishing the tangle of emotions that threaded between them. She rocked forward, touching Lucas's chest with quivering fingers. He stilled beneath her hand, his breath freezing in his chest.

"Tori." His guttural whisper ripped from his throat. Torque drew her hand down, tracing the trail of hair that ran over his belly and disappeared beneath the waistband of his pants. He groaned and she watched his Adam's apple bounce as he swallowed. His fingers gripped her wrist. "Tori, we," he said, his voice drawn on a tight breath between his lips. He shook his head. "This can't happen."

A growl rumbled from Tori's chest, and another wave of sobs crashed over her as she clawed at the barrier in her mind. *Don't do this, you can't do this.*

Torque bit back and she felt the whip of the serpent against her thoughts. *Mine.*

He's not yours, he's not even mine. You can't do this. She felt the shrug of the serpent within her and shoved against the wall in her mind, desperation building, as Torque stepped closer, rubbing her body against Lucas. The heat of his skin licked across her naked flesh. Desire pooled between her thighs, slick and wet. Her hips rocked forward, feeling the pulse of him against the dampness. A shudder rippled through her belly and Tori felt raw lust crash over her thoughts. She wanted this, she realised. She and the serpent shared their desire.

"Tori," Lucas said, his voice thick but firm. "Enough." Her head tilted again. Torque looked up at him, leaning forward to brush her lips across his mouth. Her tongue slipped between her lips and flickered across his. He gripped her arms, pushing her back. "Enough." Tori shuddered, feeling the serpent's anger rising within her. She grew frantic, rising up against the wall she thrashed at it. Inside her, Torque's fury grew.

"I want you." Tori felt her own voice as she pressed against the barrier. Shock froze her. Horror rose as she realised Torque could mimic her perfectly. The hiss, the serpent shiver that had stolen her voice was gone, replaced by a mirror of her own husky quiver.

Lucas closed his eyes. "Tori," he groaned. His fingers still laced around her upper arms. He held her at arms length, but his grip tightened. She felt the pulse of his desire ripple through him. She felt his confusion and the conflict that burned over him. She could feel his own longing.

He wants us, Torque hissed inside Tori's thoughts.

It doesn't matter! Tori shouted back. *This can't happen.*

The serpent quivered within. Tori felt its confusion shiver between them. *I want him.* Tori was not sure if the thready voice was her own or Torque's. They shared their desire.

We can't have him, she whispered. She felt the barrier in her mind weakening. *Please.*

Torque bit back in an angry hiss. *He is mine!* The chill of fury ripped through Tori, snarling against her mind. The shutter between them crashed back into place, a hard, cold wall of steel. Tori cowered from the ricochet of savage rage that rumbled through her. The serpent lashed at her. The chill of it rippling over her skin. *Mine!* It shouted against her thoughts. Tori shrank back from the pain of the crushing whip of the serpent within her. It reared, ripping from her skin.

Tori screamed, her voice bouncing back at her from the shield. A wash of agony wove through her and a fog wove over her thoughts, a chill of darkness invaded her, swirling a choking plume that swallowed her within it. Frantic, she shoved against the darkness. Her mind raced through it like a maze, searching for the clarity of her thoughts. She slammed up against wall. It quivered against her mind and she pressed on, slamming her thoughts against it again and again. Overwhelming fury threaded through Torque. The serpent writhed, tail thrashing against the tug of Tori within. They vied for control, Tori frantically threw herself across the cage in her mind while Torque tried to coil tighter and tighter around her thoughts.

Forgotten, Lucas's hands threaded over her, his palms flames against her arms. Tori felt a jolt of golden power burn through her as he shook her. The flash of it rocketed through her and Torque flinched, falling back. The ripple of scales on Tori's skin disappeared and her legs fell beneath her. She crashed to the ground. Lucas dropped to crouch beside her. "Tori."

Tears flooded from her eyes and she buried her face in her hands. Pulling her legs to her chest she curled into a tight ball. The pain in her ribs ripped through her, but she pushed the agony aside, overwhelmed by relief. "I'm sorry," she whimpered, feeling Lucas's gentle hands on her. She could feel pity rippling off him and cringed. "Don't," she said, "don't feel sorry for me. I can't stand it."

Her breath shuddered through her lungs. For long minutes she sat, waiting for the weight of her mind to ease. Pain throbbed through her head, crushing pain like a swollen thrust of energy ready to burst inside her brain. Tori cried, her thoughts running through her body. She could feel all of herself. She owned all of herself. The serpent was so far buried within her that the whisper of it deep in her core felt like a prick of anxiety tucked beneath a wave of courage.

Lucas stroked his fingers through her hair. One hand rubbed her shoulder. His heat rippled through her. "Tori?" he whispered.

She took a deep breath, letting it shudder out of her lungs as she pushed back the tears. She pushed herself upright and then felt the chill return when Lucas stepped away from her. She wiped the streak of tears that ran down her cheeks with the back of her hand. As she swung her legs beneath her, she shifted onto her knees. She looked up at him and attempted a smile. It wobbled on her lips as another trickle of tears leaked from her eyes. She sniffed, biting her lip as she forced them back, wiping the damp trail away with an angry swipe. Her breath heavy in her lungs burned and she exhaled. "I'm okay," she said. Her voice quavered. She straightened her spine and, her voice more firm, said again, "I'm okay."

He looked down on her, his eyes fixed to hers. "You're not okay, Tori. Something else happened just now."

She shook her head. "I can control it. I can." She could hear the doubt in her own voice and cringed at the compassion in his eyes.

"Let me help you, Tori."

"You did. That was you," she said. "That was you in my mind?"

"What do you mean?"

"I wasn't sure I could stop her. I felt myself growing weaker and weaker, trapped, helpless." She shuddered and he stepped forward as if he had intended to reach for her and then froze. She shook her head, "No, don't touch me." She sniffed again and then continued, "Just when I thought I was going to disappear something happened. Like a bolt of golden lightning crashing through my mind. It crashed right through the barrier." Tori stroked a finger under her eyelashes, catching another tear. "I." She sobbed, her voice trailing away.

Lucas looked as if he was not sure where to put his hands or feet. He seemed to hesitate between stepping forward to reach for her and stepping away. He shook his head. "I don't think I did anything, Tori."

She sniffed and ran a hand through her hair. "It felt like you."

"I don't know," he said. His voice was a soft caress over her. It soothed her aching skin. Lucas swallowed, then reached a hand toward her. "Come on. We need to get off this roof."

As he pulled her to her feet his warmth pulsed through her palm and wove its way down her back. The quiver of smothered anxiety deep within her swelled and Tori felt an icy wash of terror thrust through her. *No! Not again.* She pushed Lucas away, and sprinted across the roof to the door. Slamming through it, she raced down the tower of stairs.

Chapter Sixteen
The Monster Within

The steel railing of the staircase bit into her hip as she spun down it. She gripped the rail with one hand and started down the steps. As she turned another corner in the stairwell, she stumbled, only just catching herself before she fell. Her ankle twisted. Pain ripped up her leg. She winced, but did not slow down.

She heard the slam of the door above her and ran faster. "Stay away!" she shouted. "I don't want to hurt you." Tori could not hear his footsteps on the stairs above her, so she did not know if he had heard. She did not know if he would listen even if he did hear. She pushed harder. Her chest heaved with her frantic breaths. Taking the steps two at a time, she felt the pain of her injured ankle radiate up her leg each time she put her weight on it.

Tori paused at another turn of the stairwell. Against the far wall, there was a door its bar painted red. She glanced back up the stairs, but could not see Lucas pursuing her. Gasping for breath, she swallowed, looking first at the door and then down the stairwell. It seemed infinite, weaving down and down in an uncountable pit of steel spirals evenly spaced with square platforms.

Chapter 16. The Monster Within

"Tori!" Lucas called from the platform above her. Tori could not see him, but her face flushed with fear as she felt him drawing closer.

"Don't," she shouted. She hesitated, then slammed the red bar down and thrust her way into the room behind the door. The door slammed closed behind her and she swirled, jamming the lock into place. She stood, staring at the door. The whisper of the serpent grew louder within her. It urged her to go back. Tori forced herself to step backwards, to move away from the temptation to tear the door away and throw herself into Lucas's arms. Torque tormented her with flashes of erotic images, her body entwined in exotic lovemaking with sleek curves of hard muscle and soft blonde hair. Tori gasped, feeling the quiver of lust thrum through her. Another image bombarded her thoughts, soft blue eyes, dark with passion, gazing up at her and the flicking touch of his lips, his tongue between her thighs. "No," she groaned. Her hands ran over her own body. The fingers of one hand thrust deep between her thighs into her wet core, the other fondled her nipple, cupping her breast. Tori shuddered, as the serpent's hiss whispered through her mind. Her breath hissed from her in a flurry of quick, sharp bursts as the tension built up in her body. She could feel her thumb, strumming with hard strokes against her sensitive nub. She sucked in her breath, her thighs quivering as a shudder ran through her. Tori could not fight back the groan that wrenched from her lips.

You want this, why do you deny us, the serpent hissed in her mind. "I can't, we can't" she whispered back. Her slick fingers rose to her mouth, her lips wrapping around them. Her tongue licked up and down the length of them. *You want this,* the serpent whispered. Tori moaned, licking her lips as her fingers fell from her mouth. "No," she whispered, but the husky rasp of her voice betrayed her. She clenched her thighs together and shoved back at the serpent within. Torque hissed, its tail whipping against Tori's mind. The lustful thoughts flickered into darkness and Tori gasped. Her chest heaved as she tried to calm her erratic breath.

The door shuddered. She glanced up, seeing the lever of the bar rattle. "Lucas," she whispered. She turned away from the door and dashed across the room. A row of offices lined one wall and the doors of an elevator stood in another. She ran over and, with a frantic jerk of her wrist, jammed the button. The light above the door lit up. "Yes," Tori said. She stood back, watching the row of lights as the car moved, floor by floor, up the shaft. It seemed to be moving snail's pace slow. Tori tapped her foot, then pushed at the button again and again. "Hurry up!" she said, glancing behind her at the violent rattling of the door. The pounding behind it was getting louder and louder. Tori bit her lip.

As the door burst from its hinges the elevator pinged and opened. Tori caught the wave of Lucas's gaze as she stepped inside and pushed the button for the ground floor.

Lucas reached out, her name on his lips as the elevator doors slid closed. He sprinted across the room and slammed his fist against the cold, hard metal. "Dammit!" he said, grimacing. "What the hell is she doing?" He stepped back, watching the illuminated numbers dropping. Lucas ran a hand through his hair, trying to erase the thrill of hot desire that had slammed into him just minutes before. He was still hard, throbbing with pent up tension, his breathing still ragged. He pulled his hair, letting the slight tug of pain ripple over him, then grimaced again. "Damn her." He slammed his fist against the door once more then turned, sprinting back out of the room.

His legs burned as he raced down the stairs. As he rounded another level, his thoughts ran in impatient circles through his mind. *This is taking too long.* On the next platform he launched himself over the railing and plummeted down the shaft. Floors flashed past him as he fell closer and closer to the bottom of the shaft. His wings burst forth in a ripple of golden light. The plume of flickering feathers stroked across his back. Lucas tucked them close between his shoulder-blades, letting gravity pull him closer and closer to the ground. Just feet above it, he spread his wings. They snapped out. Lucas felt the jolt run down his back as the soft curve of wings caught against the rush of air. Their tips touched the edges of the shaft, brushing down them as he glided to a smooth stop on the floor below.

Glancing around, Lucas was thankful for the abandoned rooms. The reception was empty. Cold marble floors reflected the soft glow of the room's security lighting. Water splashed in a rush from a large water feature in the middle of the room. The greenery around it cast a dark shadow in the muted light. At the front of the room a pair of glass doors secured the building. Lucas's gaze flickered across to the elevator against a far wall. He strode toward it, and stood in front of the thick metal doors. Above him, the numbers slowed as the car neared the ground floor. The elevator pinged as the doors slid open. Tori rushed out, slamming into Lucas's chest. He gripped her arms, slick with sweat, and glared down at her. "Where are you going?"

Chapter 16. The Monster Within

"Lucas," Tori gasped. He felt her shudder and a wave of desire rippled through him. He pushed it away.

"Anyone would think the Hounds of Hell were chasing you."

"No," Tori said. She tried to pull herself out of his arms. "Let me go, Lucas."

"You'll only run again if I do. What are you afraid of?" He saw the desperate fear in her face. It warred with something else. There was a sheen of moisture on her lips and a flush that bloomed across her naked skin. Her dark irises pooled with wanting. His breath caught in his throat and a shudder ran through him.

"I don't want to hurt you, Lucas."

"I just want to protect you, Tori."

They both spoke at once and the flush in Tori's cheeks deepened.

"What do you mean, hurt me? How could you hurt me?" Lucas asked.

"The serpent. I said before that I can control it, but I can't. Just being around you makes her rip at the edges of my skin. She takes me over. I'm not me any more. Please, Lucas, just let me go." Tears shimmered on her eye lashes and then trickled down her cheek. Lucas wiped them away with the pad of his thumb.

"Tori, you can do this. We can do this together."

She shook her head. "I can't fight a battle I don't really want to win."

"You do want to win, Tori. No matter what else you want, you do not want to lose yourself to that darkness. I know, because I can feel every racing heartbeat, every quiver of fear, every lash of the cold blackness that threatens to swallow you whole."

"You can feel it? You can feel what I feel?" Tori shuddered. She averted her eyes, her breath hissing out of her lungs as she closed her eyes. "Oh God," she groaned. He saw the burn of embarrassment that chased across her features as she bit her lip. Her breath quickened and he felt the wave of passion that pulsed through her. He clenched his teeth. "Oh God," she groaned again.

Lucas closed his own eyes, sucking in a breath. "Give me strength," he muttered, ignoring the hot thrust of desire that rampaged through him. "It's okay," he said, his voice a groan as he tried to suppress the torment of lust that thundered through his heart, through his stomach, through his manhood. He took a deep breath, letting it out in a tortured exhale.

Her eyes were pools of shamed guilt. "I have to go back."

Chapter 16. The Monster Within

"What?" Lucas asked. He dropped his hands from her arms and stepped back.

She looked up at him. "I have to go back to the Nagaran. Lucas, you know I have to."

"Why? Why would you ever have to go back there? I'm not letting you go. I can't let them hurt you again, Tori."

"But they are hurting me, Lucas. All that exists within me now is the torment of a battle I can't win."

"You can! Dammit Tori, why won't you believe that?"

Her gaze dropped to the floor. "I think I can, and then she rises up and I'm helpless against her."

"What do you mean?"

"Torque. The monster I've become. Sometimes I don't even know if I'm her or if I'm me any more."

"Let me help you."

"I don't want you anywhere near me!" Tori shouted. "Don't you see that? You torment me. Every look, every touch. You burn through my skin and she," she paused, her breath shuddering through her chest. She shook her head. "God, she rips me apart just to be near you." He saw a thrash of pain cross her face and felt the tearing anger stir within her, it danced within the flames of her desire. "No," she whispered, her breath shuddering out of her. Her tongue parted her lips and a shadow passed over her eyes.

Tori pushing against Lucas's chest to shove past him. Lucas grabbed her arm. He tugged her toward him, crushing her against his chest. He wrapped his arms around her and held her tight. "Don't, Tori," he said. "Don't run from this. Let me help you fight her. I can help you."

Lucas bit back the groan that rumbled in the back of his throat. She felt so good in his arms. He pushed back the betraying thoughts, trying to remember his vow to protect. *I can't fall in love with her.* He closed his eyes, feeling like maybe he did not have a choice. *Like everything else I'm helpless to this.*

Tori sobbed against his chest, her body weak in his arms.He opened his eyes and looked down at her. With gentle fingers he gripped her chin and lifted her face, forcing her to meet his eyes. "Listen to me. You *can* do this."

Tori placed a finger on his lips. The fire that burned through him at the touch seemed like a furnace against the coolness of her skin. "You're always so very warm, do you know that? It's as if the sun burns within you." Her fingers brushed his chest. Hunger rose in him, he felt it within her and his own rose to meet it. He could feel the lick of warmth pooling where her body touched his. He felt her yearning, the craving she felt, and felt his own body responding to it. "I'm so very cold, Lucas," she gasped his name, her voice thick with the treacle of her desire. "You could make me warm, couldn't you?" Lucas groaned, his whole body riveted against her, hard and stiff. "You want me, don't you?"

Lucas gripped her arms, pushing her back against the wall of the elevator. Tori wriggled across his hips and he gritted his teeth. A wash of humour seemed to glimmer through her and he swallowed. Anger burned through him, anger at himself for wanting her like this, and anger at her for wanting him too. "This isn't right, Tori. What has got into you?"

He could see the conflict warring behind the dark pools of her eyes before she closed them again. He felt the waves of confusion, anger, fear, lust. The last was building as he felt Tori battling within herself. His heart grew tight and his fingers tightened around her wrists. She whimpered, her eyes closing. He felt the chaos of her thoughts and then the cold chill of the serpent. "I know you want me. You want me, Lucas," she said, her voice echoed in the room and she spat his name with a hiss. She rubbered herself against him with wanton abandon, leaning forward she drew his bottom lip into her mouth. He felt her tongue trace the curve of his lip.

His breath caught, his mouth opening and she deepened the kiss, sucking his tongue into her mouth. She curled a leg around his, pulling his hips into the damp centre of her thighs. "Tori," he groaned.

She stiffened, and he felt it, the choking coil of the serpent rearing up within her. He felt Tori attempt to clamp down on the dark shimmer of angry triumph that had woven through her. She shuddered, a frantic whisper rushed from her lips as her eyes widened, "Lucas, help me." Then she was gone. The light in her eyes glittered, dark with calculating malice. Her lips parted on a sighed hiss. Her tongue darted out, tasting her lips and her head tilted.

"You deny my hunger, Seraph," the serpent hissed, eyes sparking. Her forked tongue snaked up against his cheek. Lucas recoiled, in horror. "You are mine!" she drawled, her voice a contented purr that curled her lips in a hungry smile.

The serpent ripped through her skin and she felt it sway in the musty air of the elevator car. Her tail hissed over the soft carpeted flooring. Rising up, it loomed over Lucas, snarling down at him. "Mine!" Torque hissed. "I want him." The serpent's lips curved in a smile and it leaned into Lucas, feeling his warmth against its chest.

Lucas gasped and stepped back. He shoved against the snake's chest and moved out through the elevator door, back into the large reception room. Torque glided toward him, slithering across the cool tile. She tilted her head, her tongue darting between her lips.

"Tori," Lucas whispered, his gaze searching her face.

"I want you," the serpent hissed again.

"You control this, Tori. You are yourself."

Tori felt herself flailing against the wall in her mind. Panic rippled through her and she scratched against the barrier. *No! Let me out! Don't do this,* she cried, her voice trapped in her mind. *Please!*

Torque pushed back at her, snarling. "Mine!" The words hissed through her lips. "He is mine."

Please, don't hurt him. Tori felt herself weakening as the wall loomed up over her. It felt like a granite weight crushing her as it closed tighter and tighter around her. Her breath rushed through her lungs and the serpent twisted, writhing on the floor as the two fought mind to mind for control of Tori's body. *Please!*

Lucas stood, his back against a tall fern potted in the exotic garden feature that surrounded the splashing centre piece of the reception hall. Tori felt Torque calculate his position; if he stepped around the planter he would fall into the small waterfall-washed pool. Torque swayed to one side, slithering to his right. He turned with her, facing her, his eyes fixed to her face. "Tori," he cried, stepping backward again. "You can do this. Take control."

I can't! Tori cried from within. *I can't do this.*

"You can."

Tori felt a quiver of shock riot through her. Torque reared up, snarling a furious hiss and baring her fangs as she leaned down over Lucas. "You do not know us, Seraph." Venom dripped from her fangs. "We are not yours."

"But she can hear me." Lucas stepped backward again, staring up at the serpent above. "She knows she has power here. You are not her."

"We are one. She is mine."

"If you are one then, as she is yours, you must be hers."

Tori gasped, she could feel his words radiating into the deep core of her, a bubble of light. She shivered.

"She is not me," Torque snarled. "I am not hers."

The denial sounded contrived. Tori shoved against the weakness of the lie in her thoughts. *You are mine. You are me. We are one.*

Lucas smiled up at Torque and Tori knew he could feel the strength in her rising. "You can do this, Tori."

Chapter 16. The Monster Within

She leaned against the barrier in her mind. *I believe you, Lucas,* she whispered. The wall quivered.

Torque snarled back. "No!" A dark hiss whispered through her lips and she whipped forward, curling around Lucas. The serpent squeezed the coil of its body tight around him, forcing his arms against his sides and relished the gasp of pain that burst from Lucas's lips. His chest heaved and he struggled to free himself. The serpent's grip tightened, and she hissed, "Mine." Her eyes looked upon him, twin vertical eyes, their pupils lit with dark desire. The serpent tilted its head, looking down on Lucas. "I relish your warmth, Seraph. You are a life giver. Perhaps your blood would give my younglings warmth in the constant cold of this world."

No! Tori cried, feeling the weight of the wall slamming back into place. It crushed against her, harder and heavier than it had ever been before. She felt her thoughts darkening, as if even her own consciousness were being thrust into the darkest reaches. *No!* The wail in her thoughts tortured her. She shrank back into the recesses of her mind, trying to escape the waves of pain that threaded toward her from the barrier. She cowered, pulling herself tighter against herself, her thoughts shimmered. *No,* she whispered.

The serpent's tail coiled around Lucas. She squeezed, tighter and tighter. Her scales rippled over his muscles as she crushed. The bones in Lucas's rib cage shifted and he cried out in pain. He gasped for breath, his hand shoving against the serpent, his fingers ripping raw on the sharp scales that edged her skin. She snarled above him.

"Tori!" Lucas shouted. "Tori! Please! Fight back. You can do this."

Tori felt the tears she wanted to cry in her mind, heard her own sobbing thoughts. The tearing agony of her helplessness ripped through her. *No*, she whispered again. *Please.*

Torque called to her, the serpent's voice touching her thoughts in a gentle caress, *you are mine*. Her breath hissed through Tori's thoughts. *Mine.*

Chapter Seventeen
The Taste Of Torque

Tori's breath caught and she felt a keening hunger deep in her belly that seemed to want to enfold her entire being. Feeling a chill pulse through her skin, she shuddered and pushed away the dark memories flashing through her mind again. *Don't do this,* Tori whispered.

I want him, Torque replied. Tori's insides were pulling, her whole body tugging toward Lucas's warmth.

Please, Tori whispered.

She felt Lucas's hands come up against the scales on her chest. He shoved, pushing her away, but the serpent gripped tighter. "Tori," he said, his voice a whispered groan as the serpent squeezed tight across his lungs. "Please, Tori, you can stop this."

Torque snarled as Tori reached up from the darkness and began frantically pummelling at the thought barrier in her mind. *Damn it, let me out!* She shouted, throwing her mind against the wall. The crushing weight of the walls slammed into her, throwing her mind backward. She struck back. She felt the cold hiss of Torque through her thoughts and shivered. Her head pounded, throbbing in an agonising thrum that blurred her thoughts.

The Flight Of Torque

"No!" Torque hissed, she thrashed curling around Lucas. The serpent drew Lucas's warmth across her skin. She hummed into it, curling tighter and tighter. Tori felt a creeping chill come over him as the serpent rubbed scale on skin.

Lucas closed his eyes. "Tori," he whispered.

No! Tori shouted but the darkness was flooding her mind again and she felt the heaviness of her thoughts dragging her deeper into herself.

The serpent keened. "Mine!" it hissed, rubbing its tail against Lucas's hips. He shoved against the serpent's grasp and she hissed again with furious snarls as his inhuman strength kept the serpent from coiling her full length around him. Tori felt anger building inside her. She quivered at its burning fury and cowered.

"Don't do this," Lucas whispered. His chest laboured against the pressure on his lungs.

Torque hissed again as she reared up. She bared her fangs, sinking them deep into the flesh at the join of his neck and shoulder. He cried out, gasping. Venom shot through him, burning like acid. Tori felt as if her own blood burned through her veins. Her silent scream was trapped behind the barrier in her mind. As consciousness drained from Lucas's body, he sagged in the serpent's grip.

Torque tilted her head to look down on him, then drew away from him and let his body fall to the floor.

No, Tori said, her voice a sobbing whisper in her mind. *No!* She could feel the fire of the serpent's venom pulsing through him. Torque looked down at Lucas through impassive eyes. Her anger receded and Tori felt a wave of curious surprise wash through her, followed by remorse.

What did you do?

"He is broken," Torque replied. She slivered forward, prodding her nose against him.

You bit him, Tori cried. *You bit him. He's dying.* She felt the shudder of guilt wash through the serpent and then the crushing weight of her own human body. Her limbs, weak with exhaustion, felt every bruise that darkened her skin. Her muscles ached, screaming in protest as she tried to stay on her feet. Her legs gave out beneath her and she hit the floor. Her breath caught in her throat as the pain in her chest and ribs shot through her.

"Lucas," Tori whispered. Her own voice sounded raw and husky. She pulled herself forward, closer and closer to Lucas. When she reached him she felt the chill of his cooling body. She leaned over him, holding him in her arms as his warmth ebbed. She sobbed, her tears dripping from her face and pooling on the contours of his chest. "I'm sorry. I'm so, so sorry."

His body quivered beneath her, shuddering. His chest heaved upward and his muscles stiffened. Blood pooled against the twin punctures in his throat. A trail of blood trickled down, plopping onto the tile floor underneath him. A pallor crept over his skin and his breathing grew shallow. He moaned. Words that Tori could not hear traced across his lips. She leaned down against him, holding him closer. Tori almost did not hear the faint whisper as his lips moved again, "Tori."

"Lucas!" Tori gasped. "Please, please don't die. I didn't mean to," she whispered against his ear. Her lips brushed his cheek and her tears trickled down into his hair as she sobbed against him. She felt webs of fear weaving inside her. She felt Torque probing in her mind and shoved the beast away. "No! You did this." A sob wracked over her and tears streaked down her face. "What have I become?" Her voice wrenched out of her, aching deep into her heart. "Lucas," she said, cupping his face with her hands, "Please."

The burning ember of his body had chilled. With every moment he seemed to grow colder. She could not tell if his chest still heaved or if her hoping fooled her senses. Tears dried on her cheeks and deep within her a brush of golden reassurance trickled through her whole body. She could sense the faint thread of his life, hear the soft beat of his heart, feel the gentle rise of his lungs drawing air.

On the edges of her mind a feather touch brushed her thoughts. "Lucas," she whispered, a soft awe of wonder as she felt his warmth within her. The radiance of him seemed to glow over his skin. It held the same golden flame as his wings and curled around his body like a shimmering cloak of sunlight. Colour flushed through his cheeks and the drag of breath through his lungs seemed to grow stronger. "Lucas?" His lips quivered, parting. The glow over his skin seemed to be fading. Tori clung to him. She leaned over him, her breath warm between them. Her tears streaked down her face and stained his cheeks and lips. "Lucas," she whispered again.

With each breath he seemed to grow stronger, his colouring improved. The labour of his lungs softened, and his heartbeat slowed. The frantic tug of her fear thrummed through her and she brushed her fingers, stroking his face and brushing her fingers over his hair. The serpent within seemed to be still, but she felt Torque watching, curious, waiting. The strange scales of her alter consciousness rippled through her mind. Tori shivered, feeling the chill of the serpent within her. She tried to push the monster out of her mind. Torque seemed to lean into her. She had the strange sensation that the serpent tilted its head, an ebb of interested wonder wove through her, curling around her insides. Tori's body began to still, her shudders subsiding as her tears dried on her cheeks.

He felt the trickle of her tears on his skin, soft and warm. His breathing dragged from his lungs and pain swelled through his body. Fire burned through him, sweet, agonising flames which rushed through his blood. It reached every cell in his body, flickering to life in a thousand tingles through his nerve endings. Inside, his heart sat heavy, the beat slowing, as he realised the truth he had been hiding from. He had known it anyway, had felt it deep to his core, but even as he had tried to convince her he had been trying to convince himself. He could not lie any more. As the flush of flames flowed through him, Lucas felt himself smothered by the deep ache of guilt. *She thought I saved her, but I didn't. I couldn't save her.*

His chest felt torn, as if the flesh had been ripped out of him. The agony if it wrenched through him in sharper contrast to the numbing coolness of his fading body. He remembered the pain that had thrust through to his very soul when the Nagaran had severed his wings from his body, but this was worse. A betraying thought flickered through his mind and he felt guilty again; guilty for betraying who he was, what he was, and for failing in the most final way possible.

The dull morning light in the room glowed against his eyelids. Soft shards of light warmed his skin and threaded through his body. He felt the warmth of it and the chill that had filled him faded. His breathing evened. The tingling and burning that churned through his veins began to recede. Feeling returned; the soft weight of Tori, the trickle of her wet tears on his cheek, the brush of her fingers through his hair. He felt her breath on his face and suppressed a groan as he felt her breasts pressed against his chest. His body ached, tense and bruised. "Tori," he whispered, his throat dry and voice ragged.

She sat up, "Lucas?" Her voice shivered with surprise and a fresh wave of tears coursed down her stained cheeks. Her head fell forward. Leaning against his chest, she buried her face in his neck.

"Hey," he said, raising a hand to cup her head, he stroked the pad of his thumb down her chin. "I'm so sorry, Tori. I," he paused, a shudder of breath chasing out of his lungs. "I failed you. I failed."

Tori lifted her head, eyes full of confusion. "What?"

He closed his eyes, swallowing the ache in his chest. *She's so beautiful.* He buried the thought, buried it beneath his grief and helplessness. "I'm sorry."

"You're sorry? You, you're sorry?" Her lips trembled. "I almost killed you. You were dying."

His mouth lifted in a half smile, "Well, I am a little worse for wear."

"But you're alive," she whispered, running her fingers over his face. "You're alive." Wonder filled her voice.

He grimaced. "I'm alive."

"How?"

Lucas shrugged and winced at the pull in his shoulder. "I don't know. I felt my lungs being crushed, felt my ribs breaking, felt the jagged pain of its fangs pierce my throat." He shuddered. "I felt venom course through my veins. And then it faded, all of it. Part by part the pain ebbed away."

Tori pulled back, sitting further up she moved away from him and wrapped her arms around her knees. "You're ok?"

"I'm okay, Tori. Really?"

She burst into tears again and he pushed himself up. "Hey, it's okay."

Chapter 17: The Taste Of Torque

"I thought you were dying. I thought I'd killed you. You, the most beautiful person I've ever known. You'd already lost so much because of me. You're wings," she shook her head. "I almost took your life."

Lucas reached a hand out and touched her arm. "Not you, Tori. That wasn't you."

She looked up at him. "Sometimes I wonder," she paused, drawing a shaky breath into her lungs, then continued, "I wonder if she and I, maybe she is me. Maybe, somehow she really is just the darkest parts of me."

He sighed, "I don't know what she is. I just know that I'll do everything in my power to protect you from her."

Tori shook her head. "I don't want to be a monster. I don't want to be this thing that kills people. This thing so full of anger. So full of hate. I don't want to be her."

"I will find a way to make you yourself again," Lucas said. He raised his hand, touching her face as he pulled himself up. "You're not this, Tori. This isn't you," his voice quavered and she turned her chin into his hand. He felt the cool wash of her tears over his fingers. "Tori," he said again, tilting her chin up so she would look at him. "You're not her."

"But I am. She takes me over, I can't control it."

"We'll find a way."

She bit her lip, causing blood to pool where her teeth had cut through the soft flesh and darkened the pink flush of her lips. Her breath shuddered out of her. "I don't know how to stop her, Lucas. What if she comes again? She could hurt someone else, she could hurt you again." Her words tumbled from her lips in an agonised whisper and trailed to a sob deep in her throat.

"Listen to me, Tori. We can overcome this. I refuse to believe there is no way to deal with what they did to you."

"We have to go back, Lucas. I have to go back."

Lucas's gut wrenched, seeing the fear crossing her face. He could feel the anxiety buried deep within her. His mirrored it. "I don't want you to get hurt again. I've already failed you, but I can't do that again."

Tori swallowed, her breath a shiver through her lungs. "I have to, Lucas. If the Nagaran have a cure, if there is any way to reverse this, I want to take that chance. I need to."

He shook his head. "Not you, *you* don't have to. You don't."

Tori sighed, glancing around the room as if seeing it for the first time. "Where are we?"

"Tempany's."

"What?"

"I don't know why I brought you here. I guess it just seemed like the safest place, the closest haven."

"I don't understand."

"Tempany manages the earth-bound business of the Hierarchy. It's," he paused, assessing his words, "well, I can't really explain what it is." He sighed, pushing himself to his feet. "We should talk to Tempany. She can help us."

"Who is she?"

"Come on," he said, reaching down for her hand. "I'll show you."

"She's here? Now?"

He smiled. "She's always here. She lives here."

"Here? It's an office building."

"Down here it's an office building, up there it's several dozen high rise apartments. A whole society of sorts. The Hierarchy is a corporation of people working together. We're early, but later today this hall will fill with people."

"You mean people like you?"

He shrugged. "Some are, but some are humans who work with us in various capacities. I can't really explain and I don't think it matters too much. I see

Tempany on the floors above, I don't have to come through this part of the building to do it. Come on."

She reached her hand to him and he caught her fingers, cool and moist in the warmth of his palm. He pulled her upright and felt her sway toward him. He dropped her hand and stepped away, increasing the gap between them. "I'm sorry," she muttered, stiffening her spine. "I don't mean to do that."

"It's nothing," Lucas replied, his voice gruff. "We should go." Tori nodded.

A part of her rejoiced to see the energy and life vibrating through him, he was alive, he radiated with it. She ached inside for that part of herself that would never be the same and wondered if somehow the person she used to be was dead. *I almost killed him*. The thought trailed through her mind chased by guilt. She was half glad, half horrified. *If he hadn't been more than a man he would be dead now.*

As he lead the way across the reception to the door of the elevator, she whispered, "What did they do to me, Lucas?" She felt the wash of pained guilt riot through her. It was chased by a wave of anger. "What the hell did they do to me? What the hell did they do to you? How can your faith in getting answers be so strong when they have so much power?"

Lucas shook his head. "What would you suggest I do?" he asked, turning to face her.

"Fight. You could fight. You know we have to go back there."

"I know that I have to go back there. Not you, Tori, me. I can't protect you from them, Tori. I'll go, alone, and I'll make sure they can never hurt you again."

"What can you do alone? I can help you."

"I can't just lay down and let the darkness take you, Tori."

"Take me? I'm already gone. It already has me."

"No, I won't believe that. It cannot take you. I can't let it." He ran a hand through his hair as he turned to face her. His face was washed with shadows of exhaustion. "What would we do if they rose serpents from within their ranks? What would we do if they really did raise an army of Serpenthrope like they've been trying to do for the past twenty years?"

"They haven't succeeded."

"But they have learned, and they have succeeded, in part. They made you."

"They don't know how. We don't even know how. You heard Crey and Zara. No one knows why it worked when every other time it failed. We need to know more, Lucas. We can't do anything without understanding them better. I am one of them now, what they did to me; they would take me into their ranks, they would accept me as a Nagaran. I could hide among them. I could work with the Uprising to find answers."

"It's too dangerous." Lucas shook his head, turning away from her again. He strode to the elevator and jabbed the button. "Tori, we can't trust the creature within you."

"Torque," Tori whispered, coming to stand beside him. She glanced up at the numbers, biting her lip.

He glanced at her. "What?"

She swallowed. "Torque. That's its name."

Lucas narrowed his gaze, but he said nothing. Tori felt the anger radiating from him as he jabbed the button again. His jaw was set in a firm line and between tight lips he said, "Tempany will know what to do."

Chapter Eighteen
Rebellion Meets Prophecy

The elevator rose through the levels with a slow shudder. Lucas glanced up at the numbers as they lit each floor they passed. His breath huffed from his lungs in impatient bursts. He could feel her beside him, a cool breeze of tension. He felt his heartbeat racing with hers. The throng of her emotions wove with his own. He felt her longing. He felt the ache within her of denying herself the urges of the serpent, and fought back the echo that rose within him. She held herself stiff, and he could feel the tight grip she held over the serpent within her, as if she were afraid that even taking a breath would allow the monster to escape. Lucas wanted to reach for her hand, to hold her close. He wanted to frighten away the fear within her.

"It'll be okay, Tori," he said. The words echoed against the elevator's walls.

She glanced at him, tilting a smile. "Even you don't believe that, Lucas."

He turned his gaze away. *She's right,* he thought. *I don't know that anything will be okay ever again.*

The floors dropped away as they came closer and closer to the penthouse apartment. She sighed beside him. "It's okay, Lucas. I know what I am."

He glanced at her. Her face was calm, the wave of her emotions a cool swirl through her. "Don't give up, Tori. Please."

She smiled. "It's ok, really."

His anger rose. "It's not okay, Tori. Stop saying that. We can fix this. Tempany will help us figure out how to fix this."

She shrugged and, as the doors slid open, stepped out in front of him. She favoured one leg as she walked, but kept her spine straight, back stiff and erect. She lifted her chin. He could feel her embarrassed shame hidden behind proud bravado as she strode, naked, into the room.

The apartment was opulent, with white carpets and white walls. Sunlight streamed in from the billowing white curtains. The windows faced the sunrise and Tempany stood at them, gazing out across the rooftops of the city's skyscrapers. She turned as she heard them enter. "Oh," she gasped, seeing Tori. A soft flush crept across Tori's skin.

"I'm sorry," Tori whispered, biting her lip.

"No, of course. Let me get you something." She crossed to a nearby room and took a silk robe from the end of the large bed. She returned to Tori and draped the robe over her shoulders. "You must be Tori," she said. She glanced at Lucas, a dark look of censure burned from her eyes.

"There was no where else to go, Tempany. I told you."

"I expected you to be able to handle this, Lucas."

"Then you expected too much. I told you," he could not help the rush of anger that ran through him. The edge of it was in his voice and Tori frowned at him.

"You have a duty."

"I have a duty, one I've repeatedly failed to fulfil for the past twenty years. I told you," he said again. "Why didn't you listen to me? Anyone else," he trailed off. Most of his anger was directed at himself, he realised. It wasn't her fault, it was his. It was always his.

"I'm sorry," Tori whispered again. She pulled the robe around herself, crossing it across her chest and clinging to the edges.

"Oh Tori, it's not your fault." Tempany soothed. "Come on, let's get you cleaned up." Lucas grimaced at the gentle tone in Tempany's voice. He could feel the censure in it, as if she blamed him for the state Tori was in. The two woman crossed the room to a recessed bathroom. "A bath, I think," Tempany said, reaching for the taps.

"Really, I'm fine."

"Nonsense, you look as though you've gone through a war. Exhausted, sore, hungry," Tempany turned a smile up at her. Lucas watched Tori's face. Her bottom lip trembled and he could see a splash of tears welling in her eyes. Tempany reached into the rushing water, testing it with her fingers. "Come," she said. Tori nodded, and as she dropped the robe from her shoulders Lucas spun away from her. He felt himself hardening just thinking about the soft flush of her skin in the water. He grimaced.

Crossing the room, he stepped out of the broad twin windows and stood on the balcony. The cool breeze of the brisk morning washed over him. He could still hear the soft murmur of voices, the rush of running water, but somehow, with the sunlight beaming down on him, the world seemed larger. He drew a deep breath into his lungs and then exhaled with a soft sigh.

"Explain it to me, Lucas." Tempany came up behind him. He turned to face her. She had her hands on her hips and a furious glare in her eyes. "You were supposed to keep her safe."

"Don't look at me, Tempany. *You* lied to me."

"What do you mean?"

"She's not in this? They took her, Tempany."

"Lucas, what are you talking about?"

"The Nagaran. Don't try to tell me you don't know." Lucas watched the flush of guilt creep over her face. "Damn it, Tempany, You should have told me!" Lucas shouted.

"Don't swear at me, Lucas. I honestly did not realise it would come to this."

"You have no idea what's it's come to. No idea. She almost died."

"I'm sorry," she said, and she really did look sorry, Lucas decided. "But she didn't die. She isn't dead, Lucas. You saved her."

"I don't know that she's glad I did. I don't know if I should have. They did something to her."

"Something?"

"I don't understand it, they've transformed her somehow."

"What do you mean?"

"Some sort of ritual. They thrust a venom-laced dagger into her heart and then she transformed."

"What do you mean transformed, Lucas?"

Lucas sighed, glancing behind her into the room. Tori was hidden from sight, but he could feel her, relaxed into the frothy suds. The ache in her limbs eased in the hot water. He could feel the tremors that laced through her. She still struggled against the draw of the serpent within. He took a deep breath, turning back to Tempany. "A serpent comes out of her, Tempany." Tempany's breath caught, he saw a strange look cross her face before it fell behind the shutter of her composure. "What aren't you telling me, Tempany?"

"There are things I can't tell you, Lucas."

"Then at least tell me we can fix this."

She turned away from him, crossing to the balcony railing. She placed her hands on the rail and stared out at the glitter of sunlight on the scatter of glass and metal skyscrapers around them. "We can't fix it, Lucas. It is what it is. She is what she is."

"What," Lucas said, pausing as he tried to fight back the well of anger raging up within him. He drew another deep breath, huffing the air back out of his lungs before trying again. "What do you mean, Tempany?"

She glanced over her shoulder at him. "I'm sorry, Lucas. It's hard to explain."

"Try."

She turned back to the view. "Do you remember when Michael first left?"

"I remember," Lucas replied.

"There was a reason he left." She paused as if she were finding the words to explain.

"Tempany, just tell me."

She sighed. "It's not easy, Lucas. We have certain rules, you know that. He broke one."

Lucas's eyes narrowed. "Which one?"

She turned to face him, glancing up, "The one I suspect you're about to break."

He grimaced. "I'm not. There is nothing happening."

"The fact that you knew exactly which one I meant means something is happening. It can't happen Lucas."

"It's not," he said with a vehement shake of his head. "Tempany, tell me."

She sighed, turning away again. "Michael fell in love with his charge. She was a beautiful young woman, but something tragic happened to her and she was transformed, like Tori. He wanted revenge. You know our rules, he cannot intervene in the crimes of men. He can protect his charge, but not at the expense of a life."

Lucas slammed his hand on the railing. "You mean this has happened before? How long have the Nagaran existed."

Tempany shrugged, "So far as I understand, she was the first."

"The Uprising told us the Nagaran dogma of the Four Father's and the Sacred Mother. She had a lover, but was taken by four men. She was raped by them. Is that why Michael turned against us?"

"Look, I don't know Lucas. If I could find him, if I could bring him back here, I'd find out the truth. I'd find out where all of this started, why all of this started, but I just don't know."

"So what will happen to Tori? Are you telling me there is no way to reverse this?"

"It's not something done too her, Lucas. It's something born of her. Or, perhaps it is better to say that it's something unleashed from within her. She was always Serpenthrope, the venom simply awoke that part of herself. It's actually a strength."

"It doesn't make her strong, Tempany. It tears her apart. She's crushed by the guilt of the people the serpent within her has killed, by the lust, by the raging fury. The darkest of her emotions riot out of control and the serpent takes her completely over."

284

Chapter 18. Rebellion Meets Prophecy

"It's not supposed to be like that, Lucas. The Serpenthrope exist in symbiotic harmony with their selves. They are two identities, but they share their wants, their desires. Ultimately, for one to act on the other, they both have to have the same yearning."

"Tori didn't want to kill people, Tempany. I can't believe that she ever wanted that."

"But she did want to escape. The serpent, sensed that desperate urge within her, it shared it, and sought a way to fulfil it. Their motivation was the same. The serpent simply acts from the baser instinct, the moral compass has to come from her."

"It takes her over. It completely rules her body and mind. I can sense the turmoil within her. I feel her mind trapped behind the iron walls of the prison the serpent's razor thoughts cage around her."

Tempany's gaze snapped to Lucas, "You sense her emotions?"

"I know it's not something I've had with a charge before, but yes, with her I can sense everything that passes through her, every lance of fear, every torment of the lust the serpent forces her to feel."

Tempany frowned. "It's not something angels ever have felt with their charges. I've never heard of it happening. Not ever."

Lucas frowned. "Not ever?"

She looked at him and gave a sharp shake her head. "Never."

"What does it mean?"

"I don't know, but anything with the power to create that kind of bond between you is something of which I would choose to be very wary. I'll need to look into this more carefully," she said. She turned away from the railing and stepped toward the doorway.

Lucas turned too, he reached out a hand as if to grab her arm, but then stopped, pulling his hand back. "Our conversation isn't finished, Tempany. Michael?"

She sighed, turning back to face him. "Michael and his lover were torn apart by what happened to her. I don't know what happened, but I do remember him after it happened. He was dark, torn, as if his very soul had been ripped from him. He was a shadow of himself and he walked through the world like an angel severed from his wings." Tempany gasped, "Lucas, your wings!" He grimaced. "What on earth happened in these past few days? Tell me everything."

"We should go inside. Tori's almost finished. I can explain when she's settled." He turned away from the balcony and walked back into the room. Tempany followed.

"You can tell that sort of thing about her?" she asked. He nodded. "Does she know?"

"She knows," he said, his voice held a soft ring of regret. "She's not too happy about it. And to be honest, neither am I. I can tell where she is at all times and I know if she's safe, but, I don't know if I could stand to share her emotions forever. Not if the serpent continues to torment her. It's like she screams inside herself, walled off from the person she is supposed to be. I feel her grow smaller and smaller in her own mind. No one should be tortured like that. I don't like sharing it with her, but in a way I'm glad too, because, somehow, with me sharing it I feel as if she's not alone. I don't know if the connection works both ways. Maybe she feels alone. I don't know."

"Sometimes, sometimes I don't feel alone," Tori said, her voice a husk of timid uncertainty from the bathroom door. She was wrapped in a thick white towel that hung to the floor, hiding her toes. "I'm sorry," she murmured. "I didn't mean to intrude, but, could I borrow something to wear."

Tempany smiled at her, a broad compassionate smile. "Of course, I'll find you something," she said, holding a hand out to Tori. Tori crossed the room to her, but did not take her hand. She blushed as the towel swished against her legs.

"Thank you," she said, then bit her lip, before adding, "I don't know if I can promise to return it. The serpent," she said, her voice trailing off as if she could not find the words to explain. She sighed, and Lucas felt the pull in his gut of her fear, her guilt.

Tempany curved her arm around Tori. "I do understand, Tori."

Tori sucked in a breath. Lucas watched the shiver across her shoulders. Tempany drew her closer, holding her in a hug. Tori seemed to melt into it. The sheen of tears on her eyelids glistened in the sunlight that cascaded across the room. "I'm sorry," she whispered, as a teardrop streaked down her cheek. Lucas tried to thrust away the helplessness that came over him. *I should be used to it by now, but I'm not. Maybe I never will be.* He watched the two as they left the room then closed his eyes. Even out of sight he could feel Tori. He could feel the turmoil of her emotions.

A soft radiance seemed to emanate from Tempany. Tori leaned into it as if the glow could blank out the darkness within. The soft terry towelling on her skin felt warm and the sunlight streaming into the room made her shiver. She wanted to step into it as if she could absorb the light into herself.

Chapter 18. Rebellion Meets Prophecy

Tempany took her into a large walk-in wardrobe. Inside an array of clothes, shoes, and accessories ran the length of two walls with a mirror against the third. Tori averted her eyes from the mirror. *I don't want to know what I look like. I don't want to see how much the monster has changed me.* She closed her eyes and drew a shaky breath into her lungs.

"My clothes might be a touch too big for you, but I'll see if there is anything suitable for you to wear," Tempany said, dropping her arm from Tori's shoulder. She opened a draw and drew out two scraps of white lace, which she handed to Tori. Tori flushed at the lingerie and Tempany said, "Oh, don't worry, they've never been worn before." She turned to a rack of dresses hanging from one of the rails. Beautiful gowns, smart business suits, and soft summer dresses in a rainbow of colours flashed past her as she flicked through them. "Here," she said, drawing a soft buttercup dress from the rack. She brought it to Tori. The dress would have hemmed above the knee on Tempany, but would hang below by a modest inch, perhaps two, on Tori.

"Thank you." Tori took the dress, running her fingers over the soft cotton. She glanced at the full-length mirror and then turned away from both it and Tempany. She felt Tempany's eyes on her back.

"I'll leave you some privacy," Tempany said.

Tori glanced behind her as the door slid closed. She could hear the muted whisper of Tempany and Lucas behind it. Tori hung the dress from a hook and placed the scraps of lace on a dresser. She dropped the towel from around her chest and draped it over the back of a chair. Her gaze fell to the floor as she turned to face the mirror, then with slow deliberation she drew it up. Her naked body was flushed with the soft tint of an embarrassed blush. She drew her gaze up her legs, past her hips, her breasts. The wound in her chest was fading.

She lifted her fingers, feeling the skin where the dagger had penetrated. She looked down. "How?" The flesh was healed. If not for the faint pink scar and the slight redness around its edges it almost looked as if there had been no wound at all. Startled, Tori glanced up, her eyes meeting in the mirror. They were wide and dark. The fall of her hair around her face and shoulders was damp. She blinked, looking again, her bottom lip dropped as she gasped.

"I look the same," she said in wonder. "How can I look the same and be so different?" A trail of tears trickled down her cheeks and she wrapped her arms around herself. She drew deep breaths into her lungs, trying to control the wash of her emotions. As tears dried on her cheeks, Tori turned and reached for the clothes. She drew the dress down over herself and ran her hands over the skirt as it settled on her. The wound was just visible under the left strap.

Tori took a deep breath, looked at herself one last time in the mirror and then turned to the door. She drew it open, then paused in the threshold. Lucas seemed to radiate an air of power that filled the room. He had changed, wearing a crisp white shirt and tan corduroy pants. He stood, facing Tempany, and ran a hand though his hair. Tori listening to the heated conversation between them and watched the strange way they interacted with one another.

"I need you to do this for me, Lucas?" Tempany said. There was a hint of desperation in her voice, as if she was fighting for a last chance, as if she really did need Lucas because no one else could help her.

"You've been searching for years, Tempany. What do you expect me to find?"

"Whatever secrets Anna was hiding; Marlena and Uriel cared enough to try to find them. I expect you to discover what they missed. I expect you to uncover those secrets, Lucas."

"I can't do that right now, Tempany. I need to find answers for Tori. All we have is speculation and fanatical stories. What we need is the truth."

"You are finding answers. The answers are there, Lucas. You know who Michael is in this, you must know. The truth lies with him. We just need to find him."

"And you think Anna knew where he was?"

"I don't know what Anna knew. That's why we need to find out."

Lucas shook his head. "I can't go off on some wild chase to find something that might not even exist. I know where the answers are. I've got to go back there. I need to face the Nagaran."

"Your job is not to mete out revenge, Lucas. You have a duty to your charge."

"My duty is to protect her. That's exactly why I have to go back. I can't let them hurt her again."

"I have to go back," Tori said. Her voice seemed to echo around the sudden silence in the room. She took a hesitant step forward as Lucas and Tempany turned to her, their faces were threaded with frustration.

"Tori," Lucas said, his eyes running a trail up and down her body. She shivered under the gaze, feeling a flush steal across her skin and a pool of desire fill her belly. He swallowed, then added, "You know I can't let you go back there."

Tempany reached out a hand and touched Lucas's arm. "We'll talk about this. But first, Tori, please, come sit down. You must be exhausted. I'll send for some food."

"You mean there are others here?" Tori asked, glancing around.

"They are arriving. They are down stairs, so don't be concerned that we will be interrupted." She gestured to a chair and Tori crossed to sit in it. She saw Tempany give Lucas a stern look and he grimaced, then dropped to a chair beside her. His chin was rigid with stubborn determination. Tempany crossed to the desk and spoke with hushed tones into the phone. "There will be a full breakfast in about thirty minutes," she said as she came back to sit with them.

"Thank you," Tori said. She touched her hands to her knees, feeling awkward.

"Now," Tempany said, "Please, tell me everything that has happened. I know it might not be something comfortable to talk about, but I need to know everything if I am to help you."

Tori's gaze dropped to the floor. The other woman's eyes had seemed to penetrate deep into her, as if she could see into the darkness within. Tori bit her lip, feeling the tears shimmering on her lashes. She swallowed, trying to push them back. "I'm sorry."

"Don't, Tori. None of this is your fault. None of this was ever your fault," Lucas said.

"Then whose fault is it? If it weren't for me, if it weren't for my father," she said, then glanced down at her fingers, laced in her lap, before continuing, "None of this ever would have happened, Lucas. You heard what Crey and Zara said. I must be a child of the Nagaran."

"I heard them, but despite all that, I should have stopped it."

Tempany's soft voice interrupted them. "You could not have stopped this, Lucas. None of this is your fault. Neither of you are to blame for what has occurred."

Tori looked up at her. "I didn't mean for any of this to happen."

"Of course you didn't, Tori. I know that," Tempany assured her. "Please, start from the beginning."

With a nod, Tori began. "I'd gone to the church because my boss wanted me to follow up a story about an illicit snake smuggling racket. I really didn't think I'd find anything, especially once I was there. The church was deserted. Then they grabbed me," her voice dropped, quavering.

Chapter 18. Rebellion Meets Prophecy

Lucas cleared his throat. Tori felt the wave of guilt wash over him. He reached out to touch her, and then sat back instead. "I should have stopped them," he said. "But I couldn't. They took us both. Then they performed some kind of sick ceremony on her. Plunged a knife into her chest, and she transformed."

"But your wings," Tori protested. Lucas shook his head, but Tori ignored him. "Lucas tried to help me. They had me tied up and Lucas tried to save me but they caught him. They cut his wings off." Tears streamed from her eyes. Tempany reached out and passed her a tissue from the coffee table. Tori took it, wiping her eyes.

"It's nothing," Lucas said.

"It's not nothing, Lucas," Tempany said, her voice was quiet with reserved compassion. "You should have told me."

"I still have wings, they're different now, but I still have them. I can still fly. Zara, she's one of the members of the Uprising. She said that being an angel was something in my soul, something that could never be taken from me. She was right."

A strange light passed through Tempany's eyes before she said, "You will have to explain this to me, but what happened next?" She turned back to Tori.

Tori bit her lip. Her voice was timid and quiet. "Then I turned into a monster, and I killed the priestess."

A soft groan came from Lucas and he leaned forward, leaning on his knees. He looked right at her. "*You* did not do it, Tori. Do you hear me? None of that was ever you."

Tori shrugged. "Maybe it was, Lucas. Maybe I really wanted to kill her for what she did to me."

He shook his head. "No, I won't believe that. *It* made you do it," he said. He spat the word with such vehemence that Tori flinched. He softened his tone before adding, "That wasn't you, Tori." Tori nodded, but she could not believe his words.

Tempany's soft voice broke the quiet that had fallen between them. "I know this has been very difficult."

Lucas turned to her. "After that, they threw me in a cell and took Tori away," he said, and then, piece by piece, they told Tempany everything that had happened to that point. Everything, except the weave of emotion, the yearning, the wanting, that bound them to one another.

"So, your wings just appeared when you leapt off the roof?" Tempany asked. Tori was sobbing again. She had curled her legs up under her body and wrapped one arm around herself. With the other she dabbed another tissue on her cheeks.

"As I fell," Lucas replied. "I remember thinking that I wouldn't be able to save her. I hate that wave of hopelessness that passes through me when I realise how helpless I am." He grimaced, shaking his head, then continued. "But then, I don't know, I guess I just refused to be less than I am. And it was like they," he paused, shaking his head. "I can't describe it."

"It's like they pulse out of you from deep within the core of your being," Tori said. He turned to look at her, surprised.

"Show me?" Tempany said, standing up.

Lucas stood. He unbuttoned the crisp white shirt and turned to drape it over the arm of the chair. Tori sucked in a breath and clenched her thighs together as a rush of passion flushed through her. She saw Lucas grit his teeth and flushed with embarrassment. "I'm sorry," she whispered. He shook his head. Tori felt Tempany's curiosity as she watched the exchange between them.

"It's fine," Lucas muttered, he flexed his shoulders and Tempany gasped as his wings burst from between them. A soft golden glow flickered from the pulsing waves of energy that formed the plume of his radiant feathers. They lit the room with an eerie light that bounced off the wall like the flicker of a candle.

"Oh, Lucas," Tempany said. Her voice was hushed with wonder. "They're magnificent." She paused, running her fingers over the curve of one wing and lifting the plume of one feather. "I've never seen anything like it."

Jealousy rushed through her and Tori struggled against the dark hunger of the serpent within. Torque bubbled to the surface of her thoughts and she gasped. She shoved against the beast, fighting against the walls that pushed at her thoughts.

"Don't," Lucas said, stepping away from Tempany. The wings disappeared, tucking behind him and then sinking into his skin. He reached down, grabbed the shirt and pulled it over himself. Tori continued to fight against the dark jealousy that Torque radiated. Her breath was tight in her chest as she battled, and her head began to pound with tension. "Tori?" Lucas asked, he bent down, and touched her knee with his hand.

"I'm," she began, and then closed her eyes as another wave washed over her. *Don't,* she whispered within her thoughts. The serpent seemed to swish in her mind, its tail a flicker of annoyance as Torque slunk back into the shadows. "I'm sorry. I'm okay, really." He watched her, his eyes full of anxiety. She felt the trace of his gaze on her skin. "Really Lucas, I'm fine."

"You stopped that," he said, his voice touched with awe. "You stopped that, Tori."

"What happened?" Tempany asked, she stood looking down on them both.

"The serpent," Lucas began.

"Torque," Tori interrupted. "She calls herself Torque."

Lucas frowned then continued, "It seems to be tied by emotion. Whenever a baser instinct is triggered it rises."

"And it did this, just then?"

He nodded, then looked back at Tori. "And Tori stopped it."

"Sometimes, I don't think it really wants to hurt people. We just get so angry." Lucas flinched. "I'm sorry," Tori whispered. "It's just, sometimes I can't tell what I feel and what she feels. It's like she is me."

He swallowed. "We'll figure this out, Tori."

"I have to go back to the Nagaran Temple, Lucas. I need to. I have to find out if there is a way to undo this. If they can put that part of me back to sleep…"

He shook his head. "It's too dangerous, Tori."

Tori shook her head and looked into Lucas's eyes. "You can't stop me, Lucas."

"I can find you answers, Tori. You don't need to go back," Lucas said.

She shook her head and reached for his hand. She touched it with soft fingers and leaned toward him. "I need to do this. I could learn so much from inside their walls, Lucas. They would believe me; they would believe Torque."

Tori could feel the war inside him, as if he wanted to reach for her, wanted to reassure himself that she was real and that she would not run away again. He shook his head, his fingers clenching under her hand. "We can't trust it. You can't trust it, Tori. You can't control it."

"It's the only way."

"Crey and Zara can get me in. You don't have to go."

"And then what? You hide in the darkest recesses and hope none of the cultists see you? I need to have the freedom to find answers, Lucas. I can't do that with you there. They won't trust you."

A soft groan from the back of his throat rumbled out of him. "You can't go in there alone."

"She won't be alone," Tempany said. "I'm going with her."

Chapter Nineteen

"I Am The Charmer"

Lucas felt a blaze of shock rocket through him. His head snapped around and he stood. Tori's hand fell from his. "You?" he asked. His voice darkened with jealous anger. "Tori is my charge, Tempany."

Tempany looked back at him, a resoluteness about her that irked him. She stared him down, but he refused to let her cower him. "You asked me to give this assignment to another, Lucas."

"You no longer take charges, Tempany. You're no longer a protector."

"That doesn't make me incapable. I oversee the protectors, Lucas. I was a protector years before you became one. Trust that I can do this."

Lucas shook his head, "No, there has to be another way."

"We have limited options in this regard. Tori needs to return and she must not do that alone."

"She doesn't have to go back. It would be safer for everyone if she stayed as far away from the Nagaran as possible."

Tori reached up and took his hand. She lifted her chin so their eyes met when he looked down on her. "I need to go back, Lucas," she said. "You must see that."

"I can't let you, Tori," Lucas said.

He saw a flame flicker in her eyes and she stood, placing her fists on her hips. "You can't let me?" she asked, a dark rage fuming in her voice. He felt the serpent flicker within her.

Anger bubbled in echo within him, but hidden beneath it he sensed a quiver of fear. He thrust it down inside himself as he turned away from Tori to face his mentor. "Tempany, I appreciate that you want to help us, but even you cannot keep Tori safe in there."

"It's the best chance you both have, Lucas. Tori needs to go back. She needs answers. She needs to understand what she is, and why. Those answers will only come from the Nagaran."

Tori reached for his shoulder. She turned him to face her again. "I am going back, Lucas. You can't stop me."

He sighed before responding. "Then I'll go with you," he said. There were bare inches between them and he looked straight into her eyes. "I have to go with you, Tori. I need to keep you safe."

Chapter 19. "I Am The Charmer"

She shook her head. "You can't, Lucas. The Nagaran will let me come back. I am the Charmer. I'm important to them, but." She closed her eyes and shook her head. "You can't go back, Lucas." When she looked at him again, her eyes glistened with a sheen of unshed tears. "They would do more than cut off your wings. Lucas, they'd kill you."

"She's right," Tempany said, standing too. "Besides, you have answers to find that are not within the walls of the Nagaran."

Tori sat in Tempany's car as they drew up outside the old church. "I'll give you two a moment," Tempany said. She stepped out and closed the rear door, leaving Tori and Lucas enclosed and alone.

Tori smoothed the folds of the elegant gown Tempany had given her. "Are you sure I should be wearing this?" she asked, turning to Lucas who had been driving.

He gritted his teeth and she felt him run his eyes over the tight curves of satin covering her breasts and trace the lines down to her thighs where the dress flared out to her ankles. He swallowed, then said, "You look beautiful, Tori. Like a queen. And isn't that what we want them to think?"

She glanced out the window at the shadows around the building and shivered. "I don't know if I can do this Lucas," she whispered.

"Tori, look at me." She tilted her head, turning her tear-filled eyes to Lucas's warmth. She closed her eyes, seeing the picture of him behind her eyelids like an image burned into her memory. His fingers gripped her chin and she felt his breath as he said, "You can do this." The pad of his thumb rubbed across the curve of her lips and then fell away. He leaned back. "But it's not too late to change your mind. If you're not sure we can just drive away. We can find another way, or we could just," he paused, and she felt the ripple of his shocked surprise.

"Could just what?" she asked.

Lucas shook his head. "I was going to say we could go, just," he sighed, an echo of defeat that reverberated through his bones. "We could just go."

She reached out, running a hand through his hair and looked into his eyes. "You could never just go, Lucas. You couldn't, just as I can't ever give up. No matter how hard it gets for either of us, we can't stop fighting against the darkness the Nagaran bring. We have to do this."

"You have a choice, Tori. Right now, you have a choice."

Chapter 19. "I Am The Charmer"

She blinked her eyes open, feeling the anger build within her, resolution followed. "I'm not changing my mind, Lucas. I won't let you give up what you are. Besides, whatever they did to me, they did it for a reason, and I have to believe there is a way to undo it."

"I still think there must be another way."

"If I pretend to be on their side, if I pretend I am Torque, they will accept me."

He shook his head and turned to gaze out of the windscreen. "Tori, I won't be able to protect you once you go in there."

She leaned forward, putting her hand on his knee. "I can take care of myself, Lucas." He clenched his jaw. "Listen to me," she said, and he turned to look at her. "I can do this. Tempany, Zara, Crey, they'll help me. I promise, I'll be okay."

"You can't promise that, Tori. You have no idea what you'll be walking into."

"What other choice is there? I have this opportunity to go back in there. There is no better opportunity than this. I can't find answers out here, and I have to know. I can't stand not knowing."

"There must be another way," Lucas muttered, he closed his eyes and Tori felt the wash of helplessness that flushed through him.

"Don't, please," she said. She placed her hand on his thigh. "Lucas, this is worth the risk."

"Is it? I don't want you to get hurt, Tori. I don't want to lose you. I don't think I could survive it."

"You won't lose me. I'm not afraid, Lucas. You believed in me before, believe in me now, please?" Lucas gazed at her, as if scrutinising every expression in her face. She knew he felt what she felt, and she drew every ounce of courage like a shroud around the flittering moths of fear that fluttered in her heart. When he did not speak she shook her head. "I have to go." She turned and lifted the handle of the door.

"Tori," Lucas began, his voice sounded like it ripped out of his throat in an involuntary reflex and he reached for her, gripping her wrist in his strong fingers. When Tori turned back to him, he said, "Be careful." She smiled at him and he lifted his hand to touch her cheek. "Please, be careful, and come back to me."

She nodded. "I'll be okay, and I will come back." Tori leaned into the warmth in his hand and closed her eyes. Then whispered again, "I will come back." Tears washed her eyes as she pulled away and stepped onto the footpath where Tempany waited.

The other woman was dressed simply. Her pale golden hair was hidden beneath an auburn wig. Dark charcoal shaded her eyes and transformed her face. Her wings, hidden in the folds of a soft dress and woollen cloak, were tucked tight against her back. "Ready?" she asked.

Tori turned her face up to the late morning sunlight and felt the rays against her skin. A soft well of hunger darted through her and she knew that Lucas was watching her. She sighed, then nodded. Turning away from the light they crossed the footpath and stepped into the darkness of the shadows surrounding the church.

The heavy metal doors clanged as they approached. Tori hesitated as they swung open. A pair of sharp eyes focused on her, examining every feature with steel objectivity. Tori straightened her spine and stalked toward the man. "What are you doing here?" he demanded. His voice held a dark hint of suspicion as he looked over the two women.

Tori tried to bury the quiver of her anxiety, but it grew as she recognised Torque rising within. *I can do this*, she whispered to the serpent within her mind.

I will do this, it whispered back. Then Tori was behind the walls of her mind again and the serpent moved in her body. It stole her voice as it said, "I am the Charmer." The man's eyes narrowed. Tori's hand lifted to rest on her outthrust hip. "I demand an audience with the

High Priestess." Her dark eyes, confident smile, and careless stance made it clear that Torque expected her demands to be met.

"I know who you are. You think you have the right to ask anything of the Nagaran? We made you." The man reached out and gripped her arm in a crushing hold.

Torque wrenched her arm free with a strength that surprised them both. She balanced her feet firm on the cobblestones and hissed, "Don't dare touch me, human." The man drew up his crossbow as he stepped back against the door. Torque stared down at him. "I am the Charmer, blood of the Nagaran, you will take me to the High Priestess right now."

"Jackson?"

"I'm sorry, High Priestess, she insisted on seeing you."

"So you felt it prudent to interrupt me in my private chambers. Who has so commanding a presence as to demand my immediate attention."

Jackson stepped aside and Tori moved into the room. She felt small against the High Priestess and wished that Torque had not let go of her thoughts and body. She wanted to wrap the serpent's violent anger, arrogant superiority, and burning confidence around herself. Marlena glared down at her, drawing herself up in a way that seemed to oppose the hunch of Tori's shoulders. The serpent hissed inside Tori as Tori's thoughts betrayed her anxiety, *I can't do this.*

We must confront her. She has no power over us.

You do it. She felt the slither of the serpent in her mind as it considered her request.

You do not need us.

Tori bit her lip then glanced up under hooded lashes to see Marlena's glare. "Charmer," Marlena drawled, "We were concerned that you would keep us waiting while you gallivanted around above ground against the wishes of the temple. I am so pleased you have returned to us." She looked far from pleased, her smile forced onto her lips and a crease of angry tension around her eyes. "I see you bring a friend with you."

Tempany shifted on her feet and drew closer to Tori. Tori could sense the wary tension in the woman. There was a strength and confidence that was at odds with the timid and deferential demeanour she was depicting.

Tori lifted her chin, swallowing the lump of fear that stuck in her throat. She took a deep breath and squared her shoulders. The serpent within seemed to preen itself in her thoughts and Tori could not help feeling a quiet resentment. She ignored it. "I have," she said, straightening her spine.

"You were told that you would not be permitted to leave the temple. Explain yourself."

"My apologies, High Priestess. I," she paused, searching for an excuse. The whisper of the serpent's hunger rocked through her. "The serpent's hunger demanded abatement."

Marlena narrowed her eyes. "Oh? I have a great many dead cultists who would attest to the beast's great hunger. Were they not enough?"

"That you can count the bodies means she did not feed on them."

"And she has fed now?"

"And returned to the temple, to do her duty for the Sacred Mother."

"I suppose this serpent—"

Tori interrupted her, "Torque."

The High Priestess inclined her head. "Torque. She will need to feed regularly?"

Tori swallowed, glancing away before returning her gaze to meet Marlena's. "She will," Tori lied. She watched the uncertainty pass the High Priestess's features.

"Then I will be sure to have ready supplies for you so that you will not have to leave the temple again." Tori flinched and Marlena smiled. "Now, you requested an audience with me?"

"I did," Tori replied. *What on earth am I supposed to talk to her about?* she whispered to the serpent in her mind.

She felt the tilt of the serpent's head in her thoughts. *You seek answers,* it reminded her.

"Well? Is it to do with your friend?" Marlena asked.

Tori lifted her chin. "Tempany serves me. She wishes to become an initiate of the Nagaran in direct service to the Charmer. She will remain my constant companion." Tempany kept her head bowed in deference and remained silent. Marlena frowned but did not object, so Tori continued, "But that is not what I wished to speak with you about. Her assignment is not open for negotiation. My interest today is far more significant. I am given to believe that you have a copy of the true history, one which is not archived. I demand access to those records."

"You demand." Marlena stiffened, raising an eyebrow she glared at Tori.

"Yes."

Through gritted teeth Marlena replied, "Why do you assume I would have such records, that I would not have them kept among the archives?"

"The archives are incomplete. I have seen them myself and I believe there is a great deal that is not included."

The High Priestess's eyes narrowed. "Why do you assume such a thing?"

"You know as well as I, Marlena, that for my Serpenthrope nature to be awoken I must be a child of the Nagaran. My birth, however, is not on record." Tori could feel Marlena's anger grow. The woman flinched at the use of her first name rather than the respectful use of her title. Tori wanted to push on that nerve. She smiled, then added, "And yet, *you* knew of me, Marlena."

"You were merely a convenient accident. You came into our temple and presented yourself to us."

"Hardly. We met when you broke into my grandmother's house. Even then you called me by title. Your intrusion in my home speaks to more than convenience," Tori paced across the room a few steps then turned back to look at Marlena. She narrowed her gaze as she added, "And twenty years ago you murdered my father. I remember you. As you can see, it is not difficult to put these pieces together. My father was a Nagaran royal." Tori heard the angry resentment in her own voice. She glared at Marlena.

Chapter 19. "I Am The Charmer"

"Not your father," Marlena spat back, then froze as she realised her mistake. Tori felt a thousand thoughts whirl through her mind. The serpent hissed, whipping through her mind in an agitated flicker of disconcertion.

"What do you mean?"

"I have no need to explain myself to you. You obviously have not even begun to grasp the true extent of the Nagaran's power. You are nothing."

"I am the Charmer. True Nagaran well beyond your minuscule claim to this cause. I am certain that I outrank you here, no matter what airs you put on and what restrictions you think to place on me. Should I choose it, you would cower before the wrath of the Sacred Mother. I could force you to your knees before her with my own hands should I choose it."

She felt the quiver of Marlena's uncertainty and then the rising jealousy that coursed through her. "You know nothing of my right to my place here. I made you, you were nothing before me."

"I am Serpenthrope. I always was. This is my legacy, not yours."

"Just because your slut of a mother left a trace of serpent blood in your veins does not make you worth more than me to the Nagaran."

Tori swallowed, feeling the rush of her mother's betrayal through her veins. "My mother?" she whispered.

Marlena continued as if Tori had not spoken. "I have been loyal to the Nagaran for more years than you've been alive. I've seen the countless bastards your siblings, the children, have brought into the world. I've seen their bastards beyond that and it sickens me. You are a plague upon us, you taint the true glory of the serpent, you weaken the venom of the Nagaran's influence. Every one of you destroys us."

"What do you mean? My mother?" Tori said. She felt overwhelmed by the wave of horror that washed through her. Tempany reached out and brushed her fingers against Tori's arm before letting her hand fall again.

Marlena grimaced. "You mother is dead. The sooner you accept that the better it will be for all of us."

The serpent rose up and Tori fell behind the shield of it. Torque gripped her and Tori let the serpent move through her. "You know as well as we do, human, that the Mother is not dead. You know the Sacred Mother cannot be killed, not by weapon, nor poison, nor illness, and particularly not in the birth of a child. She is the bringer of life and death. She is the first of us, the first true Serpenthrope. She is origin."

Chapter 19. "I Am The Charmer"

Tori's thoughts raced as realisation dawned. Their frantic dance within her mind left her queasy. The wash of confusion and horror flushed her skin as the serpent's words sunk into her mind.

Marlena glared at her. "You are mistaken, Charmer," she said. "The Sacred Mother has nothing to do with Tori's birth." The quiver in her voice betrayed the lie. She seemed to shrink within the glimmer of fear in her eyes.

Torque rose up, her tail swishing out from beneath the long hem of her dress. She towered over the High Priestess. Tori felt the strange sensation of her own arms, her own hands, her own breasts and face and hair attached to the sway of scaled hips and serpent tail. "You will reveal to us the true histories, human. We will have our answers," Torque hissed. Her forked tongue darted between her lips, tasting the High Priestess's fear in the air.

Chapter Twenty
The Secrets Of Friends

Police tape still crisscrossed the library door, but the windows were ajar and the curtains fluttered open on a breeze. Sunlight streamed into the room. It was still in shambles, the desk draws ransacked, books pulled from the shelves. The coffee table was a pile of broken splinters on the carpet.

The desk was, perhaps, the most intact object. Its sturdy oak frame made it a heavy block that dominated the centre of the room. It looked familiar, Lucas realised. He crouched down, running his fingers over the wooden slats under the desktop. "This was her father's," he whispered. Looking through the slats, he pictured her, a young Tori, peering between them as she watched her father's blood staining the cream carpet before her. This room had a rich, burgundy carpet. It was larger, airier than the office that had been in the small apartment, but the desk was the same.

Lucas stood again and ran his hands over the desk's surface. He felt the smooth grain of the oak. The draws were well carved and solid. Lucas tugged them out and hefted their weight as he placed them, one by one, on the surface of the desk. Their contents were mostly strewn on the floor, but he emptied them completely, and ran his fingers over the base and walls of each draw, searching. The draws held no secrets.

"What were they looking for?" Lucas asked. The silence answered him. He imagined the ticking of the broken clock that still lay in shards of wood and glass outside the library door. Lucas frowned, glancing around the room. "There are too many places to hide things. A whole house of secrets." *But they didn't find anything in here.*

He strode around the desk and out of the room. The entry lead to the kitchen and a hall behind the stairs. The stairs lead up to the landing above and, Lucas remembered, the bedrooms. Tori's room. He took the stairs two at a time, ignoring the railing and stood at the top a moment before moving across the hall to her room.

The sheets on her bed were still mussed, her nightwear lay crumpled in a tidy pile on a chair. An array of photos lined the dresser; pictures of Tori, her friends, her family. Lucas leaned over to look at each one. Even as a child Tori had been beautiful. A dark, rich beauty with sad brown eyes. When she smiled, as she did in all of the pictures here, there remained a haunted whisper in her eyes; a secret pain.

He lifted one of the pictures from the glass. The woman in it looked like Tori. The same young face, same dark eyes, same rich wave of ebony hair, but her eyes sparkled with vibrant life. The shot was only half of what must have once been a larger picture. The woman in the embrace of a man whose face and body was gone.

Lucas tucked the picture back into place against the mirror and began searching each of the draws. He felt awkward, searching through Tori's things. A box on the dresser was open, earrings, bracelets, necklaces, and rings were scattered around it. Each of the pieces were like her. Large silver hoop earrings, and delicate silver rings. A charm bracelet decorated with dragons, stars, castles, and a scatter of magical creatures nestled in the silk lining of the box. It was as if she still believed in fairy tales, like a little girl who had never had the opportunity to grow up.

Necklaces, studded with gemstones, seemed to tumble off the edge of the dresser. Lucas glanced down at the trail of them on the floor and frowned. A fragile glass pendant was crushed into the carpet. He leaned down and brushed his fingers over the broken fragments. His jaw firmed. "Tori wouldn't have done this." He glanced around the rest of the room, wondering what else was out of place.

Chapter 20. The Secrets Of Friends

A pair of old jeans were slumped on the floor at the foot of the bed as if they had been slung over the end and were knocked to the ground. He stooped to pick them up. In one pocket, he felt a crinkle of paper. He dug into the pocket and drew out a sliver of old photo-booth-style photographs.

"Michael," he said. Lucas felt his knees weaken and let a sigh brush through his lips as he settled on the edge of the bed. He gripped the photograph in a tightening fist and stared down at the picture of Tori's mother in the arms of a dark-winged angel. His wings were hidden, of course, but Lucas recognised the anger in Michael's eyes, the stern turn of his jaw. He had always been aloof, even before all this, and yet, in this picture he seemed, almost happy. Protective, alert to danger, but in an awe of tender love. Lucas felt his own gut tingle, thinking of Tori. He clamped down on the sensation and returned his focus to the photograph. The woman was a bloom of health, ballooned with pregnancy. She had the same colouring as Tori, down to the depths of dark brown in her eyes but there was no taint of haunting memories. Pure joy. She looked up at Michael as if she could see the world in him, see the stars and the sky. "Maybe she could, if he'd told her his secret, maybe she saw that magnificence in him."

Lucas sighed and tucked the photograph back into the pocket of Tori's jeans. Pieces were coming together. Small, insubstantial pieces. Pieces that asked more questions than they answered.

A clatter from the door downstairs startled him. He dropped his hands, and rose to his feet. A flush of guilt stained his cheeks. He grimaced, shaking his head and feeling ridiculous. He ran a hand through his hair then stalked out of the room.

Taking the stairs two at a time he moved to answer the door. He drew it wide. An elderly woman stood on the threshold with her hand shielding her eyes as if she had been trying to peer through the peep hole. "Oh," she said, dropping her hand and taking a step back. "I'm sorry, the porch light was on so I thought Tori was here. Is she here?"

Lucas recognised the woman from Anna's funeral. She had spent time talking with Tori after everyone else had left. "She's not here," he said. "Can I help you?"

"I don't know, who are you?"

"I'm Detective Caelum," he replied, standing in the frame of the door.

"Oh," Jess said, her voice hitched up a few notches. "Is Tori a'right?"

I hope so, he thought, but did not answer her question. Instead, with all the authority of an officer of the law he asked, "What is your name?"

"Oh," she hesitated. Lucas lifted his eyebrows and straightened his back. He loomed over her, using his stature to dwarf the woman as he frowned down at her. She shuffled her feet, blinked, and then replied, "I'm Jess, Jessabelle MacFarlan. I'm, I mean I was, Anna's friend."

"I see, and is there a reason you came?"

He watched her pupils retract and her eyes darken as she calculated her answer. *She's working her way up to telling half a lie. She's hiding something.* "I," she began, "Well, it's just that Anna was my dearest friend. I've been so lost since she died. I once gave her a pendant and I wanted to know if Tori had found it. I always treasured the piece and I'd like to keep it in memory of Anna."

"A pendant?"

"Yes, just a little keepsake. She used to wear it on a gold chain for special occasions. I'm sure she must have left it here and I had hoped Tori might have found it as she sorted through Anna's things." Lucas could hear the drip of fabrication in the woman's lies.

"She has not mentioned a pendant, but I'll pass on your request when I next meet with her." She nodded, but remained standing on the threshold. "Is there anything else I can help you with?" Lucas asked. She glanced over his shoulder, into the darkness of the entryway.

"It's just, well, no, I suppose not," she said, shuffling her feet.

"Good day to you, Ms MacFarlan." She seemed to hesitate again and then nodded before turning away. She scurried across the yard to her car. Lucas watched her go with a mixture of amusement, curiosity, and anger. She knew something, but he couldn't do anything to find out more.

He closed the front door and clicked the lock, then leaned back against it. With a deep breath he closed his eyes and searched within himself for that part that tied him to Tori. The sense came in a strong wave of emotions, the darkest of which was anger. He exhaled a sharp breath, hating the wave of helplessness that washed over him. "At least she's safe," he muttered, opening his eyes. He pushed himself away from the door then crossed the room and headed back upstairs in search of a pendant.

"I be need'n to talk to the High Priestess," a voice shouted from beyond the door. Jess burst in. She stopped as she saw Tori. A gasp escaped her lips with the name, "Tori!"

Chapter 20. The Secrets Of Friends

"Jess? What are you doing here?"

"Indeed, Jessabelle," the High Priestess drawled. "What, *are* you doing here?"

"Apologies, High Priestess. I was concerned. I'd gone to Anna's house today, see, to acquire that thing you wanted. Tori wasn't there. I thought it was best to come to you to ask after her. I knew you had been ensuring her safety after her Grandmother died."

She knew? Tori felt the blink of betrayal in the tears in her eyes. "You knew?" she whispered. Jess looked up at her.

"They only be wanting to keep you safe, Tori. You've no idea how important you are to them."

"You knew?" Tori whispered again. "How could you know this? How could you not tell me?"

Jess shook her head. "There is so much you don't understand."

"There is so much she has no need to understand, Jessabelle. I say again, what are you doing here?"

"High Priestess, I truly did only wish to enquire after Tori's safety. I assure you. Although, I do have other news that may interest you."

"Oh? Then do stop wasting my time with your anxieties and inform me of something consequential."

Jess shuddered, shifting her feet. "Yes, High Priestess. It's just that, there's a guy, a cop, he's been nosing around. Tori went to him, but then he was at Anna's house again today."

"And this should interest me why?"

Jess glanced at Tori and tilted her head as she looked back at the High Priestess. She swallowed. "Only, you know that thing you sent me to find. I didn't find it. And now he's there."

"What is he doing there?"

"I don't know?"

"Why are you here if you know nothing, Jessabelle. You are of no use to me if you cannot find out the simplest things. You tell me a police officer is in Anna's house, probably rifling through her things and you have no idea why or what he might be looking for?" Marlena's anger was rising, Tori felt the quiver of protectiveness the serpent riled within her.

"The officer?" Tori heard her voice, before the question had formed in her own mind. Torque laced around her thoughts. She tilted her head.

"I," Jess glanced at her, a dart of surprise crossed her face and she swallowed again then glanced at the High Priestess. The other woman's back was stiff and her lips were pressed in a tight grimace. "I," Jess said again.

Chapter 20. The Secrets Of Friends

"I said, the officer, who was he?" Torque's voice rang out with command. She rose up above Jessabelle and glared down at the small woman.

"Tori?" Jess' voice was a soft croak of anxious hesitation.

The High Priestess spoke, "I believe we are speaking to the serpent who calls herself, Torque."

Torque turned, a slinking movement that swung Tori's human head and chest toward the High Priestess. She inclined her head. "Indeed. Now, human, answer my question."

Jess' mouth dropped open and her jaw flexed several times before she answered. "I, he, he said he was, ah, some detective."

"A detective. Is that all you know?"

"He was tall, blonde, very um, policeman like."

"Enough of this, what relevance has the officer on matters?" Marlena said, she waved a hand. "He is certainly nothing of our concern."

"But, Marlena," Jess said.

Marlena glared down at her. "You will not address me in such an impudent manner, Sister."

Jess bowed, and stammered, "I apologise, I did not mean any disrespect, High Priestess. It's just, the officer, the policeman, he,"

"Spit it out, Sister, he is what?"

"He," she fell silent again, glancing at Tori. Tori gazed at her from serpent eyes and Jess shuddered. Torque's amusement bubbled through her. "He might be a problem for the Nagaran. His interest seems to go above a simple home invasion."

"We have people in place to ensure the police have limited involvement in our affairs. Now, if you are both quite finished, I would like to return to my private contemplation. You are intruding in my quarters."

"My apologies, High Priestess, I did not mean, I mean, I did have to speak to you urgently," Jess said.

"Leave, now," Marlena said. She glared at Jess and pointed at the door. "And send Jackson back in here."

As she opened the door, Jess whispered to the man behind it and a moment later Jackson strode past her.

"The Charmer wishes to return to her room now, Jackson."

He inclined his head. "Of course, High Priestess. I apologise for the intrusion."

Marlena shook her head and turned away. "Take the serving girl with you. She may quarter with the kitchen staff."

Chapter 20. The Secrets Of Friends

Tempany lowered her gaze to the floor and stayed close to Tori. The serpent riled within Tori, feeling the warmth of the angel against her back. She purred within and Tori felt the brush of it through her mind as it spoke. "Tempany is not to leave my side."

Marlena raised an eyebrow and looked more closely at Tempany. "But surely you do not mean to sleep in the same bed?"

"Indeed not," Torque said, "we will have a suite." The serpent flicked its tail as it circled Marlena. It glanced around the collection of rooms that made up the High Priestess's quarters. They were far grander than the single bedroom Tori had been given. "We are certain you have more than the one, but will make do with this if choices are limited."

Tori watched as Marlena's jaw clenched. Sparks of anger glittered in her eyes and she forced her lips to relax as she replied, "We have other suites, if you insist." She turned to the crossbowman and inclined her head. "Jackson, take our guests to the Asp Suite downstairs?"

Jackson reached to take Tori by the arm. Torque turned a glare on him. "Do not touch me, human. I go where I please and am not sent to my room like a child. If you insist upon it you may accompany me, but do not think you, or your mistress, can demand anything of me."

The Flight Of Torque

Jackson swallowed and took a step back. He raised his arms and pressed his back against the door. Torque glided past him.

She turned in the doorway and cast Marlena a withering glare. "I will expect those records in my chambers before nightfall," she said. Without waiting for a response the serpent turned again and slithered out of the door. Tempany stayed close behind her. Tori felt a dry amusement as Torque's thoughts slunk back with a trailing whisper through her mind and her body became her own again. *Where are we going?* She asked the serpent.

Anywhere but where that woman wishes us to be.

Tori chuckled, and wove her way through the musty halls.

The dim caverns in this part of the temple were lit along their length by red orb candles. The reek of incense was less smothering, but the smog of it increased as they turned through the maze of corridors. Each turn confused Tori and she started to wonder if they were making any progress at all. She was just about to ask when the corridor widened. Rows of chatting worshippers sat at tables eating the evening meal. Jess perched on the corner of the long seat closest to the entry. She looked unsure if she should sit or stand. In one hand she held a bowl and she held her spoon in the other. As Tori came into the room Jess clattered both onto the table. A murky green soup splattered onto the tabletop.

"Tori," she said, darting toward her across the room.

Torque seemed to wriggle inside her thoughts. Tori straightened her back and lifted her chin as she frowned at Jess. "You lied to me."

"Oh, Tori, dear. I didna lie, I just didna tell you the whole truth."

"I told you about the Nagaran, you didn't tell me you were one of them. How could you be one of them, Jess? How could you?"

"It's more complicated than you think, Tori," Jess said.

She looked like she was about to say more but Tempany reached forward brushing her fingers over Tori's arm. She glanced around the room. "We should find somewhere more private to speak of things." Her gaze lingered on the table where Crey and Zara sat, before she brought her gaze back to Tori's face.

Tori looked around too. Several sets of curious eyes watched them. When Tori caught individual cultists glances they flushed and returned to their meals. With a slight tilt of her chin, Tori gestured to Zara and Crey.

Crey nodded. Turning to Zara, he whispered something in her ear before he stood and crossed the room to Tori. He faced Jackson and addressed the other man directly. "Thank you, Jackson. I can see to the Charmer's needs now. You should return to your normal duties." Jackson glared at him but nodded and stormed out of the room. Crey turned to Tori with a smile. "Do you require anything, Charmer? Shall I fetch your meal?"

Tori, with a regal tilt to her head, said, "My friend and I wish to have somewhere private to speak."

Crey glanced at Jess, running his eye up and down the older woman. "Of course, Charmer," he said, not taking his eyes from Jess. "I will show you to a sitting room where you will not be disturbed." Crey led the way down several hallways and came to a door that led into a small room. A few chairs were scattered around a low coffee table. "Here you are. Would you like me to bring a meal to you?" His tone of deferment felt strange, but the sparkle in his eyes showed he was enjoying their game of their subterfuge.

Tori smiled at him and nodded her head. "Yes. Tempany and I have not eaten. Thank you." As Crey left the room he drew the door closed and Tori let her shoulders drop as she sat in one of the chairs. Tempany came to stand just behind her as Tori looked up at Jess. "We can talk here. Tell me the truth now, Jess. Please, I need to understand."

Jess folded her hands in her lap as she sat on the edge of the chair opposite Tori. She glanced at Tempany then leaned forward to whisper. "What about her?"

"I trust her completely. We may speak freely. Just tell me the truth, please Jess."

Jess flickered a glance at Tempany again. It was obvious her curiosity was piqued, but she returned her attention to Tori. "It's not so easy to be talking about, Tori."

"Start at the beginning. When did you become involved with the Nagaran? Why are you here?"

She glanced at Tempany one last time before sighing. Then said, "Oh, I come here a long while back. Back before you were born. Did Anna ever tell you that I was the one who delivered you? You were a beautiful baby, even then."

Tori swallowed and bit her lip, closing her eyes. She took a shaky breath, feeling it fill her lungs. "And my mother?"

Jess' eyes went wide. "Well," she stuttered, "I never wanted you to think she died, Tori. Rick, Anna, your mother, they all insisted it be that way. I'd ha' told ye the truth if they'd let me."

"You could have told me the truth."

She sighed. "By then t'was just another lie. We'd been doing it so long that I was wondering where the truth ended and the lies began."

"I don't understand."

"You see, I joined the Nagaran after meetin' your grandmother. Anna were a sweet sort, but she 'ad a bitter anger. Her daughter, your mother," she paused then shook her head, "Well there's no point goin' into details, lets say she went through an ordeal an' Anna always felt a failure for not protecting her. When the Royals were born, Charlene was torn between being their mother, and being afraid of the darkness within 'em. They were each selfish, tortured young'ens. It broke 'er 'eart that she couldn't change 'em."

Tori leaned forward in her chair. "She raised them?"

"I suppose you could say that. Their fathers held greater influence o'course, and they'd gone back to warrin' among 'emselves so you can imagine the tension. I think that's why she founded the Nagaran. Like an 'aven from the Four Fathers, from their conflicts."

"My mother founded the Nagaran?"

Chapter 20. The Secrets Of Friends

"Yes, well it all began with her. Then, as the boys grew they went out into the world and did unspeakable things. When the children began to be born she gathered those she could find. I suppose she wanted to protect 'em, or perhaps protect the rest of us from 'em. As infants the children of the Nagaran can be," she paused, "volatile. None of them transformed, o'course, but that dark nature was always there, under the surface."

"Do you think they heard it? Talking to them in their minds I mean?"

Jess shrugged. "It's possible, some of the children were very clearly mad in it all."

Tori felt the quiver of disquiet as the serpent moved through her mind and she flinched, pushing her emotions deep into the pit of her stomach. "And my mother?"

"She did as she could to tame their inclinations, but it is impossible to quell their anger an' lust. As more and more of the children left the Nagaran they gathered followers, people who worshipped them for their drive and prowess."

"You worshipped them?"

Jess blinked. "Me? O'course not. Anna and I were always here for Charlene. Anna couldn't leave 'er daughter, no matter what happened. We protected 'er secret, and kept 'er from falling into the darkness."

"The darkness?"

With a sigh, Jess looked up at her, her eyes full of sadness. "The serpent within, once truly awoken, it can inflict a person. Your mother, she, well, I guess you could say she fell into its thrall. As time passed she became more and more the serpent, an' less herself."

"What about me?"

"You may too, in time."

"No," Tori said, shaking her head, "I mean, when she had me. Did she love Rick?"

"Rick? Lord no. Rick was in love with her of course, but he could only hope to be her friend. Charlene had only ever had eyes for Michael."

Tori felt the quiver of tension from Tempany behind her and heard the woman's breath catch.

"Michael?" Tori asked.

Jess sighed. "Your father's name is Michael, Tori. He came for Charlene, maybe a year before you were born. Carved his way through the Four Fathers to get to her. Incredible, really, he 'ad such a righteous fury."

"Did he love her?"

"More than 'eaven and earth, I expect. To see them together, it was like light shone through 'em both. Her darkness lifted and she glowed around 'im. Then you were born." She paused, looking at Tori, her eyes full of pity.

"I was born, and she abandoned me."

"She never abandoned you, Tori," Jess said, shaking her head. "Don't ever think that. She did what she did to keep you safe. Rick, Anna, even me, we all did it to protect you."

"I don't understand."

"I don't be understandin' it either, but she were certain you were not safe with the Nagaran. Michael seemed like he'd been ripped apart when she became pregnant with you, like there was some dark secret over your birth, and she was never the same either. I think it broke 'er heart to let you go."

"Why did they? Didn't they want me?"

Jess leaned forward and touched Tori on the knee. "They wanted you, but, don't you see? You were a child of the Nagaran, just as the Four Fathers, and she didn't want you raised with the influence of the Nagaran in your life."

"Why didn't she just leave them? Why couldn't she unmake them?"

"The Nagaran have served a purpose here, Tori. They still gather together the children."

"They kill them. Crey and Zara told me what the High Priestess does to children of the Nagaran. They did it to me, only I didn't die. I became something else."

"The ceremony is just a fanatical way to ensure the children of the Nagaran cannot spread their darkness through the whole world."

"So, you kill them? You kill them all? It's not their fault they were born this way. It's not my fault."

"Of course not, but it has to be done, Tori. Don't you see?"

"And my mother was doing this? She was killing these children."

"I assure you, it breaks 'er heart to do it, but what other way is there? They rise up in the world, power-hungry, immoral, violent. Their thirst for the basest aspects o' life is unquenchable. The more children reach maturity the more generations of 'em will be born."

"There has to be a better way," Tori said, she rose to her feet and gestured with her hands. "You can't believe killing them all is the only solution."

"I," Jess stopped as a soft knock on the door interrupted them. Tempany crossed to the door and held it open as Crey strode into the room with a tray.

"I've brought you all something to eat," he said.

Chapter 20. The Secrets Of Friends

Tori's chest was heaving and the serpent roiled beneath the surface of her thoughts. She wondered why Torque had not intervened in the heated discussion she and Jess had been having. She glanced at Tempany. The angel's eyes were shadowed with concern and she looked distracted as Crey handed her a bowl of soup then turned to Tori.

Crey smiled, "I did not have the opportunity to finish my own meal. May I join you?"

Jess glanced at Tori and Tori could feel the wave of rejection that hummed from the old woman's skin. Tori lifted her chin and forced a smile to her lips, "Of course, Crey, you are welcome." Jess huffed and settled back against the chair, her eyes watched Crey with hawk-like vigilance. She snatched the bowl Crey handed her, almost spilling the soup in her lap as she drew away from him. He handed Tori another bowl from the tray before settling into a nearby chair.

"Oh, I almost forgot, Zara said she would come by. She wanted to check your wound." Crey tilted his head at Tori's chest as she sat down again.

She nodded. "Thank you."

They sat in silence for several minutes as they ate. Crey was the first to place his bowl on the table. "Forgive me," he said. "I feel I have intruded on your conversation."

Tori grimaced. "It was not a pleasant one. We were discussing moralistic judgements regarding the sacredness of a life."

Crey raised an eyebrow. "Indeed? Was it regarding any particular lives?"

"The children of the Nagaran."

Tori heard Jess whimper and the woman clattered her bowl down onto the table. "I'm sure this boy doesn't need to know our conversation, Tori. The Nagaran 'ave very determined perspectives o' such things."

"I'm interested in his perspective, Jess," Tori said and then turned back to Crey. "I understand the Nagaran feel the only way to deal with the children is to kill them?" Tori asked him. Jess gasped. Her spoon quivered in her hand as she placed it back into the bowl.

Crey glanced at her and then returned his gaze to Tori, "Well, some certainly think so."

"Do you feel there may be another option?"

Crey looked as if he were trying to judge the intent behind the question. Jess fretted with the hem of her robe and kept her eyes cast down. Crey tilted his head. "Well, I do hold very certain ideals about the sanctity of life. The children? They are harder to define because, from what I've read in the archives, they have no moral compass, they do not hold anything sacred."

Chapter 20. The Secrets Of Friends

Tori closed her eyes and took a breath before opening them again. "Perhaps then, they'd be equated to demons," she said. Jess gasped, lifting a hand to her mouth. "Is that why the Nagaran kill us, Jess? Do they think we are demons?"

"I never believed any of that, Tori," she said, rising to her feet. She gasped again and then glanced at Crey. "I mean, I," she stuttered as if trying to retract the vehement statement. "Of course, I respect the choices of the Sacred Mother in her wisdom." She bowed her head as she sat back down in her seat.

"Of course," Crey said. He glanced at Tori. Tori felt the questions in his gaze. She shrugged her shoulders. A timid knock on the door interrupted them. Crey rose to answer it and Zara came inside.

"Zara," Tori said with a smile.

"I'm sorry to intrude on you. I promise it won't take more than a moment."

"Not at all, I appreciate your coming to check on my wellbeing."

"Of course, you're very important to us, Charmer." She bowed her head and then knelt on the floor beside Tori's chair. "May we have some privacy?" She turned to look at each of the others in turn. Tempany stood, her bowl and spoon forgotten in her fingers as she gazed down at Zara.

Crey's voice broke the tension that seemed to hum in the room. "I promise not to look," he said, his voice laced with dry humour. "I'd much rather discuss this further with, Tori's friend."

"I'm sure Jess will oblige, won't you Jess?"

Jess swallowed and she turned away from them. "I'm sure there is nothing more to say on the matter."

"Quite the contrary," Crey said. His voice held traces of honeyed humour. "This sort of debate rages for centuries. Surely you're not against considering the philosophical implications of such things."

Tori hid her smile behind a gasp as Zara touched her chest with chilled fingers. Tempany's gaze snapped to Tori's face and she took a step forward before relaxing. Zara's lips parted and she lifted her fingers away. "I'm sorry, I didn't mean to hurt you."

"It's nothing, really. I'm mostly healed."

Zara examined the wound, running her fingers over the soft skin surrounding the faint pink line. "It's remarkable."

"So, Jess," Crey drawled. He leaned back in the seat and steepled his fingers in front of him, brushing the tips of his fingers against his lips. "Do you believe the children of the Nagaran are demons worth only a brutal death?"

Jess gasped. "Of course not." She glanced at Tori. "Tori were always the sweetest child. I 'ave to believe that, given the right circumstances, the right upbringing, the young'ns could grow to become as 'onourable as she is."

"You said my mother tried to raise them."

"It is difficult to know what a child needs to become the person they are meant to be."

"So, having failed to raise them into kind and compassionate people, the only recourse for them is a hasty death?" Crey asked.

"You can't mean that," Zara said, turning to face him. Anger burned in her eyes.

Crey lifted his hands in a defensive gesture. "I was merely putting forward the question. I'd like to know what Jess believes."

"It is unspeakable to even consider such questions."

"But the Nagaran do consider these questions. Do you think they shouldn't?"

Jess narrowed her gaze, watching them with calculating eyes. Tori could see the way she tried to process the response she thought Crey wanted to hear. "I think we are not Gods, and should not stand in judgement as such."

"I agree."

"It really does not matter that we agree. There is nothing we can do about it. We follow the will of the Sacred Mother. This is the way the Nagaran have been, it is the way we are," Jess said.

"It was the way we were. Things can change," Crey said. He rose to his feet, and placed a hand on Zara's shoulder. "We should go."

Zara ran a finger around the edges of tape holding the fresh bandage over Tori's wound then nodded. As she gathered up the supplies she had brought with her, she said, "You're healing very well, Tori." She rested a hand on Tori's shoulder a moment. "I'll see you again soon."

Tempany moved to open the door as they were leaving. She lingered in the doorway a moment before closing the door. With a sigh she returned to the table and gathered up the finished bowls and dirty cutlery. She arrayed them on the tray and although she took deliberate care to appear nonchalant, Tori could sense the tension in her.

Ignoring her, Jess looked across at Tori with a frown. "You keep very dangerous friends, Tori."

Chapter Twenty-One
Intersecting Bloodlines

"A pendant," Lucas muttered to himself. He glanced around one of the other upstairs bedrooms. The bed had been made up with fresh sheets, but there were pale patches of wall where picture frames had been hung and empty places on the bedside table and dresser. "Where would Anna hide a pendant?" He drew out the small draws niched into the vanity and searched within them. Delicate handkerchiefs, silk scarves, and a collection of lace scattered to the floor. Lucas frowned, running his fingers across the draws. "Where?"

The window clattered open and he whipped around. "I hardly think a woman like Anna would leave something so precious lying amongst her under garments."

"Uriel?"

"You were expecting someone else? Maybe your precious charge? Oh, I heard, you let her be turned into a murderous snake."

Lucas gritted his teeth, then said with biting anger, "That's not what happened."

Uriel shrugged and stepped from the window ledge into the room. He ruffled his feathers and tucked them behind him. "It matters not. You are searching for something. I will help you."

"I don't need your help, Uriel. Did Tempany send you?"

"Tempany no longer sends me anywhere."

"So it's true, you've gone rogue?"

"I have learned we must all make our own paths."

"What does that mean?"

"It means that we were given a will of our own and we should use it."

A wave of disease ran through him as Lucas considered what Uriel had said. *What would happen if the angels stopped following the will of the Heavens and forged their own place among the people of Earth?* He shook his head, then said, "You have a duty."

Uriel's eyes flashed with the reflected light from the window as he snapped his head around. "I do not dishonour my calling, Lucas."

"Then why are you here?"

"I have my own charge to consider."

"Your charge?"

"It is none of your concern. For the moment our duties coincide and so I am willing to help you to our mutual benefit. That is all you need to know." He turned away, running his gaze over the room. Lucas followed his line of sight. The walls were papered with a pale apricot decal that ran the length of three walls. The fourth was a feature wall of earthy red brick, twin burgundy doors were closed within it, their door handles a sheen of decorative brass. "Where would the mother of a serpent hide a pendant that holds value above all things for her family?"

"I don't understand," Lucas said as he began searching through the other draws of the vanity. "What is it we're looking for?" Uriel stomped his feet on the floor. Lucas heard the resonance through the carpet into the wood beneath. The other angel bent down and tugged at the edges, ripping the carpet up from the floor. "What are you doing, Uriel?"

"You don't expect her to have hidden it in plain sight, do you? As much as Anna had aged prior her death, she was as still as cunning and sly as she'd been in her youth."

"You knew Anna?"

"In sort. Our paths crossed. Hers at odds with mine as is usually the case with the Nagaran," he said, then spat, "Vermin." The floorboards under the carpet were stained with splatters of glue and paint. Uriel grimaced. "Nothing," he muttered, then lifted his gaze to look around the room. "Perhaps?"

He strode to the twin doors and tugged on the brass handles. As they opened a tumble of papers fell to the floor and scattered, catching on the breeze through the window. Uriel batted them aside, kicking a trail through the pile that had landed at his feet. "What is it?" Lucas asked.

"What all strange dark cultists hide in their closets."

"An altar?"

"Well, no, this one does not seem to be a clandestine place of ritualistic worship, merely an archive of some kind."

"I hardly think that is normal, cultist behaviour." Lucas said. He stooped to pick up a piece of paper from the floor and scanned the page. "It's a birth certificate," he said.

Uriel grunted. "So, the mother of the Sacred Mother kept records of the children after all."

Lucas ran his gaze over the sweeping pile of papers that trailed past the door and tumbled from the strange row of shelves that streaked several feet back into the closet. "There must be thousands of them," he said, his voice dripping with quiet horror.

"Indeed. Serpents are prolific breeders."

"Are all the records here?"

"Those that can be known, I would suppose."

Chapter 21. Intersecting Bloodlines

"Even Tori's?"

Uriel looked at him. "Your charge? Hers might not be here. Her situation is, unique."

"What do you mean?" Lucas asked. Uriel grimaced. "Tell me Uriel. What do you know that I don't?"

"You know more than you think you do, Lucas. I'm sure by now you've concluded who Tori's father is?"

"Michael," Lucas said, nodding. "I understand that. Is that what makes her unique? She's the daughter of an angel?"

"It was Michael who saved Charlene. He hates himself sometimes, when the darkness overwhelms her and she's screaming in pain with the serpent ripping it's way through her skin. If he had let her die, none of this would have happened."

"So that's what makes Tori different? That's why she survived the ritual when all the other children of the Nagaran died?" Lucas wove through the boxes spread between the walls of the closet and started shuffling through one along the furthest wall.

Uriel came into the closet behind him. With a frown, he picked up a box from the upper shelf, and rummaged through it's contents, then tossed it out of the door onto the bedroom floor. "Our blood is a powerful heritage, Lucas. Why do you think there is a decree that forbids us mating with them?" Lucas swallowed. Uriel stopped, his hand in another box and looked across at Lucas. "You still have the power to choose."

Lucas shook his head. "I don't understand why Michael would betray his duty, his calling?"

Uriel lowered his head and looked at Lucas. "Do you not?"

"What we do is important, Uriel. It doesn't matter if you choose to walk your own path, you cannot deny that our cause is just. Why would he give that up? Why would he turn his back on his duty to protect people?"

"He did his duty, he honoured his charge, and his heart. That is a truer calling than any other we might pursue."

Behind one of the boxes Lucas saw the hard edges of a door in the wall. He drew the box aside, and tugged on the handle of the small wall safe. The handle stuck fast, locked. Lucas glanced behind him, Uriel was scattering the contents of another box, his back turned away. Lucas grunted as he applied a little more pressure and the handle cracked against the hinge. The little door gave way. He reached into the safe, his fingers fumbling over the contents as he watched Uriel. "You think what he did was noble?"

Chapter 21. Intersecting Bloodlines

Uriel shook his head and Lucas froze, his fingers brushing over cold metal. "I think he is a better man than I." Lucas swallowed, closing his fingers around the thick thread of chain. He drew his hand out, tilting his head to look down at the gold coiling around his fingers. The pendant that dangled from the necklace was an intricately carved serpent coiled around a vial of silver liquid laced with cloudy swirls of crimson. Lucas gasped, wrapping his fingers around it.

Uriel's head snapped up, his eyes narrowing. Lucas tucked his hand behind his thigh. "You think yourself a man then?" he asked, but inside he cringed, knowing that Uriel would not be fooled by the subterfuge.

"You found it then," Uriel said, moving to stand over Lucas. Lucas took a step back, feeling the cold wall behind him. "Lucas." Uriel glared down at him. "You have no idea what you are holding."

"Then tell me, Uriel. Why is everyone so determined to get their hands on this?"

Uriel clenched his jaw. He reached to snatch it out of Lucas's hand. Lucas jerked back. "Give it to me, Lucas. I swear," Uriel's voice held a gritty determination and he lunged at Lucas. Lucas darted out from under his arm and stepped back toward the door. He stumbled on a pile of papers and flailed his arm. The chain of the pendant swung from his fingers.

"For our mutual benefit. You said that, Uriel. Is it only for your benefit that we've worked together on this?"

"You have no need of that vial. You do not know its purpose. I told you, I am here for my charge just as you are here for yours. There are answers here, you've found them. The pendant holds the answers I have been seeking. That is why I came."

Lucas lifted his chin. "Then tell me what it is."

Uriel lunged at him again and Lucas spun away. He wrapped the chain around his knuckles and clutched the pendant in his hand. Uriel flinched, reaching a hand out, "Be careful," he said.

"Like you said, I've no idea what it is, what it does. I don't need it. So if I smash it then what do I care?" Lucas said. His voice rang with a bravado at odds with the frantic anxiety that ran through him. What on earth could drive even an angel to desperation over so tiny a thing?

Uriel swallowed, pacing around Lucas like a cat stalking prey. "You do not wish to get in my way, Lucas. I am sworn to protect my charge and I do not hold to the creeds of our people any longer. I will not hesitate to kill you."

Chapter 21. Intersecting Bloodlines

The truth of Uriel's words gutted him. "You're betraying all we are, Uriel."

"I'm doing what I must." He lunged, tackling Lucas to the floor. Lucas swung, trying to push Uriel from his chest. Uriel growled, cracking his elbow across Lucas's face. Lucas's head snapped backwards, hitting the carpet with such force that he felt the floorboards beneath crack. His jaw ached but he shoved back, rolling Uriel to one side. His head spun as he loomed over him. Uriel gasped, his wings crushing into the carpet. Lucas heard the cracking splinter of fragile bones breaking. "Lucas," Uriel groaned.

Lucas held him down. "Why are you doing this, Uriel?" Uriel grunted and twisted his body to shift the weight off his back. He gripped Lucas's shoulder, his arm crossing Lucas's chest and shoved hard launching Lucas aside. Lucas fell back, slamming against the wall. He felt the air rush out of his lungs. Pain lanced through his ribs. "Damn it," he muttered, groaning as he tried to stand.

Uriel pushed himself up from the floor. One wing dangled in a limp flutter of feathers from his back, the other flapped and he wobbled on his feet. He stumbled. Then, throwing himself against Lucas, he rammed his elbow into Lucas's stomach and drove his head up under Lucas's chin. Lucas felt his jaw crack and the edges of unconsciousness began to sweep over him. He blinked, sucking a breath deep into his lungs. He clung to the chain as hard as he clung to the blurred edges of his vision. Uriel slammed into him again and crushed the breath from Lucas's lungs. "Damn you, Lucas."

The pendant dropped from Lucas's fingers and his legs collapsed beneath him. He reached for the chain, but Uriel was there before him. Uriel slammed his shoulder into Lucas again, pinning him to the wall. He leaned against Lucas and groaned as he reached down and grasped the pendant in his fingers. He shoved himself up from the floor, holding himself upright with a hand against the wall. Lucas lay in a heap at his feet. "Uriel, why?" Lucas whispered.

"I have no choice, Lucas," he said, then turned away. He ducked through the window again, leaping from the ledge to the ground below.

"But," Lucas whispered, his voice trailing away. As unconsciousness stole over him his scattering thoughts whispered, *you make your own path.*

Tori smiled. "You disapprove of my friends?"

"You should not be talking to him, Tori," Jess said. "You've no idea who he is."

"He is Crey de Luca Vento, keeper of accounts for the Nagaran."

Jess' eyes narrowed and she tilted her head. "That is what he told you?"

"Isn't that the truth?"

"Perhaps not the whole truth. Did he tell you about his family?"

"What do you mean?" Tori asked. She felt Torque stir within her, the serpent's curiosity spiked.

Jess sighed. "It really isn't my place to be tellin' you. It's just that, you seem to be under the impression you can trust 'im, that he truly means to be you're friend. His position here is precarious and you should not associate with him."

"Why not?"

"It is difficult, Tori. You see, his parents were not Nagaran. He came to us after. Anyone who comes to the Nagaran, anyone not brought here by blood, hold a fanatical view about what the Nagaran should be. They," she paused, looking up at Tori, "They are not necessarily in a balanced place within themselves."

Tori raised an eyebrow. "You think Crey is unhinged?" Torque bubbled with a strange, swirl of chuckling humour and Tori struggled to keep the smile from her lips. She shared a glance with Tempany before returning her attention to Jess.

"His parents were murdered. That can be very damaging for a child."

"He was hardly a child when it happened, and he wasn't there to see it. Do you think I'm unhinged because I saw my father's murder?"

"It's not the same thing, Tori."

"I think it is. Crey seems to be doing just fine. He has a firm focus on the future he wants and is making a path through his life. I was trying to do that too. Trying to make a place for myself in the world even though I'd lost everyone."

Jess lifted her chin as she stood. "I see you are very set in your mind. But remember Tori, the Nagaran are your family. Crey has no Nagaran blood."

"Does Zara have Nagaran blood? Do you?"

"I," Jess paused, "It is not the same thing," she said again. "Zara's father is a significant figure here. He and Zara, their place is deserved, it has been earned. Their loyalty is unwavering."

"Despite her mother?" Tori felt the trickle of tension that wove through Tempany. The angel appeared to be focused on browsing the books on a nearby bookshelf and Tori wondered what the woman might have found that upset her.

Jess frowned, "We never met her mother."

"And you haven't wondered?"

"It is not our place to ask such things. We assumed she had passed away and that Josiah and Zara were alone in the world."

"Passed away?" Tori asked.

"Yes, Tori, why is that so difficult to imagine. I assumed that, like your father, she had joined the angels in heaven."

Tori laughed, the sound had a bitter undertone. The serpent within swirled in the dark humour. "Like my father?"

"I mean Rick, of course. The man you always knew as your father. I don't see what is so funny about it."

"No, I guess you wouldn't," Tori said, wiping the tears from her eyes. "I never even new him, not really, did I?"

Jess' eyes narrowed. "What do you mean?"

Tori shook her head. "Look," she said, leaning forward in her chair. "It doesn't matter, really. It's just, Jess, I trust them, Crey and Zara. I think we could both trust them. They could help us change things here."

Jess' voice rose several degrees and she answered, "They will never understand what we do here, Tori, how important this is. They will never understand your place amongst it all."

Swift anger rose within her and Tori stood, glaring down at Jess. "My place? I don't understand my place here. None of this should ever have happened. What happened with my mother, the children of the Nagaran, what they did to me? None of it should have happened." She felt Torque hovering on the edges of her mind, her thoughts woven with the serpent's coils of sparking fury. Tori took a deep breath, trying to calm the tension that throbbed through her. She felt a wave of soothing energy flow from Tempany as the angel came to stand behind her again. The woman's fingers were a warm balm on her shoulder. Tempany trailed her fingers against Tori's spine sending tingles of relaxing energy through her. Tori let that warmth sink into her soul, soothing the serpent within.

"You can't begin to know how important you are," Jess said.

Tori turned tear-filled eyes on her. "So important that my mother abandoned me in favour of raising an army of demons? What kind of family is that? At least Crey, Zara, they had parents who loved them, who wanted them."

Chapter 21. Intersecting Bloodlines

"They are not truly with us though, are they?" Jess asked, her eyes narrowed and she looked up at Tori, searching her face.

Tori glared back. "They want to make a positive change in this world. What is so wrong with that? It's what my mother, what my father should have done in the beginning." Tori spun away from Jess and strode across the room. Tempany followed close behind her.

When she reached the door she yanked on the handle, pulling it open, Jess called out, her voice a soft husk, "I have to believe it's not too late."

Tori turned around, holding the door between them. Tempany passed through it as Tori replied, "Then why aren't you making it right, Jess? Why aren't you fighting for the future we should have?" Jess stood, mouth open, as Tori stepped out of the door and slammed it behind her. As the clang of it reverberated down the hall, she drew a shaky breath and closed her eyes. A tear streaked down her cheek as she whispered, "I'm throwing away my family."

Tempany lifted a hand to Tori's cheek. "You're not alone in this, Tori. We'll figure it out, together."

Tori lowered her chin, letting Tempany's voice sooth the tension in her body. "Who were my parents, Tempany?" she asked, looking up into Tempany's sky blue eyes. "The mother I thought was dead my whole life is a deranged murderer. And my father?" Tori paused and ran a hand through her hair. "Who is he? I don't know what I am any more. I don't know who I am."

"You're the daughter of two remarkable people, Tori. Your mother is Serpenthrope and your father," she paused, letting her breath rush from her lungs. "Tori, your father is an angel."

Chapter Twenty-Two
Blood Traitors

"The essence of an Angel," Crey whispered, more to himself than to Tori, Tempany, or Zara as he paced down the corridor in front of them. He turned to face them, glancing at Tori, "I've heard of it before, once, as a child. My father had a book that talked of the guardian spirits, those who watched over humans on Earth, guiding and protecting them in times of great peril. In the story, a great warrior fought in a battle. He was guided by the virtue of a guardian angel. When he was mortally wounded and should have died, the angel sacrificed his wings, his essence, and ultimately his immortality, to heal his charge."

"So you think Angel's blood protects me against the Serpent?" Tori asked, turning to Tempany.

"I don't know, Tori," she replied. "It's difficult to understand how this works. Charlene, your mother, she was not born of an angel and yet she survived."

"She had Michael," Zara said. "Don't you see? Your mother had Michael, Tori. When he found her dying he would have done anything to save her. He must have done."

"But in the story, to save his charge the angel had to sacrifice his wings," Tori said.

Crey inclined his head as he ducked under a low beam that supported the rock ceiling above them. "Yes, that is what the story says."

"It has always been unclear to us how the sacrifice works," Tempany said. "There are many deeds that can lead to an angel becoming fallen, wingless, but choosing to give up one's wings to save a charge, it is only in our oldest mythologies that such stories exist."

"But Michael didn't lose his wings," Tori said.

"Perhaps he should have," Crey replied, "perhaps he would have if they'd discovered his secret."

"Maybe he did," Zara said. Crey and Tori looked at her. "I mean, it's been so long since anyone saw him. Maybe, when he saved her, maybe he did lose his wings."

The four fell silent. Tori felt the serpent's agitated caress. *Is it possible? Did Michael give up his wings for my mother?* She could not stop the wave of her thoughts as they turned to Lucas. Torque called his image up behind her eyelids, but Tori pushed back the thoughts. She did not want to consider the similarities between the two angels, torn apart by emotions they had no power to control. "Maybe that's why he never came back." The silence up and down the corridor seemed to throw her words back at her. A tingle of apprehension crept over her skin. Tori glanced behind her. "This doesn't feel right," she whispered.

Crey paused, he lifted a finger to his lips and the women fell silent, listening to the eerie quiet of the empty corridors. He shook his head. "It is just your nerves. It can be unpleasant to return to a place you would rather avoid."

Zara shook her head. Tori could feel the air move against her skin and shivered. "It's more than that, Crey," Zara whispered.

Tempany took a defensive stance and glanced down the corridor in both directions. "I feel it too. We should go back."

Crey turned to look at her. Tori watched him. His eyes filled with concern. A trace of fear flickered through him. She felt the faint wash of it roll off him and felt Torque quiver inside her, swishing its tail back and fourth in her thoughts. "Come on," Crey said, gripping Zara's hand in his own, he squeezed her fingers and pulled her forward. They crossed through a dark room toward a glowing ember of light that flickered from the hall beyond.

As they stepped into the light, Tori froze and spun around at the sound of a hard footfall just behind her. Thick fingers gripped her shoulder. "Now," a thick voice drawled, "Ya wouldn't be tryin' to run away again would ya, Charmer?"

"Let her go, Orton," Crey demanded. He pushed Zara behind him and stepped beside Tori then flinched as a short dagger was pressed into the groove of his back. Tori winced, seeing the tip of the dagger dig into his flesh. He grimaced, his head twisting to look at his assailer. "Jackson."

"I don't recommend moving, Crey. This blade is so close to your spine that one false step could see you unable to ever walk again."

"What is the meaning of this?" Zara asked, her voice echoed off the walls with a haughty tone and Tori blinked in surprise. "I demand you let them go at once."

"Now, why would we want to do that, Sister? What we have here is a trio of blood traitors. The High Priestess was very clear about her insistence that they be brought before her," Jackson drawled, he dug the blade another few millimetres into Crey's back.

Crey swallowed. "Zara, stay out of this."

"But she ain't not got no choice, has she?" Zara gasped as Carny's hands gripped her wrists and dragged them behind her. "You know Zara, I always did take a fancy to you. Maybe we ought to linger a while 'afor I take you to the High Priestess. We could, you know," he leered at her and she kicked back at him.

"In your dreams, Carny. Get your hands off me."

He grunted as her foot connected with his shin. He grappled with her, pulling her off balance and she gasped. He chuckled. "Always did like 'em a bit feisty. It ain't not no fun if they lay there and take it."

"Remove your hands from the girl, right now," Tempany said. She moved to stand in front of Carny.

Carny laughed. "Yeah, sprite of a woman like you? You got nothing."

Crey spun out of Jackson's grasp and swung his fist against Jackson's jaw. He lunged at Carny, shoving him into the wall. His fingers gripped around Carny's neck. "If you touch her, I swear, I will kill you." Carny's face turned ashen, his eyes wide with fear. He tried to swallow, his throat convulsing under Crey's fingers.

"Crey," Zara whispered, tugging on his arm. Crey's lips twitched, anger dark in his eyes, but he let his fingers fall away and instead wrapped his arms around Zara. He glared down at the other man. Zara leaned into the curve of his arm and they backed away.

Jackson grunted, rubbing his chin. "Lucky shot, Crey. You might as well give in gracefully. We've got orders, and you're not getting out of this without shackles around your wrists and ankles. The only question is how many bruises you'll be wearing with them."

"Yeah, ya ain't not going no place 'less we be saying so."

"Right on, Carny," Orton said. Tori struggled against his grip as his fingers tightened around her arms.

Carny lifted his chin as he stalked toward them. "See, Orton's got little missy Charmer so it ain't no use fight'n."

Tori glared at him, her breath rose and fell in gasps as she felt the serpent rising up within her. She struggled against Orton's grip and tried to pull away from him. With a sharp jerk she felt her body rock forward, yanking out of his grasp. She almost stumbled, but felt Torque take control of her limbs as her body drew up to tower above him. "What," she said, the snarling voice of Torque hissing between her lips, "is the meaning of this?"

"I," Orton began. He cowered back, then glanced up at Jackson. "Jackson?"

"Take her in hand, Ort."

"But," he began, glancing up at Tori. His voice shook with an uneasy tremor. "She's," he paused.

Tori swung, feeling the serpent shiver through her limbs as its tail whipped out from behind her. She leaned forward, looming over Orton. She tilted her head and peered down at him. "We are what?" she drawled.

The crack of heels on the stone echoed against the stone walls. Torque turned, in one fluid motion, to face the new threat. Marlena stood at the end of the corridor. Her chin lifted and she glared at Tori. Their eyes met, Marlena's dark with fury and Tori's mirroring the flame of her anger. Marlena's voice rang down the hall, "You, are nothing more than a child who never had a mother to show you how to be a woman."

Tori felt the slap of her words and was glad for the wall Torque had put between her mind and the biting acid of Marlena's statement. The serpent rumbled, low in her throat. "You would be well to mind your tongue, human," she spat. "I see you, I know what you are, burning for the loving affection and acceptance of anyone. You cower in the corner of your thoughts because you know nobody can stand you."

Marlena flinched, a flicker of pain darting through her eyes. She lowered her voice, "Bitch! You are under arrest for conspiring against the Nagaran. You are a blood traitor. Seize them!"

Jackson slapped his hand against his fist as he moved toward Crey. "Just give me a reason."

Crey put an arm across Zara and swung with the other. Jackson stepped out of the way and swung back, his fist cracking against Crey's jaw. The crunch of bone bounced off the walls and Zara gasped, reaching frantic hands toward Crey. "Don't," she whispered. Tempany stepped forward to draw her back, but Jackson grabbed Zara's arm and pulled her toward him. He wrapping the fingers of one hand around her throat as he backed away from Tempany and Crey. Zara swallowed, her eyes wide.

Carny chuckled. Rushing forward he rammed his shoulder into Crey's stomach, slamming him back against the wall. He gripped Crey's shoulder, punching him in the gut again and Crey doubled over. Crey yanked away from him and Carny stumbled before lifting a dagger to Crey's throat. Zara gasped again. "Crey, please."

"Yeah, you ain't not better try nothing. Even your woman knows that."

"Leave her alone," Crey cried out as Jackson pushed Zara against the wall. "Zara!"

"Crey?" Zara called back. She turned her head, her eyes wide with fright.

Torque slithered forward and Jackson stepped backward, dragging Zara with him. He never took his eyes from the serpent. She glared at him as he said, "Stay away. I swear, I will slit her down the middle if you come near me." He held a wicked serrated dagger against Zara's hips. Zara gasped, as he yanked her back against his chest. Torque hissed. Anger burned in her slitted eyes as she slithered forward. "Don't," he said. Zara whimpered as a trickle of blood welled against the soft pale folds of her robe.

"No!" Tempany cried out in alarm her arm instinctively reached out to Zara.

Tori's head tilted and the serpent's tongue flickered from between her lips. "Unhand her, human."

The High Priestess, stepped between them, glaring at Tori. "Not even twenty-four hours after we condescend to give you accommodations, you have betrayed out trust. I will take your frail corpse before the Sacred Mother and she will be pleased with me, for I will have dealt with the violent infection you have brought amongst our people."

"Infection?"

Marlena sneered. "You understand perfectly. Before you, we never had any dissension among our people and yet, immediately after you come to us we have two drawn into your fallacy. You brought this third traitor amongst us from outside our very walls. What did you say with your charming tongue to temp them away from the words and the honour of the Sacred Mother?"

"We've worked against you for months!" Zara shouted.

Crey struggled against Carny's grip. He winced as the blade nicked his neck. Carny pushed him harder against the wall. "Zara, there is no use saying these things to protect the Charmer," Crey said. He glanced up at the High Priestess. "High Priestess, please, we meant no harm. We felt we were doing the Sacred Mother's bidding. The Charmer assured us you had sanctioned her actions or we would never have aided her."

Zara glanced at him, a look of betrayed shock crossed her face. He gave an almost imperceptible shake of his head.

"I will not fall for your lies and nonsense Crey de Luca Vento. You are known to us now. More than you thought to reveal. Your father was Vincento Marque Sonto, Count de Luca Vento. I know you."

"My title, my heritage, does not bond me to my people, High Priestess. I serve our Sacred Mother faithfully."

"You are a de Luca Vento. None of the decedents of that line were ever loyal to the Sacred Mother. Your family betrayed your heritage a long time ago. You are nothing more than the bastard of a human woman, nothing more than the coupling of royalty with beast."

Chapter 22. Blood Traitors

Crey's anger grew. Tori could feel it pulsing from within him. "I am heir to my family's honour and I will not be spoken down to by one who bares no blood of the Mother what-so-ever. Who are you to condemn me for the circumstances of my birth?"

Marlena crossed to him in two swift strides and struck him across the cheek. The force rocked his jaw and he turned to spit a mouthful of blood on the floor beside him before raising his smouldering gaze back to her face. She turned to Orton and nodded her head. "Bring them," she said, then glanced back at Jackson. "And take Zara and the servant girl to my chambers."

Jackson nodded. He looked across at Tempany and gestured down the hall with the dagger. "You heard the High Priestess, her chambers, and if you try anything I swear I'll split Zara through the middle."

Helpless frustration chased across Tempany's features. She glanced at Tori.

Torque swayed and Tori could feel her thoughts whirl as the serpent calculated the distance across the floor to the High Priestess. The brief moment of concern that flickered through Tempany's eyes as her mouth fell open distracted her. Then a splitting pain ripped through the back of her head and she crumbled to the floor. Tori's human limbs slammed against the hard stone. Orton leaned over her, a cruel grin on his face, the splinters of the broken chair still in his fingers. "Not so tough now, eh?" He tossed the shards away, and curled his lips in a smug grin. Tori felt waves of dizzy sickness wash over her as she tried to sit up. She retched, her stomach heaving as Orton gripped her hair and pulled her up to her feet. "Come on, bitch."

Tori could hear Crey's raised shouts behind her, but could not make out his words. Darkness was closing in around her and, swirling in the mist of her fragmented thoughts, the serpent snarled and hissed.

Lucas lay in a heap on the soft carpet of Anna's bedroom floor. Pain, deep in his bones, and the deeper ache of betrayal and confusion, weighed him down. He felt the throbbing of his jaw and the tight knot of his muscles. With each breath his ribs and lungs burned a laser of agony through him. He drew another shallow breath before pushing himself upright. He leaned back against the wall, tilting his head to rest it on the soft yellowed wallpaper.

He tried to focus, fighting against the sensation of spinning that left him uneasy. He groaned as he dragged his legs forward. His limbs felt weak. That weakness wove deep into his core. His head ached and, as he battled with turgent waves of helplessness, he felt a heavy darkness threading through his thoughts. Behind his eyelids flashed the images of his fallen charges. One by one they battered through him, breaking his heart.

"I'm sorry," he whispered. He clenched his eyes tight, pressing the heels of his hands against his eyelids. "Please, I'm sorry."

The long strokes of the sun sunk behind the horizon as the minutes passed. Lucas drew shallow breaths. He let the bombardment of his failures smother him. With every tortured memory he felt weaker, smaller. "I can't," he whispered, seeing behind his eyes the image of Tori draped in white silk, strung down on the sacrificial alter with tears streaming from her eyes.

Tempany broke through the flogging screed of his memories. The image of her standing resolute, but frustrated passed through Lucas's mind. Her sharp words echoed through his thoughts, "So you won't even try?"

Lucas blinked his eyes open and dragged a thick, heavy breath deep into his lungs. He blinked again as his eyes adjusted to the darkness around him. A hint of moonlight pierced the windows. It cast shadows around the room. Lucas felt his heavy limbs. He flexed his fingers, then arms. Inch by inch, sensation returned, flooding around his aching body. The sting of returning awareness woke up his other senses and he reached, with instinctive expectancy, for his connection to Tori then grew frantic when the trail did not reach her.

In the misery of his own agony he'd lost touch with Tori and as that realisation dawned on him he thrust out a panicked thread of his senses, hunting for her. "No. Tori?" His voice croaked, dry and rough. "Dammit!"

He grimaced, closing his eyes as he traced a path of emotions through the air, down into the depths of the Nagaran temple. When he finally caught the edges of Tori's consciousness he felt a fuzzy obscurity to the connection. He drew in a deep breath, then winced as pain sliced across his chest again. He dropped the tendrils of their connection and his link with Tori faded.

"No," he groaned. He pushed himself up against the wall until his unsteady legs held him upright. "No," he said again. "I have to figure this out. She needs me."

The stone beneath her was cold. Tori felt the chill seeping into her bones. Her head spun, a crashing headache ringing through her ears. The thrumming hum of voices seemed like waves of fire over her thoughts. She groaned, trying to lift her heavy eyelids.

"Tori," Crey whispered beside her. "Tori?"

Chapter 22. Blood Traitors

"Crey." She gasped as flickering red-gold light of nearby braziers pricked her eyes. She groaned, blinking back the sharp stabs of brightness. "My head." She tried to lift a hand to touch her brow, then grimaced as a cord dragged around her wrists holding her arms down. "What happened?"

"They took Zara. I tried to stop them."

"They hit me with something."

"I thought you were dead. I cannot believe you are alive. The bastard, he hit you with a chair."

She closed her eyes, feeling his voice ricocheting thought her mind like the pounding thrum of a thundering freight train. "Where are we?" The hum of voices grew louder and Tori groaned. "I hate that sound. What more could they possibly want to do to me?" She opened her eyes again, peering out at the writhing crowd of worshippers. They scraped and bowed beneath her, their red robes an ocean of crimson.

"Nagaran, you see before you two blood traitors!" A voice called, dark with reverent fury.

Tori winced as she tilted her head to see the priest who stood facing the crowd. Then gritted her teeth as the crowd roared. "Blood traitors!"

"These blood traitors are the darkest betrayal. They come to us, take safe harbour within our walls. We welcome them into our fold, make them as one with us. Her, we gift with the sight of the serpent. How do they repay our kindness?"

The roar of the crowd crashed around her in an undecipherable torrent of bitterness. Crey's soft words were almost lost in the wave of sickness that washed through her. He leaned close, his lips bare inches from her ear, "That is Josiah. Zara's father."

"Her father? But I thought?"

She could hear the sigh in Crey's voice, "He's always been a reverent fanatic. Even before she was born."

"But," She fell silent as another wave of nausea hit her. The reek of incense burned through her nostrils as she sucked in a breath. Her head throbbed, thoughts wavering. The light blurred in front of her eyes.

"You see the blood traitors, they dared to plot against us. They rise from within our walls in search of our destruction. We must cut this taint from our flesh before it can infect the tender hearts of our people." The roar of ascension that rose from the crowd ripped through Tori's temples and she cried out with the pain. They seemed to become even more frenzied as she moaned and writhed on the dais before them. "The Sacred Mother has already deemed to make her suffer for her crimes against us. See her helpless in her human form, tangled in the agony of the serpent devouring her from within."

Tori felt the serpent's angry hiss through her thoughts. She could feel the way it pressed against her mind, trying to get past the throbbing wall of tension and pain within her. She thrashed, hissing, but Tori could not hear her words. She closed her eyes, feeling the darkness close to the surface of her thoughts. "Help me," she whispered, hearing her own voice on her lips.

The faintest trace of the serpent whispered through her mind, *I cannot.*

A tear trickled down her cheek and she curled into herself, giving herself over to the pain that flogged every inch of her with a tingling agony. "Please," she whispered. Inside her mind the serpent seemed to thrash even harder, fighting against the waves of darkness that swamped through her, dragging down her thoughts.

"The Sacred Mother decrees we punish those who seek to defy our way of life. What punishment should traitors of the blood deserve but death?" The crowd cheered, voices lost in a rolling wave of thunderous applause. Tori winced, curling even tighter into a ball. She wished she could drown out the noise as she struggled against the bindings that held her wrists and ankles.

"Let me go!" she shouted, but her voice whimpered from her throat, her breath torn from aching lungs.

The priest laughed, turning to face her he waved his hand at her then turned back to the crowd. "See her brought down by the suffering the Sacred Mother delivers. Their deaths will be a service to the Sacred Mother. We will see this temple cleansed of their hatred. Tomorrow, at dawn, we will awake a new sister, and at her feet lay the bodies of these blood traitors as tribute."

Chapter Twenty-Three
The Darkness Below

Tori fell hard against the stone floor as Orton threw her into the cell. The heavy iron door clanged closed, it's new hinges gleaming in the flickering torchlight. Crey grimaced, and leaned down to help her up. She shook her head. "Don't, I'm fine. Where's Zara?"

"She's not here. I heard the guards say the High Priestess was keeping her close." He slammed his hand against the back wall.

"Hey, shut it, both o' you," Orton said.

Crey turned and crossed the cell to stand before him. His lip curled as he spat back, "Filthy bastard.

Tori lifted herself on one arm. The dizziness lingered and her weakened muscles quivered. She leaned against the bars and glared at Orton. "You have no idea, do you? No idea what this is all about. You just do what you are told like a good little lap dog, like the stupid grunt you are."

"Watch yer mouth. You're the filthy one. Damned blood traitor. Ain't nothing either of you ever did to deserve the kindness the Nagaran've shown you. Should'a slit ya throats like we did his father."

Crey reached for Orton through the bars. He jerked Orton forward by the shirtfront and pulled him close so they stood faces inches apart. "What do you know about my father's death?"

Orton smiled, curling his thick fingers around Crey's. He loosened Crey's grip and yanked himself backward out of reach. "I know the High Priestess took it nice and slow. She made right sure they regretted betray'n us. Should've known ya was a blood traitor. Came from tainted stock, no matter the royal in yer veins."

Crey looked bewildered. His mouth opened as if he were trying to form the words for a response but he did not speak. Tori pushed herself up against the bars as she asked, "What are you talking about?"

"She don't even know, does she? Don't deserve to, neither. You'll both die traitor's deaths, right you will. First thing a'morrow." Orton turned away and stomped up the stairs, taking the light with him. Tori's breath heaved ragged in her lungs as she pushed herself to her knees. She bit her lip between her teeth and wiped the back of her hand against her tear-stained cheek.

"I'm sorry, Crey. This is all my fault."

"You are not to blame Tori."

She could hear him pacing up and down the length of the cell. "But I have ruined it, haven't I?" she asked.

"I've ruined us, you, the uprising." She drew a shaky breath. "Tomorrow they will kill us both."

He stopped and she could feel the warmth of him standing close to her, then his hand on her arm. "Tori, listen to me. This is not your fault. I, the Uprising, we have been reckless. More and more we undertook dangerous quests for our people. Various cultists had grown suspicious of our actions. We would have been discovered regardless."

"But if," she began.

"No, we do the right thing. The High Priestess must have known about the Uprising well before this. You heard Orton, they never trusted me. They knew all along who I was."

She shook her head. "How can you be sure of that?"

"Orton does not have the brains to lie creatively. Trust me, Tori. It is right."

Crey paced the room. Tori could feel the tension radiating from him as he walked the length of it and then the breadth. She heard his hands tracing the rock and the clatter of the iron bars as he shook them. "So, any ideas?" she asked as he came to a standstill against the back wall.

He huffed a sigh. "None, you?"

Tori shook her head then realised he could not see her. "No."

"Then we wait. The Uprising is not just one man. The others will come for us."

"What if they don't? What if they can't?"

She felt the anger vibrate from him as he started pacing the cell again. "They will come," he muttered. "I must believe."

Tori crawled across the cell, feeling the hard rock beneath her fingers. There were only a handful of feet between her and the back wall. When she reached it she ran her hand up the wall and drew herself upward. It felt like every muscle in her body was crying out. Inside, the pain dulled the serpent, but she could still feel it riling within, trying to escape. Waves of dizziness swept through her and her legs wobbled. She slid down the wall, her back scraping against the rock. Her breath hissed out of her and she drew her knees up to her chin, rocking forward.

"Tori?" Crey called in the darkness.

"I'm okay," she whispered back. The lie quivered through her as another wave of dizziness roiled in her stomach like a wash of nausea. She felt the touch of it at the back of her throat and bit back the dry retch with a breath of musty air. She shivered as the cold of the stone crept through her skin and felt the fuzziness in her mind dragging her down. Her eyelids were heavy and she leaned her head back against the wall.

"You must not sleep, Tori. You must be awake," Crey said. She could hear his footsteps. He paused beside her. She knew he must be leaning against the wall. "I know you are tired, but you must not sleep."

"I'm okay," she whispered again. He sighed, his breath rasping in the dark silence.

"They will come," he muttered again, spinning away from the wall. His footsteps echoed as he paced back and forth. Tori listened, feeling the steady beat of them through the floor.

I can't let myself believe him. I want to, but I can't. The thought chased through her mind and she felt the serpent hiss in response. The anger that thrummed through her felt like a burning wash of energy, but it faded as the cold of the stone swept through her again. She felt the chill dragging her down, felt herself growing sleepier with every moment. She wrapped her arms around her legs and tipped her head to her knees. *I can't fall asleep.* "Can't," she whispered. The darkness of her dreams were already filling the shadows behind her eyes.

She ran, screaming, through the woods. Her legs felt heavy beneath her. She felt every footfall, every twig snapping beneath her bare feet, every snag of vine that tried to drag her down. A stone cut deep into her foot and she gasped, twisting her ankle as she tried to stop herself from falling. Her breath burned through her lungs, but she pushed herself faster, and faster. Somehow, she knew she could not let herself be caught by them. She glanced backward at the emptiness behind her.

"But the snakes," she whispered. Then felt them coiling around her fingers, her legs. She shuddered, sweeping them away with her hands as more and more wrapped themselves around her. Their tongues flickered against her skin. "No!" she shouted, throwing them off. With every snake she tossed away two more took their place. "Get off me!"

"We are one," a dark voice hissed. She spun, searching for the voice in the shadows of the trees around her.

"Who said that?"

"I am you, you am I, we are one." The voice coiled around her like the snakes. The serpents trickled away from her hands, pooling at her feet before slithering away. Her breath heaved through her and she turned again, searching.

Chapter 23. The Darkness Below

"I don't know what you mean," she whispered.

She screamed as she felt her skin tearing away from her body. Then the darkness slammed against her mind. *Mine*, it hissed within her thoughts. She glanced down, her hands and feet were gone. Her body was a writhing mass of coiled scales.

No! she shouted, but heard the echo of her cry on the walls of her mind. She whimpered, feeling herself curl into a ball in the dark recesses of the deepest parts of herself. She felt herself recoil, seeking oblivion in the shadows. She clenched her eyes closed, bit her lip and pressed her hands over her ears. *No*, she sobbed. But she knew no one could hear her cries.

Then the darkness was gone. She was in the arms of her mother again, and beside her a dark shadow loomed over them. "Traitors," it cried, its face a camouflage of shadows.

"Who are you?" Tori cried, but instead of words she heard the cry of an infant.

"Hush, Tori," a woman's gentle voice crooned. She felt warm fingers caress her face. Dark eyes above her, full of tears. "She's so beautiful."

"She's a monster, she's a monster, she's a monster." The dark refrain echoed through the glowing red corridors. "She's a monster." Tori was running again.

He legs tangled in the white of flowing robes. Everywhere she turned the corridors stretched further and further ahead. A maze of long halls, broken only by the smouldering embers that burned in braziers between the lengths of rock.

She slammed against a wall, and turned searching for a way out. Soft voices broke the throbbing echo of reverent chanting. "She doesn't even know," Josiah said.

"I know," Marlena replied. A husky chuckle followed her words. "Don't you see? That's the best part. She doesn't even know what she is, or why. She doesn't even realise that her mother began all this. She doesn't even know that her blood runs with the poison of a thousand deaths. She doesn't even know."

Tori gasped, slamming her head back against the wall. Tears streamed down her face and she scrambled backward, but felt the cold press of wall behind her.

"Tori! Tori! Are you okay?" Crey's frantic voice seemed to echo in the darkness. Tori's hands reached out, searching the shadow.

"Crey?"

"I am here," he said. And he was. His fingers brushed her arms.

Chapter 23. The Darkness Below

"I'm so sorry, Crey. What I've become. What I always was. I should have," she said, her voice trailing off. She shook her head, tipping it forward against her arms, folded over her knees. She could not say the words, but they echoed in her mind. *I should have let them kill me. I should let them.*

"Stop. This is not your fault. This is their doing. They are at fault."

"Don't you see, Crey? This all began with my mother. My mother." She bit her lip and shook her head, trying to push back the tears.

"Tori, even as your mother, she did not raise you. She did not make you. This? The Nagaran? None of that is in you."

"Isn't it? Blood traitor, that's what they call me. As if my very blood is enough to make me one of them. I don't know, maybe it is enough. I'm a monster, don't you see?"

"I do not believe. Even as the serpent, you defend us. You are loyal, to yourself, to Zara and I. Monsters do not take sides."

"I don't know what she is. I can't control her. I don't know what she wants. She has her own mind, her own thoughts. They chase around inside me as if they're part of me. She changes who I am, just as much as she forces my body to change to her will."

"You are still you, Tori. Just as I am me. We've all made our own choices. I am here because I chose to be here."

"You chose to be in a cell, in the dark, with me?"

She heard the warmth of his chuckle. Somehow, even despite all that had happened, he could still laugh. "Well, I must admit I didn't quite plan things this way. But I do not regret the decisions that led us here, Tori. And I will not believe we are defeated. Not until I draw breath no longer. You will see. The others will come for us."

"What if they don't come in time?" she asked, her voice a bare whisper.

"Then we will find another way. We must."

"We only have until dawn."

"Then we have a few hours still. Rest, there is no more we can do in this moment."

Tori leaned her head back against the wall and let her eyelids close again. She lifted a hand to stroke a tear from the corner of her eye with her thumb and let her thoughts wander. Sleep refused to come, but as she reached out through the darkness she felt warmth and light. She felt Lucas and wondered if she did sleep, if she did dream.

Chapter 23. The Darkness Below

The church seemed eerie in the moonlight. The gargoyles on the high cornices leered down with violent, repugnant faces. Their glassy eyes reflected the silver moonlight, twinkling as if they sparkled with life. Lucas glanced around the building, hunting the darkness. Somehow, he could not help feeling eyes on him. He glanced up at the gargoyles again and then shook his head. He strode across the cobblestones and thrust the doors aside. They crashed against the wall, the chain binding them splintering into shreds like torn paper. The echo of the clanging metal on stone shook the walls. Splinters of glass trickled down from the windows. The pews stood in silent homage to the darkness within the church.

The light of the moon through the stain glassed window seemed to mock him. He glared up at the angel in the glass. The moonlight made it seem like he was glowing with power, a tower of strength with glorious wings unfurled. The infant in the angel's arms gazed up with admiration and awe. Trust burned bright in its eyes and the angel held the child tight as if unable to betray that trust. Lucas felt his gut roil, and he swallowed the lump of fear that tightened his throat. He drew a breath, feeling the tingle of cold air against his skin. He grimaced, then took a deeper breath, feeling the chill air soak his lungs. *Even now, I've never felt more like a man, a mere, powerless, human.*

He closed his eyes, drowning out the thoughts chasing through is mind. Behind his eyelids the stained glass apparition stung and he blinked the image away, hiding for a heartbeat in the darkness. He drew another breath, this time allowing it to swell his lungs, sink into his stomach, and thrum through his veins. He felt the air tingle through him, felt the rippling tug of Tori drawing him onward. He felt a weave of power flood through him. Light washed across his eyelids and he opened his eyes to see the soft glow of light radiating from his skin. His breath evened, chest rising and falling in rhythm with his beating heart.

He closed his eyes again, this time searching through the shadows, through the rock beneath his feet, through the echo of flickering fire from the braziers below him. He let his mind search through the layers of sleeping worshippers, sinking deeper and deeper into the earth, until he found it, the faintest trickle of her. He felt close to her, as if just sensing her like this made her breath brush against his skin; as if his heart beat in time with hers; as if their souls brushed up against each other.

"Tori?" He threw out his senses again and felt them tumbling through the layers of temple beneath his feet. He closed his eyes, tracing back along the thread of their connection until he found the source. "I'm coming, Tori" he whispered. The silence of the old church echoed back to him.

Chapter Twenty-Four
Break Out

"Lucas?" Tori whispered. She lifted her head. Her neck and arms felt stiff. She winced feeling the ache of her muscles as if every one had frozen in place. She stretched her back and winced again as pain throbbed through her like fire. Then her head snapped up. There it was again, the faintest whisper of warmth through her skin. "Do you hear that?"

"Mi scusi?" Crey asked.

Tori blinked. The darkness was absolute, but she could sense Crey nearby. Her skin tingled as if she could feel him through the distance between them. She blinked again. "Crey?"

"It is me Tori, we are still here."

"I know, I mean, don't you hear him?"

Silence fell around them again and lingered. Then Crey broke it, his voice echoing around the room. "I do not hear anything."

Tori shook her head. "No, I suppose not. I must be imagining it."

"What did you hear?"

"Nothing. I was probably just dreaming."

Chapter 24: Break Out

"Well, dreams, they are better than nightmares, no?" Crey began pacing again. Tori wondered if he had slept, or even paused long enough to rest his legs.

"How long has it been?"

"An hour, maybe two."

She sighed. "It'll be morning soon."

He did not answer. Tori wondered if he had nodded his head. The air moved with his agitated steps. She closed her eyes again and leaned back against the wall. Then gritted her teeth as the hard stone bit into her back and shoulders. She ran her tongue across her lips, swallowed, then let her mind wander.

Somehow, in the cold darkness she felt warmth and light. She reached out, wondering where Lucas was, what he was doing. Then gasped as she felt Torque stir within her mind. It was like the serpent was waking from a dream. *Warm, so warm*, it hissed within her thoughts.

Tori's breath quickened. *Go away*, she whispered back, her thoughts turning frantic.

She could feel the slither of the serpent in her mind. Felt the tilt of its head as if it were moving her own body. *I have slumbered in the winter, but he is the sun.*

What do you mean?

The flicker of Torque's tongue through Tori's thoughts sent a shiver down her spine. *Your angel.*

Leave him alone, Tori cried back. The serpent flicked its tail and Tori felt her mind recoil from the beast within her. *Please.*

She felt Torque pause, and then retreat. As she faded, she flickered a final hiss, *You must call to him.*

Tori's breath caught. *What do you mean?* But the serpent was gone again. Lost in the shadows of the dark places in her mind. Tears trickled from her eyes and Tori whispered, "What do you mean?" Her breath stirred the soft layer of hair on her arms, then faded into the silence around her. She closed her eyes again. *Lucas? Please Lucas, help me.*

Lucas gasped as Tori's voice echoed through his thoughts. "Tori?" He glanced around, but the dark shadows were empty. He closed his eyes, feeling her deep in the core of the temple below him. He could feel the cold rippling through her, the ache of her bones, the pain cutting her skin. He groaned, pushing back the wave of helplessness that flooded him. "No," he said, gritting his teeth. "I can do this."

He strode across the room and slammed against the hidden door. It clattered, hinges buckling. Lucas yanked the door from the frame. Stone crumbled around his fingers as he tore the door from the wall. The noise of it clanging against the stone floor rang down into the temple below. He took slow steps down the tiny stairs and inched his way into the corridor. Along with the flickering hiss of the burning embers in the brazier, he heard the echo of ringing metal disappear into the halls beyond.

Lucas moved with hasty, but quiet, footsteps down the hall. He reached out for Tori again, feeling her drawing him closer and closer. The air around him stank with acrid smoke and sweaty bodies. He passed closed doors and listened to the gentle breathing of the cultists behind them. As he crossed another intersection he heard his own boot tread on a crunch of glass and glanced down at the shards of a small vial. His eyes narrowed and he glanced around. Then he heard a shuffle of footsteps up the hall.

"Be quiet, they'll here you," a voice whispered.

"You're the one who dropped it."

"We should have used the vial tray like I told you."

"At least it wasn't the oil of vitriol. Come on, we have to get down there before everyone else wakes up."

"Should we be doing this, Ronny?" The young woman's voice quivered, "You know what they'll do to us if they catch us."

"You know what they're going to do to Crey in the morning, Kayleigh. We can't let them kill him."

The Flight Of Torque

Lucas crept forward, listening to the soft echo of voices trickling back to him. He glanced around the corner. Two young women stood in the light of a brazier. A petite pixie-faced blonde held a small collection of glass vials in one hand. The woman beside her was voluptuous with a short crop of copper hair. Her robe, unlike any of the others Lucas had seen, clung tight to her curves and was cut low to bare her shoulders and ample cleavage. She stood with her back against the wall, half turned as if ready to run away. Lucas stepped back out of sight.

"But maybe they're right, Ronny?" the blonde said.

"What are you talking about? Of course they're not right. What have we been fighting for all these months?"

"It's just, the High Priestess, if she finds out."

"She won't find out. At least not if we're fast. Come on, Kayleigh. I need you."

Their footsteps whispered down the hall like the shuffle of mice along the wall of a room. Lucas glanced around the corner just as a wisp of ash blond hair and the trail of a satin robe disappeared around the next corridor. He stepped into the hall and moved along it, following them. The tug of Tori drew him on behind them and his brow furrowed as they moved further and further down through the bowels of the temple and closer and closer toward Tori.

Chapter 24: Break Out

Lucas stumbled to a stop as the redhead's voice rang back at him, loud in the quiet. "Orton," she said, her voice held a faint tremor.

"Ronny," Orton replied. His gruff voice was rich with welcome, "whatcha doing out so late?"

"Oh, Orty," Ronny replied, her voice dripped with honey. Lucas stepped back against a wall. He could just see the redhead lean down across the table. The top of her soft cream breasts spilled from the low cut of her robe. Orton sat with his chair rocked back on two legs, his feet propped on the table. He stiffened, his eyes drawn to the woman's cleavage. His hands clenched in his lap as, with a coy voice, she added, "We just came to see the blood traitors. You'll let us, won't you?"

"Ronny," Orton replied. He swallowed the husky tension in his voice before continuing, "They ain't no side show. Ya know the High Priestess don't want no one talking to 'em."

"Who said anything about talking?" Ronny said, her scarlet lips curved in a smile full of invitation. "Kayleigh got some veliserum from the lab. We wanted to see if that bastard's skin will burn off if we throw it at him."

Orton chuckled. "Kayleigh, woman scorned, huh? I hear you an' he had a thing. You know, 'fore Zara."

The treacle of Kayleigh's laugh seemed to bounce off the wall with a ring of falsity. Lucas smiled.

"She's got a thing coming to 'er in the morning too, d'ya hear? Better have plenty of the serum left for the ritual."

"Speaking of morning," Ronny said, running a hand down Orton's arm. She looked over his bald head and gave Kayleigh a pointed look. "They'll want them brought up soon. Sunrise in what? Fifteen? Twenty? Come on, Orty, can we go down, just for a few minutes?"

He looked at them, his eyes wandering over Ronny, at the short crop of her red hair, the full curve of her breasts. He groaned, "Come on then. But don't be tell'n no one I let you see 'em."

Lucas leaned back against the wall as Orton lifted the torch from a scone beside the door. As the other man turned to unlock the iron door, Lucas leaned forward and whispered, "Hey." Ronny glanced back, fear flittering across her face before her eyes narrowed.

Ronny's lips moved so fast Lucas almost did not catch the silent words, "What are you doing here?" He nodded his chin toward the door. She sighed, lifted a finger and nodded, then turned to Orton. "Can you go down first, Ort? I'm," she leaned forward, "You know, a little afraid of the dark."

Orton seemed to lean into her, inhaling her breath, his grin lopsided on his face. "Sure thing, Ronny. Wouldn't want ya to be scared." He turned, and stretched the torch out in front of him as he stepped on the first stair. Ronny turned back to Lucas and jerked her chin toward Orton's back. Lucas stepped forward past her and Kayleigh, who held the vials clutched to her chest. He shoved the man, hard. Orton rocked forward. He slammed his face against the stone above the stairs and then tumbled down them. Lucas heard the crunch of his bones as he crumbled in a heap at the bottom. The torch rolled down the steps behind him.

"Damn, boy. Don't know you should have killed him," Ronny drawled.

Lucas swallowed. "I guess I don't know my own strength. Besides," He glanced down at the body beneath them. "He's not dead, but he'll have one hell of a headache and a few broken bones when he wakes up."

"Jerk deserves worse than that. I saw what they did to you."

Kayleigh smiled. "I'm glad Crey could get you out," she said.

He tilted his head forward in a bow of acknowledgment. "Thanks to you. Come on, time to return the favour."

Tori glanced up at the clatter of noise from the stairs and stared in shock as Orton's body slammed against the floor. The light from the burning torch stung her eyes. She could see Crey stride up to the bars. "I told you," he said. "I knew they would come for us."

Two women stepped over Orton's body. The curvy redhead gave him an ineffectual kick in the ribs. She smiled up at Crey. "So, I hear someone broke into the lab, stole some stuff. Bet there'll be a big shindig about it at some point. I'd rather you weren't here when it happens."

"I would prefer you and Kayleigh were vacant also, Ronny," Crey said. "Gracias."

"Of course, didn't think we'd leave our fearless leader behind, did you?"

Kayleigh bit her lip. "Come on," she said, glancing up the stairs. "We don't have time."

"We have time to introduce our guest," Ronny said.

Lucas strode past them and Tori pushed herself up from the floor. She reached toward him. A wave of dizziness came over her and her stomach roiled. She gasped as she fell forward from the dizzy spell. She caught herself with an outstretched hand. "Damn," she said, her breath huffing out of her.

"Tori," Lucas cried, concern deep in his voice. His shoulder slammed against the bars of the door as he reached for her. The door clattered in its hinges. "Damn it, can we get this thing out of the way."

Kayleigh stepped forward, running her hands over the hinges. "Oh no," she whispered. Lucas jerked around to look at her and Crey stepped forward.

"What is it, Kayleigh?" Crey asked.

"Steel. I didn't think. At this concentration the oil of vitriol won't work."

"What do you mean? It worked before."

"Yes, on iron. Even at this relatively high concentration the acid oxidises and corrodes iron. It causes the iron to rust which weakens the metal, but on steel it will cause a tough layer of iron oxide to coat the metal which will protect the bars from further corrosion. At this concentration the oil of vitriol will make steel stronger, not weaker."

Lucas looked at the hinges and yanked on the door. He slammed the heel of his hand against the bars, then glanced around. "What about these other bars? The lock."

Crey shook his head. "The lock is reinforced steel also."

"It'll work on the bars, but it'll take too long to rust through that much iron. We only have minutes before they'll come for you."

"Kayleigh and I can't be here when they do," Ronny said. "You know that, Crey. You need us to maintain our cover."

"I want you both to leave the temple, Ronny."

Ronny ignored him. She looked Lucas up and down. "What about you, tough guy? I saw what you did to Orton. You're strong."

"Step back," Lucas said. Crey stepped back to the wall and drew Tori away from the bars. Lucas slammed into the door with his shoulder and shoved against the bars. The clang of metal grinding on metal echoed up the stairs. "Damn it." He gritted his teeth, and gripped the bars. A soft glow surrounded him and his muscles clenched as he pulled and then pushed the bars. The iron bars groaned, the slight bend in the metal almost imperceptible, but they did not break. He shook his head as the light around him faded. His breath chased through his lungs. "I'm not strong enough. Damn." Tori could see the wave of frustration chase through his eyes and feel the ripple of anger that rushed through him.

Chapter 24: Break Out

"Lucas, it's okay," she said. "Just go. They'll come for us, for me. When they do, you can get Crey out of here."

He shook his head. "I'm not here for Crey, Tori." He glanced at Crey. "Sorry."

"Not at all, you have your duty, as I have mine."

"I need to get you out of here Tori." Lucas reached out to her again.

Tori bit her lower lip. She stepped forward and reached through the bars to touch his fingers. She could feel the pulse of heat from his skin. She could feel the warmth of his breath against her lips and face. A strand of hair fell across her eyes and he reached up to tuck it behind her ear. "I have to get you out," he whispered, his lips close to hers.

Tori felt the serpent stirring within. Her whole body seemed to rock forward. Her lips brushed against his and she felt his gasp as he sucked air into his lungs. Their breath mingled and she felt the cold iron against her skin as she tried to draw closer to him. Torque rippled through her. She gasped and thrust herself backward, clamping down on the raging sensations that rumbled through her. "I can't Lucas," she said, her chest heaving. "I don't want to hurt you. You have to go."

"Tori, that's it!" A sparkle of light lit his eyes. "I can't do it. I'm not strong enough. But you can. I've felt your strength. You, she, you could break these bars."

"What are you talking about?" Tori said, shaking her head. "I don't understand."

She gasped as the serpent reared up in her thoughts. She lifted a hand to her head as the whip of the serpent's tail lashed through her mind. It slithered through her thoughts.

"Of course, Tori. Do you not see?" Crey asked. "The strength of your serpent could bend these bars. You can free us."

She shook her head and gritted her teeth against the sense of scale scraping across the surface of her mind. "I can't control her when she takes over, Crey. There is no way to make her do what we want."

Lucas reached out to her, but Tori stepped back again shaking her head. "Tori, remember what Tempany said. The serpent acts on baser instinct. You both want to escape. It will act to that end."

Tori felt tears trickle down her cheeks as she shook her head again. "Then what? Even if she can get us past the bars. What then?" She gazed up at Lucas. "I don't want to hurt you."

Kayleigh glanced up at the door. "We have to do something, there's no time."

"Trust yourself, Tori." Lucas said. She felt his warmth pulse toward her, felt the soothing balm of him caress her skin even across the feet between them. "You can do this." Tori's tear-filled eyes pleaded with him and she could see the helpless hope in his. She knew they were right. Either the pain of holding Torque at bay would kill her, or she had to find out how to take on the form without losing herself to it. "Just, relax," Lucas said. He leaned close. "I will take care of you."

"Please, take care of yourself. I don't want her to hurt you." Tori gritted her teeth, her muscles tensed as she pushed back the serpent riling in her thoughts.

"Let go, Tori," Lucas whispered.

She drew a deep breath and then with a slow exhale forced her muscles to relax. She stretched her back and closed her eyes, searching within her thoughts for the caress of the serpent. *Please, don't hurt them,* she whispered in her mind as she let the serpent wrap itself around her and weave its thoughts with her own. She felt her limbs grow heavy and her skin taut. Her stomach clenched as she expected a wave of tearing agony, but none came. As she opened her eyes she felt like she was peering through a mask. She could see the world through serpent eyes. She gasped, and a cool hiss parted her lips. A forked tongue flickered, tasting the heavy air.

Chapter Twenty-Five
White Silk Sacrifice

Torque reared up, hissing. Kayleigh and Ronny gasped, stepping back from the bars. Ronny's hand lifted to her mouth and Kayleigh kept backing away until she tripped over Orton's unconscious body and caught herself against the far wall. Even then she did not take her eyes from the serpent. Tori felt the loathing Torque felt for them trickle through her mind. *Weak*, the serpent whispered within her.

Torque turned on Crey. She slithered forward and Crey stepped back, he tilted his head to look up at her. His hands came up as if ready to fend her off. Lucas stepped close to the bars. "Tori," he said, his voice tasted of frantic concern. "Listen to me, Tori. You're still there." In a slow, graceful curve, Torque's head turned. She slithered forward, toward the bars. Lucas swallowed, but he held his ground. "You control this, Tori."

Tori pushed at her thoughts. She took a deep breath and felt the serpent's lungs fill with air. She nodded and the serpent's head nodded too. Lucas's breath exhaled and Torque's tongue flickered, tasting the heat of moist air as it left his lungs. "Seraph," the serpent hissed. The sinew of serpentine muscle flexed as Torque reared up. The brush of her scales rasped across the hard ground and her head brushed the earthen ceiling. Torque sneered and hissed. She slithered the length of the cell. Her tail flickering with anger.

"Tori?" Crey asked. He pressed back against the bars. The serpent spun and moved its head close to Crey. He swallowed.

Torque tilted her head. "She is here, Human." Her tongue flickered again as she turned away. "Foul creature, she has displeased me," she said, her voice a cool hiss of contained anger.

"None of this is Tori's fault," Lucas said.

Torque turned and looked down on him. "Not us, Seraph," she hissed, tongue flickering between twin fangs. "Her." Torque lifted her nose up toward the ceiling. Her tongue flickered through the air again. "We smell her, even now, danker than the rank odour of burning embers. Her filth permeates this place." She swished her tail and slithered, rubbing her belly against the bars. "Let us be gone from here."

The bars were cool and brittle against her scales. The cold iron bit with chill. A growl rumbled in the back of her throat as she snaked her tail around them, coiling her length between the gaps in the bars. Crey moved closer, his steps cautious. "Can you free us?" he asked.

Chapter 25. White Silk Sacrifice

"The chill of death is on these bars, but we must not sleep." She flickered her tongue and tilted her head at Lucas. "Your warmth, Seraph. We will need it."

Lucas stepped closer. A glow like sunlight lit his skin and a wave of warmth pulsed through Torque. The radiance filled Tori's mind and she felt the serpent curl into it. "Like this?" Lucas asked.

"Yes," the serpent hissed. She flexed against the bars as his heat rippled through her.

"Can you break them?" Crey asked.

"Be patient, they bend." A faint creak filled the cell as the hard metal groaned. The bars curved between the coils of her tail and she wrapped more of her length around them. The serpent's muscles clenched and Torque closed her eyes. She hissed, stretching her neck as pieces of rock crumbled above her. The bars touched, bent in a strange curve and Torque tilted her head at them. "Strange man things these." She uncoiled and drew a third bar against the first two. The ceiling dropped chunks of dark earth. She shook the dirt from her scales with a majestic flick of her head. All three bars pried loose and as she pushed herself through, the bars clattered to the floor like toothpicks.

"You did it," Crey said, touching the bar beside the gaping hole in the cell.

In an agile curve of scale, Torque spun and bent her head low to him. "Do not doubt me, Human."

Crey lifted his hands again. Torque's tongue flickered between her fangs, but she turned away. Lucas watched her, his eyes full with concern. "We should go," he said.

Tension roiled in his gut. Seeing Tori transform into a giant serpent unnerved him. Although she had not cried out, Lucas could not help but feel as if his own skin peeled away as she did it. Torque slithered across the room. Her tail flickered in the air. The sound of scale grinding on rock echoed off the walls and sent a chill down Lucas's spine. He swallowed, then took a deep breath before stepping up beside her.

"Seraph, we must not linger." The serpent said, turning her head to peer down at him.

"Tori?" Lucas said. His voice quavered, but he stood tall, looking into the strange slitted iris of the serpent's eyes.

"I am Torque," it replied. Torque tilted her head, her tongue flicking between her lips.

"I'm sorry," Lucas said. "Torque, is," he paused.

A shiver ran over the serpent's body and it bowed its head as if sighing. "She is here, Seraph. Do not fear for her." He nodded. Torque's head whipped around, gazing up the scattering of stairs. A short hiss quivered from her lips, then she said, "They come." With a swish of her tail she slithered across the floor and wove her way up the stairs.

Lucas turned as she passed. Crey stepped up beside him and placed a warm hand on his shoulder. "She will be fine."

Lucas nodded. "We should go after her."

"But," Kayleigh stuttered, then fell silent.

Crey glanced at her. "We must go, Kayleigh. They must not find you here."

Kayleigh looked up at him. "They don't know I helped you, Crey."

Crey shook his head. "You must not stay. The danger exceeds the benefit. The High Priestess is aware of us and will seek to eradicate any who have aided the Uprising."

"She won't know I'm part of this. How could she? I'll put these vials back and no one will know they were taken. No one will know we were here."

Ronny stepped forward touching Kayleigh's elbow. "Orton will know, Kayleigh. When he wakes up, he will know."

Kayleigh swallowed and looked down at Orton. "He won't remember. Besides, even if he does, you could sweet talk him, Ronny."

Ronny shook her head. "He's loyal to the High Priestess, no matter how much his manhood might wish he weren't. We need to go Kayleigh. We have to."

"But," Kayleigh began.

Crey interrupted, "There is no choice, Kayleigh."

Lucas felt a quiver of anger rush through him and clenched down on it in surprise before he realised it came from above, from Torque, and from Tori within her. A rush of guilt followed it, tainted with a curl of lust and a taste of hunger. The riot of emotions welled up inside him and he gasped for breath feeling the dank air fill his lungs. "We have to go," he said, his voice tight.

"What is it?" Crey asked.

"Torque. Come on." He took the stairs two at a time, then passed through the doorway and dashed down the hall. Torque was out of sight. Lucas sprinted forward drawn through the maze by the coil of emotions that wrapped around his insides. The strange link that connected him to Tori was like a magnet on a chain drawing him deep into the bowels of the temple.

He rounded a corner and stumbled, as he tried not to fall over the curves of Torque's serpent tail. Her thick body curved in a crushing grip around the body of one of the cultists. The blade he had held gripped in his fingers dropped to the floor as he gasped for breath. Blood still oozed from twin punctures in his throat.

From the corridor opposite the desperate cries of a young female voice echoed through the temple. "Zara!" Crey shouted, running into the room behind Lucas. Lucas stepped in front of him, throwing one arm across the man's chest to hold him back. "Don't Crey."

"Let me go!" Crey shouted. "We must save her." He clawed at Lucas's arm.

"Wait, Crey," Lucas said. He grimaced as Crey's fingernails dug into his skin.

"Make way, Lucas. I must pass."

"Listen to me, Crey. Torque, the serpent, she's acting on base instinct. She'll kill you as well as she'd kill anyone that gets in her way right now."

Torque flinched, turning her head she hissed at Lucas. Her tongue flickered between her fangs. "Seraph, do not think to know me."

Lucas felt Crey hesitate. He half turned to face the serpent that stood between them and the corridor opposite. Lucas watched Torque. "Tell me you are in control of yourself," he said. He could feel his connection to Tori wavering through the air between them. Torque tilted her head, her slitted eyes gazed at Lucas. "Torque, tell me Tori has some power here."

The serpent paused, tilting her head a moment as if considering the question. She shook her head and Lucas felt the wall between Tori's thoughts and body crumble. Inside her mind she seemed to gasp and the serpent's lungs filled. "She is mine," the serpent whispered.

"She is her own, Torque. And you need her."

Torque nodded. "We need her. She is mine."

Torque twisted, her scales curling around the body grasped tight within her coils. Lucas winced as he heard the man's bones break. He could sense Tori's desperation as if she pleaded with the serpent. Torque rose up over him. She turned her nose down, peered at the man still gripped in her coils, then sniffed the cooling flesh.

The serpent's grip loosened and she swirled away as the body of the cultist crumpled to the floor. A wash of confusion rippled through her. "He grows cold."

"Yes, Torque," Lucas said. "His life is gone."

Silence seemed to linger after his voice faded. Torque swayed side to side, her tongue flickered through the air, tasting the tension, the fear, the sadness. "His warmth is gone." She said. Her whole body stilled as she lingered over the corpse.

Chapter 25. White Silk Sacrifice

A crooning song began to emanate from the corridor opposite them. Torque swung toward the sound. She seemed to move in time to the rising crescendo of voices in the distance. A heavy hum broke through the quiet in the room. The chanting cadence bounced from the walls. Zara cried out again, her words lost in the din of worship. Torque snapped upright. "They call me," she hissed. With a flick of her tail she turned her back on Lucas and wove her way down the hall.

Lucas sprinted across the room. "Torque, wait!" She slithered ahead, disappearing behind another turn in the corridors. Tori's churning emotions were frantic and Lucas felt the waves of it against his skin as he chased down the halls. Crey raced with him. They wove their way through the temple.

As they moved through the halls the light grew brighter. More braziers broke the shadows along the walls. Heat smothered his lungs, burning with the acrid taste of seared embers and the bitter incense that filled the air. A throbbing sound bounced down the corridors. It grew louder and louder as they drew closer to the humid warmth of the chambers ahead.

The muted sounds of scale on dirt filled the corridor. Tori could feel the brush of earth against her as if she swam in waters of sand. Her vision flickered between slitted eyelids and she fought for control. *Let me go.* Her words were a whisper in her mind.

The people, they sing for me, Torque replied, her voice a brush of scale through Tori's thoughts. She paused, swaying in rhythm with the chanting voices that pulsed down the corridor toward them.

They want to kill me! Tori shouted back.

Torque tilted her head. "She," the serpent spat, "the one you call High Priestess, she is our enemy. She would have us killed. But these are my people, they sing of the serpents. They sing of our mother, a woman of snakes, Naga. They sing for me."

But they follow the High Priestess.

"They are mine!" the serpent snarled. "The High Priestess is a usurper of their affection. She is our enemy." Torque's tail flickered as she jerked forward.

Tori gasped within her thoughts. *Don't! We have to escape. Let me go!*

"I follow their voices to the surface. They sing for me." Her lips curved as she slithered forward, turning another corner. As they swished down corridor after corridor through the maze of temple halls the sound of the reverent chanting grew louder. A bubble of warm joy threaded through the serpent as she drew closer. "Their warmth, I will have it."

Please, Tori begged, frantic within the walls Torque had erected in her mind. *Don't hurt them.*

The snake swayed, gazing over the worshippers with her slitted eyes. "They are mine. I will have their warmth. They give themselves to me."

But they don't know what they are doing. They're misguided, not evil. Torque, you can't hurt them. Please. We should get out of here.

Torque paused at the edge of another corner. The throng of voices were like a wash of heat over the serpent's scales. She swayed to the beat of their hearts as if they were a snake charmer's drum. *They call to me.* The vibrations of the melodic ritual soaked through her scales, enlivening her blood. "They sing so sweetly," she hissed. Her head swayed back and fourth.

A voice rose over the din of the worshippers chant. It rang in pious, self-absorbed clarity. The man's focus clung to the altar. "And so, today, it is with great honour and compassion this daughter of the Nagaran is submitted unto the Sacred Mother. Her sacrifice strengthens our people. She gives herself in the service of our heritage and the grace of our family. We will remember her, as the holiest of Nagaran, who willingly offers her blood to nourish our people. We raise her up, a child of the Nagaran, to the honoured ranks of noble sacrifice. For while her blood is tainted with darkness her soul is still pure with the light of the Nagaran. She will be reborn, cleansed of her sins."

The Nagaran cheered, their voices vibrated in the musky air. The words were lost in the pulsing rhythm. Together, their voices rang out as they took up their chant again. The chamber throbbed with the resonance of hundreds of voices. Chanting in unison, their eerie echo reaching a climatic cadence that shook the earthen walls dropping dust and grime through the corridors and over the oblivious worshippers.

Torque lay, belly close to the ground and slithered into the chamber with slow, deliberate movements. Torque hissed a sharp breath. Her tongue flickered between her lips. She rose to full height, peering over the crowded Nagaran. Her slitted eyes narrowed, her focus drawn to the altar, draped with sheer white silk.

What are they doing?

"They waste the warmth of the one you call Zara."

Tori gasped within her mind. *How do you know it's her?*

"Her fear clings to her scent, her heart shudders in a frenzy of frantic beats. The flicker of her vibrance glimmers in the darkness of this dank, foul grave. They shall not steal her warmth, it is mine." The serpent's body clenched in a tight clutch of muscle. Tension built in her coils and she quivered.

The serpent's breath shuddered from her lungs and Tori felt the weight of the serpent's heavy body as their thoughts touched within her mind. "We have to save her," Tori whispered and her words shivered from the serpent's lips.

Torque nodded. "Time grows close," she hissed as she wove her way forward. She slithered further into the chamber, unseen by the nearest worshippers only because their gazes were fixed on the altar across the room. Torque rose up, looking over the sea of worshippers who seemed to hum with anticipation. Tori swallowed and the serpent's throat flexed, as their eyes gazed over the thrashing white silk robes that caressed Zara's skin. She struggled against the ropes binding her wrists and ankles to the altar.

Kneeling on the stone at the foot of the altar, Tempany struggled against cords lashing her hands behind her back. She shook her head, biting down on the strip of fabric tied across her mouth. She winced with the pain of each movement. Although still hidden, the fragile bones in her wings crushed together between her shoulders because of her confinement. Despite the obvious pain she felt, her wide eyes remained fixed on Zara's writhing form and she continued to struggle to free herself.

Chapter Twenty-Six
Brightness Fades

The throbbing hum of chanting voices echoed back through the corridors while Lucas sprinted through them. Layers of thick red dirt clung to his skin as it tumbled in dusty motes from the earthen ceiling. "Lucas," Crey called from behind him. "Wait. The chanting, it is not right." Lucas ignored him, sprinting further and further ahead. As he disappeared around another corner he heard the echo of Crey's voice shout behind him. "Lucas! We must move with caution."

As he rounded another corner Lucas halted, almost tripping over the serpent's scaled tail again. She had risen up, feet taller than any man, and was gazing out over an ocean of worshippers. They stood ranged before him, chanting in an eerie reverberation of reverence. Torque, her tail poised, seemed to sway with the pulse of the chant. Vibrations ran through his feet and up his legs. The serpent seemed to caress the floor as if absorbing the rhythm through her scales. Her belly close to the ground, she slithered with slow, deliberate movements.

As one, the worshipper's chanting ceased. A quiet whimper drifted between the cultists and Lucas could hear the frantic tears of a woman. The woman's desperate terror drew his gaze to the dais.

Josiah stood behind the altar, raised above the worshippers. He leaned close to Zara. She thrashed across the altar, tugging against the bindings that held her down. Josiah's gaze remained intent on the poised knife he held inches from her breast. His voice, thick with fanaticism, broke over the hushed silence, "Sacred mother, grant us beauty. Sacred mother, grant us wealth. Sacred mother, this we offer; blood for blood and health for health."

Crey slammed into Lucas's back as he rounded the corner and Lucas stepped aside, gripping the other man's arm to steady him. Crey looked up with a frown. Torque hissed, her tail flickering.

"What is it?" Lucas whispered.

"The chant. It is somehow wrong. I have never heard the Nagaran so devout, so feverish. Something has happened."

Torque's slitted eyes narrowed. "They are desecrating the one you call Zara. They will steal her warmth."

"No!" Crey burst forward. Lucas gripped his arm, pulling him back.

"Careful, Crey."

Chapter 26. Brightness Fades

"But they have Zara!"

"Hush, Human. You will not best their number."

"We need a plan, Crey. If we just burst through them they'll have us back in the dungeon."

"Lucas," Crey said, his voice filled with a desperation that glimmered in the sheen of tears Lucas knew the other man was refusing to let fall. Crey took a deep breath, drawing heavy air into his nostrils and sighing as the air burst from his lungs. "Help me."

"We'll get her out of this, Crey. We will." Lucas met his eyes, refusing to allow the quiver of doubt that fluttered in his belly to touch his voice or expression. "We'll save her."

Torque tilted her head. Her slitted eyes gazed down at him. "I will end this." She slithered forward, her scales brushing between the shoulders of the cultists standing nearest them.

Lucas reached out to stop her. "Torque!", he said, his voice low. His fingers brushed against the cold chill of her scales before she moved out of reach. "Damn, what is she doing," Lucas said with a grimace as the worshippers gasped and stumbled aside. Torque wove through, parting the red sea of robes. The room fell quiet, but for the hysterical whimpers of Zara, bound to the altar, and the fear that wove through the worshippers as Torque moved past them. Torque wove closer and closer to the front of the room where the dais rose up from the floor.

Crey stared ahead, his gaze fixed on Zara. He strained against Lucas's grip on his arm. "Crey," Lucas whispered, "be smart." Lucas nodded at the line of pillars that curved around the room. The worshippers stood circled by them. There was a gap of a few feet between them and the wall. Crey nodded back and they turned together to move around the cultists toward the dais.

"Crey?" Kayleigh asked, her voice a soft whisper that seemed to bounce off the walls. The worshippers gazes were fixed ahead, on Torque, but Crey lifted his finger to his lips as he spun to face her. She stepped close and whispered, "Where are you going?"

"Kayleigh, you and Ronny must leave this place. While everyone is distracted you must go."

"What are you going to do?"

"I have to help Zara."

"Zara? But," Kayleigh replied.

Crey shook his head, cutting her off. "You must go."

"Come on, Kayleigh," Ronny whispered. She grabbed Kayleigh's hand.

Kayleigh glared at Crey and shook off Ronny's grasp. "We're not going."

"Do not be ridiculous, Kayleigh. You must go. It is not safe here."

"You need us, Crey. You need me."

Torque drew closer to the dais and Lucas turned to Crey. "We don't have time to argue."

Ignoring him, Crey stretched one arm and pointed to the dark corridor. "I will not endanger you. Go!"

Kayleigh's eyes filled with tears and she lifted a hand to her mouth as she caught back a sob. She turned and ran away down a darkened corridor. Ronny sighed. "God, Crey, you can be a real bastard sometimes." She sighed again then added, "Go save Zara, I'll deal with Kayleigh." Ronny sprinted to the hall where Kayleigh had disappeared and followed her into the darkness.

"Come on," Lucas whispered. Crey grimaced and turned to follow him. He moved from column to column behind Lucas. The two men circled around the cultists, moving closer and closer to the dais.

With sure movements, the graceful curves of Torque's serpentine body slid across the floor. The worshippers parted, mouths dropping open, eyes wide, as she passed. Torque swung low, turning to face one of the warm bodies at the foot of the dais. She hissed in the man's face and he fell back, stepping into the people behind him. Tori could feel Torque's pleasure ripple through her as the serpent swept away and slithered up the steps.

Marlena stood at the foot of her throne. Her mouth hung open, chest heaving. Her hands clenched beside her, fingers white with the tension in her knuckles. Torque wove forward toward her then reared up, towering above the woman. Her serpent's tongue flickered in the air, tasting the threads of anxiety radiating from the High Priestess's body. Marlena swallowed. As a sharp inhale filled her lungs she straightened her back and put her hands on her hips."What is the meaning of this?" she asked, her voice starched with haughty pride. Torque's tongue flickered as she heard the fallacious bravado in the woman's words.

"Foul creature, you dishonour us."

Marlena laughed. The sound rang false in Torque's ears. Torque hissed, glaring down at the High Priestess. Marlena shivered, and leant away from the serpent as she replied, "You? What are you to me? Nothing more than a traitor, a blood-tainted soulless creature whose very existence soils the honour of our Sacred Mother."

"We?" Torque's hissed chuckle sounded like an eerie echo of laughter remembered through a veil of insanity. "How could we be a traitor to the Nagaran? We are the very essence of our people. We are Serpenthropy. The blood of the Mother courses through us like a raging torrent of primal essence. You, filth, are unworthy to even speak in our presence."

The High Priestess cringed. Her face grew dark. She clenched her hands either side of her and her spine straightened. She rose inches higher, but Torque still glared down on her. "I am Marlena, High Priestess to the Nagaran. The blood that runs through my veins is generations rich with loyal service to the Four Fathers."

"You, human, are a pitiful worm with no blood to claim of the Nagaran. You claim service to the Four Fathers? Theirs is a taint to dishonour your very soul. You serve them only, and owe allegiance only to them, never to the Sacred Mother." Torque hissed, her tail flickering. "You scramble for the praise and acceptance of my people, but you are nothing, raised to your status only under the generosity of the Sacred Mother. You are no longer worthy of her consideration, nor ours." Torque turned away from her. Her sharp tongue flickered between her teeth as she tasted the fear that wove through the worshippers. She addressed them, "Who of you are loyal to the Nagaran?"

Timid, the cultists shuffled their feet. Their gazes flickered between the giant speaking serpent and their

High Priestess. Marlena glared at the intricate weave of scales running the length of Torque's back. Her thoughts were visible in the race of emotions across her face; anger, vengeance, hatred, fear, loathing, jealousy, desperation. "How dare you?" She shrieked. Her voice quivered with fury. Rage came alive in her eyes.

"We are the child of the Sacred Mother." Torque swirled on her, slitted eyes narrowed as she watched the High Priestess shiver.

"Then you should stand witness, for it is with great honour and compassion we submit this child to the trials." She waved a hand toward the altar. "Our sacrifice, the Sacred Mother's sacrifice, will give birth to the true Children of the Nagaran."

Torque rose a few inches higher. She slithered close to loom over Marlena. The High Priestess tilted her head up and looked as if she would have stepped back, but instead held herself with stiff resolution, spine straight with pride. "This child?" Torque hissed, dark fury pulsing through her. Torque flicked her head to the altar where Zara, tears streaming down her face, struggled against the ropes binding her to the cold rock. Tempany kneeled beside her. She leaned close to the young woman, her eyes now closed. Zara whimpered. Torque lifted her chin. "She is not your play thing," she said, turning her head to face Marlena again. "You think you honour the Sacred Mother? You torment and murder her children, you steal from them their heat. How is that honourable?"

"They give their life in the service of our heritage, our family. We will remember them, the holiest of Nagaran, who willingly offer their blood to strengthen all."

"Willingly?" Torque sneered. "She does not appear willing."

Marlena glared at Torque. "She will rise, more powerful than any before her." The High Priestess's voice, raised in pious, self-absorbed clarity glanced past Torque to the crowd of worshippers. They cowered beneath the dais and watched with horror-filled faces as the debate volleyed between these two figures of power. "My glorious Nagaran, you give your blood, your breath, your life and soul to the Sacred Mother, do you not? You are all here, in the service of the Nagaran." The worshippers remained silent, their eyes wide as they stared up at the serpent. Their bodies quivered with fear, their breath held in unison.

Torque's tongue flickered, tasting the tension in the air that hummed around them. "They give no answer."

Marlena's jaw clenched and she swallowed. "They're afraid of you," she snarled.

"Perhaps, but they are not yours to command."

"Enough!" Marlena growled. She turned and nodded at Josiah who stood beside Zara, dagger still poised in his hand.

He gave a single nod in response, then lifted the dagger high above him and doused the blade in acrid venom. "Sacred mother, grant us courage. Sacred mother, grant us guile. Sacred mother, so anointed; tooth for tooth and bile for bile."

Torque hissed, then swirled on him in a slither of scale. "Filthy human, cease! You displease me."

He lifted his chin and glared at her. His eyes sparkled with conviction. "You? You betray the Sacred Mother. You murder her most beloved and loyal. You are a monster in the flesh of an angel. You defile our heritage. You dishonour the scale that clothes your pathetic wraith of flesh." He turned his sharp glare down on Zara's bared chest. He lifted the dagger high. "Sacred mother, grant us glory."

"Zara!" Crey shouted from across the room. He and Lucas sprinted forward, closing the distance between them and the dais.

"Enough!" Torque slithered forward with a swish of her tail and towered over him.

"Sacred mother, grant us might. Sacred mother, take our daughter; life for life and blight for blight." As the final word burst from his lips, Josiah thrust the dagger downward.

"Josiah, no!" Tempany's quivering voice broke through the tingle of silence that had fallen over the worshippers. She flung herself over Zara. Her crystal blue eyes glittered with tears, the stains of which trailed down her cheeks. The cloth that had muzzled her hung loose around her neck. Her body hit Zara hard as she fell forward. The auburn bob she'd worn over her blonde shimmer of hair tumbled to the floor. She gazed up at Josiah, desperation in her eyes.

Shocked recognition rushed across Josiah's face. He flinched, the blade no longer sure in his fingers, but the downward stroke continued. Thick cords still bound Tempany's hands behind her back. Above them, her wings beat, tearing through the fabric of her cotton dress. A scatter of pale feathers burst through as her wings tangled in the knots of her clothing. Her muscles clenched as if she tried to bring her arms and wings up to defend herself, but she was helpless to ward off the blade. It plunged deep into her chest.

Tempany gasped, her eyes frantic and wide. The crimson flow of her blood ebbed out in stains of dark contrast against the pale cotton of her dress. Her breath burst from her lips as she whispered, "She's our daughter."

A hum of tension, fear, and horror flooded toward the dais from the wave of worshippers. Confusion spread among them. Tempany's soft voice faded. Then, as her body began to thrash, her voice keened in a piercing cry. Worshippers clutched their hands across their ears. Frantic, many scattered, disappearing down the corridors that lead away from the chamber. Others forced themselves to remain. Calm, devout, perhaps even eager for brutality, violence, and death, they lingered, gazes fixed in hungry anticipation.

"Tempany!" Lucas called out. He rushed forward from the side of the dais and sprinted up the steps.

Fury rose up in Torque. Tori felt as if she was drowning in the anger coursing through her. Her body rocked forward. Torque wrapped her length around Josiah. He froze with fear as her serpent body coiled tighter and tighter around him. He blinked, swallowing. His hand quivered. The dagger slipped from his fingers. It skittered across the floor. Torque could smell the rank odour of his terror seeping from his flesh. "No," he whispered, his voice a strangled gasp. Torque gripped him, crushing his lungs beneath her scales.

Chapter 26. Brightness Fades

No, Torque, we're not this, Tori pleaded. Her thoughts bombarding against the walls that had slammed down around her as Torque's body flooded with rage. *We're not murderers.*

They have harmed the bright one. The cold echo of Torque's voice swirled through Tori's mind. *They are filth.*

Crey darted forward to Zara's side. She sobbed as he began tugging away the bindings that held her to the altar. With a hand free she clung to him. He held her close against his chest.

Zara's whimpers almost masked Tempany's soft murmur. "Tori," she whispered. The serpent snapped her head toward the altar.

Lucas leaned down over Tempany's trembling body. His hands covered the wound in her chest and he leaned into her, applying pressure. Tempany shuddered, her whole body convulsing. Lucas's voice hitched with concern. "Tempany, stay still, you're losing too much blood."

Spasms wracked through her and she shuddered. Between clenched teeth, and dragged from the tightness of her aching lungs, she whispered again, "Tori."

Torque slithered close. Still clutched in the serpent's coils, Josiah's thrashing resistance was growing still. Torque tilted her head close to Tempany. "She is here, bright one."

Tempany's breath lingered in short sighs. "Don't, I love him. Please don't," she paused, drawing another laboured breath, "don't hurt him."

"He has harmed you. Your warmth is fading even now."

"He's my daughter's father," she whispered. She grimaced as a wave of pain wracked through her body. Her eyelids fluttered closed.

Lucas grimaced. "Dammit, why won't you heal. Tempany, stay with me." Lucas reached down and with thick fingers he tugged away the black cord binding her hands behind her back. Tempany groaned as her shoulders pulled tight then relaxed. Lucas lifted her wrists, placing her hands over the wound before adding his own above them. "Help me, Tempany, use your power. Heal."

Her eyes fluttered open. She sighed. A sad smile curved her lips. "It would take more than either of us have," she said.

"What do you mean?"

She shook her head. "One last charge, Lucas."

He gazed down on her. "I don't know what you mean."

Chapter 26. Brightness Fades

"Just one more," she whispered. Her breath caught between each phrase as she struggled to find the strength to speak. "Please, you can't save me, but you can keep her safe. Promise me." Her breath hitched in her throat and another shudder of pain washed through her.

Lucas gritted his teeth then let his breath hiss between his lips before he asked, "Who, Tempany?"

"My daughter, Zara."

Lucas's breath shuddered out of him. "You want me to keep your daughter safe?"

"You can do this, Lucas. You have to. Please." She reached out, placing a blood-stained hand on his shoulder. The warmth of her hand felt like sunlight on his skin. He looked down at her, watching the glow of her power shimmer across her skin. She closed her eyes and let the heat flow through him as she faded into the darkness of the room's shadows. Lucas felt his heart leap and grow heavy at the same time. Somehow, the room had grown dimmer as her light faded. Somehow, feeling a wave of power rush through him, he knew he had taken something from her that left her less than herself.

"No, Tempany. Don't do this." Lucas leaned over her as her breath became shallow. Her limbs grew heavy and her fingers fell away from his shoulder. Her chest still rose and fell beneath his hands, but her face relaxed as she slipped further and further from consciousness. "No, Tempany. Wake up, stay with me."

Josiah's limp body fell to the floor in a heavy heap as Torque uncurled herself from him. The man gasped, crying out in pain. Torque turned away from him, slithering close to Tempany and Lucas. "She fades, she grows cold."

Josiah scrambled on hands and knees across the floor to her. Torque hissed at him, but Lucas shook his head. The man grasped Tempany's hand. "Tempany, oh, Tempany. What have I done?" His voice rushed from his lungs in pained gasps. He leaned close over her, burying his face in the cool skin at her throat. "I'm sorry, please, I'm sorry. What can I do?"

With a final sigh, Tempany's breath eased from her lungs on whispered words, "Our daughter, love her." Her body grew still, her chest no longer rising and falling. Lucas's hands shook on her motionless skin. Josiah broke down. Tears streamed from his face and he clutched Tempany close to his chest as he sobbed over her.

Chapter Twenty-Seven
Descent Into Madness

A piecing screech broke through the chaos of cultists. Marlena, whole body vibrating with her fury, strode toward the altar. Her blood-bleached fingers gripped the ceremonial dagger. "How dare you?" she shouted, thrusting the dagger toward Josiah. "Finish the ritual!"

Zara clung to Crey, who held her close as a fresh wave of tears rocked her. He lifted his gaze to glare at Marlena. "You will not touch her," he said.

Josiah stood. He faced the High Priestess and straightened his spine. "I won't harm her."

"You are a priest of the Nagaran, you will do as I say?"

"I won't harm her," Josiah said again. "She's my daughter." Although he stood firm, resolve dark in his eyes, his whole body shrunk against the black rage Marlena directed at him.

"Then you'll join them, blood traitor. Jackson!"

The crossbowman stepped away from the small collection of cultists who ringed the dais. "High Priestess?" he asked.

"Arrest these miscreants."

Jackson nodded. He drew his crossbow and levelled it at Josiah. Josiah raised his hands. "Don't do this, Jackson," he said.

"You've betrayed our order, Josiah. You defy the orders of your High Priestess. You are under arrest as a blood traitor."

"Please, I'm just protecting my daughter. She's done nothing wrong. We've already killed too many innocent children."

Carny stepped up onto the dais beside Jackson. "We ain't not done nothing wrong," he said. "We be servin' the High Priestess. Followin' orders, like we're a'sposed to."

Lucas lowered Tempany's body to the stone before he stood. "You don't have to follow orders, Carny. You have a choice."

"This is not a discussion," Marlena said. Her voice pitched with strain.

"Are you afraid you words won't hold their loyalty, Marlena?" Lucas asked.

She glared at him, her fingers turning white around the dagger. "I have nothing to fear. I am tired of your interference in the affairs of the Nagaran. *I* am High Priestess." She lifted a hand and gestured to Jackson as her bitter voice snapped, "Kill them."

Chapter 27. Descent Into Madness

Jackson's jaw clenched, but he nodded. He squeezed the trigger of his crossbow sending a bolt across the distance toward Josiah's heart. Torque hissed. She whipped her tail across the priest and shoved him aside. He fell back against the altar. The bolt glanced from the rock beside him and he flinched away. Jackson grimaced and reached to reload the crossbow as Torque crossed the space toward him. She reared up. With a whip of her tail, she flicked the crossbow from his hands. It clattered across the floor and settled at the foot of the throne.

"Dammit," Jackson growled. He swung at Torque with a heavy fist.

The serpent backed away, hissing at him. "You will not harm the bright one's lover. He must live."

Carny screeched as he sprinted across the dais and flung himself at the serpent. In one fluid motion he leapt several feet from the ground and wrapped his arms around Torque's throat. Torque hissed and thrashed in an attempt to throw him from her back.

Jackson turned to swing at her again but Lucas was there. Jackson stumbled backwards as Lucas's fist connected with his chin. The man growled. He spun on one ankle and kicked Lucas through the middle. Lucas gasped and stepped back. He raised his hands as he kept distance between them. "You can walk away, Jackson," Lucas said. "Right now, you can walk away from all of this."

Carny cried out as Torque gripped his legs between her coils. Jackson glanced at him, his eyes sparking with indignant anger. "Call off your snake."

Lucas shook his head. "I don't control her, she's defending herself."

With a wild swing, Jackson thrust forward. Lucas darted out of the way, but Jackson's feint distracted him. He caught a kick to the side of the head as another cultist intercepted them. Others, those who had ringed the dais to prevent worshippers crowding onto the stage, circled around them. Some sported weapons, blades and whips with wicked serrated edges. Lucas glanced between them and circled to keep the most dangerous in his field of vision. As cultists darted in to strike at him he fended them off.

Zara whimpered in Crey's arms and he crooned to her. "All is right, you are safe, I have you." She sobbed, clinging her free arm around his neck. He reached out and untethered her other hand.

"No!" The High Priestess screeched. She darted forward and thrust down with the dagger she still held in her clenched fist. "No! She must be sacrificed!"

Chapter 27. Descent Into Madness

Crey moved to draw Zara away but the young woman's feet were still bound to the altar. Marlena wrenched the dagger downward, crushing her fist into Zara's chest. Zara groaned, her face white, as shock and pain pulsed through her.

"Zara!" Josiah cried out. He rushed to her side.

"No," Zara whispered. Her voice hitched and she shuddered. Marlena stepped backward. Her lips curved in a maniacal grin. Her eyes glittered with malice as Zara's whole body began to shudder.

Torque hissed. Carny still clung to her. His arms pulled tight around her neck. She wove back and fourth, flicking her head in an attempt to loosen his grip. He snarled, clenching harder.

The circle of cultists that had gathered around Lucas blocked his path. He tried to ease through them, to find an opening, but they clustered tight around him. He raised his hands to fend off another kick and caught a blow to the solar plexus from the cultist opposite his original attacker. Another darted in and Lucas shifted away but the blade in the man's hand nicked his shoulder. Every time he moved to defend himself another assailant took the opening to attack.

"Lucas, help me!" Crey shouted. Lucas spun to avoid another fist, then turned to kick his attacker. As his foot booted the man backward several feet, another man swung the hilt of a sword down against the back of his neck and shoulders with a crushing blow. The heavy metal left Lucas's ears ringing. His eyes filled with tears and he blinked away the blurry haze as another fist swung toward him. He flinched away, ducked under the blow, and brought up his own fist under the defence of the aggressor. "Lucas!" Crey shouted again. His voice was filled with growing desperation.

"Dammit!" Lucas shouted. He shoved one of the men that stood between him and the altar. "Let me past." The man stumbled, but another gripped Lucas from behind. He wrapped his arm around Lucas's shoulders and pulled tight against Lucas's windpipe. Lucas gagged. He reached behind him and gripped the assailant behind the neck. In a fluid movement he tipped his whole body forward, grounded his feet, and tossed the man over his shoulder.

Zara quivered just feet away from him, but between them there were still several cultists. *No, not again. Dammit!* The torture of his thoughts bleed through and he felt panic rising inside him. Desperation, and the drowning sense of helplessness that had become so familiar over the past twenty years, built up within him. It blurred reality as flashes of his failures crowded his mind. He glanced at

Tempany's body knowing that in every moment, as Zara grew closer and closer to death, he was failing his mentor.

Another blow struck the side of his head and then Jackson took out his legs from beneath him. "Come on pansy," Jackson taunted. "If you're so tough, fight back."

"If it were fair odds you wouldn't be so cocky, Jackson." Lucas glared at the other man as he rolled away and pushed himself back to his feet.

"You're a celestial being, Seraph. What are the fair odds for that? Aren't you supposed to be strong? Fast? Powerful?"

Lucas spun to deflect a blow from a cultist behind him then shoved away the kicking leg of another. Another and another rained down on him and he moved in a fluid flow of defensive stances avoiding most strikes, but taking other glancing blows as the attackers outnumbered him.

"Come on, I thought you're a protector?" Jackson stepped back and let other cultists move in closer to Lucas. Lucas focused on the mob assaulting him and, one by one, fought off their attacks. He spun to kick one in the stomach, then turned to punch another. As he raised his fist again he gasped. A stab of pain pierced through his gut. He looked down, blood cascaded from the wound. Jackson chuckled as he lowered his spent crossbow.

Torque hissed. She snarled, snapped at Carny, then released her grip on him as she thrust herself forward and flicked her head away. Carny's grip faltered and Torque flung him across the room. His skull cracked as he hit one of the stone pillars and crumpled to the floor in a groaning heap. Dazed, he lay there, sprawled on the ground at the foot of the dais.

Torque turned toward Lucas. "Seraph?"

Lucas gripped one hand over the wound as he fending off blows with his other. He groaned, feeling the mob of cultists overwhelming him. He lifted his arm to shield his head and as they pummelled him he shrank, curling into a ball to protect himself.

"Lucas! Help me!" Crey cried out again.

Lucas's breath rasped in harsh gasps through his aching lungs. Blood flowed over his fingers and stained his clothes. "No," he whispered, feeling the fists of the cultists against his back and shoulders. "I have to save her."

"Seraph," Torque began. She wove forward, tossing aside the cultists. Some scattered as she neared.

Crey called out, "Please! She is dying!"

The serpent stilled. She turned her nose toward Crey and sniffed the air. She tilted her head, her forked tongue flickering from between her lips. "No, human, she does not die."

Zara's piercing screams broke through the turmoil and chaos in the room. The cultists lifted their hands to their ears and turned to face the altar. Against the cold stone, Zara's body shook and shifted. The cords binding her feet fell away as her limbs disappeared. A lithe, serpent body formed in their place. It's scales, a soft white and yellow glimmer, tore through the fine threads of her clothing. Crey stepped back, his eyes full of tears. "No, not this."

The cultists fell to their knees as the serpent rose up above them and peered out over them. Marlena stood frozen in place as she, like everyone else in the room, watched with horror. She released the breath held in her lungs in a gentle huff as wonder began to brighten her eyes. "It's the blood," she whispered. She glanced down at the blade still clutched in her hand. A smile formed on her lips.

"Sister, you are one of us," Torque said. She slithered close to the other serpent. The creature tilted its head and sniffed the air. Tori's thoughts raced through her mind. Confusion, horror, and sorrow wove in a subtle blend within her.

Oh, Zara. Her thought brushed like a whisper through her mind as she looked for the young woman she had known in the serpent that now swayed before her. *I'm so sorry.*

Tori? Zara's soft voice broke through Tori's thoughts. The pale-scaled serpent swayed, tilting its head as it met Torque's gaze. *Tori?* The voice inside Tori's head quivered.

Shocked, Tori could not form a thought for several seconds. With tentative wonder she let her mind brush against the presence within her. *Zara?*

What am I? Oh, God, what have I become?

Zara's voice fell silent as her desperation rose. Tori tried to break through the shroud that rose up around Zara's thoughts. She was blanketed by her panic. *Zara, you need to calm down. The harder you fight it the less control you have.*

The walls around Zara's thoughts came crashing down as Zara's limbs began forming beneath her. She fell, her human legs unable to catch her weight. Torque lifted her tail to catch her before she hit the ground. Crey darted forward to hold her.

Josiah reached out to brush his fingers over her hair. "Zara," he whispered, stroking his cool hands over her face.

Chapter 27. Descent Into Madness

"She slumbers, but she will wake again," Torque said.

"Angel blood," Marlena said. "That's the answer isn't it. Angel blood tempered with human." Torque spun to look at her. The High Priestess had a sharp grin on her face. Both hands clenched the dagger between them as she held it poised over her own heart. "That's been the secret all along."

Lucas groaned. He knelt on the floor still feet away from the altar, and reached a blood-covered hand toward the High Priestess. "Don't Marlena!" he cried out.

Marlena shook her head. "You can't stop me, Seraph. All along, she knew the secret, she kept it from me. But now, now I know." Her words fell away on a whisper of wonder. The muscles in her arms clenched as she yanked the blade forward. It slipped between her ribs, cutting through her flesh. She gasped, then sighed, plunging the blade deep into her own chest.

Marlena closed her eyes. She fell back against the altar as her body began to quiver and writhe. A keening cry broke from her lips. It echoed around the chamber. Most of the remaining cultists scattered, some still on their knees, prostrated themselves. Bowing low, they kept their foreheads pressed to the ground as they quivered and wailed in terror and subjugation. Torque sniffed the air.

"She is not one of us."

"No, but there is angel blood on that blade. Tempany's, Zara's, what is in them will course through her," Lucas said. He pushed himself up from the ground, holding one hand over the wound across his belly.

"It is not enough. She will die." Torque said.

Lucas turned to face her. "Are you sure?"

Torque tilted her head.

"You're not sure, are you?" Lucas asked. He turned back to Marlena. His brow furrowed as he watched her squirming and flailing. He winced with each step as he crossed the distance between him and the altar where Marlena writhed, groaning in agony. He ran the fingers of one hand over her forehead, then placed his hands either side of the dagger still protruding from Marlena's chest. A soft glow tingled across his skin. Torque swayed toward the warmth radiating from him.

"You waste your warmth on her. She will die."

"You don't know that," he said.

Marlena's body convulsed. Her eyelids fluttered open and her glassy eyes gazed up at the earthy ceiling above them. Her shoulders shuddered. The curve of her lips broadened as laughter bubbled out of her. She keened again, a slow, drawn out, agonising scream that tore its way from her lungs. Her whole body writhed against the stone as her skin flaked, shedding. Beneath it, scales glistened, coated in her blood.

Lucas focused his attention. Pulses of energy flooded through his fingers. The bruises over his own body faded. The ragged flesh at his stomach knitted, healing. Where his hands touched Marlena her human skin radiated outward. As light and heat spread over her, the scales faded beneath healthy, human skin. Elsewhere on her body scale continued to burst from her flesh in rivers of gold tinged with crimson. It trailed across her, veining her body and bombarding the healing flesh to reach her core.

Torque leaned close to the strange mixture of human flesh and serpent scale. She sniffed the air. "She is deformed. She will die. You cannot heal her."

"Die?" The word burst in a hiss from Marlena's lips. Her face, a mixture of crazed expressions, grinned up at the ceiling.

Lucas stepped backward. His hands fell to his side and the glow tingled away from his skin. Darkness smothered the light that had settled over Marlena. The bones in her chest began to crack and her chest split open. Lucas's breath caught and he backed away again.

"I become," the strange serpent-beast hissed from between Marlena's lips. Then, from within her a giant snake formed. It ruptured from her chest, rising up. The husk of Marlena's human body fell away as if it were a skin shed by the serpent within. The beast drew itself up and peered down on Lucas and Torque. An eerie voice burst from the serpent's scaled lips, "immortal."

Chapter Twenty-Eight
Devouring Insanity

Jackson stumbled forward. His mouth hung open as he gazed at the beast rising up before him. Her head turned toward him. Her eyes, dull and lifeless, gazed down on him. He scrambled backward, shaking his head back and forth. The creature hissed. With a snarl it slithered across the dais. It left Marlena's body in a desecrated heap as it moved. Then it lanced forward, crushing Jackson between its jaws. The fangs of the giant snake pierced through his chest and hip. His ribs cracked beneath the pressure and his whole body hung limp and frail in the creature's mouth. The snake lifted her chin, flicking Jackson's body up as she opened her jaws. His heavy limbs and thick torso slipped backward into her mouth. With a flex of its throat and a flick of its tongue he disappeared, devoured by the beast.

Lucas stumbled backwards as the scaled creature turned toward him. It hissed; its tongue flickered close to Lucas's face as if she tasted his breath. Torque shoved Lucas back with her head and moved to rise up between seraph and snake. "Mine!" Torque snarled at the beast. She swayed before the snake. Her slitted eyes watched the creature as its monstrous lips curved in a hideous smile.

"You claim, yet you do not take," the beast replied. It tilted its head, lifted its nose and flicked its tongue. "You are weak."

"I am strong. His warmth has value to him, to us."

"Weak!" the beast snarled. In a spring-like movement the snake lunged forward, striking down at Torque with sharp fangs. Torque backed away, hissing.

"Tori!" Lucas called out, he moved to step forward but Torque shoved him backwards with her tail.

"Do not intervene, Seraph. She has venom."

A haunting hiss of laugher jangled through the air as the snake chuckled. The streak of venom that trailed down its teeth was dark with filthy toxin. The creature tilted its head to look past Torque at Lucas. "I wish to taste him."

"He is mine!"

"I wish to taste him," the beast snarled again, lifting her gaze to meet Torque's. "I wish to taste them all." The snake spun away from Torque and Lucas. It swept forward in a slither of curves to circle around the collection of cultists who remained, faces bowed to the dais, in reverent and horrified worship.

Torque licked the air, tasting their fear and the foul scent of their sweat and urine. She hissed. "You will not touch them. They must live."

"They are unworthy! I will have them." The snake's fangs, stained with trails of dark venom, seemed to elongate as they stretched close to a timid worshipper. He quivered, his whole body shrinking away from the beast as she hovered over him, her tongue flicking between her fangs to trace the smooth curves of his ear.

"No, please, no!" the cultist pleaded.

"Filthy worm, do you not respect the great honour? I would give your warmth to the Sacred Mother."

He whimpered, cowering away.

"He does not want to die," Lucas said. Torque snarled, shoving him back as he tried to cross to stand beside the man. Lucas pushed her away. "Let me past, we have to help him."

"The danger is great," Torque said. Shoving him back again.

"And even greater to the Nagaran worshippers. We have to help them."

Torque snarled and hissed. She slithered forward, placing herself between Lucas and the giant snake again. "Sister, you will not harm them."

The Flight Of Torque

The snake rose up, turning its head to face Torque. "Sister? We are not as one. You are tainted with the streak of mortal blood within you. I am true, truer even than the Sacred Mother herself. Remove yourself from my presence."

"I will not! You will leave the mortals, you will leave this place."

The snake's rough laughter echoed from the walls as it lifted is head. "I? I will do no such thing. This place is mine; these people are mine!" The giant snake rose up, swirled in place, then struck the cowering worshipper.

His limp, lifeless body crumpled to the floor as Torque lurched forward. She shoved the cultist's body away from the snake, then darted forward, fangs drawn. The tough scaled hide of the snake deflected her. The beast spun in a lithe twirl. It clamped it's sinewed muscles around Torque's body. Torque writhed in the iron clench of the creature. She swayed, flicking her tail and twisting her head to fend off the attack.

"Torque!" Lucas cried out, stepping forward.

"Stay back, Seraph!" Torque hissed. She struck at the snake again, scales glistening in the light from the braziers. Her fangs sunk deep into the snakes hide. It shrieked and tossed, untwining its length from Torque's body.

Chapter 28. Devouring Insanity

Torque clung to the creature as it thrust against her in an attempt to throw her off. "No!" howled the beast. It writhed across the dais. Its tail flicked, striking prone cultists as it twitched and spasmed. Torque clung to the creature, jaw crushing down against the beasts scales, as it swayed and slithered around the room. It slid from the dais, plunging into the small crowd of cultists that still prostrated themselves on the floor of the main chamber. They scattered, crawled away, and cowered behind the stone pillars as the two serpents thrashed against each other in the centre of the room.

Lucas felt dark with frustration as he watched the two. Every time he stepped closer Torque hissed, warning him off. He could sense her triumph and confidence as the beast seemed to grow more and more frantic. As he watched them, he noticed the creatures frenzied movements became more precise. Each movement seemed to be calculated with careful deliberation. The beasts own fangs glistened as the creature raised its head and glared down at Torque.

"Torque!" Lucas cried out, stepping forward. Torque spun, hissing at him again. The beast struck in that moment of distraction and Lucas winced as the creatures sharp fangs pierced Torque's throat. The serpent snarled, shaking off the beast with a flick of her head. She shook the creature, which had curled its length around her. Entwined, they seemed to dance around the room in an embrace of deadly intent.

Torque swayed. Her movements slowed. Lucas cast around for a way to intercede that wouldn't illicit Tori's instinct to protect him. Crey still knelt beside the altar. He wept over Zara's unconscious body in his arms. Josiah hovered nearby. Lucas put a hand on Crey's shoulder. He let a tingle of warm energy move through him into the other man. "She's alive Crey."

"But she is no longer herself. She is the creature."

Lucas shook his head, but Crey didn't look at him. "No," Lucas said. He crouched beside them and stroked a finger across Zara's forehead to push aside a stray strand of hair. The soft glow in his fingers left a trail of golden light across her skin. "She is Serpenthrope, Crey. Like Tori. Even inside the serpent she is Zara."

Crey looked up at him. "Did you not see her? Violent, impulsive, her hunger raged. Zara was not present. It was nothing but beast."

"That," Lucas said. He thrust his hand out to point at the disfigured snake that still writhed in the strange unified grasping dance with Torque. "That there, Crey, that is beast. The monstrous abomination that ripped out of Marlena is the beast. Zara's serpent-form is beautiful. She'll be revered like a Goddess, but that." He glanced again at the creature twined in Torque's coil of scale. "That is a beast. And we have to stop it."

"We can do nothing against it. Even your charge in serpent form fails to best the creature."

Lucas looked down on Zara's cool, calm features. He wondered why he'd never seen Tempany in the young woman before. She was in the soft curve of the girl's nose, the pale cream of her skin, the gentle angle of her cheekbones. His mentor's daughter, part angel, part serpent. "You're right, we can't fight the snake. But maybe two against one would swing the odds in our favour."

"You and I would make three against one," Crey said. "But even a Seraph's considerable strength would do little against that monster and I would be nothing more than a toothpick with which she would clean her teeth after dealing with you."

Lucas rested his hand against the side of Zara's face and let the rich light and warm energy pass through him. "Two serpents," Lucas whispered as the power Tempany had passed into him gathered within him. His fingers tingled as it flooded through him into Zara. She blinked open her eyes and drew a long breath into her lungs. The glow of golden light seemed to fill her. Her eyes sparkled and she gazed up at Lucas.

"What happened?" she whispered. Lucas drew back. He let his hand fall away as the energy settled around her.

"Zara." Crey groaned her name as he pulled her close. "Thank God, you are alive."

"Crey? What happened?"

"What do you remember?" Lucas asked.

"Remember?" Zara shook her head. "No, it was a dream. I must have been dreaming." She glanced around the room. The braziers still flickered with flames. She gasped as she saw Torque and the beast's erratic twirl of tooth and scale. She shook her head, muttering over and over to herself, "No, it was a dream, just a dream."

"Zara," Lucas said, his voice gentle. "Torque needs your help. Tori needs your help."

"Look at them! I can't do anything!" Zara's voice pitched with anxiety on the edge of hysteria.

"Your serpent form could help us all, Zara. You just have to reach inside to call it out of you."

"No!" Zara shouted. She scrambled backwards into Crey's arms and clung to his shoulder. "No, I don't want to be a monster."

"Zara, you can help them," Josiah said.

Chapter 28. Devouring Insanity

"Enough," Crey interrupted. He clutched Zara close, pulling her tight against his chest. "She must do nothing."

Torque hissed and snarled. Lucas spun to see the beast's fangs sinking deep into Torque's flesh again. He turned back to Zara. "Please Zara, Tori needs your help. You're the only one who can."

Tori felt a strange peace within her as she, as Torque, battled the monstrous snake. It was as though her thoughts moved as one with Torque, their minds in harmony with every breath and motion. As the beast's fangs sunk deep into Torque's flesh, Tori's mind jarred with the pain. For an instant they were two, separate beings again, then as Torque and Tori counter-moved to throw off the creature their minds melded again.

Torque rocked sideways, thrusting away the snake with a flick of her head. The beast snarled and clung with vice-like grip around Torque's body.

"Release me, beast!" Torque snarled.

"You cling to me as tightly as I cling to you, sister." The drawling voice of the creature used the endearment as a sarcastic insult.

"We are equally matched."

The beast's strange, manic laughter filled the room. Tori felt it tingle through her like and unpleasant creep of chill. "Equal? You and I will never be equals. I am immortal, a Goddess, a Queen!" The beast rose up, uncoiling from Torque's body as it pulled itself to full height. "You will bow in worship! You will all bow before me." She turned a lithe circle in place to incorporate every presence in the room. Then narrowed her eyes as she spied Lucas and Crey crouched beside Zara. "Seraph!" she snarled.

Torque whipped her tail forward, striking out at the creature. The blow glanced off the beast's scales, but the angry gaze of the beast spun back to her. Dark, soulless, eyes glared at her. Torque hissed. "Do not think yourself better than us, creature."

It tilted its head. "Better? I am superior in every way. This world will be my feast and the bones of my conquests will be my throne!"

Torque lunged forward. The creature moved to meet her and they began again their riotous dance. Torque's sharp fangs bit deep into the flesh of the creature, her body curled in coils around it. Over and over she lifted her head, readied her fangs, and pierced the creatures scales leaving pockmarks across her throat and body.

Chapter 28. Devouring Insanity

The creature snarled. It echoed each move and with every penetration of twin fangs, venom sunk into Torque's flesh and pumped around her body. She felt the staining darkness filling her. She felt her muscles weakening, her vision blurring, as the venom took hold of her. She shook her head, trying to clear the fuzzy haze that ebbed over the thoughts.

"Are we equal, sister?" The snake's lips curled in a manic smile of conquest and triumph as Torque clung on her with loosening grip.

"You cannot steal their warmth, you cannot have these people," Torque hissed, her breath short in her lungs.

The creature's laughter filled the room. "I can have what I please. All is mine!" It gripped Torque, the strength crushing as it rose high in the air. "It is all mine!"

Torque blinked, her vision a blur of scale and fire. Her head hung limp in the creatures clutches. She glanced past the beast as a ghost-white shadow raised up behind them. It struck forward, plunging stained fangs over and over into the thick scales of the creature's back.

The creature reared away, snarling. It spun to face the new assailant. Zara's serpent form swayed before them. Her glorious white scales glistened with muted gold and red in the light from the braziers. It snarled, empty pale eyes stared as if she saw through the beast, through Torque, into an unknown other universe. "Release my sister," she snarled.

"You dare rise against me? You dare?" The beast snarled back. It thrust Torque aside and wove forward to meet the pale serpent.

"I am Nariath and I do as I please." The serpent bared her fangs. Her tail flicked from side to side behind her.

"You cannot hope to best me."

"I need no hope. Your death is already certain. Do you not feel it? Do you not see the cowled face of him standing beside you?"

The beast cast a terror-filled glance either side of her then shook her head. "Your confidence will not save you. My venom will penetrate you, just as it did the other. See her there? If death has come it is for her."

Nariath smiled. "Her strength returns, even now. No, death is here for you today, and no other." She lunged forward. Her fangs, dripping with a pungent, viscous honey, sunk deep into the creature's flesh. Her jaw clenched tight and she whipped her tail forward to curl the creature in a crushing coiled embrace.

The beast writhed but could not move beneath the heavy grasp of Nariath's clutch. Torque slithered forward.

Chapter 28. Devouring Insanity

She twined her own coils around the remaining feet of the beast's length and sunk her fangs past the thick layer of scale, deep into the muscle and sinew at the base of the creature's throat. Together, the serpents squeezed and wrenched their iron jaws and razor fangs to tear the scales from the beast's flesh. Piece by piece they tore her apart as she snarled and hissed. In its final moments the beast cried out with Marlena's cold human voice. The sound keened through the temple, echoing off the walls, until it sunk into silence.

Chapter Twenty-Nine
Into The Light

Lucas and Crey rushed forward as Tori and Zara's human limbs crumpled to the earthen floor amidst the blood-soaked scatter of scale, flesh, and venom. Tori braced herself as she fell. She lay, half sitting, her eyes glazed with half-conscious confusion as she gazed down on Zara. The young woman blinked as Crey flung the sheet of altar silk across them. His fingers brushed over her arm and he knelt beside her.

"Zara!" Relief burst from his lips as she looked up at him. Her lip trembled and he pulled her close into a tight embrace.

"Lucas?" Tori asked.

"I'm here, Tori," he said. He reached down to brush a smear of blood from her shoulder. She trembled and he pulled her into his arms.

"I didn't want to kill her," she said into his shoulder. She sobbed, then shuddered as she added, "We didn't have a choice. She was crazy."

"No, you didn't have a choice," he said, sadness echoed in his voice as he felt the trails of grief and guilty relief that wove through her. "Come on, lets get out of here." He stood and reached down to take her hand. She pulled herself up.

Zara glanced at him. "Is it over now?"

Crey brushed her hair away from her face with gentle fingers. "No, mi amore, this is just one sect, one single people. The Nagaran range far, it will never be over, not for us, not for a very long time."

Tori reached down to Zara, "It's over for now, but there are too many unanswered questions. If my mother really is alive, if she is the Sacred Mother, then I have to find her."

Lucas felt anger rise within him. "Why? Dammit Tori, why do you have to? Hasn't this been enough? You can walk away, right now, you can leave all this behind."

"And do what?" she asked, turning to face him. Her eyes sparkled with fire and she put a hand on her hip.

"Just live your life, Tori."

She laughed, the sound hollow in her throat. "This is my life now, Lucas. Do you really imagine I could go back?"

"Yes, you could try. You could forget all this and just live a normal life."

Crey cleared his throat before he spoke. "She will always be Nagaran, Lucas. She will always be Serpenthrope."

Lucas glared at him. "She can choose to leave all this behind. Wouldn't you want that for you, for Zara?"

Zara pushed herself upright and stood, dragging the altar cloth with her. "Do you really think she could do that, Lucas? Do you really think she could walk away from the truth, to ignore it? How can any of us know the wrongs inflicted and not try to right them? How can you?"

He swallowed, hearing Tempany in her daughter's voice. Now he knew the truth he could see his mentor in the woman's eyes as well. She held the same poise and had the same giving heart. He sighed.

Tori brushed her fingers down his arm. "You can't walk away any more than I can, Lucas. We have to find my mother, we have to find Michael, we have to find out where all of this goes."

He shook his head, but it was not a denial. He turned to face her, feeling anger recede he realised it had masked his fear. "I don't want to lose you, Tori. You've already come close to being lost so many times. I can't lose you."

"I'm still here, but you can't give up who you are any more than I can. We have to find the truth."

From the edges of the room, and the mouth of the gaping corridors, straggling cultists moved forward. Their eyes wide, they whispered among themselves and pointed at the two women. Crey frowned as more and more worshippers gathered around them. The quiet that had fallen upon the room earlier darkened into a frenzied din.

"They killed the High Priestess!" A cultist shouted, thrusting a pointed finger at Tori and Zara. Zara cringed backward and Tori held her with a firm arm around her shoulders. She lifted her chin to glare at the man.

"She would have killed you all."

Zara lifted her head, her voice wavered as she said, "You can all go home now. You're free of this place."

Her words sent a ripple of chatter between the cultists. An elderly woman moved forward to stand before them. Her grey eyes shone with tears. "Free? Where would we go? This is our home."

"You can make a life in the real world, Erica," Josiah said. He reached a hand to touch the older woman's shoulder.

"You can find your family," Zara added.

"This is my family. I don't have anywhere else to go. We gave our lives to the Sacred Mother. Was it all a lie?"

The murmur in the room rose again as other cultists echoed her words.

"But we saw them, giant serpents, it's real." A young cultist shouted from the back of the room. "The Nagaran are real!" His triumphant roar was echoed by others amid the confused clamour of voices.

Zara glanced at Tori. Tori lifted her head to catch the gaze of the young man. "There have been too many lies. I won't lie to you. What you saw, yes, it was real, but that doesn't make it something to worship. A gift of the blood? It's a mutation in our genetics, nothing more. When you go from this place, that is the message I want you to spread. The Nagaran don't have to be ruled by fear and fanaticism. The Sacred Mother, the Four Fathers, the Children of the Nagaran, none of us are Gods, we're just like you."

Another cultists standing near them said, "Where would we go? Our lives are here."

Lucas sighed. "They're so entrenched in routine, it will take time to unravel their loyalties so that they can walk away from this place."

"We don't have time," Tori said. "We're stealing their lives from them every moment they stay here. We have to find my mother, we have to put a stop to all of this. In other sects there are children still being slaughtered."

Chapter 29. Into The Light

"I'll stay," Zara said. Tori glanced at her. Zara met her gaze and smiled with a shrug. "This is my home too. It's the only home I've known. I'll stay and help them find the way back to the light."

Crey stepped forward. "They've been too long in the service of others."

"They will need a leader," Josiah said.

"You want them to follow you? To serve you like they did the High Priestess?"

Josiah shook his head. "No, not me, but they will follow Zara," he said. "She is Serpenthrope and their honour would insist upon it. They will support you, Zara. I will support you."

Crey took Zara's hand in his. "But we will lead them into the light; we will guide them to their freedom. We will do as you said, Tori," Crey said, turning to Tori, "we will spread the word and bring truth where before there were lies."

Zara smiled up at him. "It's what the Uprising always wanted."

Tori looked at her. "Can you do it, Zara? Lead these people without, you know, the darkness taking over?"

Zara blinked, a sheen of tears sparkled in her eyes. "I don't know what I am now, Tori. I don't know what it means to be what you are. It scares me. But I can't abandon these people. They're my family."

Several of the cultists rushed forward. Sobbing, they clung to Zara and Tori. "Please," one pleaded, "please."

Lucas took the woman's arm. Tori felt the warm tingle of his golden energy brush through her as he created an aura of peace around them. "Be calm," he commanded. A hush came over those nearest them. He raised his voice. "Nagaran, listen." The noise in the room faded as cultists gathered close around them, pushing forward to fill the light.

Tori turned to face the worshippers. "Nagaran, hear me. You're free to leave this place, if you choose. But if you stay, know this! There will be no more sacrifice, there will be no more death, the ceremonies are over." Whispers rose up among the cultists.

"Did you hear?" Zara called out. "It's over."

The worshippers shuffled their feet for a few moments longer, then began to disband in packs. Tori turned to Zara. "Thank you," she said.

Zara nodded, then smiled. "You'll be back you know and they'll remember you. No matter what you say, you'll always be a Goddess in their eyes."

Chapter 29. Into The Light

Tori smiled. "You will too, Zara." She sobbed then pulled the other woman into a tight hug. "Please, be careful, that kind of adoration—" She shook her head.

Zara lifted a hand to hold Tori's as she stepped back from the embrace. "Truth," she whispered, her voice catching. "That's what I'll always remember. We'll bring truth; We'll return the Nagaran to the light."

Chapter Thirty

Ever The Charmer

Tempany's apartment was light and airy. The morning sunlight streamed in from the open balcony window and a gentle breeze fluttered the curtains. Lucas stood in the glow, letting the sunlight warm his skin. He gazed out of the window and across the blue sky. It extended past the tall buildings, over the river, the distant suburbs, and out past the rolling hills.

"You worry too much," Tori said, coming to stand beside him. She was dressed in her own clothes now; denim jeans and a simple cotton shirt. Lucas gazed down on her. He shoved away the urge to tuck a stray strand of her hair behind her ear and tilt her chin so he could see her eyes. She flushed, glancing up at him beneath her lashes. "We're safe now you know."

"I know, it's not us I'm thinking about." He turned away to look out of the window again. "I don't know what happens next. With Tempany gone and Michael still missing, the Hierarchy falls apart."

"You're still here."

He shook his head. "No, I promised I'd stay with you."

Chapter 30. Ever The Charmer

"Lucas," Tori began. She placed a hand on his arm.

"I know," he said, interrupting her. Beneath her fingers his skin tingled and he wondered if she felt the way her touch burned through him. He swallowed, then turned to face her. "I have a duty to my people, but I have a duty to you too, Tori. You're my charge."

"I'm safe now. You don't have to protect me any more."

He sighed as she turned away to walk between the curtains and out onto the balcony. She stood by the railing with her hands resting on the cool iron. "What about your mother, Tori?" he asked, as he followed her outside.

She shook her head. "I don't even know where to find her," she said. She glanced over her shoulder at him as he came to stand behind her, then returned her gaze to the skyline. "And the other sects, where are they?"

"The answers are there, Tori, in the temple archives or in Anna's records. We'll find them together."

Tori turned around. She leaned her hips against the railing and looked up at him. Her body brushed against him. Lucas swallowed, pushing away the betraying dart of lust that arrowed through him. He glanced down as her pink tongue darted across her lips.

"Together, Lucas?" she asked. His breath caught and he felt himself sway toward her.

"Tori," Lucas said, his voice wrenched from him in a wary groan. He closed his eyes and tilted his head back as he took a deep breath. The sunlight filled his face and warmed his skin. Her desire mingled with his inside of him and he clenched his teeth as he tried to reign in the emotions coursing within him. He looked down on her again as he spoke. "I have to protect you," he said again, his voice a horse scratch in his throat.

Her lips parted and the rich chocolate of her eyes gazed up at him. "Lucas," she said. His name was almost a sigh on her lips. "Will you kiss me?"

Tension thrummed through him and he sucked another breath into his lungs. "We can't, Tori." He closed his eyes again, drawing air through his nostrils as he tried to calm the yearning, hers and his, rioting through him. "It's forbidden."

Tori sensed the echo of her own emotions within him. "I've tried, Lucas. I've tried not wanting you, but I can't," she said. Desire pooled within her as she felt his fingers brush against the hairs on her arm.

"We shouldn't, Tori."

Chapter 30. Ever The Charmer

She sighed. "I want you Lucas, we can't keep trying to pretend this isn't real."

"But the serpent—" he began.

"I'm not afraid any more, Lucas."

"You're not?"

She smiled, shaking her head. "She won't hurt you, we can't, because I love you, Lucas." She felt the way his breath snagged in his chest. Inside, her emotions tingled like butterflies in her belly. Torque swirled within them as if basking in the warmth.

Tension clenched Lucas's jaw again. "Tori—" he groaned.

"No, listen. I love you, Lucas," she said again, "I'm not afraid to say that."

"It's forbidden."

"What can they do to me, Lucas? I'm not afraid." He closed his eyes. "And I'm not afraid of Torque," she said, touching the palm of her hand against his cheek. He opened his eyes and looked deep into hers. "I love you," she said. The words came easily now and a smile curved her lips as she added, "and because I love you she does. When we act as one it's almost as if she is me. We're of the same mind, my thoughts are no longer separate from hers. We are one. She could never hurt you, because I would never hurt you."

He groaned in the back of his throat. She felt the rumble against her lips and smiled as he leaned forward. His breath rushed from his lungs; it mingled with hers, warm on her face. He pulled her close, his lips crushing down on hers. She clung to him.

Inside her, Torque seemed to coil in her belly as if wrapping her serpent body around his warmth. Tori leaned into him, opening her mouth as his tongue traced her lips. She sighed, her whole body softening against him.

Long moments passed. Tori's soft curves felt cool and pliant in his arms. His body, rock hard against her, seemed to hum with energy. The golden glow of his aura flamed around them and his wings burst into a cascade down his back as his entire being rejoiced. Lucas deepened the kiss, letting his tongue taste the moist warmth inside her mouth. He drew her lower lip between his teeth.

A guttural cry echoed above them and Uriel's voice sliced through the air, "Lucas!"

Lucas and Tori sprang apart. Drawing air deep into their lungs, they looked up. The thick muscled, red-winged angel plummeted from the sky toward them. His wings, one tattered and broken, batted against the air above them as he attempted to slow his descent. He tumbled toward them, then crashed into the hard concrete at Lucas's feet.

"Uriel?" Lucas asked. He knelt down beside the man.

Uriel groaned. His body, a mess of blood and feathers, seemed to quiver. "Lucas," Uriel gasped, "Help me. He is coming."

Dear Reader,

Since publishing The Flight of Torque in 2014, life got in the way of my finishing the series in a timely manner. But that actually proves to be a good thing because over those years the sequel to Tori and Lucas's story evolved into a rich and dynamic story world where romances and thrilling tension abounds. Those stories are well into production now and life has given me the space to devote a strong focus on my fiction so that I can finally give this series the attention it deserves.

If you'd like to receive updates and notification when new books in the series are released, join the Nagaran at http://www.rebeccalaffarsmith.com And discover a whole new world of paranormal romance.

Sincerely,
Rebecca Laffar-Smith
P.S. If you loved this story, please leave a review.
Your review means the world to me and also helps readers discover new stories they can know they'll love.

Acknowledgements

There are so many people who made this book possible.

Forge, we started writing this book together in 2006. Although our journey as co-writers ended early, I hope the final version of the book has some resemblance to the first imaginings we created together. Those embryonic beginnings lead to this final version. This book could not exist without you.

Matt, you are a candle that lights up my life. Whenever the depth of my own inner darkness descends you bring the sun. In your eyes I am radiant, and because of the way you see me I want to be that version of myself. There is a lot of you in Lucas. 8/3 forever.

Mum, you've always supported my dreams and given me the room to chase them in my own time and my own way. You always want what is best for me. I admire the courage you've shown through your life and hope to be as courageous through mine. Thank you for helping me discover who I want to be and what I can accomplish.

Kaylie, I'm so blessed to have a daughter like you. I love sharing our passion for literature. We have similar tastes; what you love, I love. It makes shopping for books a little easier. Of course, the speed with which you devour books may be problematic. I love that you insist I write so that you will have more to read. You help keep me on track and prevent me wandering too far away from the page. Your own writing fills me with pride.

NaNoWriMo - Australia :: Perth :: South writers. November 2012 was amazing. 50,000+ words of this book belong, in part, to you. You pushed me forward. You kept me writing. You stayed with me through the hard nights, and kept the fire of writing lit through the entire month. I never felt I might not be able to do this that month. You continue to motivate and inspire me. I look forward to many more Novembers with you.

And all of you, my readers. Thank you.

About The Author: Rebecca Laffar-Smith

Born to the magical beauty of her sunburnt country home in Western Australia, Rebecca Laffar-Smith always yearned to explore the wonders of this world and beyond. After twelve years as a freelance writer and editor, she gave up writing about the non-fiction world in favour of the fantastical creatures and fanciful things she could create and immortalise in fiction. Now she writes in the moments she can steal away from homeschooling her son, raising her daughter, and volunteering as an events coordinator and mentor for her local writing community. She dreams of someday running a farm-stay writer's retreat on the outskirts of Perth and writing her stories in a detached, hexagonal room with floor to ceiling bookshelves and plenty of natural light.